LA BODEGA

LA BODEGA

(THE FRUIT OF THE VINE)

𝔄 𝔑𝔬𝔳𝔢𝔩

BY

VICENTE BLASCO IBAÑEZ

TRANSLATED FROM THE SPANISH BY

Dʀ. ISAAC GOLDBERG

WILDSIDE PRESS

INTRODUCTION

"LA BODEGA," written in 1903, is the third of the notable series in which Blasco Ibáñez attacks important questions of the day. It was preceded by "La Catedral" (The Shadow of the Cathedral) and "El Intruso" ("The Intruder"), and was directly followed by "La Horda" ("The Horde"). The first of these books deals with the retrogressive influence of the Catholic Church upon Spain; the second, with the Jesuits. "La Bodega" is a double assault: first, upon the vice of drunkenness, and second, upon the propertied interests that willfully keep the lower class in ignorance. That same directness of purpose and vehemence of expression as characterize the author in "The Shadow of the Cathedral" and in "Blood and Sand" (*Sangre y Arena*)—which considered from the point of view of its subject matter belongs with the thesis novels—are also present in "La Bodega." In this work, however, there is something more. There is a breath of the regional novel, reminiscent of the author's earliest efforts, in the love story of Rafael and María de la Luz; there is a fountain of poetry not only in the amorous passages, but also in the passionate presentation of the rights of common humanity. The hovering figure of Fernando Salvatierra, despite the extreme nature of his views, impresses the reader, even as he impresses his enemies, with the feeling that the ascetic revolutionist is indeed a lay saint. Writing sixteen years ago of a small section of Spain, Blasco Ibáñez seemingly foresaw much of what to-day is agitating the whole world. Perhaps, even as he forecasted the evils, he has given us a glimpse of the remedy.

The novel comes with particular timeliness during days when the question of prohibition is uppermost in the public mind. It should be noted that the Spaniard does not here attack the use of drinks, but rather their abuse, particularly as such abuse affects the working-class in its struggle against ignorance and exploitation. The Blasco Ibáñez of the present novel would hardly subscribe to the quatrain of the Rubaiyat:

> Waste not your Hour, nor in the vain pursuit
> Of This and That endeavor and dispute;
> Better be jocund with the fruitful Grape
> Than sadden after none, or bitter, Fruit.

To him the "fruitful Grape" is a source of bitter fruit indeed; he summons the humble and lowly to forsake the illusory joys of the beverage—to "endeavor and dispute" in a noble pursuit that is far from vain.

It is of interest to note that the city about which the action of the novel centers—Jerez de la Frontera—gives the name to sherry. The former spelling of Jerez was with an X, anciently pronounced like sh. The full name of the town signifies Jerez of the Frontier. It is situated some fifteen miles from Cádiz. Another point of interest in connection with wine-manufacture in this district is that the bodegas, or wine-sheds, are above ground.

Rather than interrupt the text of the novel with intrusive notes, I have thought it preferable to list the explanations in a glossary at the end of the book. For the explanation of such foreign terms as are not clarified by the text the reader is referred to the glossary.

—I. G.

CONTENTS

LA BODEGA

LA BODEGA

(THE FRUIT OF THE VINE)

CHAPTER I

HURRIEDLY, as when he used to be late to school, Fermín Montenegro entered the office of the house of Dupont, the leading wine-dealers of Jerez, known throughout Spain; "Dupont Brothers," manufacturers of the renowned wine of Marchamalo and makers of the cognac whose merits were emblazoned upon the fourth page of the newspapers, on the multi-colored posters at the railroad stations, on the walls of old houses that had been invaded by advertisements and even upon the bottom of decanters in the cafés.

It was Monday, and the young clerk was an hour late. His office associates barely raised their eyes from their work when he entered, as if they feared by word or look to render themselves accomplices in this astounding lack of punctuality. Fermín looked uneasily about the spacious headquarters and at last rested his gaze upon an adjoining private office, where there rose in solitary majesty a *bureau* of shining American wood. "The boss" had not yet arrived. And the young man, eased by the knowledge, sat down before his desk and began to classify his documents, arranging the work for the day.

That morning the office seemed to be something new, even extraordinary, to him, as if he were entering it for

the first time—as if he had not spent fifteen years of his
life within its walls, ever since he had been hired as an
errand-boy; this had been during the life of don Pablo,
the second Dupont of the dynasty, the founder of the
famous cognac that opened "a new horizon to the wine
business," in the pompous language of the company's
prospectus, which spoke of him as of a conquistador—
the father of the present "Dupont Brothers," kings over
an industrial state that had been formed by the effort
and the good fortune of three generations.

Fermín saw nothing new in this room, of a Pantheon-
like whiteness, cold and raw, with its marble floor, its
bright, stuccoed walls, its large windows of frosted glass
that reached to the very ceiling, imparting a milky soft-
ness to the light from outside. The closets, the desks
and the files—all of dark wood—furnished the only
warm tone in this glacial decorative scheme. Hanging
beside the desks, the wall-calendars displayed large
images of saints and of virgins, printed in colors. Some
of the clerks, flinging discretion to the winds, in order
to flatter their employer had pinned up near their desks,
next to the English almanacs with their modernist figures,
prints of miraculous saints, which contained at the bottom their corresponding prayer and the memorandum of
indulgences. The great clock, which from the rear of
the room broke the silence with its ticking, was shaped
like a Gothic temple, bristling with mystic spires and
medieval pinnacles, like a cathedral adorned with gold
and precious stones.

It was this semi-ecclesiastical decoration of a wine and
cognac establishment that aroused a certain amazement
in Fermín, after his having looked upon it for years.
His impressions of the day before were still vivid. Up
to a late hour of the night he had been with don Fernando
Salvatierra, who had returned to Jerez after serving

an eight years' sentence in a penitentiary of northern
Spain. The noted revolutionist came back to his province modestly, without any ostentation whatever, as if
he had spent the past eight years in traveling for pleasure.

The young man found the revolutionist almost the
same as he had been at their last meeting, before Fermín
had gone off to England to complete his English studies.
It was the don Fernando he had known in his boyhood;
the same gentle, paternal voice, the same generous smile;
clear, calm eyes, sometimes blurred with tears because of
their weakness, shining through a pair of light blue
spectacles. The privations of prison life had turned his
reddish hair gray at the temples, and whitened his thin
beard, but the serene expression of youth still glowed
upon his features.

He was a "lay saint," as even his adversaries confessed.
Had he been born two centuries earlier, he would have
been a pious mendicant preoccupied with the sorrows of
others, and perhaps would at last have come to figure
upon the altars. Plunged into the activities of a period
of strife, he had become a revolutionist. He could be
moved to tears as easily as a child. A stranger to selfishness, he considered no act unworthy if it could aid the
unfortunate; nevertheless his name roused indignation
and panic among the rich. It was enough for him to
appear, in his wandering existence, for several weeks in
Andalusia; whereupon the authorities would grow
alarmed and the public force would be mobilized. He
journeyed hither and thither like a Wandering Jew of
revolt, incapable himself of doing harm, detesting violence, yet preaching it to the lower classes as the only
means of salvation.

Fermín recalled his latest adventure. He was in
London when he read of the capture and the conviction
of Salvatierra. The rebel had appeared in the country-

side of Jerez, just as the field laborers had begun one of their strikes.

His presence among the insurgents was his only crime. He was seized, and upon being questioned by the military judge refused to swear by God. Suspicion of complicity in the strike and his monstrous atheism were enough to send him to jail. It was an example of injustice that social fear permitted itself with a dangerous person. The judge struck him during an interrogatory, and Salvatierra, who as a young man had fought in the insurrections of the revolutionary period, limited himself to requesting, with an evangelical serenity, that the violent judge be placed under observation, since he must be suffering from some mental affliction.

At prison his habits caused stupefaction. Devoted by preference to the study of medicine, he served as a physician to the prisoners, moreover sharing with them his meals and his clothes. He went about in tatters, almost naked; whatever was sent to him by his Andalusian friends passed immediately into the possession of his less fortunate associates. The guards, seeing in him the former deputy, the renowned agitator who in the period of the Republic had refused a place in the ministry, called him don Fernando with instinctive respect.

"Call me just Fernando," he would say, simply. "Address me familiarly, as I address you. We're nothing more than men."

Upon arriving at Jerez, after having remained several days in Madrid among the journalists and his former acquaintances in political life, who had succeeded in procuring his pardon without paying any heed to his remonstrances, Salvatierra went in search of the friend who still remained loyal to him. He had spent Sunday in a small vineyard near Jerez, owned by a wine merchant, a former comrade in arms in the period of the

Revolution. All of his admirers had flocked thither upon learning of don Fernando's return. There came from the wine-stores old *arrumbadores,* who as young men had marched under Salvatierra's orders, over the rough passes of the neighboring mountains, firing their muskets in defense of the Federal Republic; there were young field laborers who revered the don Fernando of the second epoch, speaking of the division of the land and of the irritating absurdities of private property.

Fermín, too, had gone to see the master. He recalled his childhood days; the respect with which he listened to that man who was so greatly admired by his father, and who had lived in his house for numerous long periods. He was filled with gratitude upon calling to memory the patience with which Salvatierra had taught him to read and write—how he had given him his first lessons in English and had inculcated in him the noblest aspirations of his soul: that love for humanity with which the master seemed to flame.

On beholding Fermín after his long incarceration, don Fernando extended his hand, without a trace of emotion, as if they had met but recently, and asked after the young man's father and his sister in a gentle voice and with a placid countenance. He was the same man as ever, insensible to his own pains and moved by the sufferings of others.

All that afternoon and for the greater part of the night the group of Salvatierra's friends remained together in the vineyard cottage. The host, glowing with pomp and enthusiasm at the return of the great man, knew how to celebrate the reunion. Dozens of gold-colored tumblers circulated around the table that was laden with plates of olives, slices of ham and other dishes that served to arouse a thirst for wine. All drank, between one word and another, with that prodigality which is

characteristic of the province. At the close of the celebration several appeared to be befuddled; Salvatierra
alone was serene. He drank only water, and as for
food, he refused everything except a slice of bread and
another of cheese. This was his meal, twice a day,
since he had left prison; his friends must respect it.
Thirty *céntimos* were sufficient for his daily needs. He
had decided that as long as the social maladjustment
lasted, and millions of his kind were slowly starving to
death, he had no right to any more.

Oh, inequality! Salvatierra grew fervent, and cast
off his genial calm at thought of social injustice. Hundreds of thousands of human beings died of starvation
every year. Society pretended not to be aware of this,
because they did not fall suddenly in the middle of the
street, like stray dogs; but they died in the hospitals, in
their hovels, apparently victims of divers diseases; in
reality, however, it was hunger! All hunger! . . . And
to think that the world contained plenty of food for all!
Cursed social organization that consented to such
crimes! . . .

And Salvatierra, amid the respectful silence of his
friends, eulogized the revolutionary future, which would
belong to Communism—a generous dream in which men
should at last find material happiness and spiritual peace.
The evils of the present were a result of inequality.
Diseases themselves were but another effect. In the
future, man would die through the running-down of his
mechanism, without knowing illness.

Montenegro, listening to his master, called to mind
an episode of his youth—one of the most famous paradoxes of don Fernando, before the latter had been sent
to prison and Fermín had gone to London.

Salvatierra was addressing a meeting, explaining to
the toilers the nature of future society. No more op-

pr_ _ors and deceivers! All the honors and the profes-
sions of the present were to be abolished. They would
do away with priests, the soldiers, the politicians, the
lawyers. . . .

"And the doctors?" asked a voice from the rear of
the hall.

"The doctors, too," affirmed Salvatierra with his cold
tranquillity.

There was a murmur of surprise and amazement, as
if the public that admired him was about to burst into
ridicule.

"Yes; the doctors, too, for on the day that witnesses
the triumph of our revolution diseases will cease."

And feeling that his audience was about to explode in
an outburst of incredulous laughter, he hastened to add:

"Diseases will cease because those that now exist are
due either to the ostentation of the rich, who eat more
than their bodies require, or to the fact that the poor eat
less than is necessary to the sustaining of life. The new
society, dividing the means of subsistence equitably,
avoiding surfeit on one hand and dearth on the other,
will balance life and do away with diseases."

And with such conviction, such faith did the revolutionist infuse his words, that these and similar paradoxes
imposed silence, being received by the believers with the
same credulity as that with which the simple medieval
audiences listened to the enlightened apostle who announced the imminent reign of God.

Don Fernando's companions in arms recalled the
heroic period of his life—the exploits of the mountain
band, each one greatly exaggerating his deeds and his
sufferings, through the illusion of time and the exuberance of the southern imagination, while their chief
smiled as if he were listening to the account of childhood
games. That had been the romantic epoch of his

existence. Battling, struggling for forms of government! . . . There was something more important on earth. And Salvatierra brought to mind his disappointment in the short-lived Republic of '73, which could do nothing and had borne no fruit. His comrades of the National Assembly, who every week overthrew one government and set up another for their amusement, had desired to name him minister. He, minister? And why, pray? The only reason he could have for accepting the post would have been to end a state of affairs like that in Madrid, where men, women and children were forced to sleep in winter exposed to the inclement weather, taking refuge in doorways and corridors, while the large hotels on the Paseo de la Castellana were closed down and served no purpose at all, and their wealthy patrons, hostile to the government, had gone off to Paris near the Bourbons, to plot for their restoration. This ministerial program, however, had won no support.

Afterwards, his friends, going back in their recollections to the conspiracies at Cádiz, before the mutiny of the troops, recalled Salvatierra's mother . . . Mamma! The revolutionary's eyes grew moist, and glistened behind his blue spectacles. Mamma! . . . His smiling, genial countenance faded into an expression of pain. She had been his whole family, and had died while he was in prison. They were all accustomed to hearing him speak, with childish simplicity, of that dear old woman who never had a word of reproof for his rash exploits and always assented to the philanthropic largess that caused him to return to his home half naked every time he found a comrade in need of clothes. She was like the mothers of the saints in the Christian legends— smiling accomplices of all the madly generous impulses and extravagant gifts of their sons. "Just wait till I tell ma, and I'll be with you," he would say, hours before some revolutionary attempt, as if this were his one personal precaution. And mamma had without protest seen him expend the modest family fortune in these enterprises, and had followed him to Ceuta when his sentence of death had been commuted to life imprisonment. Ever courageous, not permitting herself to address the slightest reproach, understanding that her son's life must perforce be of such a nature, she did not wish to vex him with gratuitous advice; she was even proud, perhaps, that her Fernando could command men by the power of his ideals and affright his enemies with his virtue and his disinterestedness. Mamma! . . . All his celibatic affection—that of a man who, dominated by a humanitarian passion, had been too busy to notice woman —Salvatierra concentrated upon his spirited old mother. And he would never see mamma again! He would nevermore behold that old woman who enveloped him in motherly endearments as if she looked upon him always as an eternal child! . . .

He wished to go to Cádiz to see her grave: the mantle of earth that hid his mamma from him forever. In his voice and in his glance there was an air of despair: the grief of not being able to accept the consolatory illusion of a future life—the certainty that beyond death lay the eternal night of nothingness.

The sadness of his solitude caused him to cling with all the greater tenacity to his rebellious enthusiasm. He should devote the rest of his life to his ideals. This was the second time they had secured his release from prison, but he would return thither as often as his people desired. As long as he could stand he would battle against social injustice.

And Salvatierra's last words, denying future existence, declaring war against private property and against God—the mask of all the world's iniquities—still echoed

in the ears of Fermín Montenegro when, on the next
morning, he went to his post in the firm of Dupont. The
radical difference between the fairly monastic atmosphere
of the office, with its silent employees bent before the
images of the saints, and that group surrounding Salvatierra, composed of veterans of the romantic revolution
and young warriors in the conquest of bread, disturbed
young Montenegro.

From long association he knew his office mates well—
their cringing submission to the imperious character of
Pablo Dupont, the head of the firm.   Montenegro was
the only employee who allowed himself a certain independence, doubtless because of the affection which the
proprietor's family professed for his own.   Two foreign
employees, one a Frenchman and the other a Swede, were
tolerated as being necessary to the foreign correspondence; but don Pablo treated them with a certain aversion,
the one because of his lack of religious belief and the
other because he was a Lutheran.   The rest of the office
force, composed of Spaniards, lived subject to the will
of the chief executive, more concerned with being present at all the religious ceremonies that don Pablo organized in the church of the Jesuit fathers than with the
office routine.

Montenegro feared that by this time his employer had
learned where he had spent Sunday. He knew the customs of the establishment: the espionage practiced by the
employees for the purpose of ingratiating themselves with
don Pablo.   Several times he had noticed that don
Ramón, the office manager and publicity director, had
eyed him with a certain suspicion. He must have been
informed about the reunion; but Fermín was not afraid
of this person. He knew don Ramón's past: his youth,
spent in the lowest stratum of Madrid journalism,
battling against existing conditions without earning a

crumb to lay aside for old age, until, wearied by the struggle, overcome by hunger and in the throes of pessimism induced by failure and poverty, he had taken refuge in the office of Dupont, where he edited the original advertisements and the blatant catalogues that popularized the products of the house. Don Ramón, through his advertisements and his pretensions to piety, had become the confidant of the elder Dupont; but Montenegro did not fear him, knowing the beliefs of his past, which still persisted in him.

The young man devoted more than an hour to the examination of his documents, anxiously eying, from time to time, the neighboring private office, which was still unoccupied. As if he desired to postpone the moment in which he must see his employer, he sought a pretext for leaving the department and picked up a letter from England.

"Where are you going?" asked don Ramón, seeing him leave the room after having arrived so late.

"To the department of *referencias*. I must explain this order."

And he left the office for the wine depositories that formed almost a town, with their bustling population of *arrumbadores,* shippers and coopers, working on the platforms, in the open air, or in the covered galleries, between the rows of casks.

The wine-sheds of Dupont occupied an entire section of Jerez. They consisted of groups of old structures that covered the slope of a hill, amid the trees of an extensive garden. All the Duponts had continued to add new buildings to the original establishment, to keep pace with the growth of business, and thus the primitive, modest shed had, in the course of three generations, been transformed into an industrial city, smokeless, noiseless, tranquil and smiling beneath the luminous blue sky, with walls of shining white and flowers growing between the hogsheads ranged along the spacious stretches.

Fermín passed by the door of the structure called the *Tabernacle*,—an oval-shaped pavilion with a glass skylight, situated next to the main building that harbored the counting-room and the shipping office. The *Tabernacle* contained the choicest products of the concern. A row of upright casks bore upon their oaken paunches the names of famous wines that were used only for bottling; liquids that glittered with all the varied shades of gold, from the reddish splendor of the sunbeam to the pale, velvety gleam of old jewels; wines of gentle fire which, imprisoned in glass dungeons, were destined to be poured out in the misty atmosphere of England, or under the boreal splendors of the Norwegian sky. At the rear of the pavilion, opposite the door, loomed the giants of this silent, motionless assembly: the *Twelve Apostles*, enormous casks of carved oak, as highly polished as if they were the costliest of furniture; presiding over them was the *Christ*, a cask adorned with oak strips fashioned to represent vine branches, similar to the Bacchic bas-relief of an Athenian sculptor. Within its hoops slept a veritable tidal wave of wine;—thirty-three *botas*, according to the firm's records,—and the colossus, in its immovability, seemed to be proud of its blood, which was enough to deprive an entire population of its senses.

In the middle of the *Tabernacle*, upon a round table, were ranged in a circle all the bottles of the firm, from the almost fabulous wine,—a century old,—which is sold at thirty francs for the stormy celebrations of archdukes, grand-dukes and worldly celebrities, to the popular Sherry that grows to a sad old age in the show-windows of restaurants, and helps the poor man in illness.

Fermín cast a glance over the interior of the *Taber-*

nacle. Nobody. The motionless casks, swollen with the ardent blood of their stomachs, labeled with their marks and coats-of-arms, seemed like ancient idols surrounded by an ultramundane calm. The rain of sunlight, filtering through the glass of the roof, formed about them a nimbus of irised light. The dark carved oak seemed to smile with the tremulous colors of the sunbeams.

Montenegro walked on. The bodegas of the Duponts formed a graded series of structures. From one to the other extended the esplanades, and on them the cask pilers were arranging the rows of barrels so that the sun should heat them. This was the cheap wine,—the ordinary Sherry,—which, in order that it might age rapidly, was exposed to the sun's warmth. Fermín thought of the amount of time and labor needed to produce a good Sherry. Ten years were necessary to create the noted wine: ten strong fermentations were required for its formation, with its sylvan aroma and the slight taste of filbert that no other wine could duplicate. But the exigencies of commercial rivalry, the aim of producing a cheap article, even if it were bad, obliged the house to force the aging of the wine by hastening its evaporation through exposure to the sun.

Montenegro followed the meandering paths formed by the rows of casks, arriving at length at the wine-shed of the *Giants,* the chief warehouse of the firm,—an immense construction containing the liquids before they were endowed with form or name,—the Limbo of the wines, when their spirits hovered in the vagueness of uncertainty. The vats, painted red and ringed with black hoops, reached to the top of the high ceiling; towers of wood resembling the besieging-towers of the ancients; giants that gave their name to the department and contained each within its bowels more than seventy thousand liters. Steam pumps drew the liquids off, blending them. The rubber hose stretched from one giant to the other like absorbent tentacles that sucked the very essence of their lives. The explosion of one of these towers could at once flood the entire warehouse with a fatal stream, drowning the men who were chatting below. The workers saluted Montenegro, who, through a side door of the *Giants'* wine-shed, passed to that called "Export Division," where was stored the unlabeled wine for the imitation of all marks. It was a grandiose nave, the vault sustained by two rows of pillars. Beside these were ranged the casks in three tiers, forming alleys.

Don Ramón, head of the counting-house, recalling his former predilections, compared the shipping shed to a painter's palette. The wines were primary colors: but along came the expert, who was in charge of the blending, and taking a little from here and a little from there, he created Madeira, Oporto, Marsala,—all the wines of the world, according to the purchaser's order.

This was the section of the Duponts' industry devoted to industrial fraud. The necessities of modern commerce compelled the monopolists of one of the chief wines in the world to stoop to these trickeries and combinations, which, together with cognac, constituted the bulk of the firm's exports. At the rear of the export shed was the formula room, "the library of the house," as Montenegro called it. A row of shelves with glass doors displayed, in compact rows, thousands upon thousands of tiny flasks, carefully sealed, each labeled and dated. This collection of bottles was like the history of the firm's business. Every flask contained the sample of a shipment; the formula of a liquor manufactured in conformity with the consumer's desire. For a repetition of the shipment the customer had only to recall the date, and the man in charge of the *referencias* would look up the sample and have a new supply of the wine made.

The shipping house comprised four thousand *botas* of distinct wines intended for blends. In a gloomy chamber, containing no other light than that from a window with a red pane, was the "dark room." Here the expert examined, through the luminous ray, the glass of wine from the recently opened cask.

According to the *referencias,* or the formulæ sent from the head office, he blended the new wine with various liquids and afterwards chalked upon the heads of the casks the number of jars that needed to be extracted from each one to form the mixture. The *arrumbadores,* sturdy youths in their shirt sleeves, their arms bared and their black sash well girded about their loins, went from one side to the other with their metal jars, transferring the wines of the blend to the new cask containing the order.

Montenegro had from childhood known the man in charge of the blending. The expert was the oldest employee of the firm. In his boyhood he had seen the first of the Duponts, the founder of the establishment. With the second Dupont he was on terms of close intimacy, and the present head, young Dupont, he had held in his arms; to his paternal familiarity was added the fear that don Pablo inspired with his imperious character of an old-fashioned master.

The blender was an old man, who seemed to have been inflated by the atmosphere in which he lived. His skin, fretted with wrinkles, glistened with an everlasting moisture, as if the volatilized wine had penetrated through all his pores and were trickling down the edge of his mustache in the form of tears.

Isolated in his bodega, compelled by his long seclusions

in the dark room to keep silence, he was seized with an
intense desire to speak whenever any one came from the
office, especially Montenegro, who, like himself, might
consider himself a son of the firm.

"And your father?" he asked Fermín. "Always in the
vineyard, eh? . . . It's better there than in this damp
cave. He'll certainly outlive me."

And noticing the paper that Montenegro offered him,
he made a wry face.

"Another one of your petty orders!" he exclaimed
sarcastically. "Wine blended for export. Fine business, good Lord. Once upon a time we were the leading house in the world,—unique,—because of our wines
and our *soleras*. Now we manufacture mere blends, export wines,—Madeira, Oporto, Marsala,—or else we imitate Tintillo de Rota and Málaga. And it is for this
that God creates the liquors of Jerez and gives bounty
to our vineyards! That we may deny our name! . . .
Bah! I could almost wish that the Phylloxera would
ruin all the vines, so that we shouldn't have to put up
with any more lies and falsifications! . . ."

Montenegro was accustomed to the old man's com-
plaints. He never delivered a foreign order without an
outburst of curses from the *técnico* against the degenera-
tion of the wines of Jerez.

"You didn't know the place in the good old times, my
dear Fermín," he continued. "That's why you're so indifferent to these matters. You belong to the moderns,
—to those who believe that things are going well because
we sell plenty of cognac, like any of the firms of those
foreign countries, whose vineyards produce only filth,
and to whom God grants nothing that even remotely resembles Jerez wine. . . . Tell me, you who have traveled a bit. Where have you seen grapes like our *Palo-
mino,* or our *Vidueño,* or *Mantuo de Pila,* or *Cañosaco,*

or *Perruno,* or *Pedro Ximénez?* . . . You'd search in
vain! They grow only in this country: they're a gift
of God. . . . And with all this wealth, we manufacture
cognac or wines in imitation of others, because Sherry,
the real Sherry, has gone out of fashion, according to
what these foreign chaps tell us. These buildings here
aren't wine-sheds any more. They're distilleries, apothe-
caries' shops, anything you please, except what they once
were,—and, the deuce!—I feel like flying off never to
return when you come along with these scraps of paper
and ask me to concoct another adulteration."

The old man waxed indignant at Fermín's replies.

"These are necessities of modern commerce, señor
Vicente. Business has changed, and so has the public
taste."

"Then let 'em stop drinking, the louts, and let 'em stop
bothering us, and not require us to disguise our wines;
we'll keep them stored and allow them to age in peace,
and I'm certain that some day people will do them justice and come begging for them on their knees. . . .
But all this has changed. England must be ruined. You
don't have to tell it to me. I notice it here only too well
from the callers I receive. In former days less Englishmen visited the place; but the travelers were persons
of distinction: lords and ladies, the least of them. It
was a joy to see with what a noble air they got drunk.
A glass of wine here for a sample! A glass there for a
purchase! And thus they went through the establishment, as serious as priests, until by the time they were
through you had to lift them into their carriages and
have them brought to their hotel. They knew how to
sample the wines and do justice to the good stuff. . . .
These days, when a shipful of Englishmen lands at
Cádiz, they come in a flock, headed by a guide; they try
everything because it's free, and if they buy anything,

they're satisfied with three-peseta bottles. They don't know how to get drunk respectably: they shout, they begin to wrangle, and go through the streets making S's, trailed after by the urchins. Before I used to think that all the English were rich, and here I see that these people who travel in gangs are something different: London cobblers or shopkeepers who run off on a holiday with their year's savings. . . . And that's how business goes."

Montenegro smiled as he listened to the old man's incoherent lamentations.

"Besides," added the blender, "in England, same as here, the old customs are falling into disuse. Many Englishmen drink only water, and, from what I've been told, it's no longer considered elegant for the women to go off in another room to chat, while the men remain guzzling until the servants take the trouble to remove them from under the table. They no longer require, as a 'night-cap,' a couple of bottles of Sherry that cost a good fistful of shillings. Those who still get drunk to show that they're real gentlemen use what are called light beverages—isn't that so, you who have been there? —nasty stuff that costs but little and lets you drink and drink before you get intoxicated; whisky and soda and other nauseating mixtures. Commonness rules over them. No more do they ask for 'Sherrrrrry,' except when they come here and get it for nothing. Only we of this country can really appreciate Sherry, and before long we'll be the only purchasers of it. They get soused on cheap stuff, and that's how their affairs go. In the Transvaal they were almost defeated. Some fine day they'll be dumped into the ocean, with all their swaggering courage. They're degenerating. It isn't like the good old days when the firm of Dupont was a wineshed little larger than a hut, yet exported its bottles and even its casks to Sir Wm. Pitt, to Lord Nelson, to Wellington and other famous personages whose names figure in the oldest *soleras* of the chief warehouse."

Montenegro continued to laugh at these plaints.

"Laugh, sonny, laugh. You're all the same. You never knew the good old days and are surprised that we old fellows should find the present so bad. Do you know how much we formerly received for a cask of thirty-one *arrobas?* Well, it came to 230 *pesos;* and now, some years we sell it for as low as 21 *pesos*. Ask your own father. He isn't as old as I am, but he, too, knew the golden age. Money circulated in Jerez just like air. There were wine-growers who wore conical hats and lived like paupers in a suburban shanty, with nothing but a brass lamp for light, but when they paid an account they pulled from under the pine table a sack that looked as if it were filled with potatoes, and out came the golden ounces! The vineyard laborers earned thirty to forty *reales* per day, and they allowed themselves the whim of driving to work in a gig and wearing patent-leather shoes. None of your newspapers and incendiary talks and labor meetings. Wherever the workers got together you could hear the guitar, and every *seguidilla* and *martinete* sounded so sweet that God's own flesh quivered with delight. . . . If your father's friend, Fernando Salvatierra, had showed up then, with all his chatter about rich and poor, division of the land and revolutions, they would have offered him a goblet and said: 'Take your place in the crowd, friend; drink, sing, dance with the lassies if you please, and don't worry about our life, which is by no means of the worst. . . .' But the English scarcely patronize our wines; less and less money comes into Jerez, and when it does, the wretch hides so well that nobody can see him. The vineyard laborers get ten *reales* a day, and they have faces as sour as vine-

gar. And in a quarrel as to whether they shall prune
with a knife or with shears they kill each other; there's
a Black Hand society and in the prison yard they garrotte
men,—something that hasn't been seen in Jerez for many
a year. Just say a word to the laborer and he bristles
like a porcupine, and the employer is worse than ever.
You no longer can see gentlemen shoulder to shoulder
with the poor in the vintages, dancing with the girls and
courting them like young gallants. The Civil Guard pa-
trols the field just as in the times when the highways
swarmed with bandits. . . . And why all this, señor?
Because of what I say: because the English have taken
to that accursed whiskey and overlook the good *palo
cortado*, the *palma*, and all the other excellent products
of this blessed soil. . . . What I say is, Money. Let
money come; let the pounds, the guineas and the shillings start to roll in this direction, as of old. And that'll
put an end to strikes, and the sermons of Salvatierra
and his adherents, and the dark faces of the Civil Guard,
and all the troubles and disgraces that we witness
now! . . ."

From the interior of the bodega issued a shout, summoning señor Vicente. It was an *arrumbador* who was
in doubt as to certain of the white numbers marked
upon the head of a cask, and he asked the old man's aid.

"I'm coming, sonny!" shouted señor Vicente. "Take
care to make no errors with the medicine!" . . .

And turning to Montenegro, he concluded, "Leave that
paper in the dark room, and I hope your hands fall off
before you bring me any more prescriptions, as if I were
a druggist."

The old man walked away with slow and wavering
step, and Montenegro left the shed, passing through the
cooperage before returning to the counting-room.

It was a wide yard with lean-tos, beneath which the

coopers were striking with their mallets the hoops that imprisoned the wood. The half-constructed casks, with only their upper parts girded by the hoops, opened their staves above a fire of wood-shavings that was heating them, causing them to curve and thus making it easier to put the remaining hoops in place.

The firm's volume of trade kept this workshop continuously busy. Hundreds of casks left it every week to be shipped from Cádiz, carrying the Dupont wines all over the world.

At one side of the yard arose a tower formed of staves. At the very top of this fragile edifice were two apprentices receiving the staves that were handed to them from below, placing them in criss-cross fashion and adding new height to the structure, which had reached higher than the surrounding roofs and threatened to topple over, shaking at the slightest movement, like a tower of cards.

The superintendent of the workshop, a robust man with a genial smile, approached Montenegro.

"How is don Fernando? . . ."

Ever since his days as an ordinary workman he had felt a deep respect for the agitator. The favor of the Duponts and the pliability with which he yielded to all their hobbies had enabled him to rise above his comrades. But as a compensation for this servitude that had transformed him into the foreman of the workshop, he cherished a secret affection for the revolutionist and all his comrades in the days of poverty. He inquired minutely as to how Salvatierra looked and felt on his return from prison, and into the nature of his plans for the future.

"I'll go some day to see him," he said, lowering his voice, "when it's impossible for the chief to learn of it. . . . Yesterday we had a great celebration at the church of the Jesuits and in the afternoon I went with

my little daughters to visit his wife. . . . I know that
you spent the day well. They've told me here, in the
bodega."

With the concern of a well-fed servant who fears to
lose his sinecure, he gave counsel to the youth. "Keep
your eyes open, Ferminillo!" There were many inform-
ers among the employees. Since he knew, it certainly
would not be surprising if don Pablo was by that time
fully aware that Montenegro had visited Salvatierra.

And as though he feared to say too much, lest some
one be spying upon him, he hurriedly left Fermín, turning towards the spot where the coopers were hammering
the casks. Montenegro continued on his way, entering
the principal depository of the firm, where the old
soleras were kept and the best wines were aged.

The interior was like a cathedral, but a white, bright,
luminous cathedral, its five naves separated by four rows
of columns with simple capitals. The noise of one's foot-
steps was magnified by the echo, as in a temple. The
vaults thundered with the sound of voices, sending them
back in increased volume. The walls were set with large
windows of white glass, and in the two façades there
opened two ample rose windows, also white, through one
of which penetrated the sun, in whose strip of light
quivered the restless, rainbow-colored particles of dust.

Along the pillars was ranged in rows the wealth of the
firm,—the triple tiers of reclining casks, upon whose tops
was inscribed the year of the vintage. There were venerable hogsheads covered with cobwebs and dust, with
the wood so moist that it seemed on the point of
falling apart. They were the patriarchs of the shed:
they were christened with the names of the heroes who
happened to be enjoying universal fame at the time of
their birth. One cask was called *Napoleon;* another
Nelson; these had been decorated with the royal crown

of England, because British monarchs had drunk of their contents. One very ancient cask, completely isolated, as if contact with the others might cause it to collapse, bore the venerable name of *Noah*. It was the chief antiquity of the establishment, going back to the middle of the XVIIIth century, and the first of the Duponts had himself acquired it as a relic. Near to it were placed other casks that displayed under the Royal Arms of Spain the names of all the monarchs and *infantes* that had visited Jerez in the course of the century.

The rest of the shed was filled with samples of all the vintages, beginning with the first years of the century. One lonely cask exhaled an acrid odor that, as Montenegro said, "made one's mouth water." It was a renowned vinegar, one hundred and thirty years old. And with this dry, pungent smell blended the sugary perfume of the sweet wines and the soft leathery aroma of the dry wines. The alcoholic vapor that filtered through the oak of the casks and the odor rising from the drops spilled upon the floor during the blending of the wine, impregnated with an incense of sweet madness the peaceful atmosphere of that wine-shed, as white as a palace of ice under the tremulous caress of the windows aflame with the sun.

Fermín crossed it, and was about to leave by the opposite door when he heard some one call him from the rear. He was somewhat startled as he recognized the voice. It was "the boss," who was showing some strangers about. With him was his first cousin Luis, a Dupont who, though but a few years younger than don Pablo, looked up to him as the head of the family, without for this reason renouncing the privilege of causing that worthy gentleman much displeasure by his unruly conduct.

The two Duponts were showing the establishment to

a newly-wed couple from Madrid. The husband was an old friend of Luis,—a companion in the gay life of Madrid who had at last married and settled down.

"You've got to leave drunk," young Dupont was saying to the newly-weds. "It's obligatory. We would consider it an affront if a friend left this place as sober as he entered."

And the elder Dupont received his cousin's words with a patronizing smile, enumerating meanwhile the excellent points of each famous wine. The man in charge of the bodega, as rigid as a soldier, stood before the casks with two glasses in one hand and in the other the *avenencia*, a short iron rod tipped with a narrow scoop.

"Draw, Juanito!" ordered the owner, imperiously.

The *avenencia* disappeared into several casks, and with a single stroke, not a drop being spilled, the glasses were filled. The luminous golden wines sparkled in the air, crowned with jewels as they were poured into the glass, filling the atmosphere with an intense odor of antiquity. All the shades of amber, from soft gray to pale yellow, glittered in these fluids, as thick as oil to the sight, yet of a glistening transparency. A faint exotic perfume, which summoned to thought fantastic flowers of a supernatural world, rose over the liquids extracted from the mystery of the casks. Life seemed to expand upon tasting them; the blood began to burn, bounding more quickly through the veins; the sense of smell, quickened to unknown desires, grew excited as if scenting a new electricity. After resisting Luis's invitations with weak protests, the traveling couple drained their glasses.

"Ho there, rascal!" cried Dupont the younger as he caught sight of Montenegro. "How's your family? I'm coming over to the vineyard one of these days. I'd like to try out a horse I bought yesterday."

And after clasping Montenegro's right hand and slapping him several times across the shoulder, happy at having been able to display the strength of his hands before his old friends, Luis turned his back to Fermín.

Fermín was very intimate with the young man. They had been brought up together in the vineyard of Marchamalo, with that familiarity of intercourse which the Duponts accorded to the Montenegro family.

With don Pablo the case was different. The owner was but a half dozen years the senior of Fermín; he, too, had seen Fermín run about the vineyard in his childhood, while the deceased don Pablo was alive; but now he was the head of the family, the director of the firm, and his was the ancient conception of authority, as grim and indisputable as that of God, with shouts and paroxysms of anger upon the occasion of the slightest disobedience.

"Remain here," he commanded Montenegro curtly. "I've got something to say to you."

And he wheeled about, continuing to harangue the visitors upon his treasure of wines.

Fermín, obliged to follow them silently and as humble as a servant in their slow progress among the casks, looked at don Pablo.

He was still young, not yet forty, but his body was already disfigured by corpulency, despite the active life in which his enthusiasm as a horseman engaged him. His arms appeared too short as they reposed, somewhat turned in against the massive contour of his body. His youth was visible only in his chubby-cheeked face, with fleshy, protruding lips, upon the upper one of which manhood had traced only a thin mustache. His hair curled over his forehead, forming a thick lock, to which he frequently raised his fleshy hand. He was, ordinarily, genial and peaceful, but it was enough for him

to imagine that he had been disobeyed or opposed, whereupon his countenance would grow red and his voice
would rise to the flute-like tones of anger. His conception of authority, his habit of issuing orders from
early youth, when by the death of his father he had become the head of the wine industry, led him to become
tyrannical toward his subordinates and even toward his
own family.

Fermín feared him, without hating him. He considered him a sick man, capable of the greatest extravagances because of his religious exaltation. To Dupont,
every master held his position by divine right. God desired the existence of rich and poor, and those at the
bottom should obey those at the top, because it was so
ordained by a social hierarchy of celestial origin. He
was not niggardly in money affairs; on the contrary, he
was generous in his reward of services, although his
largess was very willful and sporadic, depending more
upon how he was impressed by the persons than upon
their deserts. Several times, on meeting in the street
workmen who had been discharged from his bodegas,
he would wax indignant because they did not bow to
him. "You, there!" he would cry domineeringly. "Even
if you're not in my employ, it's your duty to bow to me
always, for I was your master."

And this don Pablo, who through the industrial power
accumulated by his ancestors and through the impetu-
osity of his character was the nightmare of a thousand
men, showed the deepest humility and even abject submission whenever any secular priest or the friars of the
various orders established in Jerez visited him in his
office. He tried to kneel as he kissed their hands, prevented from doing so only because they forbade him
with a bounteous smile; he exulted, with an expression
of satisfaction, over the fact that the holy visitors ad-

dressed him in intimate terms, calling him Pablito, as in the days when he had been their pupil.

Jesus and His Holy Mother above all commercial combinations! . . . They watched over the interests of the firm, and he, who was but a lowly sinner, limited himself to receiving their inspirations. To them alone should be attributed the good fortune of the early Duponts, and don Pablo was filled with a burning desire to redeem the religious indifference of his predecessors by his own fervor. It was the heavenly protectors who had suggested to him the idea of founding the cognac distillery, which had communicated a new impulse to the business; they, too, had brought it about that the trade-mark of the Duponts, with the aid of plentiful advertising, had spread all over Spain, without fear of rivalry. A great favor this, for which every year he returned thanks, devoting a part of his profits to the aid of the new religious orders established in Jerez, or helping his mother, the noble doña Elvira, who always had some chapels to restore or a luxurious cloak to be made for some Virgin.

Don Pablo's religious extravagances furnished laughter to the whole town; but there were many who laughed with a certain fear, for, since they were more or less directly dependent upon the firm's industrial power, they needed his business support and feared his displeasure.

Montenegro recalled the stupefaction of the townsfolk a year before, when one of the dogs that watched over the wine-sheds at night had bitten various employees. Dupont had come to their aid, fearing lest the bites produce hydrophobia; to avoid this, he made the victims at once swallow, in the form of pills, the print of a miraculous saint owned by his mother. The affair was so incredible that Fermín, although he had been present, began to doubt as time passed by whether it had really taken place. It is true, of course, that don Pablo afterwards paid the victims' traveling expenses, when they went to a noted physician to be cured. Upon being confronted with this circumstance Dupont explained his conduct with disconcerting simplicity. "First, Faith. Then, Science, which sometimes accomplishes great things, only because God permits it."

Fermín was amazed by the inconsistency of this man, —an expert in business, who advanced the great industrial exploitation inherited from his ancestors, adding to it certain successful innovations; who had traveled and was possessed of a certain amount of culture, and who nevertheless was capable of the most monstrous extravagances of superstition, believing in supernatural intervention with all the simplicity of a lay brother.

Dupont, after accompanying his cousin and his cousin's friends through the wine-shed, decided to withdraw, as if his proprietorial dignity permitted him to show only the most select section of the establishment. Luis would take them through the other buildings, the cognac distillery, the bottling department; he had some business waiting for him at the office. And saluting the visitors with an expression of haughty, seignorial kindness, which Montenegro had often noticed in don Pablo's mother, doña Elvira, the redoubtable Dupont beckoned his clerk to follow him.

Don Pablo, once out of the bodega, stopped; the two men were now in the open air, their heads uncovered, standing in the middle of an esplanade.

"I did not see you yesterday," began Dupont, frowning as his cheeks colored.

"I could not come, don Pablo. I was detained . . . some friends . . ."

"We'll discuss that later. Do you know what a celebration we had yesterday? You would have been moved by the sight."

And with a sudden outburst of enthusiasm, forgetting his displeasure, he began with an artist's delight to explain the ceremony of the day before in the church of those whom, by antonomasia, he called the Fathers. The first Sunday of the month. Extraordinary ceremony. The crowded temple; the office force and the laborers of the firm of Dupont Brothers were there with their families; almost all of them (eh, Fermín?) almost all; very few were missing. Father Urizábal had delivered the sermon,—a wonderful orator, a savant who made everybody cry (eh, Montenegro?) everybody! . . . except those who weren't there. And then came the most touching scene of all. He, like a commander, approaching the sacred table about which were seated his mother, his wife, his two brothers who had come from London, the staff of the house, and behind them those who ate the bread of the Duponts, together with their families; while above, in the choir, the organ poured forth the sweetest melodies.

Don Pablo grew ecstatic as he recalled the beauty of the ceremony. His eyes glistened, moist with emotion; he inhaled the air as if he still perceived the odor of wax and incense and the perfume of the flowers that his gardener had placed upon the altar.

"And in what excellent spirits such a rite leaves you!" he added with delight. "Yesterday was one of the most precious days of my life. Can there be anything more holy? The revival of the good old times, of simple customs: the master communing with his servants. To-day there are no longer masters, as formerly, but the wealthy man, the captain of industry, the commercial head, should follow the old example and present himself to God, followed by all those to whom he gives bread."

Then passing from tenderness to rage, with all the vehemence of his impulsive nature, he glowered at Fermín, as if up to that moment, engrossed in his description of the ceremony, he had forgotten his clerk.

"And you didn't come!" he bellowed, red with indignation, eying him sternly.—"Why? . . . But don't speak. Don't lie. I warn you that I know everything!"

And he continued to reprimand Montenegro in menacing tones. Perhaps it was his own fault, he said, since he tolerated disobedience in his office. He had two heretic clerks, a Frenchman and a Scandinavian in charge of foreign correspondence who, under the pretext of not being Catholics, furnished an evil example to the others by not attending the Sunday services. And Fermín, just because he had traveled, because he had lived in London and read several crazy books that had poisoned his soul, thought he had the right to imitate them. Perhaps he was a foreigner? Hadn't he been baptized at birth? Or could it be that because Fermín had gone to England at the expense of his employer's deceased father, he thought himself superior to the rest? . . .

"This must come to an end!" continued Dupont, excited by his own words. "If these foreigners don't go to church like the rest, I'll discharge them. I object to their giving a bad example to my office, and affording you a chance to show off your heresy."

Montenegro was not intimidated by these threats. He had heard them often. After any of the special Sunday ceremonies the proprietor always promised to discharge the foreigners; but afterwards, his commercial convenience caused him to postpone this resolution in view of the efficient services they rendered in the counting-room.

What did alarm Fermín, however, was to see don

Pablo change expression and to hear him ask several times, with cold irony, where he had spent the previous day.

"Do you imagine I don't know?" he continued. "No excuses, now, Fermín. No lies. I know everything. A Christian employer should occupy himself not only with the material life of his employees, but also with their soul. Not content with having fled from the house of God, you passed the day with Salvatierra, who has just been released from prison, where by all rights he should have spent the rest of his life."

Montenegro grew indignant at the scornful tone in which Dupont spoke of his master. He blanched with anger, trembling as if he had just been struck by a whip, and he looked straight into his employer's eyes with a certain arrogance.

"Don Fernando Salvatierra," he replied, in a voice that trembled with his efforts to restrain his indignation, "was my master, and I owe him very much. Moreover, he is my father's best friend, and I'd consider myself a heartless ingrate not to have gone to see him after all the misfortune he's been through."

"Your father!" exclaimed don Pablo. "A simpleton who will never learn how to live! . . . May no harm come to his old gray head! And I'd like to ask him what good it ever did him to go marching over the mountains and through the streets of Cádiz firing shots in defense of his Federal Republic and his don Fernando. If my father hadn't taken a liking to him for his simple ways and his honesty, he certainly would have died of hunger long before this, and you, instead of being a young gentleman, would be toiling in the vineyards."

"But your own father, don Pablo," answered Fermín, "was also a friend of don Fernando Salvatierra, and more than once he ran to him, asking help in those days of insurrections and cantons."

"My father!" rejoined Dupont with a certain indecision. "He was a queer sort; the son of a revolutionary age, and a bit lukewarm in what should be man's chief concern: religion. . . . Then again, Fermín, times have changed. The Republicans of those days were many of them fanatic persons, but excellent at heart. I knew several who couldn't bear to miss mass, and they were pious men who hated kings but respected the priests of God. Do you think, Fermín, that the idea of a Republic frightens me? I am more of a Republican than you; I am a modern."

And with violent gestures, striking his breast, he spoke of his convictions. He had no sympathy whatever for present rulers; they were a set of thieves, and as far as religion was concerned, a band of hypocrites that pretended to support Catholicism because they considered it a power. The monarchy was a social banner, as his friend Father Urizábal averred. Very well. But banners and colors mattered very little to him; the important thing was that God should be over all,—that, whether the form of government was monarchial or republican, Christ should reign, and the officials be submissive sons of the Pope. He wasn't afraid of the Republic. He looked with sympathy upon some of the South American republics,—ideal, happy peoples where the Most Pure Conception was captain-general of the armies and the Heart of Jesus figured in the flags and the uniforms of the soldiers, the governments being formed under the learned inspiration of the Fathers of the Company. As far as he was concerned, a republic of this kind might come whenever it wished. Indeed, he would contribute half of his fortune to its triumph.

"I tell you, Fermín, I'm more of a Republican than

you, and with all my heart I would have joined those
good men that I've known since childhood, and those
others who were looked upon by the people as vagabonds, and who yet were excellent persons. . . . But
the Salvatierra of to-day! And all you scatter-brained
young men that listen to him,—you whippersnappers who
think it a small matter to be Republicans and speak of
equality, of dividing up everything, and say that religion
is all very well for the old folks! . . ."

Dupont opened his eyes very wide, to express the
amazement and the repugnance inspired in him by the
new rebels.

"And don't imagine, Fermín, that I am of those who
are scared by what this Salvatierra and his friends call
social revindications. You know very well that I don't
quarrel about money matters. Do the workers ask a
few *céntimos* more per day, or a new rest-period in
which to make a cigarette? Well, if I'm able, I grant it
to them, since, thank the Lord who watches over me so
well, the least I lack is money. I'm not like those other
employers who, living in perpetual uncertainty, trade on
the very sweat of the poor. Charity, plenty of charity! Let people see that Christianity can arrange everything. . . . But what makes my blood boil is this pretending that we are all equal, as if hierarchies didn't
exist even in heaven,—this chatter of Justice when they
come asking for something, as if when I helped out a
poor man I were doing no more than my duty to him,
and as if my sacrifice weren't a kind action. And above
all, this infernal mania of opposing God, of taking away
from the poor all their religious feelings, of making the
Church responsible for all the troubles that occur,—
troubles that are the work of this cursed liberal-
ism. . . ."

Don Pablo grew indignant as he brought to mind the

impiety of the rebellious folk. He refused to compromise on the point. Salvatierra and the rest that
opposed religion would have him to reckon with. In his
business, anything but this. He still trembled with **rage**
as he recalled how, two weeks before, he had discharged
a cooper—a blockhead spoiled by reading—whom he
had surprised in the act of boasting before his shop-
mates of his unbelief.

"Imagine! He said that religions are born of fear
and ignorance: that man, in his early days, had no belief in any supernatural agency, but that not being able
to explain the mystery of lightning and thunder, fire and
death, he had invented God. Heavens! I don't know
how I kept from giving him a good drubbing! Apart
from these follies he was a fine young man who knew
his business. But he's doing proper penance, as nobody in Jerez will give him work for fear of displeas-
ing me, and he'll have to wander about starving. He'll
certainly wind up by throwing bombs, which is the ulti-
mate fate of all who deny God."

Don Pablo and his employee walked slowly toward the
main office.

"You know what I've decided upon now, Fermín,"
said Dupont before entering. "I like you because of
your family and because we've been friends almost from
childhood. Besides, you're like a brother to my cousin
Luis. But you know me. God above everything else.
For His sake I am capable of abandoning my family.
If you are dissatisfied with any of the conditions here,
speak up; if you think your salary is too low, say so.
I don't haggle with you, for I'm fond of you despite
your silly notions. But don't be absent Sunday from
the firm's mass; keep away from Salvatierra and all
the outcasts that accompany him. And if you don't,

we'll have a falling out. Understand, Fermín? You
and I will separate."

Dupont returned to his private office, whereupon don
Ramón, the publicity manager, entered hastily, handing
his chief a packet of papers, with the smile of an old
courtier.

Montenegro, from his desk, watched the head of the
firm engaged in discussion with the office director,
thumbing the papers and making inquiries about business with a directness that revealed how intensely concentrated were all his faculties upon the welfare of the
industry.

More than an hour had passed, when Fermín was
summoned by the chief. The firm needed to adjust an
account with another wine company; it was a drawn-
out affair that could not be discussed over the telephone,
and Dupont was sending Montenegro as a confidential
employeé. Don Pablo, already calmed by work, seemingly wished with this distinction to efface the harsh
threats he had made to the youth.

Fermín donned his hat and cape and left the office in
no particular hurry, having the entire day at his disposal for the execution of his task. The head of the
firm was not exacting when he saw that he was being
obeyed. The November sun, as warm and balmy as on
a day in spring, brought out in sharp relief under its
shower of gold the white houses with their green balconies, cutting off the line of their African roofs across
a deep blue sky.

Montenegro noticed a graceful rider in country costume approaching him. It was a swarthy, robust youth,
dressed like the smugglers or the magnanimous high-
waymen that exist now only in popular legends. As
his horse trotted along, the tails of his short jacket, made
of Grazalema corduroy, flapped in the air; the elbows

were patched with black cloth trimmed with silk, and
the crescent pockets were lined with red. His hat, with
a wide, stiff brim, was held in place by a chin strap.
He wore yellow leather boots with large spurs, and his
legs were protected from the cold by several strips of
skin tied around them, like aprons, with leather straps.
From the pommel of his saddle hung folded his dark
blanket with large tassels; on the crupper, the saddle
bags, and on one side the double-barreled musket peep-
ing out from under the animal's belly. The horseman
rode elegantly, with all the grace of an Arab, as if he
had been born on the back of the steed, and the latter
and his rider formed a single body.

"Ah, there, my fine horseman!" shouted Fermín, as he
recognized him. "Good day to you, Rafael, old boy."

The rider checked his horse so suddenly that the animal's haunches touched the ground, while at the same
time its forelegs rose in the air.

"A splendid animal!" commented Montenegro, stroking the charger's neck.

And the two young men stood there silently, watching the animal's restless, nervous behavior, with the fervor of persons who love horse-riding as man's most perfect state and consider the horse their best friend.

Montenegro, despite his sedentary life as a clerk, felt
atavistic enthusiasm stir within him at sight of a spirited steed; it was the admiration of the nomad African
before the horse, his constant life companion. Of all
the wealth of his master don Pablo, he envied only
the dozen horses—the dearest and most famous in all
Jerez—that stamped in his stables. Even this stout person, who seemed to feel no enthusiasm other than that
inspired by his religion and his wine business, for an
instant forgot both God and cognac upon beholding a
beautiful horse not his own, and smiled with pleasure

when he was praised as one of the first horsemen in all
the Jerez countryside.

Rafael was the steward of Matanzuela, the most valu-
able of the estates that remained to Luis Dupont, the
scandalous, prodigal cousin of don Pablo. Bending over
the pony's neck, Rafael explained to Fermín the reason for his visit to Jerez.

"I've come to buy a few things for my place, and
I'm in a hurry. But before returning I'll gallop over
to the vineyard to see your father. I always miss it
when I don't see my godfather."

Fermín smiled ironically.

"And won't you see my sister? Don't you miss it
when a few days pass without your seeing María de la
Luz?"

"Naturally," confessed the young man, reddening.

And as if he had been overwhelmed by a sudden embarrassment, he spurred his horse.

"Good-by, Fermín, and try to call on us at the farm
some day."

Montenegro watched him disappear rapidly down the
street, in the direction of the country.

"He's an overgrown child," he thought. "Much he
should worry about Salvatierra, and the fact that the
world is ill managed and must be turned, so to speak,
upside down! . . ."

Montenegro walked along la Calle Larga, the main
thoroughfare of the city: a broad way flanked by houses
of dazzling white. The seignorial eighteenth century
façades were carefully whitewashed, as were also the
coats of arms on the keystones. The leaves and twigs
of the carved stone were hidden beneath a coat of mor-
tar. Upon the green balconies at that hour of the morning appeared the heads of dark-complexioned women
with large black eyes, and flowers in their hair.

Fermín followed one of the spacious sidewalks bordered by rows of tall orange trees. The principal clubhouses of the city and the best cafés opened their large glass windows upon the street. Montenegro cast a glance into the *Círculo Caballista*. It was the wealthiest club in Jerez, the rendezvous of the rich, the refuge of the young set that had been born into the possession of country estates and wine industries. In the afternoons the worthy assembly discussed its favorite interests: horses, women and hunting dogs. The conversation did not touch upon any other theme. There were a few periodicals upon the tables, and in the obscurest corner of the secretary's office there was a bookcase whose glass doors were never opened, containing hand-tooled books with gilded backs. Salvatierra dubbed this rich man's club the "Moroccan Atheneum."

A few steps ahead Montenegro noticed approaching him a woman who, with her lively gait, her proud mien and the seductive carriage of her body, seemed to excite the street. Men stopped to eye her and follow her with their glances; women turned their heads with affected disdain, and as soon as she passed, began to whisper, pointing her out. From the balconies the young women called into the houses and other maidens hurried out, their curiosity aroused by the call.

Fermín smiled at noticing the inquisitiveness and the confusion which the young woman left in her wake. From between the lace in her mantilla peeked forth several blond locks, and under her dark, fiery eyes a little pink nose seemed to defy the world with its dainty contractions. The audacity with which she gathered her skirts, accentuating the most opulent curves of her body and displaying a generous view of her stockings, irritated the women.

"God be with you, my winsome marquise!" greeted Fermín, barring her advance.

He had spread his cape, assuming the air of a gallant *majo*, happy at the opportunity to stop, upon the central street of the town and within full sight of all, a woman who provoked so much public gossip.

"Marquise? No, my boy," she replied with a charming lisp. "I'm tending pigs now . . . and many thanks."

They chatted with the familiarity of two good comrades, smiling with the frankness of youth and not looking about, yet rejoicing to think that they were the target of many eyes. She spoke with numerous gesticulations, threatening him with her pink nails every time he dared to say anything "strong," and accompanying her laughter with a childish stamping of the foot when he praised her beauty.

"Always the same. But how very, very fine you're looking, boy! . . . Come to see me some time; you know I like you . . . in a nice way, like fond brother and sister. And to think that my brute of a husband was jealous of you! . . . Will you come?"

"I'll think it over. I don't care to have a quarrel with the hog merchant."

The young woman exploded with laughter.

"You're quite a gentleman; do you know it, Fermín? You are worth more, with that mountain cloak of yours, than all these dandies of the *Caballista*. I'm for the common folk; there's much of the gipsy in me. . . ."

And giving the youth a playful slap with her caressing little hand, she went on her way, turning back several times to smile at Fermín, who was following her with his eyes.

"The poor girl!" he said to himself. "Despite that silly head of hers, she's the best one in her family. And

don Pablo, with all his pride in his mother's nobility! . . . This one and her sister are of those who console us by disgracing their proud lineage. . . ."

Montenegro continued on his way, amid the amazed
glances or the malicious smiles of those who had witnessed his chat with the Marquesita.

Reaching la plaza Nueva, he passed by the groups that
habitually gather there: wine-dealers and live-stock
brokers; cereal merchants, vineyard laborers out of a
position—lean, tanned fellows waiting for some one to
hire the inactive arms that were crossed against their
breasts.

A man stepped out of a group, calling to him:
"Don Fermín! Don Fermín!" . . .

It was an *arrumbador* from the Dupont warehouses.

"I'm not there any more, d'you know? They discharged me this morning. As soon as I came into the
shed the superintendent told me, for don Pablo, that I
wasn't needed. After four years of hard work and good
conduct! Is that what you call justice, don Fermín?" . . .

As the latter with his looks asked the reason for this
misfortune, the worker continued excitedly:

"It's all the fault of their nasty bigotry. Do you
know my crime? . . . Not going to hand in the slip
that they gave me with my pay on Saturday."

And as if Montenegro were not acquainted with the
customs of the firm, the good man related, in detail, what
had happened. On Saturday, when the wine-shed
workers received their week's wages, the foreman presented them all with the little slip: an invitation to be
present the following day at the mass which the Dupont
family was celebrating at the Church of St. Ignatius.
If the ceremony was with general communion, the invitation was more difficult than ever to evade. On Sunday

the foremen of the various warehouses collected the slips from each workman, at the very church door, and upon going over them they could tell who had been absent.

"And I didn't go yesterday, don Fermín; I was absent, just as I've been on other days; I don't care to get up early Sunday mornings, for on Saturday nights I like to have a time with my friends. Why does a fellow work, if not to have his little bit of fun? . . ."

Besides, he was master over his Sundays. His employer paid him for his labor; he did his work and there was no reason for cutting in upon his day of rest.

"Is that fair, don Fermín? Just because I don't act a farce with all those confounded spies and lickspittles who go to don Pablo's mass, together with all his family, and take communion after passing the night in a carousal, they throw me into the street. Be plain spoken; tell the truth; and even if you work like a dog, you're a rascal. Isn't that a fact, gentlemen?"

He turned to the group of friends who from a short distance were listening to his words, commenting upon them between curses against Dupont.

Fermín continued on his way with a certain haste. The instinct of self-preservation warned him how dangerous it was to remain there among persons who hated his employer.

And while he hurried toward the office where they were awaiting him for the settling of the accounts, he thought of vehement Dupont, so fervent in his religion that his very ardor seemed to harden his heart.

"And at bottom he's not bad," he murmured.

Certainly not bad. Fermín recalled the capricious, unmethodical generosity with which Dupont aided persons in unfortunate condition. His kindness, however, was extremely narrow: he divided poverty into castes; and in exchange for his money he demanded absolute submission to all that he thought and loved. He was capable of despising his own family, of besieging it with hunger, if he believed that he was thus serving God—that God to whom he professed such immense gratitude because He visited prosperity upon the firm and was the support of the social order.

CHAPTER II

WHENEVER don Pablo went with his family to spend a day at the renowned vineyard of Marchamalo, one of his diversions was to call upon señor Fermín, the old overseer, together with the Fathers of the Company or the Dominican friars, without whose presence he believed it impossible to make a felicitous trip.

"Let's see, señor Fermín," he would say, taking the old man out upon the spacious terrace before the houses of Marchamalo, which formed almost a town. "Shout your command; but arrogantly now, just like when you were with the reds and marched across the mountains as a *guerrillero*."

The steward smiled as he noticed that the employer and his companions of the soutane or the cowl showed great pleasure in hearing him; but none could tell whether his sly, countryman's smile was one of jest or of gratefulness for the master's intimacy. Happy to grant a rest-period to the young men who were stooping among the vines on the slope, raising and lowering their heavy hoes, he advanced several steps toward the parapet of the esplanade with comical rigidity, bursting into a prolonged, thundering shout:

"Time for a smoke!"

The steel of the hoes ceased to glisten among the vines and the long row of laborers, bare at the breast, rubbed their hands, calloused by the handle of the tool, and from their sashes slowly extracted their smoking provisions.

The old man followed their example, and receiving

43

with an enigmatic smile the gentlemen's praises of his
stentorian voice and commanding intonation, he continued to roll his cigarette, smoking it in leisurely fashion
so that the poor fellows down below might have a few
additional seconds of repose at the cost of their master's
good humor.

When only the end of the cigarette was left there was
a new diversion for the visitors. The overseer once
again strode toward the parapet with purposely exaggerated stiffness, and his voice woke the echoes in the
neighboring hills:

"Back to work!" . . .

And with this traditional summons to resume toiling,
the men once again bent over their tasks and the tools
flashed above their heads, simultaneously, in rhythmic
curves.

Señor Fermín was one of the curiosities of Marchamalo that don Pablo took delight in exhibiting to his
friends. Everybody laughed at the aged fellow's sayings,
the rare, well-chosen terms of his expressions, his advice
uttered in pompous tones; and the old man accepted the
ironic praise of the gentlemen with the simplicity of the
Andalusian peasant, who seems still to live in the feudal
epoch, a slave to his master, crushed by large property
and lacking the stubborn independence of the modest
tiller whose land is his very own.

Moreover, señor Fermín felt himself bound for the
rest of his life to the Dupont family. He had seen don
Pablo in swaddling-clothes, and although he treated him
with all the respect that the master's domineering character imposed, the latter to him was always a child and
the overseer received his peculiarities with a paternal
indulgence.

Señor Fermín had suffered a period of dire poverty
in his earlier days. As a young man he was a vine-

grower, enjoying the good old days—when the laborers went to work in carriage and patent-leather shoes—which the old wine-blender of the Duponts recalled in such a melancholy voice.

Abundance made the toilers of that day generous; their minds were fixed upon lofty thoughts, which they could not succeed in defining, but the grandeur of which they felt, in a confused fashion. Besides, the nation was in open revolt. At a short distance from Jerez, on the invincible ocean whose breezes blew to the very vineyards, the government ships had fired their guns to announce to the queen that she must abandon her throne. The firing at Alcolea had awakened all Spain; "the spurious race" had fled: life was sweeter and the wine tasted better at the thought (consolatory illusion!) that each individual possessed a minute share of the power formerly held by a single person. Besides, what soothing music for the poor! What eulogy and adulation of the people, which months before was nothing and now was all! . . .

Señor Fermín was touched upon recalling this happy epoch, which was that of his marriage to "the poor martyr," as he called his deceased wife. The groups of workers gathered in the taverns nightly, to read the newspapers, and the goblet of wine circulated fearlessly, with all the generosity of abundant work and good pay. A tireless nightingale flew from place to place, mistaking the cities for forests, and its divine music turned the people crazy, causing them at the top of their lungs to demand the Republic . . . but a federal Republic, eh? . . . Federal or nothing. Castelar's speeches, read in these nocturnal meetings, with his curses for the past, and his hymns to the mothers, the hearth, to all the tender themes that move the simple heart of the people, caused more than one tear to fall into the wine-glasses.

Then, every four days, there arrived, printed on a loose sheet, with narrow lines, one of the letters that "citizen Roque Barcia directed to his friends," with frequent exclamations such as "hear me well, good people," "come nearer, my poor comrade, and I will share your cold and your hunger," which softened the hearts of the toilers, inspiring them with great confidence in a gentleman who treated them with such brotherly simplicity. And to wash themselves clean of such lyrism, of so much compressed History, they repeated the clever sayings of the Orense patriarch—the witty Marquis of Albaida—a marquis who sided with them, with the vine-dressers and the field-laborers, who were accustomed to respect with a certain superstitious fear, as creatures born on another planet, the aristocrats who possessed the soil of Andalusia ! . . .

The solid respect of the hierarchy, inherited from their ancestors and transmitted to the innermost part of their souls by long centuries of servitude, influenced the enthusiasm of these "citizens" who at all hours spoke of equality.

What most flattered the elder Fermín in his youthful enthusiasm was the social category of the revolutionary leaders. Not one of them was a laborer, and this he considered a merit of the new doctrines. The most illustrious defenders of the "idea" in Andalusia came from the classes which he respected with atavistic loyalty. They were young gentlemen from Cádiz, accustomed to the easy, pleasure-seeking life of a leading port; caballeros of Jerez, owners of farms, robust persons, expert horsemen, skilled in arms and indefatigable attendants at *juergas:* there were even priests in the movement, who affirmed that Jesus was the first Republican and that as he expired on the cross he proclaimed something like "Liberty, Equality and Fraternity."

And señor Fermín did not hesitate for a moment when, from the meetings and their journalistic oratory, read in a loud voice, it was necessary to pass to sallies over the mountain with a musket on his shoulder in defense of that Republic which was refused acceptance by the very generals who had expelled the Kings. And he had to run about the mountains for many days, firing against the very troops which months before he had acclaimed when, in rebellion, they passed through Jerez on the way to Alcolea.

It was during this adventure that he made the acquaintance of Salvatierra, becoming inspired with an admiration that had never cooled. Flight and a long time passed in Tangier were the sole result of his enthusiasm, and when at last he was able to return to his land, he kissed Ferminillo, the first child that the "poor martyr" had presented to him a few months after he left for the mountains.

He resumed his labor in the vineyards, somewhat disillusioned by the unsuccessful outcome of the rebellion. Moreover, paternity made him selfish, and he gave more thought to his family than to the sovereign people, which could liberate itself without his assistance. Upon the proclamation of the Republic in 1873 his ardor was born anew. At last, it had come! The good era was here! . . . But a few months later Salvatierra, like many others, came to him. Those at Madrid were a set of traitors, and the so-called Republic was a fiasco. It must be made federal, or destroyed; they must proclaim the cantons. And once again Fermín placed the musket on his shoulder and fought at Seville, at Cádiz and in the mountains, for things which he did not understand, but which nevertheless must be truths as clear as the sun, since Salvatierra proclaimed them. From this second adventure he had not escaped so easily. He was caught, and spent many months at the *Hacho de Ceuta,* mingling with Carlist prisoners and Cuban insurgents in a confusion and a wretchedness which he still recalled with horror, despite the passing of many years.

Upon regaining his liberty, he found life in Jerez sadder and gloomier than in prison. The "poor martyr" had died while he was away, leaving her two children, Fermín and María de la Luz, in charge of relatives. Work was scarce; there were too many "hands," and the agitation against the "dangerous firebrands" of the country had not yet subsided; the Bourbons had just been restored to the throne, and the wealthy owners were afraid to admit to their estates the men whom they had lately seen with guns in their hands, menacing the owners with glances and treating them as their equals.

Señor Fermín, in order not to come with empty hands to the relatives who were caring for his little ones, took to smuggling. His companion, Paco el de Algar, who had been in the mountain warfare with him, knew the trade. Between them existed the relationship of the baptismal font, that of godfathership—more sacred among the country folk than ties of blood. Fermín was the godfather of Rafael, the only son of Paco, whose wife had also died during the days of flight and imprisonment.

The two friends undertook together their arduous expeditions as poor smugglers. They went on foot, through the most abrupt paths of the range, making use of the knowledge they had acquired in the complicated marches of the revolutionary campaign. Their poverty prevented them from riding on horseback, like others, in a platoon, carrying on the crupper of their strong steeds two huge bales of tobacco, and on the pommel of the saddle-bow a musket full of shot so as to get the contraband goods at any cost. They were only humble *mochileros* who, upon arriving at San Roque or at Algeciras, slung three *arrobas* of tobacco over their backs and undertook to return to the village by avoiding the roads, seeking the most dangerous paths, journeying by night and hiding by day, crawling over the crags, imitating the habits of wild beasts, bemoaning the fact that they were men and thus unable to tread the verge of the precipices with the same security as animals.

Oh, the hard life of continual risks, the necessity of earning bread struggling against darkness, tempests, and man, who was the worst of enemies! A distant sound, a voice, the fluttering of a nocturnal bird, the cry of the invisible beasts, the bark of a dog—forced them to seek hiding, to stretch themselves prone among the sharp brambles, suffocated by the weight of their burdens. On leaving the Gibraltar boundary they paid to cross the lines. The venal guards imposed fees according to the class to which the smugglers belonged: so many *pesetas* for the men on foot, so many for those on horseback. They all left at the same time, after having deposited their offering in certain hands that stretched forth from gold-braided sleeves; whereupon peons and riders, all the smugglers' army, opened up like the ribs of a fan into the shadow of the night, taking separate roads, spreading through Andalusia. But the worst part was yet ahead: the danger of encountering the flying night-patrols that had not shared in the bribery and were doing their level best to intercept the defrauders and make a good catch of their booty. The smugglers on horseback inspired fear because they answered the "who goes there?" of the guards with bullets; so that it was the poor *mochileros* who bore the brunt of the pursuit.

It took the two men two whole nights to make their way to Jerez, crouching, perspiring in the middle of winter, their ears buzzing and their chests oppressed by

their burdens. Certain mountain passes, where their
enemies lurked in hiding, they approached panting with
uneasiness. They trembled with fear upon entering
certain ravines in whose obscurity flashed the discharge
of a gun or a bullet whizzed by, if they refused to obey
the *"Boca abajo!"* of the ambushed guards. Several
of their companions had met their death in these fateful
passes. Moreover, the enemies avenged themselves for
the long waits in hiding and the fear they felt of the
mounted smugglers, by drubbing mercilessly those who
plied the trade on foot. More than once the nocturnal
silence of the mountains was rent by howls of pain
caused by the barbarous blows with the butt-end of the
guns, delivered at a venture, in the dark, far from any
habitation, far from all law, in a savage solitude. . . .

But these dangers were the least that the godfathers
feared. The thought of losing their load terrified them.
Lose their load! Their only means of existence—the
capital of their business! To find themselves suddenly
without the profits accumulated by dint of exposing their
lives night after night, to be forced to beg a loan again
and begin anew the struggle to pay the money-lender,
taking it out of their bread and the bread of their little
ones! . . .

They ventured perilous ascents in the darkness, so as
not to lose their packages. At the least alarm they fled
from the ravines, taking circuitous courses through almost inaccessible places, which inspired horror when beheld by the light of the sun. The crows, far above,
cawed in fright at hearing the noise of unknown animals
crawling in the darkness. The young eagles fluttered
about on finding their dreams cut short by the dragging
of strange quadrupeds who, wearied by their humped
position, advanced along the thread of the precipices
with their bruised hands, scattering the loose rocks into

the emptiness of the gloomy depths. The recollection of a former companion who had lost his life in these difficult passes froze their blood. "So-and-so lies down there." *Down there,* at the bottom of the black chasm upon the verge of which they were groping, like blind men depending upon their sense of touch—where only the crows could see him, little by little leaving his bones white under the weight of the knapsack, while at his home his hungering family, moved by a distant hope, waited for him to appear some day or other.

The thought of those who waited in vain for their dead comrade infused them with new energy. They, too, had their dear ones who could wait forever, if they fell in a fatal pass. "Forward! Forward!" And with the indomitable valor that is inspired by the struggle for one's children, the two humble smugglers advanced through peril and the night.

Ah! All the dangers señor Fermín had run in his life —all the misery of the prison, among persons from all lands, who killed each other with sharpened spoons to vary the monotony of their incarceration! Of the fear of being shot, after they captured him upon the defeat of the party, he remembered nothing with such melancholy as the three times that he was surprised almost at the city gates, by the guards, who relieved him of the load which for three nights he had been carrying on his back. And afterward, when he sold his tobacco to the idlers, the gentlemen of the casinos and the cafés, they even grudged him a few *céntimos!* Ah! If they only realized the cost of those packages, as hard as bricks, in which the sweat of a beast of burden's fatigue and the chills of fear seemed to have become petrified! . . .

Misfortune, wearied of the invariable cunning with which the two friends had been able to escape her, commenced to batten upon them. It was in vain that, at the risk of their lives, they escaped the difficult mountain passes at night. Three times they were surprised near the city, in the meadows of Caulina, when they imagined themselves already safe. They were rudely buffeted about when relieved of those bundles which represented life for their little ones, and were even menaced with being shot if they repeated the offense. The loss of their tobacco intimidated them more than the threats. Farewell, savings! These three failures left them poorer than when they had gone into smuggling, harassed by debts that seemed enormous. Nobody was willing to advance them anything to continue the *business*.

Paco, taking by the hand little Rafael, who was now quite a boy, walked off to Algar, his mountain hamlet, to seek work as a farm-laborer—that is, if they would engage him when they saw how old and sickly he was.

To señor Fermín no place of refuge other than Jerez remained, and early every morning he went to la plaza Nueva to join the group of toilers who were waiting for work, receiving resignedly the scornful glances of the overseers, who refused him because of former reputation as a revolutionist and because of his recent adventures as a smuggler, which had netted him several days in prison. Ah! Those unhappy mornings passed on the square, shuddering with the cold of dawn, without any other nourishment in his famished stomach than a glass of Cazalla brandy to which he had been treated by friends! And then the dispirited return to his hovel, the children's innocent smile and the sadness of his poverty-stricken sister-in-law when she beheld him appear at an hour in which the rest were at work.

"Not to-day either?"

"Not to-day. . . But be patient, woman. Just do as well as you can for yourself, and don't think of me."

It was at this time that Fermín made the acquaintance

of his "guardian angel," as he called him—of the man
who, next to Salvatierra, was the master of his will: old
Dupont, who, on seeing him one day, was struck by a
vague recollection of certain marks of respect—certain
small favors to his house and to him personally, at the
time when that unhappy fellow was going about Jerez
with the air of a master, proud of his Phrygian military
cap and his arms, which he made resound at every step
with all the racket of old ironware.

It was the patronizing generosity of a grand gentleman, the caprice of a millionaire who felt admiration
for himself at thought of providing bread for a desperate
fellow who found all the roads to a livelihood barred
against him. Fermín procured a position in the vineyard
at Marchamalo, the great estate of the Duponts. Little
by little he won the confidence of the owner, who watched
his labors closely.

When the former rebel had risen to the position of
overseer of the vineyard, he had already suffered a
marked transformation in his ideas. He considered himself a part of the firm of Dupont. He was filled with
pride by the importance of don Pablo's wine-vaults, and
commenced to recognize that the upper class was not
so evil as the poor believe. He almost abandoned his
high opinion of Salvatierra, who at that time had fled
beyond the Spanish frontier, and dared to confess to
his friends that things weren't going at all bad after the
collapse of his political illusions. He was the same as
ever, a Federal Republican; above all, federal: until a
federal republic should come about, Spain would not be
happy. But, until that happy day, despite evil governments and the fact that "the poor people was oppressed,"
he considered himself in a better position than formerly.
The little girl and his sister-in-law lived in the vineyard,
in an old country-house, as roomy as a barrack; the boy

went to school at Jerez and don Pablo had taken him under his wing and promised to "make a man of him," in view of his wide-awake intelligence. He received three *pesetas* per day, without any other duty than to keep the pay-roll account, hire men and watch over them so that the lazy louts shouldn't take a rest before he shouted the command to begin smoking.

From his days of poverty there remained with him a sympathy for the laborers, and he pretended not to notice their carelessness and their deficiencies. But his actions spoke louder than his words, for, desiring to display his great interest in his master, he spoke harshly to the field workers, with that excess of authority displayed by the humble man as soon as he is elevated above his associates.

Señor Fermín and his children imperceptibly made their way into the master's family, even to the point of being confused with it. The simplicity of the overseer, happy and exalted, like that of all Andalusian farmers, led him to gain the confidence of the master's household. The old don Pablo laughed at his tales of flights through the mountains, sometimes as a *guerrilla* fighter, others as a smuggler, and always pursued by the guards. The proprietor's children played with him, preferring his tomfoolery and his peasant wit to the glum countenance of the English governess who had charge of them. Even proud doña Elvira, the sister of the Marquis de San Dionisio, always frowning and in seignorial bad humor, as if she thought herself degraded by having joined her lot with that of a Dupont, conceded a certain intimacy to señor Fermín. She listened to him with an expression resembling that she had seen at the theater when a lady deigned to hold converse with an old squire, the confidant of her thoughts.

The overseer believed that he was living in the best

of possible worlds whenever he contemplated his children scampering over the paths of the vineyard with the two little ones of the house, while the oldest—the future proprietor—despite the fact that he was still a child, clung to his mother's side, imitating her haughty demeanor. There were days on which don Pablo arrived in a cloud of dust, with his four spirited steeds galloping at full speed, to deposit at Marchamalo a cartload of children—almost a schoolful. With the Dupont children came little Luis, the orphan of one of the brothers of don Pablo, whose ample fortune took care of the child; also the daughter of the Marquis de San Dionisio—two rebellious girls with frank eyes and insolent mouths, who quarreled with the boys and chased them with pebbles, revealing in their impetuous fearlessness the character of their notorious father. Little Fermín and María de la Luz played with these children, who were heirs to large fortunes, upon terms of equality, with the simplicity of childhood, which seems a reminiscence of the times when men lived like brothers, before social castes had been invented. The overseer followed them in their games with tender glances, swelling with pride to think that his children addressed the children and the relatives of the master in terms of genuine intimacy. The dreamed-of Equality had arrived—that equality for which he had exposed his life, and which at last had come to him, to him alone.

From time to time came the Marquis de San Dionisio, and in spite of his fifty years he turned everything topsy-turvy. Pious doña Elvira was proud of her brother's noble titles, but she looked down upon the man for his wild escapades, which had brought a sad celebrity to the noble name of Torreroel.

Señor Fermín, influenced by his old respect for historic hierarchies, admired this noble, happy liver. He

was devouring the last remnants of his family's vast
fortune, and had been instrumental in the marriage of
his daughter to Dupont, so as to provide thus a place
of refuge when the hour of total ruin overtook him.
His nobility was of the oldest in Jerez. The banner of
Las Navas de Tolosa which, upon certain festal occasions,
was pompously brought out from the City Hall, had been
acquired through sturdy blows of the ax by one of his
ancestors. His title of Marquis bore the name of the
city's patron saint. His lineage boasted every grade of
splendor, even friends of monarchs. There were gov-
ernors who struck terror into the Moors, viceroys of the
Indies, holy archbishops, admirals of royal galleys; but
the marquis rated cheaply so many honors and such
illustrious forebears, believing that it would have been
better for him to possess such a fortune as that of his
brother-in-law Dupont, although without the obligations
and labors of the latter. He lived in a lordly mansion,
the sole remainder of a Saracen fortress, restored and
transformed by his ancestors. In the halls, almost empty,
there remained as memories of the former magnificence
several repulsive tapestries, dark paintings of bloody
saints in hair-raising postures, chairs in Imperial style,
their silk all raveled; in short, everything that had been
refused by the Sevillian dealers in antiques, to whom
the marquis had recourse in his moments of financial
embarrassment. The rest, triptychs and panels, swords
and armor belonging to the Torreroels of the Reconquest, exotic wealth brought from the Indies, and gifts
that the various monarchs of Spain had made to his
ancestors—ambassadors who left at the courts a recollection of their princely ostentation—had all gradually
disappeared after the terrible nights in which Fortune
turned her back upon him at the gaming table. To con-

sole himself for these adversities, he gave noisy feasts which were the talk of all Jerez for days afterward.

A widower since early youth, he gave his two daughters into the care of young governesses, whom the little wards more than once surprised in the embrace of their papa, and addressing him familiarly. Señora Dupont, on learning of this scandalous procedure, waxed indignant and took her nieces in under her own roof to remove them from the sight of such evil example. But they, like true daughters of their father, longed for their free surroundings, and protested with such desperate weeping and such writhings upon the floor, that they succeeded in being returned to the absolute independence of that old mansion through which money and pleasure sped like a hurricane of madness.

The most notorious gipsy bands camped in the historic palace. The marquis felt himself fascinated and dominated by the women with their olive-colored skin and their eyes as fiery as glowing coals, who attracted his affections with a mysterious magnetism. He ruined himself covering, with jewels and bright shawls, gipsies who had worked on the farms, hoeing the fields and sleeping in the immodest promiscuity of the workers' dormitories. The endless tribe of each of his favorites pursued him with servile whining and the insatiable greed of their race, and the marquis allowed himself to be plundered, laughing at the cleverness of his illegitimate relatives, who fawned upon him, declaring that he was a pure *cañi*, more of a gipsy than any of them.

The most popular bull-fighters passed through Jerez to honor with their presence the Marquis de San Dionisio, who organized pandemoniac celebrations in their honor. Many a night the little daughters awoke in their beds, hearing at the other extreme of the house the strumming of the guitar, the wailing of the deep *cante*,

the shuffle of dancing feet, and through the illuminated
windows on the other side of the patio, which was as
large as a square, they could see men passing in shirt
sleeves, with a bottle in one hand and a tray of glasses
in the other; there were women, too, with their hair
disheveled and trembling, crushed flowers stuck behind
their ears, running about with inciting movements to
evade the pursuit of the men, or waving their Manila
shawls as if goading them on like a bull. Some mornings the little girls, upon arising, even found unknown
men sprawling upon the divans, snoring with their
mouths wide open, their sweaty exhalations covering
their ears, their trousers unbuttoned, and more than one
with the remains of an ill-digested supper at a short
distance from his face. These orgies were admired by
some as a simple display of the marquis's popular tastes.

Señor Fermín was among these admirers. A personage of such noble lineage who could, without dishonor,
make love to a princess, amusing himself with village
maidens or gipsies; choosing his friends from among
horsemen, bull-fighters and cattle-raisers, and clinking
a glass of wine with the first poor fellow that came along
to ask for it! This was pure democracy! . . . And to
the enthusiasm for the plebeian tastes of this nobleman,
who seemingly desired to indemnify the common people
for the haughtiness and the pride of his snobbish ancestors, was added the almost religious admiration which
physical vigor always inspires in country folk.

The marquis was an athlete and the foremost horseman in Jerez. It was a sight worth seeing to behold
him on horseback, in mountain costume, with his broad-
brimmed hat shading his grayish, gipsy-like side whiskers,
and his *garrocha* stretched across his saddle. Only
Santiago of the legendary battles could be compared
to him, when, for lack of Mussulmans, he overthrew the

bravest bulls and sent his mount galloping through the most intricate sections of the pasture-ground, passing like a flash among branches and trunks, without any too much pains. Whatever man he let his fist down upon fell to the ground; any wild colt whose back he pressed against with his legs of steel might just as well rise on its hind legs, bite the air and foam with rage, for it would sooner collapse, beaten and panting for breath, than succeed in freeing itself of the weight of its conqueror.

The bravery of the first Torreroel of the Reconquest and the bounty of those who lived afterward in the court ruining themselves in the entourage of the kings, came to life again in him like the last flicker of a race on the point of extinction. He was capable of the same feats as his ancestors had performed when they conquered the banner at *Las Navas* and he was hastening to his ruin with the same indifference as that of those ancestors who had sailed to reëstablish their fortunes by governing the Indies.

The Marquis de San Dionisio was well content with his ostentatious display of strength, and his rough jests, which usually ended in injuries to his companions. When they admiringly called him a brute, he smiled, proud of his race. Brute, yes; just as his most illustrious ancestors had been—just as the caballeros of Jerez had always been—the very model of Andalusian nobility, arrogant horsemen produced by two centuries of daily battle and continuous attacks upon the land of the Moors, for not without reason was Jerez called de la Frontera. And recapitulating in his memory all that he had read or heard about the history of his family, he laughed at Carlos V, the great emperor, who on passing through Jerez had desired to break a few lances with the noted horsemen of the province, who do not enjoy mock battles, taking them seriously as if they were still struggling with the Moors. In the very first encounter they ripped the Emperor's clothes—in the second they drew blood, and the Empress, who was watching from the tiers, called in great fright to her august husband, begging him to reserve his lance for persons who were not so rough as the knights of Jerez.

The marquis's predilection for practical jokes enjoyed as great fame as his muscular prowess. Señor Fermín would laugh as he related the Marquis of San Dionisio's funny pranks to the vineyard toilers. These were all jests of action in which there was always a victim; cruel tricks, worthy of a crude people's enjoyment. One day, as the marquis passed through the market-place, two blind beggars recognized him by his voice and greeted him with pompous phrases, hoping that he would come to their aid, as usual. "Here's something for both of you," and he continued on his way, not having given anything, while the two mendicants heaped insults upon each other, each believing that his companion had received the alms and was denying him half, until, tired of verbal injuries, they raised their sticks.

Another time the marquis had the news spread that on his birthday he would present a *peseta* to every lame man who came to his house. The notice spread like wildfire, and the patio of the mansion was on the appointed day crowded with lame persons from the city and from the country, some leaning on crutches, others dragging themselves along upon their hands, like human larvæ. And when the marquis appeared upon a balcony, surrounded by his boon companions, the stable-doors were thrust open and there issued forth, foaming at the mouth with anger, a young bull that had previously been goaded. Those who were genuinely lame made for the corners, huddling together in a heap, gesticulating with

the madness of fear; the pretended lame ones dropped
their crutches, and with ludicrous agility climbed over
the grating. The marquis and his friends laughed like
children, and for a long time all Jerez spoke of the marquis's excellent sense of humor and of his habitual
generosity, for, once the young bull was returned to his
stall, the nobleman distributed coins by the handful
among the lame folk, genuine and false, so that they
might all be cured of their fright with a couple of glasses
drunk to his health.

Señor Fermín could not understand the indignation
with which the marquis's sister looked upon his idiosyn-
crasies. Such a man ought never to die! . . . But at
last he died. He died when there was nothing left for
him to squander; when the halls of his house contained
not an article of furniture; when his brother-in-law
Dupont really refused to make him new loans, offering
him all that he needed, as much wine as he desired, but
not the slightest amount of cash.

His daughters, who were now almost grown to woman-
hood and attracted attention by their roguish beauty and
their freedom of manner, abandoned the paternal roof,
which had a thousand owners (since all the creditors of
the Marquis de San Dionisio disputed possession of it)
and went to live with their pious aunt, doña Elvira. The
presence of these adorable little imps produced a series
of domestic troubles that embittered Pablo Dupont's
final years. His wife could not endure her nieces' un-
restrained habits, and Pablo, the oldest son, and his
mother's favorite, added his protests against these relatives who had come to disturb the tranquillity of the
home, as if they brought with them an odor, an echo of
the marquis's customs.

"Why do you complain?" don Pablo would ask, with

displeasure. "Aren't they your nieces? Aren't they your blood? . . ."

Señora Dupont was content with her brother's last moments. He had died like the man he was—a Christian gentleman and a decent person. His mortal illness had surprised him in one of his orgies, surrounded by women and guitar-players. The blood of his first hemorrhage had been wiped away by his woman friends with their shawls adorned by Chinese embroidery and fantastic roses. But upon recognizing the approach of death and hearing the counsel of his sister, who after an absence of many years had consented to enter his home, he wished to "give a good example," and leave the world with a dignity befitting his rank. And priests of every garb and canon hastened to his bedside, standing aloof when a guitarist or some woman friend came to sit down beside him; the fathers spoke of heaven, in which, certainly, a seat of distinction awaited him because of his ancestors' merits. The countless confraternities and brotherhoods of Jerez, in all of which the gay nobleman held hereditary office, were present at Extreme Unction. At his death, his corpse was dressed in friar's costume, and upon his breast were heaped all the medals that Dupont's wife judged to be of greatest efficacy in preventing a long delay in, or obstruction to, this high liver's ascension into eternal glory.

Doña Elvira could not complain of her brother, who at the end had given proof of his noble blood up to the very last breath; she could not complain against her nieces, restless birds that fluttered their wings with a certain impudence, but who accompanied her submissively to masses and novenas, with such gracious unction that she could have smothered them with kisses. But she was deeply grieved by the recollection of the marquis's past and by the giddy behavior of her wards in

the presence of young men; their shameless words and
looks, which were like an echo of what they had heard
in their father's home.

The noble woman was mortified by anything that could
alter the majestic harmony of her existence and of her
salon. Her very husband gave her cause for displeasure
because of his business man's habits—always desirous of
rest, and that serious and somewhat eccentric nonchalance
which he had acquired from his English correspondents.
She felt for him only a feeble affection, similar to that
inspired by a business partner. She was united to him
by a common interest in the children—by a certain gratitude upon seeing that his labors assured the wealth of
her descendants. She had concentrated upon her oldest
child all the love of which her proud, austere soul was
capable.

"He is a Torreroel: he is my son; mine alone. There's
nothing of the Duponts in him."

And with these words, indicative of a vehement
maternal pride, she thought she was liberating her son
from a danger; as if, after having accepted marriage
with Dupont for the sake of his great fortune, she was
now filled with repugnance for him.

She thought with pride of the millions that her children would inherit, and at the same time despised those
who had amassed them. Mentally, and with a certain
sense of shame, she recalled the origin of the Duponts,
and what the old folks of Jerez said whenever they
mentioned their huge wealth. The first of the dynasty
had come to the city at the beginning of the century,
like a beggar, to enter the service of another Frenchman
who had established a wine business. During the war
of Independence the owner fled through fear of popular
anger, confiding all his fortune to his compatriot, who
was a confidential employee. The latter, by dint of vilify-

ing his native country and cheering the name of Fernando VII, succeeded in winning the respect of the people and in making the wine business prosper, becoming accustomed to consider it his own. When, at the conclusion of the conflict, the real owner returned, Dupont refused to recognize him, alleging to himself, to soothe his conscience, that he had acquired the ownership of the firm fairly, by facing all the dangers. And the confiding Frenchman, grieved to the point of illness by this betrayal, disappeared forever.

The business of the house increased and developed with the beneficent fruitfulness that almost always attends an evil deed skillfully executed. Then commenced the honorable career of the Duponts, excellent persons, as generous as are all those who need not stoop to baseness in order to insure their commercial prosperity, and whose virtue is not put to proof by misfortune.

Noble doña Elvira, who never lost an opportunity to boast of her illustrious ancestors, experienced a certain shudder upon calling this story to mind; but she was immediately tranquillized by the thought that with her pious generosity she dedicated a part of the vast fortune to God.

The death of don Pablo solved her problem. She was now more free of preoccupations and twinges of remorse. Her oldest child had just married and he would be owner of the firm. The fortune no longer belonged to the Duponts, but to a Torreroel, and with this it seemed to her that its shameful origin had been effaced, and that God would watch more than ever over the business of the firm. Pablo's commercial aptitude, his initiative, and especially the new distillation of cognac that made the name of their industry famous, seemed to confirm the good woman's hopes. Dupont on the sign, but Torreroel in the soul! Her son appeared to her

a great gentleman of yore, of those who with all their
nobility were cultivators of the soil and served God
plow in hand. The business would now serve this
descendant of viceroys and holy archbishops in affirming
his social importance. The Lord would bless the cognac
and the wine-sheds with His protection. . . .

The overseer of Marchamalo felt the death of his
patron more than all the family. He did not weep, but
his daughter María de la Luz, who was growing up into
quite a young lady, walked behind him, seeking to cheer
him up and rouse him from his sad lethargy, so that he
would not spend hour after hour seated in a corner of
the vineyard with his chin in his hands and his gaze lost
in the horizon, as spiritless and downcast as a dog that
has lost its master.

The daughter's condolence was fruitless. Never
should he forget his protector, who had lifted him out
of misery! That blow was a decisive one; it could be
compared only to the grief that the death of don Fernando would cause him. María de la Luz, to raise his
spirits, drew from the depths of a closet one of those
bottles that the young gentlemen overlooked when they
came to the vineyard, and the overseer regarded the
golden liquid in the glass with tearful eyes. But upon
filling the glass for the third or fourth time, his sadness
took on an accent of gentle resignation.

"What we humans are! To-day you . . . to-morrow I."

To continue his funereal monologue he kept drinking
with the calm of the Andalusian peasant, who looks upon
wine as the greatest of riches, smelling it and examining
it until, after a half hour of this solemn, refined tippling,
he abandoned Dupont and fixed his attention upon
Salvatierra, commenting upon his adventures and his
travels, in which he propagated "the idea" in such a

manner that for the greater part of the time he lived in prison.

But not for this reason did he forget his benefactor. Ah, good old don Pablo, how well he had treated him! Through him, his son Fermín had become a gentleman. Old Dupont, seeing the industry that the boy exhibited in the office, where he had begun as errand-boy, desired to help him along. Young Fermín had taken advantage of Salvatierra's presence in Jerez to acquire some learning. The revolutionary, returning from a voyage to London, yearning for the sun and the peace of country life, had come to live at Marchamalo, in company with his friend the overseer. Sometimes, when the millionaire visited the vineyard, he encountered the rebel enjoying the hospitality of his property without any permission whatever. Señor Fermín believed that, since it was a matter of so gifted a man, it was unnecessary to solicit the master's authorization. Dupont, on his part, respected the honest, generous character of the agitator. Besides, his foresight as a business man counseled him to be benevolent. Who could tell whether these fellows would again acquire the reins of government on the day least expected! . . .

The millionaire and the leader of the poor calmly shook hands after not having seen each other for so many years, as if nothing had happened.

"Hola, Salvatierra! . . . They tell me that you're little Fermín's teacher. How's the student doing?"

Ferminillo was making rapid progress. Many evenings he did not care to stay in Jerez, and undertook a walk more than an hour long to go to the vineyard in quest of don Fernando's lessons. He devoted his entire Sundays to his instructor, whom he adored with a fervor equal to that felt for his father.

Señor Fermín did not know whether it was upon the

advice of don Fernando or upon the proprietor's own initiative; but Dupont, with the imperious manner in which he offered benefactions, one day expressed his desire that Ferminillo go to London at the firm's expense, to spend a long time at the branch which was situated there.

And off went Ferminillo to London, revealing in his occasional letters his satisfaction with that sort of life. The overseer predicted a brilliant future for his son. He would return from England knowing more than all of the fellows who scribbled in the Dupont counting-room. Moreover, Salvatierra had given him letters to friends he had in London—all Poles, Russians and Italians—refugees in that country because their native lands would have none of them: men who were considered by the overseer as influential personages, whose protection would surround his son as long as he lived.

Señor Fermín, however, languished in his seclusion, unable to converse with any others than the vine-dressers, who treated him with a certain reserve, or with his daughter, who gave signs of developing into an attractive maiden, and thought only of her dress and the admiration of her person. Scarcely did he begin, at night, to spell out by the light of the kitchen-lamp some of the pamphlets of the good old epoch—the short lines of Barcia, which filled him with enthusiasm, like a resurrection of his youth—when the girl fell asleep. From afternoon to afternoon there would appear don Pablo the younger, who directed the great firm of Dupont, allowing his younger brothers to divert themselves at the London branch; or doña Elvira would come with her nieces, whose love affairs had turned the young set of Jerez upside down. The vineyard seemed to have changed; it was more silent, more sad. The little children that in past days used to scamper about the place now were en-

grossed in other preoccupations. Even the farmhouse
at Marchamalo had grown to a sad old age; its rude,
aged construction, more than a century old, was yielding
to cracks. The impetuous don Pablo, in his fever of
innovation, spoke of having it demolished and rearing
some grandiose, lordly structure, that should be a veritable castle of the Duponts, princes of industry.

How sad! His protector had died, Salvatierra was
wandering over the face of the globe, and his friend
Paco el de Algar had abandoned him forever, having
died of a cold yonder on a farm in the heart of the
mountain range. Paco, too, had improved his worldly
position, although not attaining to señor Fermín's good
fortune. By hiring himself out as a farm-hand and making the rounds of the workmen's shelters, wandering
about like a gipsy with his son Rafael, who did the work
of a *zagal*, he had reached the post of steward of a poor
farm: a matter, as he said, of killing hunger without
having to double up before a furrow, weakened by premature old age and by the cruel necessities of the conquest of bread.

Rafael, who was already a youth of eighteen, hardened
by labor, came to the vineyard to apprise his godfather
of the bad news.

"Well, boy. And now what are you going to do?"
asked the overseer, concerned as to the future of his
godchild.

The young man smiled upon hearing him talk of going
to work upon another farm. No tilling the soil for
him! He detested it! He was fond of horses and guns
—with all the childish enthusiasm of any youth belonging
to the *Círculo Caballista*. When it came to breaking in
a colt or sending a bullet to the target he aimed at, he
admitted no rival. Besides, he was a thorough man; as
much a man as the best of them; he liked brave fellows

so that he could match his strength against theirs; he longed for adventures, to show that he was the son of Paco el de Algar. And as he said this he swelled his chest and crossed his arms, boastfully exhibiting the vital energy and youthful aggressiveness stored in his body.

"In sum, godfather, with what I've got, nobody dies of hunger."

Nor did Rafael die of hunger. He, die! . . . His godfather thrilled with admiration when he saw him arrive at Marchamalo, mounted on a strong, costly, sorrel-colored horse, dressed like a farmer of the mountains, with the conceit of a country gallant, with costly silk handkerchiefs sticking through his jacket-pockets and his musket hanging from the saddle-bow. The old smuggler's heart bounded with pleasure on hearing the youth relate his deeds of prowess. The boy was avenging his former companion and him for the terrors they had suffered in the mountain and for the blows that they had received from those whom señor Fermín nicknamed "the bailiffs." They certainly would think twice before facing this lusty fellow and relieving him of his burden! . . .

The youth was of the mounted smugglers, and did not limit himself to dealing in tobacco. The Jews of Gibraltar advanced him credit, and his sorrel-colored horse trotted along with bundles of silk and bright Chinese shawls on its crupper. Before the open-eyed godfather and his daughter María de la Luz, who looked at him intently with her glowing eyes, the youth drew forth fistfuls of gold coins—English pounds—as if they were mere *ochavos*, and finally would extract from his saddle bags some sightly shawl or intricate piece of lace, as a gift for the overseer's daughter.

The two young persons looked at each other with a certain intensity; but as they conversed they felt a great

timidity, as if they had not known each other since childhood—as if they had not played together when señor
Paco would come of an afternoon to the vineyard, or on
a visit to his old companion.

The godfather smiled slyly as he noticed the agitation
of the young couple.

"It seems you've never seen each other. Speak without fear, for I know that you're seeking to be something
more than my godchild. . . . Too bad you're in that
business!"

And he advised the youth to save, since luck seemed
to be with him. He must hold on to his earnings, and
when he had accumulated a little capital, they would talk
over the other matter—that which was never named, but
which the three understood. Save! . . . Rafael smiled
at this advice. He had that same faith in the future
which is possessed by all men of action who are sure of
their strength; the spendthrift generosity of those who
make their money defying man and laws; the easy largess
of the romantic bandits, of the ancient slave-traffickers,
of the smugglers, of all those who, prodigal with their
lives and accustomed to face death, consider worthless
what they acquire in their game with death. In the
countryside taverns, in the miners' mountain huts, in
every place where men gathered to drink, he generously
paid the entire bill. In the taverns of Jerez he organized
noisy bouts, astounding the young men with his generosity. He lived like those mercenary lansquenets who,
condemned to death, devoured in several nights of Panta-
gruellian orgy the price of their blood. He had a thirst
for life, for enjoyment, and when in the midst of his
hazardous existence he was assailed by doubts as to the
future, he closed his eyes and beheld the gracious smile
of María de la Luz, and heard her voice, which always
said the same thing whenever he came to the vineyard.

"Rafael. They tell me lots o' things about you, and all bad. . . . But you're good! And you'll change, won't you?"

And Rafael would vow to himself that he must change, so that he would not be gazed upon with such pained, large eyes by that angel who watched him from the top of a hill near Jerez, and who, no sooner did she spy him from afar, galloping over the dusty road, ran down the slope through the vines to meet him.

One night the dogs of Marchamalo howled wildly. It was near dawn, and the overseer, grasping his musket, opened a window. A man in the middle of the little square was clutching at his horse's neck, to keep standing. The animal was gasping, and its legs quivered, as if it were about to collapse.

"Open, godfather," panted the man in a weak voice. "It's I, Rafael—I'm wounded. It seems that they've shot me through and through."

He entered the house, and María de la Luz, appearing at the percale curtain of her room, uttered a scream. Forgettting all modesty, the maiden came out dressed only in her chemise, to help her father; the latter could scarcely support the youth, who was as pale as death, his clothes spattered with blackish blood, while a fresh, red stream trickled down his jacket, dripping on to the floor. Exhausted by his efforts to reach the place, Rafael fell in a heap into the bed, managing to tell the story in chopped words, before swooning away.

An encounter with the guards in the mountains before daybreak. He had wounded a man to open a passage for himself, and as he made off a bullet struck his back, below the shoulder-blade. At a wayside inn they had patched him up somehow or other, as if he were a beast, and on hearing with his finely developed mountaineer's ear the sound of the enemy's horses in the silence of the night, he had remounted his saddle to avoid capture. A gallop over leagues, desperate, mad, straining every nerve to keep himself in the stirrups, pressing his legs tightly together with the throat-rattle of a will that is about to give way; everything whirling before his eyes, seeing red clouds in the darkness of the night, while over his chest and his shoulder flowed something warm and sticky, which seemed to suck his very life, with a painful, tickling sensation. He wished to hide, so as not to be caught, and for this purpose there was no place like Marchamalo, during the idle season, with the vine-dressers all absent. Besides, if he was fated to die, he wished it to be among those whom he loved best of all in the world. His eyes dilated as he said this; between his tears of pain he tried to caress the daughter of his god-father with them.

"Rafael! Rafael!" moaned María de la Luz, bending over the wounded man.

And as if misfortune caused her to forget her habitual modesty, she came near to kissing him right before her father.

The horse died on the following morning, exhausted by the mad race. His master recovered after a week of hovering between life and death. Señor Fermín had summoned a doctor from Jerez, a great friend of Salva-tierra, a comrade of the heroic epoch, accustomed to such situations. The wounded youth suffered deliriums that made him scream with the terror of nightmare, and when after long periods of coma he would turn his eyes about, he would see María de la Luz seated at his bedside, bent over his head, as if watching in his breath for the arrival of the vital reaction that would save him.

His convalescence was not long. Once the danger was past, the wound healed rapidly. The overseer declared, with a certain pride, that his godson had the hide of a dog. Any other fellow would have been ground to powder with such a shot. But what were bullets to him —the handsomest chap in all the Jerez countryside! . . .

When the wounded man was able to rise from his bed, María de la Luz accompanied him in his vacillating walks about the front of the house and the neighboring paths. Between the two there had reappeared that bashfulness of peasant lovers, that traditional reserve which makes sweethearts adore each other without speaking of their affection, without declaring their passion, limiting themselves to the mute expression of it through their eyes. The maiden, who had bandaged his wound, and who had seen his bare breast, pierced by that scratch from the violet lips of the bullet, did not dare now to offer her arm to him when he staggered along, leaning upon a cane. Between the two was left a wide space, as if their bodies instinctively repulsed each other; but their eyes would meet, caressing each other timidly.

At nightfall señor Fermín would seat himself upon a bench, under the arcades of the old manse, with his guitar upon his knees.

"Come over here, Mariquita de la Luz! We've got to cheer the invalid up a bit."

And the maiden would burst into song, her countenance grave and her eyes rolling upward as if in fulfillment of a priestly rite. She smiled only when her gaze met that of Rafael. The youth listened to her in ecstasy, accompanying the melancholy strumming of señor Fermín's guitar with a soft clapping of the hands.

Oh! The voice of María de la Luz! A solemn voice, echoing with sad intonations—the voice of a Moorish maiden habituated to constant seclusion, singing for the invisible listener behind the thick curtains. It quivered in its modulations with liturgical gravity, as if it were stirred by the vision of a mysterious religion, known to her alone. Suddenly it grew thinner, winging like a flash toward the heights, until it was converted into a shrill scream—a scream that wandered in serpentine paths, forming complicated arabesques of wild grotesquerie.

The popular couplets heard so often by Rafael in his carousals with the gipsies, sounded like new strains from the lips of María de la Luz. They acquired a touching sentimentality, a religious unction, in the silence of the fields, as if that gay, ingenuous poetry, wearied of rolling over tables stained with wine and with blood, found new youth as it stretched out sleepily upon the furrows of the soil under the canopy of the vines. The voice of María de la Luz was renowned throughout the city. During Holy Week, the people who watched the passing of the processions of hooded monks at the late hours of the night, ran to hear her from close by.

"That's the daughter of the Marchamalo overseer who's going to shoot a *saeta* to Christ."

Coaxed by her frineds, she would open her lips and incline her head to one side with a tearful expression upon her face, similar to that of the Dolorosa; and the silence of the night, which seemed to be intensified by the emotion of a gloomy piety, was rent by the slow, melodious plaint of that crystalline voice which bewailed the tragic scenes of the Passion. More than once the audience, forgetting the sanctity of the night, burst forth into eulogies of the girl's skill and into benedictions upon the mother that had borne her, without respecting the inquisitorial apparatus of the Holy Interment, with its black-hooded friars and its funereal tapers.

The voice of María de la Luz aroused no less enthusiasm in the vineyard. When the men heard her under the arcades they were touched and their simple souls opened to the breeze of the twilight's poesy, while the distant mountains were tipped by the colors of the sunset and Jerez tinged its whiteness with the splendors of a conflagration, standing out against a violet sky in which the first stars were already beginning to twinkle.

The plaintive, melancholy song of the sad peoples awoke inexplicable recollections, echoes of a previous existence. The Moorish soul in them trembled upon hearing those couplets that sang of death, blood, hopeless passion and swaggering threats. The old overseer, fired by the voice of María de la Luz, seemed to forget that she was his daughter, and laid his guitar aside to throw his hat at her feet.

"Olé, my fair one! Long life to your golden beak, and to the mother that bore you . . . and the father, too!"

And recovering his solemnity, he would say to his godson, in the tone of a professor who is imparting truths of universal transcendency:

"This is the real *cante jondo*. . . . A pure Jerez product! And if they tell you it comes from the Sevillians or the people of Málaga, say that it's idle talk. Jerez is the home of song. That's what all the wise men of the world say."

As soon as Rafael felt his strength returning, this period of tender intimacy came to an end. One afternoon he had a private conversation with señor Fermín. He could not remain there; soon the toilers would return, and the place at Marchamalo would again bustle with all the animation of a little village. Besides, don Pablo announced his intention of having the old house demolished, so that he could construct the castle of which he dreamed as a glorification of his lineage. How could Rafael explain his presence in the vineyard? It was a shame for a man of his strength to tarry there, without any occupation, living on the bounty of his godfather.

His encounter with the guards seemed to have been

forgotten. He did not fear persecution, but was, never-theless, resolved to abandon his former life.

"Once is enough, godfather; you were right. This is no way to earn an honest living, nor is there any woman who's going to tie up with a fellow, no matter how much money he brings into the house, when he's always in danger of meeting a violent death."

He wasn't afraid. That, never! But he had his plans for the future. He wished to raise a family, just as his godfather had done, and not pass his life roughing it about the mountains. He would seek a more honest, and more tranquil occupation, even if it meant hunger.

Then it was that señor Fermín, using his influence with the Duponts, procured Rafael the place as steward of the Marchamalo estate, which was the property of the deceased don Pablo's nephew.

That nephew, Luis, had returned to Jerez grown to manhood, after a continuous wandering through all the universities of Spain, seeking ample-sleeved professors who would not make it a point to "flunk" future lawyers. His uncle had imposed upon him the obligation of follow-ing some career, so while the old man lived Luis re-signed himself to living the life of a student. He ad-justed himself to the niggardly remittances of money, supplying their deficiencies with atrocious loans, for which he signed, with his eyes closed, as many documents as the usurers cared to present to him. But upon finding his cousin Pablo at the head of the family, and seeing that his own age of majority was approaching, he flatly refused to continue the comedy of his studies any longer. He was wealthy, and had no desire to waste his time upon matters that did not interest him in the slightest degree. So, taking possession of his fortune, he initiated that untrammeled career of pleasures of which he had dreamed in his necessitous days as a student.

He journeyed over all of Spain, but this time not for the purpose of sampling a course of lectures here and another course there. He aspired to a position of authority in the taurine art—to be a great man in *la afición*—and he went from bull-ring to bull-ring at the side of his favorite matador, witnessing all his exhibitions. In winter, when his idols rested from their labors, he lived at Jerez, caring for his hacienda; this care consisted of spending every night at the *Círculo Caballista,* heatedly discussing the merits of his bullfighter and the inferiority of his rivals, and with such vehemence, that in an argument about a sword-thrust given years before to a bull whose very bones no longer existed he was ready to stake his life, and would whip out his revolver upon the spot, and his knife and the rest of the arsenal which he carried always on his person, as a guarantee of the bravery and the high-handed manner in which he settled his affairs.

He bought up every beautiful and costly horse in the stables of Jerez, outbidding his cousin, who was the richer of the two. At night the mountaineers in the taverns would see him come flying in like the presage of a tempest, certain that he would end by smashing bottles and plates and throwing chairs into the air, to show that he was a real man and could afterwards pay for all the damage done, and three times over. It was his great ambition to be the successor to the glorious Marquis de San Dionisio, but at the *Círculo Caballista* they said that he was no more than that man's caricature.

"He lacks the noble touch—that *something* which the blessed Marquis possessed," remarked señor Fermín upon being told of the escapades of Luis, whom he had known as a child.

Women and bullies were the young man's two passions. Nor did he act very generously toward them. He wished to be worshiped for his skill as a horseman, believing in all good faith that every balcony in Jerez trembled with the palpitation of hidden hearts whenever he passed by mounted upon his most recent purchase.

Toward the suite of sycophants and hectors that followed him about he was somewhat more kind. There was not within the limits of Jerez a single bully of questionable notoriety that was not attracted to him by his liberality. Those who had just been released from prison had little need to worry about their lot; don Luis was a good friend, and in addition to giving them money he showered them with admiration. When, in the wee small hours, at the end of the gluttonous feasts in the restaurants, he felt drunkenness coming over him, he was deluged with disgust for his favorite mistresses and transferred his affections to the brawny giants that accompanied him. He had them display the scars of their wounds and relate to him the tales of their heroic frays. Many a time, at the *Círculo Caballista,* he would point at an evil-faced fellow waiting for him at the door.

"That's *el Chivo,*" he would declare, with the pride of a prince who speaks of his great generals. "A mighty dangerous and brave chap. Between bullet-wounds and stabs he can show more than fifty scars on his hide."

He would then look about with insolent superiority, as if his friend's scars bore testimony to his own bravery, and he lived happy in the thought that in all Jerez there was none who could dispute his popularity with the men and his good luck with the women.

When the overseer of Marchamalo spoke to him in favor of Rafael, the young man engaged him at once. He had heard talk of the boy; he was one of his own (and as he said this he assumed a patronizing air); he recalled certain shots in the mountains and the fear in which the youth was held by the guards. Never mind. Let the fellow be kept. That's the kind of men he liked.

"I'll put you on my farm at Matanzuela," he said, stroking Rafael with his palms in friendly fashion, as if the youth were his pupil. "The steward I've got there now is a half-blind old codger, and the workers make fun of him. And you know what those laborers are: the evil souls! With them, it's a case of bread in one fist and the club in the other. I need a fellow like you to take them in hand and watch over my interests."

And Rafael went off to the estate, returning to the vineyard only once per week, when he went to Jerez to talk over with his master the various affairs of the farm. Many times he had to hunt him up at the home of one of his lady favorites. Luis received him in bed, propping himself up on a pillow, against which another head was also resting. The new steward inwardly laughed at the swaggering affectation of his master, who was more concerned with recommending harshness to him, and telling him to "take in hand" the lazy fellows that worked in his fields, than with learning about the agricultural operations. He would blame the farmhands for the bad harvests; they were a set of ruffians who did not care to work, and wished their masters to become the servants, as if the world could turn topsy-turvy.

Don Luis even forgot his suite of bullies and his amorous exploits when he touched upon the subject of the country boors, who, incited by false apostles, desired to divide up everything. He had studied—so he declared pompously in the *Círculo Caballista,* unaware of the smiles of his listeners—and he knew that the things these laborers wished for were all *utopias;* that's what they were: *utopias,* and he repeated the word with a certain pleasure. All the trouble that was taking place

these days was the fault of the government officials who
didn't "take the workers in hand"; also, it was due to
a lack of religion. Yes, sir—religion. This was the
only check upon the poor, and as there was less and less
all the time, those at the bottom, with the pretext of
hunger, aimed to destroy those on top.

At these words his fellow-members of the *Caballista*
no longer smiled; rather they approved the sentiments
with fervent gestures, with all the faith of their position
as wealthy landowners, who shrugged their shoulders
when some deluded dreamer proposed dams and canals,
and every year went to the expense of great feasts to
the Virgin of Mercy, turning to her in prayer as soon
as their fields began to lack water.

Despite the ideas that Luis propagated in his moments of serious thought, affirming that things would go
better if he were at the helm of the government, don
Pablo Dupont detested his cousin, considering him a disgrace to the family.

This relative, who revived the scandals of the Marquis
de San Dionisio—exaggerating and degrading them, according to doña Elvira, because of his plebeian origin
—was a calamity to a house that had always inspired
respect because of its nobility and its pious deeds. And
to add to the misfortune, there were the marquis's
daughters, Lola and Mercedes. The many times that
their aunt nearly suffocated with indignation, surprising them at night at a low grille-window of their little
palace, speaking with their sweethearts, who changed
almost monthly! Now they were cavalry lieutenants,
now young men of the *Caballista*, or English youths,
employed in some office or other, who were most enthusiastic about flirting in the style of the country, and
made the girls laugh at their Britannic jabbering of the
Andalusian dialect. There was not a young man in

Jerez who did not have his little conversations with the giddy-pated *Marquesitas.* They greeted everybody: it was enough to stop before their grating, whereupon they would engage the person in conversation, and those who passed by without stopping were followed by laughter and sarcastic hissing that sounded at their back. The widow of Dupont could not restrain her nieces, and they, on their part, became more and more impudent toward the pious woman as they grew up. It was in vain that their cousin prohibited them from going out to the window-grating. They poked fun at him and declared that they had not been born for the nunnery. They listened with sanctimonious countenance to the sermons of doña Elvira's confessor as he recommended obedience, and made use of every subterfuge to communicate with the gallants, both on foot and on horseback, who hovered about the street.

One young gentleman of the *Caballista,* the son of a wine-merchant, a great friend of the firm of Dupont, fell in love with Lola, begging her hand at once, as if he feared she would escape him.

Doña Elvira and her son accepted the proposal. At the *Círculo* the courage of the young man, in marrying one of the daughters of the marquis, caused universal comment.

This marriage served as a deliverance for both daughters. The maiden marched off with the other, happy to be free at last from her unbending, pious aunt, and a few months later, at the home of the husband, the sisters resumed the habits with which they had scandalized the Duponts. Mercedes spent the nights at the grating in close intimacy with her wooers. Her sister accompanied her with a certain air of an older woman, and in order not to waste her time, spoke with other men. Her husband protested, in token of rebellion.

But both women were highly offended with him because he dared to interpret these innocent diversions in a manner that injured their modesty.

What great displeasure the two *Marquesitas,* as they were known in the city, brought upon the austere doña Elvira! ... . Mercedes, the bachelor-maiden, eloped with a rich Englishman. From time to time vague news arrived that caused the noblewoman to blanch with anger. Sometimes Mercedes was seen at Paris; others, at Madrid, living the life of an elegant *cocotte.* She frequently changed paramours, for she attracted them by the dozen with her roguish fascination. Besides, the title of the Marquise de San Dionisio, which she had added to her name; the nobiliary coronet with which she embroidered her nightgowns, and the sheets of a bed that was as much frequented as the sidewalk of an important thoroughfare, produced a great impression upon certain vainglorious men.

When the widow Dupont learned these things she thought she would die of shame. Good Lord! And was it for this that the illustrious men of her family had been born—viceroys, archbishops and great captains who received titles and lorddoms from monarchs! And was all this glory to serve only as advertising for an evil woman! . . . And she was the better of the two daughters! At least she had fled so as not to insult her family in their very presence; and if she lived in sin, it was among men of a certain lineage, with persons of rank, as if even in her very debasement she were influenced by a certain respect for her family's high standing.

But there was the other—the elder, the married one —and she was determined, it seemed, to do away with all her relatives by killing them with shame. Her conjugal life, after Mercedes' elopement, had been a hell. Her husband dwelt in perpetual jealousy, groping about blindly in his suspicions, not knowing whom to decide upon, for his wife looked with equal pleasure upon all men, speaking to them with a freedom that incited them to all manner of audacities. He was jealous of Fermín Montenegro, who had just returned from London, and who, resuming his childhood friendship with Lola, visited her frequently, attracted by her picaresque language.

Domestic scenes led to blows. The husband, advised by friends, had recourse to slapping and the stick, to tame "the wicked beast." But the so-called beast justified her sobriquet, for, turning upon her mate with the vigor and the combativeness that she had acquired in a bold childhood worthy of her illustrious father, she gave him back blow for blow so well that it was always the husband who came out second best.

Often he appeared at the *Círculo Caballista* with a face marred by scratches or dark contusions.

"You can't do anything with her," said his friends in a tone of comic compassion. "She's too much for you."

And they praised Lola's strength, admiringly, with the secret hope of some day becoming one of her favorites.

The scandal became so great that the husband returned to the home of his parents and the *Marquesita* was at last able to live very much as she pleased.

"Off with you," said her cousin Dupont to her one day. "You and your sister are the disgrace of our family. Flee far, far away, and wherever you'll be over yonder I'll send you enough to live upon."

But Lola replied with an immodest gesture of her fingers, rejoicing at the opportunity to mortify her pious relative. She hadn't the least desire to leave, and she did not. She was very *flamenca;* she liked the place and its people. To go away would be little less than dying.

At various intervals she would go to Madrid on a

visit to her sister, but her stay was always of short duration. She was a *cañí*, a legitimate daughter of the Marquis de San Dionisio. They weren't going to deprive
her of her little sprees that lasted till dawn, holding
hands and beating time to the music, sitting down, with
her skirts upon her knees! They weren't going to take
away her wine of the soil, which was her blood and her
joy! If the family fumed, let them fume! She wished
to be a gipsy, like her father. She detested the young
gentlemen. She was fond of men with wide-brimmed
hats, and if they wore leather aprons, all the better;
but they must be men, every inch of them, smelling of
the stable and the sweaty male. And she continued to
show her beauty—her auburn hair and her skin as
smooth as porcelain—at the restaurants and the cheap
country inns. She treated the singers and the prosti-
tutes that took part in her orgies with exaggerated familiarity, demanding the utmost intimacy of address.
She laughed with the hysterical enjoyment of the
drunken woman when men, besotted with wine, drew
forth their knives, and the women huddled into a corner, trembling with fear.

This life of drunkenness, noise, brawls and alcoholic
caresses she had glimpsed as a child, under the paternal
roof, and perhaps because of this an ancestral influence
worked upon her, following her remorselessly about, as
if she were carrying on a family tradition. In her nocturnal excursions, on the arm of some rustic gallant who
was for the nonce enjoying her affection, she would encounter Luis and his train of merrymakers. They called
each other cousins because of their distant relationship;
they got drunk together, and Luis declared that he would
fight a pistol duel with any one who refused to confess
that the *Marquesita* was "the finest woman in the province." But despite Lola's liberties, which permitted the

scatter-brained young man to appreciate her most hidden physical secrets, and to accompany her more than once through the deserted streets, to the very door of her house, while she made the most strenuous efforts to contain the hysterical impulses that were driving her on to a scandalous deed, their relations never passed the bounds of friendly intimacy. Luis experienced a certain deadening of his desires, leaving for some future time that facile conquest, as if he were restrained by the recollection of the childhood days they had spent together.

The entire city discussed the *Marquesita's* scandalous conduct, and she rejoiced exceedingly at the agitation of the quiet folk.

She was the same, whether they saw her upon the principal streets of the town, dressed in elegant array, or at the Campo de la Feria, in a sumptuous carriage, her hair disheveled and her figure wrapped in a cloak, imitating the fashion of the loose women, and answering the attentions of the men with words that made more than one blush. She took particular pleasure in smiling with an expression of mysterious complicity upon sober gentlemen that passed by in company with their families. Then she would laugh like a madwoman, thinking of the domestic quarrels that would burst forth when these solemn and respectable fathers reached home. For she had had dealings with more than one of the husbands when she was still living with her own. On a sidewalk of la Calle Larga, before the tables of the principal club-houses, she had kissed a friend with exaggerated transports of passion, amid the shouts of the people who ran to their doors.

Her most recent love affair had been that with a young fellow who dealt in pigs—a flat-nosed, heavy-browed giant, with whom she lived in the suburbs. This strong man fascinated her with a secret power. She spoke of him with pride, taking pleasure in the contrast between her own birth and her lover's occupation. From time to time she suffered attacks of willfulness and absented herself from the suburban cottage for a few days. The clownish sweetheart did not seek her, feeling certain that she would return. And when the capricious bird came back, the entire quarter was alarmed at the blows and the shouts that resounded from the cottage. The *Marquesita* would appear at the balcony with her hair hanging down, crying for help, until a brutish paw would drag her away from the railing and thrust her inside, there to continue the flogging.

If any of her friends jocularly referred to these amorous castigations, she would reply with pride:

"He beats me because he loves me, and I love him because he's the only one that understands me. My hog-dealer is every inch a man."

The *Marquesita's* uproarious behavior made some persons indignant and caused others delight. The common folk regarded her with a certain sympathy, as if her degradation flattered the equalitarian instincts of the under dog. The wealthy and pious families who could not deny their relationship to the San Dionisios, since formerly they had sought to establish it as a source of pride, remarked resignedly, "She must be crazy. God will touch her soul and guide her to repentance."

The Duponts, however, could not resign themselves; every time they saw Lola's auburn tresses and insolent smile upon the streets, don Pablo and his mother returned to their mansion in ill humor and in confusion. It seemed that people had lost their respect for them because of this evil woman, the disgrace of the family. They even imagined that they detected in the servants a certain smile, as if they, too, were pleased with the stain

that the madcap was bringing upon her relatives. The
members of the Dupont family ceased to frequent the
city streets, spending many days at their Marchamalo
estate, so as to avoid all encounter with the *Marquesita*
and the persons who gossiped about her eccentricities.

This absence from Jerez permitted Dupont to realize
his dreams in regard to Marchamalo. He had the old
house thrown down and ordered the construction of new
wine-press houses, a beautiful structure for the family,
a chapel as spacious and richly fitted out as a temple,
and a square battlemented tower, dominating the undulation of the vine-clad hills that formed the great
realm of Marchamalo. Everything was new and solid,
constructed with a most lavish indifference to expense.
The only old structure left standing was the wine-labor-
ers' house, so that the estate should not lose entirely its
traditional character, preserving the kitchen that had
been blackened by the smoke of many years, and in which
the workers slept about the hearth, upon a rush mat—
the only bed provided for them by their employer.

Fermín Montenegro, going upon festal days to visit
his family, always found the proprietors. Thus his relations with don Pablo were gradually growing. Amid
the vineyard, under the deep blue sky, the character of
Dupont seemed to soften, causing him to treat his subordinate with more kindliness than in the office.

Before the waves of vines that submerged the whitish
slopes, the wealthy merchant admired the fertility of
his estate, modestly attributing it to the protection of
God. Several wasted tracts extended their tragic deso-
lation amid the foliage of the vine-branches. These were
the signs of the havoc wrought by the *Phylloxera*, which
had devastated half of Jerez. The wine-growers,
ruined by the drop in wine prices, had no means with
which to replant their vineyards. This was an aristo-

cratic, costly soil, which only the rich could cultivate. To begin anew the tilling of an *arranzada* cost as much as to keep a family decently provided for a whole year. The house of Dupont, however, was opulent and could combat the plague.

"Just look, Ferminillo," said don Pablo. "I'm going to plant all those open spaces with American vines. In that way, and above all with the aid of God, you'll see how well things will go. The Lord is with those who love Him."

Doña Elvira did not condescend to take the Montenegro family into her confidence, but she deigned to speak with a certain frankness, which amazed her city servants. Living in the country caused the noble woman to feel a softening of her pride. She spoke to señor Fermín, desiring to learn which church in Jerez María de la Luz attended for mass. . . . Noting how the daughter of the overseer sank into abstraction, with her thoughts far, far away at the farm where Rafael dwelt, the good lady interpreted this sadness as a desire for retirement from the world, and offered the maiden her protection.

"No, señora," replied the girl, smiling. "I don't care to be a nun. Life attracts me."

To Fermín Montenegro the displeasures of a spiritual nature and the great contradictions that the widow of Dupont suffered because of the business were no secret. Her son found himself compelled to deal with persons of every type: heretics and men without religion; foreigners who used the firm's wines and who, when they passed through Jerez, desired to be received with all the hospitality that good customers deserve. . . . To be servants of the Lord and yet have to treat their enemies as if they were equals! In vain did the fathers of St. Ignatius church seek to dissipate these scruples by recalling the importance of business and the influence exerted upon the religious spirit of Jerez by so powerful an establishment. Doña Elvira could be reconciled to their famous *bodegas* only when, annually, a cask of wine, as sweet and thick as syrup, started out towards Rome, destined for the Pontiff's mass, and recommended by several bishops, friends of the firm. This honor served to console her. But even then, what anguish she suffered because of those repulsive, red-faced foreigners who had the audacity to read the Bible in their own fashion and in their own tongue, without believing in His Holiness and not going to mass! . . .

Montenegro had heard of one of the most recent annoyances suffered by the pious lady, which had been spread about by her domestics.

The Duponts had a Swedish traveling-representative, the best advertiser of their business. He sold thousands and thousands of bottles of the *vino de fuego* that Marchamalo produced, in those northern countries of nights that are almost eternal and days of full sunlight that last for months. The salesman, having come to Spain, made it a point to visit Jerez, so as to make the personal acquaintance of the Duponts. Don Pablo had considered it impossible to avoid inviting him to dine with his family.

It was a horrible torture that his mother underwent before this stranger, enormous in build, ruddy-complexioned and of a talkative nature, with that childish delight of men from the north when they come into contact with the sun and the vines of the warm countries.

Doña Elvira received with a hypocritical smile the incessant chatter of the stranger in labored Spanish; his exclamations of amazement as he commented upon the appearance of the country; so many churches, so many monks and priests, so many beggars; the fields cultivated in an almost prehistoric manner; the barbarous, picturesque customs; the main squares of certain towns crowded with men whose arms were crossed against their breasts, each with a cigarette stuck between his teeth, waiting to be hired.

Dupont coughed, pretending to be absorbed in thought, as if he did not hear what his guest was saying, while his mother dumfoundedly followed the havoc that the foreigner was wreaking upon the dishes. What a manner of eating! No Christian could act like that. Besides, he was red, like Lucifer and Judas,—the color of all of God's enemies. His face, congested because of his hearty meal, recalled to her the evil spirits that gesticulated so horribly in the illustrations of her devotionary. And to have to do business with heretics of this sort, who make fun of a Christian country because it still preserves, pure and intact, the reminiscences of more happy times! To be obliged to receive him smilingly, because he was the chief customer of the firm! . . .

When Dupont, after the meal, took him away, the pious lady had servants hurriedly remove the tablecloth, the vases, and all that had been served to the foreigner, without daring to touch any of it herself. Let all *that* never again appear upon the table! Business was one thing, and the soul another, which must be preserved inviolate, removed from all impure contact.

And when the servants returned to the dining-room they beheld doña Elvira, with the font of holy water from her boudoir, diligently sprinkling the chair that had been occupied by the impious red ogre!

CHAPTER III

WHEN the dozen dogs, all told, belonging to the
Matanzuela farm—greyhounds, mastiffs and hunting-
dogs—scented at noon the return of the steward, they
greeted the patter of the horse's hoofs with loud barking and fierce tuggings at their chains; summoned by
these signals, tío Antonio, known by the nick-name
Zarandilla, appeared in the archway to welcome Rafael.

The old man had been steward of the estate for many
years. He had been taken into service by the former
proprietor, the brother of the deceased don Pablo Dupont; but the present owner, the merry don Luis, desired to surround himself with young persons, and taking into account *Zarandilla's* years and his failing eyesight, had substituted Rafael for him. And many thanks
—as the old steward would say with his farmer-like
resignation—for not having sent him begging over the
roads, allowing him instead to live at the farm with his
wife, in exchange for her taking care of the poultry that
swarmed in the corral and his assuming charge of the
hog-pens that were lined up at the rear of the building.
A beautiful end to a life of incessant toil, his spine
broken by the curvature brought on through so many
years of weeding the fields or sowing wheat!

This pair of invalids from the battle with the soil
found no other consolation in their wretchedness than
Rafael's excellent character. Like two old dogs, to
whom from sheer pity a pittance is doled out, they
awaited the hour of death in their hovel close by the
entrance to the farm. Only the kindness of the new

steward served to make their lot endurable. *Zarandilla* passed the hours seated upon the benches at the side of the door, looking fixedly with his opaque eyes at the fields of endless furrows, without being called to task by the steward for his senile indolence. The old woman was as fond of Rafael as if he were her own son. She mended his clothes and served his meals, and he repaid these small services most generously. Blessed be the Lord! The youth, both in his kindness and his handsomeness, resembled the only child that the old couple had ever had: a poor fellow who had died in a Cuban hospital while serving as a soldier, in times of peace. Nothing seemed good enough to *señá* Eduvigis for the steward. She would scold her husband because in her opinion he was not kind and solicitous enough toward Rafael. Before the dogs in chorus announced his approach she could hear the trotting of the horse.

"You blind old fool!" she shouted to her husband. "Don't you hear Rafael coming? Run and hold his horse for him, you wretch!"

And the old man went out to meet the youth, gazing straight ahead with his motionless eyes, which perceived only the silhouette of objects through a gray film, and moving his hands and his head with that trembling of weary, exhausted old age which had earned him the sobriquet *Zarandilla.*

Rafael rode through the gateway upon his spirited horse, as erect and arrogant as a Centaur; with a great clanking of spurs and a rustling of leather he dismounted in the yard, while his steed pawed the stones, as if it were ready for a new gallop.

Zarandilla removed the musket from the saddle-tree; more than once the steward had been obliged to bring the weapon to his cheek so as to impose respect upon the muleteers who were bringing down charcoal from

the mountain and who, upon stopping at the side of the
road, allowed their beasts to pasture in the *manchones*—
uncultivated lands reserved for the cattle of the farm
when they were not upon the pasture-grounds. Then
he picked up the *chivata* that had fallen to the ground
—a large olive-branch that the horseman carried across
his saddle, using it to goad along the cattle that he found
in the corn-fields.

While the old man led the horse to the stable, Rafael
removed his leather apron, afterwards entering the old
folks' kitchen with all the merriment of youth and a
keen appetite.

"Well, mother Eduvigis, what have we got for to-
day?"

"Just what you like, you rascal. Hot garlic sauce."

And they both smiled, sniffing the odor that rose from
the saucepan, where some well-ground bread and garlic had just been cooked. The old woman prepared the
table, smiling at the eulogies with which Rafael was
celebrating her skill as a cook. She was only a wreck
now; the young man might make all the fun of her he
pleased; but in former days the gentleman that came
with the deceased master to see the colts at the farm had
said even better things than these in praise of the meals
she cooked for them.

As *Zarandilla*, having returned from the stable, sat
down before the table, the first look from his opaque
eyes was for the bottle of wine, and his quivering hands
instinctively went forward. This was a luxury that
Rafael had introduced into the meals at the grange. It
was easy to see in all this his ebullient youth, accustomed
to dealing with the gentlemen of Jerez, and his visits to
Marchamalo, the renowned vineyard of the Duponts!
. . . The old steward had spent year after year with no
other enjoyment than stealing away from his wife to the

roadside inns, or going to Jerez under the pretext of carrying a basket of eggs or a brace of capons to the master's family—journeys from which he returned humming a tune, with sparkling eyes, unsteady legs and in his head a supply of merriment sufficient for all of the following week. If he had ever dreamed of possessing a fortune, it was with no other ambition in mind than drinking like the richest man in town.

He adored wine with the enthusiasm of country folk who know little food beside brown bread, the bread of the *gazpachos* or the hot garlic sauce; compelled to wash down with water this tasteless meal, containing no other fat than the ill-smelling oil of the seasoning, they dream of wine, beholding in it the strength of their existence, the delight of their thoughts. The poor long for this blood of the soil with all the vehemence of anemic bodies. The glass of wine stills hunger and with its fire for a moment gladdens life; it is a veritable sunbeam entering the stomach. For this reason *Zarandilla* was more interested in the bottle than in his wife's cooking, holding it within reach of his hand, calculating in advance, with infantile greed, just how much of it Rafael would drink, and assigning the rest of it to himself, without the slightest consideration for his wife, who took advantage of the first opportunity to remove it, keeping a share for herself.

Rafael, unable because of the habits formed in his earliest youth to accustom himself to the sobriety of the farmhouse, ordered the *sobajanero* (a boy who made daily trips to Jerez upon a young ass) to renew the supply of wine from time to time; but he kept it under lock and key, fearing the incontinence of the old couple.

The meal was eaten amid the solemn silence of the field, which seemed to filter into the house through the open door. The sparrows chirped upon the roof; the

hens clucked in the yard, with spread feathers and peck-
ing at the interstices of the cobble-stone pavement.
From the large stable came the neighing of the stallions
and the braying of the jackasses, accompanied by stamp-
ings and snorts indicative of stomachs sated before the
feed in the manger. From time to time a rabbit appeared at the door of the hovel, its ears drooping, fleeing
in fear at the slightest sound, with its little tail trembling upon its silky buttocks. From the distant hog-
pens came loud roars, revealing a struggle of greasy
shoves and treacherous bites around the tubs of hog-
wash. When these evidences of life would die out, silence would return in all its religious majesty, but faintly
broken by the cooing of the doves or the tinkling from
a drove of beasts being driven over the near-by road,
which cut the immensity of the yellow fields like a river
of dust.

Amid this patriarchal calm, smoking their cigarettes
(another excellent custom for which the old man was
indebted to Rafael) the two men discussed in leisurely
fashion the various labors of the farm, with all the
gravity that country folk impart to matters of the soil.

The steward was reckoning the journeys he would
have to make to one of don Luis's pasture-grounds,
where the herd of bulls and the horses belonging to the
grange had their winter quarters. The responsibility
reposed upon the keeper of the breeding mares; but don
Luis, who was more interested in his animals than in all
his crops, wished to be kept fully informed as to the
condition of his mares, and every time he met Rafael,
his first question concerned their health.

Upon his return from such a trip Rafael would speak
with a certain admiration of the keeper and of the *vela-
dores* under him, who watched over the animals at night.
They were men of primitive honesty, their spirits pet-

rified by the solitude and the monotony of their existence. They spent days without speaking, with no other
evidence of thought than the shouts addressed to the
animals in their charge. "Here, *Careto!*" . . . "Go
somewhere else, *Resalá!*" And the bullocks and the
mares obeyed their voices and their glances, as if the
continuous communication between beast and man had
at last elevated the ones and degraded the others, amal-
gamating the species.

The former smuggler felt that he brought back a supply of new life when he went down to the plain, in the
field of endless furrows, over which there bent perspir-
ingly a turbulent, wretched multitude, devoured by hatred
and necessity.

The mountain range was the scene of his youthful adventures, and upon returning to the farm he recalled
enthusiastically the mountains mantled with wild olive
trees, cork trees and oaks; the deep glens with their
thickets of evergreens; the tall rose-bays bordering the
streams, across which large fragments of ancient columns adorned with arabesques, which the water was
slowly effacing, served as a footbridge; and in the background, upon the summits, the ruins of Moorish palaces,—the castle of *Fátima,* the palace of *The Enchanted
Mooress,*—a sight that brought to mind the tales told in
the winter twilights, beside the farmhouse hearth.

The insects buzzed above the restless bushes of the
coppice; the lizards dragged themselves along among the
stones; from afar came the sound of bells accompanied
by the bleating of sheep. From time to time, as Rafael's mount trotted along paths that had never known
the wheel, the curtain of the thicket on the top of a hillock was opened, revealing the horns and the slavering
snout of a cow, or the head of an inquisitive calf; the

animals seemed to be surprised at the presence of a man who was plainly not a shepherd.

At other times it was the mares with their long tails and loose manes that for a moment trembled with wild surprise upon beholding the horseman, and sped down the hillside with violent undulations of their haunches. The colts followed them, their legs grotesquely covered with hair, as if they were wearing trousers.

Rafael gazed in astonishment at the shepherd sons of the mountain. They acted timid and shy before the persons who came from the plain, whom they regarded with a certain suspicious fear, as if they possessed the secret of life's mystery. They were pieces of Nature, of a rudimentary, monotonous existence. They went about and lived as a tree or a rock might have done were it endowed with movement. Within their brains, rebellious to all but animal sensations, the necessities of life had scarcely been able to grow the slightest moss of thought. They looked upon the great warts of the cork-trees as miraculous fetiches, fashioning from them *dornillos,* natural saucepans for the preparation of *gazpachos.* They hunted for old snake skins, abandoned among the stones at the time the reptiles sloughed their integuments; they would festoon the mountain springs with these whitish coverings, attributing mysterious influence to their offering. The long days of immobility upon the hills, watching the animals at pasture, slowly extinguished every human attribute in these men.

When, once a week, the oldest of the herdsmen came down to Matanzuela to get provisions for the cowherds and horsekeepers, the steward liked to converse with the uncouth, somber fellow, who seemed like a survivor of the primitive races. Rafael would always ask him the same question.

"Let's see, now. What is it you prefer most of all? What do you wish?"

The sturdy youth replied without hesitation, as if beforehand he had well determined all his desires:

"Marry, fill up, and die. . . ."

And as he said this, he showed his teeth, as white and strong as those of a savage, with an expression of ravenous hunger: hunger for food and the flesh of woman, yearnings to cram himself in one great feast with all those marvelous things which, according to vague accounts, the rich devoured; to taste in a single gulp the brutal love that disturbed his dreams,—those of a powerful, chaste youth; to know woman, the divinity whom he admired from afar upon coming out of his mountain seclusion, and whose hidden treasures he thought he divined when he contemplated the lustrous, agile cruppers of the mares and the pink and white udders of the cows. . . . And then, die! As if, after these mysterious sensations had been experienced and fathomed there was nothing worth while left in his life of arduous toil and privations.

And these swains, condemned to a savage existence from very birth, like those creatures who are deformed for the purpose of exploiting their ugliness, earned thirty *reales* per month, in addition to a sad pittance that could not still the tremblings of hunger in their stomachs, excited by the mountain air and the pure water of the springs! And the men above them—the keepers of the mares and the cowherds—received two and a half *reales* more, with not a holiday during the year; every day the same, living in isolation, with their wretched wives, who brought little savages into the world, within huts that were black with soot—veritable coffins with a hole for an entrance, walls fashioned out of loose rock and a roof of cork-tree leaves! . . .

Rafael admired the youth's honesty. A man and two young herdsmen living in this wretchedness, watched over flocks that were worth many thousands of *duros*. On the pasture-grounds of the Matanzuela estate the men earned no more than two *pesetas* on an average, and had entrusted to their care eight hundred cows and one hundred bullocks, a veritable treasure of flesh that could sicken and die away as the result of the slightest neglect. This flesh, over which they watched, was destined for unknown persons: the tenders ate of it only when a beast fell a victim to filthy diseases that did not permit of its fraudulent conveyance to the cities.

The bread received at the farm hardened in the huts for days and days; this, plus a handful of chick-peas or kidney-beans and the foul oil of the country, composed their entire nourishment. Milk nauseated them, for they were satiated with its abundance. The old herders even felt their sense of honor rebel when some younger man helped an animal to its death, through the desire to partake of meat. Where could better, more resigned persons be found?

When *Zarandilla* heard these reflections from Rafael, he supported them most enthusiastically.

There was no honor like that of the poor. And yet folks were afraid of them, thinking them evil! . . . He laughed at the honor of the city gentlemen.

"See here, Rafael, how is don Pablo Dupont, for example, with all his millions, entitled to any credit for being good and not robbing anybody? The real good people are those poor wretches who live like cannibal Indians, never seeing a human face, dying of hunger, watching over the wealth of their masters. *We* are the good folk."

But the steward, having in mind the farms of the plain, was not so optimistic as the old man. The toilers there also lived in poverty and suffered hunger, but they were hardly so noble or resigned as those of the mountain, who maintained their purity amid their isolation. The others possessed the vices that are born of herding men together; they were suspicious, beholding enemies on all sides. He himself, who treated them like brothers in poverty, and many times exposed himself to a scolding from the master because he favored them, was looked upon by them with hate, as if he were an enemy. And above all, they were lazy and had to be driven just like slaves.

The steward's talk roused the old man's ire. And what did he expect of the laborers? Why should they have any interest in their work? . . . He, thanks to his position on the farm, had lived to a fair old age. He was not yet seventy and was far worse than many gentlemen of more years who nevertheless looked like his sons. But he could recall the days in which he and Eduvigis worked in the fields and had become acquainted during the promiscuous nights of the workers' shelter, finally marrying. Very few of his companions in misery were left—men or women; almost all had died, and those who remained were similar to skeletons, with twisted spines and withered, deformed, powerless limbs. Was that a life for Christians? To work all day under the sun, or shivering with the cold, for two *reales*, and five as extraordinary, unheard-of remuneration at harvest time! It was true that the master provided the meals, but what meals for bodies which from sun to sun showered all their strength upon the soil! . . .

"Do you call that eating, Rafael? That's merely deceiving your hunger; merely getting your body ready for death to take."

In summer, during the gathering, the workers were given chick-pea porridge—an extraordinary dish that they remembered for the rest of the year. During the remaining months their food consisted of bread—only bread. Dry bread in their hands and bread in the saucepan, in the form of fresh, hot *gazpacho*, as if in all the world there were nothing but wheat for the poor. A small measure of oil, as much as could be contained in the tip of a horn, had to suffice for ten men. To this was added a few slices of garlic and a pinch of salt, whereupon the master felt that the supply was enough for men who required to renew energy exhausted by labor and the climate.

Some farms were managed upon a plan called *pan por cuenta;* here each man received three pounds of bread. Six pounds of brown bread was the only food for two days. Other estates employed the *pan largo* system; there was no restriction; the laborer could eat as much as he pleased, but the farm oven was used only every ten days and the bran-filled loaves were so hard, and solidified in such a manner that the master, who prided himself upon being a generous soul, came out the gainer, for nobody dared to sink his teeth into them, unless moved by the most desperate straits of hunger.

The toilers had three meals per day, all consisting of bread; food fit for dogs. At eight in the morning, after they had put in more than two hours of work, came the hot *gazpacho,* many times more than an hour on its journey from the house, and soaked with rain on winter mornings. The men pulled out their horn spoons, forming a wide circle about the food. There were so many of them, that in order to avoid interfering with one another they kept at a great distance from the tub. Every spoonful meant a journey. They had to come forward, bend over the tub, which was placed on the ground, scoop out their share and return to their places to devour the sops, which were repellently lukewarm. As the men approached, their thick boots raised the dust or clods of earth, and the last spoonfuls tasted like the soil itself.

At noon the *gazpacho* was cold, prepared in the very fields. Bread once more, this time floating in a broth of vinegar, which usually was wine of the previous harvest that had soured. Only the herders and the field laborers, in the prime of youth, dipped their spoons into it on winter mornings, gobbling it down while the cold breeze chilled their shoulders. The older men, veterans of labor, with stomachs weakened through long years of such feeding, held aloof, munching at a dry loaf.

And at night, when they returned to the dormitory for rest, another hot *gazpacho:* cooked bread and dry bread, the same as in the morning. When some animal died at the farm, and no other use could be made of its meat, it was presented to the toilers, and that night the colic of overeating would disturb the mass of human beings herded in the lodge. At other times those who were most brutal in this battle with hunger, if they succeeded in stoning a crow to death in the fields or killing some other bird of prey, carrying it in triumph to the farm, cooked it and celebrated this sumptuous banquet with the laughter of despair.

The men began their apprenticeship to this crushing fatigue and to this deception of hunger in their earliest years. At an age in which more fortunate children were attending school, they were already farm helpers, at one *real* and three meals of *gazpacho* per day. In summer they served as *rempujeros,* walking behind the carts, carrying ripe grain, just like the mastiffs that go behind wagons; they picked up the sheaves that fell upon the road and dodged the whips of the drivers, who treated them like beasts. Then they became field laborers and worked the soil, devoting themselves to this task with all the ardor of youth that needs activity and an opportunity

to display its strength. They were prodigal with their
vigor, and their masters took advantage of this generosity. They always preferred for such work the inexperi-
ence of the youths and the maidens. And when they
had not yet arrived at their thirty-fifth year, the toilers
felt old, broken up inside, as if their life were fading
away; their services began to be rejected at the various
granges.

Zarandilla, who had lived through all this, objected to
having these Andalusian workers accused of laziness.
Why should they work harder? What incentive did
their labor offer them? . . .

"I have seen the world, Rafael. I've been a soldier.
Not one of your fellows of to-day who ride on the trains
like gentlemen, but of those who wore a high helmet and
traveled on foot over the highways. I've covered the
whole nation, killing ants, and I've seen a great deal in
my travels."

Whereupon he evoked the recollection of the cam-
paigns in the Levant, the plains of Valencia and of Mur-
cia, as thickly populated as cities, with the belfries of
neighboring towns visible from every village; every field
had its rustic dwelling, and under its roof lived a care-
free, well fed family, drawing its food from tracts of
land so small that he, with his Andalusian hyperbole,
compared them to pocket handkerchiefs. The men
worked nights as well as days, assisted by their families,
in noble seclusion, with neither the rivalry of groups nor
the fear of a steward. Here man was not a member of
a slave gang; the farm hand was hardly known in those
parts. Each man cultivated his own strip of land, and
neighbors helped one another in difficult tasks. The
toiler worked for himself, and if the land had a master,
the latter limited himself to collecting the rent, trying,

from force of custom and through fear of the poor folks' solidarity, not to increase the old prices.

The recollection of these fields that never lost their green color gladdened old *Zarandilla* after the lapse of so many years, passing like a luminous vision before his weak eyes.

Then he spoke sadly of the province in which he lived. Immense fields whose borders were lost in the horizon; furrows that came together and then were lost in the distance, spreading out like the ribs of a fan, unfettered by boundaries. As far as the eye could reach—meadows or hills, cultivated tracts or strips of pasturage—it all belonged to a single proprietor. A man might travel for hours and hours before walking beyond the property of this one owner. These fields were not for men; they were vast extents that could be cultivated only by giants such as appear in the fairy tales, tilling them with beasts possessed of feet and wings. And all about reigned solitude: not a town, and no dwellings except the farmhouse. One would have to journey for hour after hour before reaching the boundary of another estate.

There were entire provinces in Andalusia that belonged to a mere hundred landowners. And the earth, a dark soil which bore in its bowels a vital reserve accumulated during many centuries because of the weak, indolent tilling of mercenary arms, sought escape for its excess of vitality in a vast flourishing of harmful parasitic growths that sprang up between harvests. Weeding could barely cope with this florescence of wasted energy.

The owner of the land resigned himself to accepting whatever the soil was pleased to yield. The extension of the property supplied the deficiencies of routine cultivation. If the harvest was bad, economies were effected by reducing the pay of the hands and the quality of their food. Slaves anxious to offer their services were never lacking. Down from the mountains, in droves, came men and women begging for work.

The sky was bluer and more serene than in those lands of eternal verdure and incessant harvests that he recalled. The sun shone with greater force, but under its shower of gold the soil of Andalusia appeared sad, as solitary as a cemetery, as silent as if death weighed upon it, with a flight of black birds above, and below, in the limitless fields, hundreds of men lined up like slaves, moving their arms with automatic regularity, guarded by an overseer. Not a church spire, not a group of white cottages such as were to be seen in the provinces where real workers dwelt! Here there were only serfs toiling upon hated land that would never be theirs; preparing harvests of which they would not own a single grain!

"And the land, Rafael, is a woman; and as to women, if you want them to be happy and well, you've got to love them. And no man can love land that doesn't belong to him. He leaves his sweat and his blood only upon soil that gives him his bread. Am I right, boy? . . ."

Let this immense tract of land be divided among those who worked it, let the poor toilers know that they could draw from the furrows something more than a few *céntimos* and three *gazpachos* per day, and then you'd see whether the men of the province were lazy!

They were bad workers only because they slaved for others; because they were forced to protect their wretched existence for a few years more, saving their bodies arduous toil, prolonging the rest-periods granted to them for a smoke, arriving as late as possible and leaving as early. For what they received! . . . But if they only had their share of the land, they would cer-

tainly give it proper attention, combing it and dressing
it at all hours as if it were a daughter, and before daybreak they would be in the field, tools in hand. In the
middle of the night they would arise and proceed to urgent tasks; those plains would be transformed into a
paradise, and every poor man would have his cottage, and
the lizards would not drag along their corrugated, dusty
backs for days and days without encountering a human
habitation.

Rafael opposed objections to the old man's dreams.
The lands that *Zarandilla* had seen were very beautiful,
with their little plots sufficient to feed a family. But in
those places there was plenty of water.

"And here, too!" shouted the former steward. "You've
got the mountain range here, and no sooner do four drops
fall from the sky than it overflows in every direction."

Water! . . . Ships sailed up the rivers of Andalusia,
reaching far inland, while on these shores the fields
were parched with thirst. Wasn't it better for men to
fructify the soil and eat with the surfeit of abundance,
even if the boats had to unload in the coast ports?
Water! . . . Let them give the land to the poor and
they would bring it water by hook or crook, impelled by
necessity. They would not be like the wealthy owners,
who, however bad the harvest turns out, always have
enough on which to live because of the vast amount of
land they possess, and are content to use the same meth-
ods of cultivation as were employed by their grandfathers' grandfathers. The fields that he had admired
in other sections of the country were inferior to those
of Andalusia. They did not contain in their bowels the
concentration of energy capable of producing plenty; they
were exhausted and required much care and continual
treating with fertilizer. They were, according to *Zarandilla*, like those fine ladies of Jerez that caught his eye:

elegant and trim with the fascination of careful attention and the artifices of luxury.

"And this soil of ours, Rafael, resembles the girls that come down from the mountains with the *manijero*. They just reek with the wretchedness of the workers' lodge; they don't wash their hair; they have horrible table manners. But just train them in polite behavior, and you'll see how good looking they are."

One afternoon in February the steward and *Zarandilla* were chatting about various farm matters, while *señá* Eduvigis was washing the dishes in the kitchen. The sowing of chick-peas, bitter vetch and chickling vetch had been finished. Now the gangs of maidens and farmhands were busy weeding the cereal fields. As yet, they were able to sustain their side in the combat against the parasitic growths. Later, when the wheat would begin to grow, they would have to tear the weeds up by hand, bent over all day long, their loins wracked by pain.

Zarandilla, whose weakness of sight had sharpened his hearing, interrupted Rafael, cocking his ear to hear better.

"Boy, it seems to be thundering."

The broad sash of sun upon the stones of the yard grew pale; the hens ran about in a circle, clucking as if they wished to flee from the squalls of wind that ruffled their feathers. Rafael, too, listened intently. It was surely thundering; they were going to have a storm.

The two men walked out to the gate of the farmhouse. Toward the mountains the sky was black and the clouds scurried along like a curtain of gloom, darkening the fields. It was not yet mid-afternoon and all objects began to be enveloped by the diffuse vagueness of nightfall. The sky seemed to have lowered, touching the mountain-tops, engulfing them in its obscure bosom, as if

decapitating them. The birds of prey flew by with strident cawings, flocking together with the terror of flight.

"Comrade! . . . We're in for an awful storm!" exclaimed *Zarandilla,* who no longer could make out anything, as if night had fallen upon him.

The old trunks of the century-plant, the only vertical
lines that broke the monotony of the fields, bent forward one after the other, as if they were ready to break,
and a steady, chilling, impetuous blast howled against
the farmhouse. The doors trembled, and there was a
noise of windows being shut violently; the dogs set up a
mournful howling, tugging at their chains, as if with their
animal sight they could behold the tempest entering
through the gateway, shaking its raincoat and flashing
its eyes.

A vivid burst of flame illuminated the atmosphere, and
the thunder crashed over the farmhouse with a dry
detonation that shook the very foundations, rousing in
the stables an echo of mooing, whinnying and stamping
of hoofs. Then suddenly the rain descended in dense
masses, as if the heavens had burst, and the two men
were forced to seek refuge under the arch of the entrance, able to see only a strip of field through the horse-
shoe of the gateway.

From the ground, lashed by the torrent of water, arose
a warm vapor; the scent of moistened earth, the perfume
of violent rainstorms. Far, very far off, through the
furrows that had been transformed into streams, unable
to contain the full measure of water, groups of persons
were dashing toward the farmhouse. They could
scarcely be seen through the liquid cloak of the atmosphere.

"Jesú!" exclaimed *Zarandilla.* "Those poor fellows
will be drenched to the skin! . . ."

The powerful wind seemed to thrust them forward.

The light from every flash showed them nearer; they stampeded beneath the downpour like a routed drove. As the first groups arrived they ran past the gateway, headed for the workers' dormitory. The men were wrapped in cloaks, and from the brims of their misshapen, faded hats dripped streams of water; the women scampered by squeaking like rats, covered by the various folds of their ragged skirts, spattered with mud, and revealing their legs encased in the men's trousers which they wore while weeding.

Almost all the bands of toilers had reached the farmhouse, and in the doorway of the lodge they were shaking their coats and their skirts, spilling streams of dirty water, when Rafael's attention was caught by several stragglers who were wearily approaching under the slanting curtain of rain. There were two men and a donkey laden with a pack, beneath which its ears and tail were scarcely visible.

The steward recognized one of the men, who was tugging at the beast's halter to hasten his gait. He was called Manolo el de Trebujena, and was a former farm hand who, after an uprising of the field laborers, had been blacklisted by the employers as an agitator. Deprived of work after the strike, he earned his living going from farm to farm as a hawker, selling to the women ribbons, thread, cloth remnants, and to the men wine, brandy and radical periodicals carefully hidden in his bundle—that heterogeneous storehouse which, on the back of the donkey, wandered from one side to the other of the Jerez district. Only at Matanzuela and a few other farmhouses could Manolo enter without causing alarm and encountering opposition.

Rafael looked at the hawker's companion; it seemed that he knew the man, yet he could not place him. The stranger walked with his hands in his pockets, his coat collar raised and his hat pressed down over his eyebrows, dripping water from every extremity of his raiment, crouching and shivering with the cold, and unlike his companion, without a cloak. But despite this, he walked with a steady, rhythmic gait, as if disturbed by neither the rain nor the wind that attacked his frail person.

"Greetings, comrades!" saluted Manolo as he passed before the gate of the farmhouse, dragging his beast along. "What terrible weather for poor folk! Eh, *Zarandilla?* . . ."

It was at this point that Rafael recognized the peddler's companion, noticing his anemic, ascetic countenance, his thin beard and the gentle, fireless eyes behind the blue spectacles.

"Don Fernando!" he exclaimed in astonishment. "Why, it's don Fernando! . . ."

And coming out of the gateway into the downpour, he seized Salvatierra by the arm to lead him into the farmhouse. Don Fernando offered resistance. He was going to take shelter in the lodge, just like his companion; he must not be opposed, for such was his pleasure. Rafael, however, protested. The great friend of his godfather, who had been his own father's leader! . . . How could he pass by the door of the house without entering? . . . And almost by force he dragged him into the house, while Manolo continued on his way.

"Go, you'll do a good business to-day," said *Zarandilla* to the hawker. "The boys are simply dying for your papers, and they'll have something to occupy themselves with while it's raining. It's going to last quite a while, it seems to me."

Salvatierra went into the kitchen; as he sat down, he left a large pool of water that trickled from his clothes. *Señá* Eduvigis, filled with compassion for the "poor gentleman," hurriedly lighted a fire of small wood in the hearth.

"Let's have plenty of light, woman, for the stranger deserves that and much more," said *Zarandilla*, proud of the visit.

And then, with a certain solemnity, he added:

"Do you know who this gentleman is, Eduvigis? . . . Much you know! Well, this is don Fernando Salvatierra, the fellow who's mentioned so often in the papers —the defender of the poor."

The countenance of the old woman, as she turned for a moment from the fire to glance at the newcomer, glowed more with curiosity and astonishment than with admiration.

Meanwhile, the steward looked here and there for a certain bottle of choice wine that his godfather had presented to him several months before. At last he found it, and filling a glass, offered it to don Fernando.

"Thanks. I don't drink."

"But this is of the finest quality, señor! . . ." interjected the old man. "Drink, your grace; it will do you good after the drenching you've received."

Salvatierra shook his head.

"Thank you again; I have never tasted wine."

Zarandilla gazed at him in stupefaction. . . . What a fellow! Most justly did folks consider this don Fernando an extraordinary man.

Rafael asked the guest to eat something; he spoke to the old woman about frying some eggs, and taking down a certain ham that the master had left upon one of his visits; but Salvatierra forestalled him. It was needless; he carried in his pocket his provisions for the night. And from his jacket he extracted a soaked package, which contained a crust of bread and a slice of cheese.

The cold smile with which he refused to accept these

marks of attention precluded any insistence. *Zarandilla* opened wide his obscured eyes, as if to obtain a better view of this astounding personage.

"But at least you'll have a smoke, don Fernando!" said Rafael, offering him a cigarette.

"Thanks. I've never smoked."

The old man could no longer restrain himself. Didn't he smoke, either? . . . Now he could understand the amazement of certain persons. A man with so few needs inspired as much terror as an animal from the other world.

And while Salvatierra drew near to the fire, which was beginning to crackle with a merry blaze, the steward left the kitchen. Somewhat later he returned, bearing his mountain cloak on his arm.

"At any rate, permit yourself to be properly clothed. Take off those dripping garments."

Before the man could refuse, Rafael and the old woman relieved him of his jacket and his vest, wrapping him in the cloak, while *Zarandilla* placed the wet clothes before the fire, which sent up a thin steam from them.

Soothed by the warmth, Salvatierra became more communicative. He was grieved to think that his sober habits should offend these simple persons who besieged him with their hospitality.

The steward was surprised to see him at the farm, as if the storm had brought him. His godfather had told him some days previous that don Fernando was at Cádiz.

"Yes. I was there a short while ago. I went to visit my mother's grave."

And as if he desired to glide hastily over this recollection, he explained how he had come to the farm. That morning he had left Jerez on the mountain *góndola*—one of those coaches that ran along the nearby road

loaded with passengers and bundles. He wished to see
señor Antonio *Matacardillos*, the owner of the "Jackdaw" tavern, situated on the road, near the farm; a
brave spirit who as a young man had followed him in all
his revolutionary adventures. He was sick with heart
trouble, his legs swollen so badly that he could hardly
move them, and was unable to reach the door of his
cabin without countless stumblings and groans. When
he learned that Salvatierra was living at Jerez, his pain
seemed to have increased with the despair of not being
able to see him.

The old tavern-keeper had wept, when his former
leader came to his cabin, embracing him with such vehement emotion that the family feared he would die. Eight
years without having seen his don Fernando! Eight
years, during which he had sent, every month, a paper
covered with scrawls to that northern prison, between
whose walls his hero was confined! Poor *Matacardillos*
knew that he was liable to die at any moment. He no
longer slept in bed; he choked, living almost artificially
riveted to his straw armchair, unable to serve a glass,
receiving with a melancholy smile the muleteers and the
farmhands who commented upon his healthy looks and
his corpulency, assuring him that he complained out of
sheer perversity. Don Fernando must return some time
to see him. He would trouble Salvatierra but little
longer; he was going to die very soon; but his friend's
presence would gladden the little life that remained to
him. And Salvatierra had promised to return as often
as possible, to visit the *veteran*, in company with Manolo
el de Trebujena (another of his loyal comrades) whom
he had met in the "Jackdaw." Together with him he
had undertaken the return to Jerez, when the storm overtook them, forcing them to seek refuge at the farm.

Rafael spoke to don Fernando regarding his strange

habits, which he had often heard his godfather mention: his sea baths at Cádiz in the middle of winter, before the onlookers, who shivered with the cold; his returning home in his shirt sleeves after having given his coat to a needy comrade; his scant diet, which could not cost more than thirty *céntimos* per day. Salvatierra listened impassively, as if he were being told of another man, and only when Rafael expressed surprise at his meager diet, did he open his lips in gentle protest:

"I have no right to more. Don't these poor fellows who are herded in the workers' lodge fare worse than I? . . ."

A protracted silence followed. The steward and the old couple seemed ill at ease in the presence of this man of whom they had heard so much. Moreover, they were inspired with almost religious awe by that smile which, according to *Zarandilla,* "seemed to come from another world," and the firmness of the man's refusals, which allowed no opportunity for further urging.

When Salvatierra saw that his clothes were almost dry, he removed the cloak and put them on again. Then he turned to the door, and despite the fact that the rain was still falling, he desired to go to the lodge, in search of his companion. He intended to spend the night there, since it was impossible to return to Jerez in that weather.

The steward protested. A man like don Fernando in the workers' shelter! . . . Rafael's bed was at his service, and if that was not good enough, he would open the master's room, which was as fine as any in Jerez. . . . The shelter! What would his father say if he tolerated this absurdity? . . .

Salvatierra's smile, however, deprived the youth of all hope. He had said that he would sleep with the laborers, and he was equal to spending the night in the open if they did not permit him to please himself.

"I couldn't sleep in your bed, Rafael; I have no right
to rest upon mattresses while, under the same roof, others
sleep upon mats."

And he tried to evade the objections raised by the
steward, who barred his passage. Old *Zarandilla* intervened.

"It's a few hours before bedtime, don Fernando.
Then your grace may go to the workingmen's dormitory
if that's your pleasure. But now," he added, turning to
Rafael, "show the señor about the place; the horses'
stable is a sight worth seeing."

Salvatierra accepted the invitation, since this did not
violate his ascetic sobriety—the one luxury of his existence. "Let's go and see the horses." He was not greatly interested in the animals, but he was grateful to these
simple folk for their earnest desire to please him and
show him the best in the house.

They crossed the inner yard under the pelting shower,
followed by several dogs who shook the rain from their
shaggy hair. A whiff of warm, thick air, smelling of
manure and animal perspiration, struck the faces of the
visitors as the stable door was opened. The horses
stamped and neighed, turning their heads upon noting
the presence of strangers behind their cruppers.

Zarandilla worked his way in among them, divining
them by touch, groping in the semi-gloom of the stable,
patting some upon the flanks, and rubbing others over
the forehead, calling them by pet names and instinctively
evading the kicks of impatience and joy that they gave
with their shod hoofs. "Quiet, there, *Brillante!*"—"none
of your tricks, *Lucero!*" And crouching under the bellies of the animals, he crossed to the other end of the
stable, while the steward explained to Salvatierra the
value of these treasures.

They were pure-blooded horses of Jerez stock, genuine

stallions of that district; and he praised their intelligent faces, their darting eyes, the trim elegance of their figures, their firm step. Some were dapple-gray, others silver-gray, silky and glossy, and every one of them quivered from leg to crupper with violent tremors, as if he could not contain his excessive energy in this seclusion.

Rafael spoke admiringly of the wealth which these animals represented. A veritable fortune; the señorito was a man of taste, a cultured gentleman who gave no heed to money when it was a matter of disputing the possession of a fine horse with the wealthiest men in the *Círculo Caballista*. He had even outbid his cousin don Pablo for a noted animal. And pointing each of them out, he spoke of thousands upon thousands of *pesetas*, beaming with pride that such treasures should be confided to his care.

The *hierro* of Marchamalo, the mark with which horses coming from that estate were branded, was worth as much as the certificates of the oldest cattle-breeders.

Meanwhile *Zarandilla*, with resounding slaps and grotesque nicknames, was addressing two stallion jackasses, as bony and angular as if they had been carved out with an ax; they were flat faced, their eyes almost hidden under a hairy entanglement, and their ears hung limp—two monstrous, fantastic, ugly beasts that seemed to have arisen from an apocalyptic vision. The old man, leaning against them, spoke of the springtime, when the mares came down from the pasture-grounds and entered the stable, and the chief breeder risked dangerous positions under the menacing hoofs in the exercise of his professional functions.

"Right before you," said the old man, "your grace beholds all the good fellows who produce the colts and the asses of Matanzuela."

He spoke of the reproductive mysteries of that stable,

with the naturalness of country folk, so timid and bashful
in human encounters and yet frank to the point of indecency when speaking of intercourse between animals.
And as if the old man's words brought to the dilated
nostrils of the horses a faint perfume of the longed-for
spring, they commenced to neigh, to jump, to bite at one
another, to shake their bellies with rhythmic movements,
to rest their forelegs upon the nearest cruppers, making
determined efforts to free their heads which were fas-
tened to the rings. Several blows delivered at random
by *Zarandilla's* stick brought this noise of kicking and
neighing to an end, and the beasts once more aligned
themselves before the mangers, venting the rest of their
agitation in roars and tremblings.

The steward led Salvatierra to a large room with
whitewashed walls that served as his office. Night was
beginning to fall and he lighted an old Lucena oil-lamp
that was on a table on which could be seen an enormous
porcelain inkholder, with a pen at least as thick as a finger.
Here he made out his accounts and in a nearby closet
were "the books," of which Rafael spoke with great respect. Every laborer had his own account. Previously the
arrangements had been administered with patriarchal
simplicity; now, however, the workers were particular
and mistrustful. Besides, it was necessary to keep careful track of the days that had been spent entirely in
labor, those on which there had been but a half day's
work because of the rain, and those on which it had
rained all day long, and during which the toilers remained in the shelter, eating their meals without per-
forming any toil.

Next came the stud book, the most precious of the
establishment, which might be called Matanzuela's letters-
patent of nobility. And from the closet the steward
drew an ample volume, which contained the genealogy

and the history of every horse or mule that had come from the estate, with its name, sires and grandsires, description of its appearance, shape, skin, color of its eyes and all defects, which were generously confessed upon the paper, to be guarded secret, leaving it to the purchaser's acuteness to discover them.

Then Rafael showed the other jewel of the farm: a long stick topped by an iron mold, whose receding and projecting edges presented the vague idea of a design. It was the Matanzuela breeding brand—*the iron!*—and Rafael's reverential fondling of it was a sight to behold. A cross upon a half moon adorned the flanks of all the Matanzuela stock.

He spoke enthusiastically of the branding operation, which don Fernando had never witnessed. The breeders cast their lassoes of bristle over the untamed colts, catching them by the ears, while the brand was being heated in a fire of dry cow-dung; when the brand had become red —Zas!—it was applied to the animal's side, burning through the hair and leaving the skin marked forever with the cross and the crescent. And with a certain commiseration for Salvatierra, who knowing so much was yet ignorant of several matters that were to the steward the most interesting in the world, he continued to explain the system to which the young horses were subjected; all the functions that he himself voluntarily performed in his enthusiasm as a horseman.

First, upon the arrival of the horses from the freedom of the pasture-grounds, they were taught to eat from the manger; then they were led out into the open space before the farmhouse, with bridle and a long halter, to run about as if in a riding school, and learn how to place their hind leg where their fore leg had just been, or even further forward, if possible. After this came the most important operation of all: placing the saddle upon their backs, habituating their wild nervousness to this servitude; accustoming them to the crupper and the stirrups. And at last they were mounted, and allowed to walk up and back at first without loosening the rope, then by guiding them with the reins. The colts that he had tamed—animals so savage that they frightened most men! . . .

He spoke proudly of the combats his strength and will had waged against those of ferocious beasts who neighed and bit the air, pawing about, rising vertically or lowering their heads to the earth while they kicked into space, without being able for all this to free themselves from the pressure of his steel legs. At last, after a mad run, in which they seemed to seek obstacles against which to smash the rider, they returned bathed in perspiration, conquered, submitting themselves completely to the hand of their rider.

Rafael suddenly stopped in the narration of his prowess as a horseman, noticing the outlines of a person in the doorway, against the violet light of the dusk.

"Ah, is that you?" he asked, laughing. "Come in, *Alcaparrón*, don't be afraid."

Whereupon there entered a lad below medium height, advancing cautiously, with his back to the wall, as if he feared to scrape it. In his submission he seemed to beg pardon in advance for anything that he might do. His eyes shone in the darkness, even as did his strong, white teeth. He approached the light of the oil-lamp and Salvatierra was struck by the coppery color of his face, with the corneas of his eyes, which seemed stained with tobacco, and with his hands—of two colors—the palms pink and the backs of a black that grew blacker still under the nails. Despite the cold, the newcomer wore a summer blouse, a plaited smock, still wet from the rain, and upon his head he wore two hats, one within the other, of distinct color, like his hands. The inner one appeared grayish white, and brand new in the under part of the brim; the upper one was old, of a reddish black, with frayed edges.

Rafael seized the youth by the shoulder, causing him to waver, and presented him to Salvatierra with mock gravity.

"This is *Alcaparrón*, of whom you have surely heard,— the most thievish gipsy in all Jerez. If there were any- thing like justice, he would have been flogged long ago in the square before the prison."

Alcaparrón tried to wrench himself loose from the steward's grasp, moving his hands with feminine ges- tures, and at last making the sign of the cross.

"Uy! *Zeñó Rafaé*, and what a wicked man you are! . . . Jozú! Such things this fellow says!"

The steward continued with a frowning countenance and a solemn voice:

"He has been working at Matanzuela with his family for many years, but he's a thief, like all the gipsies, and he ought to be in prison. Do you know why he wears two hats? To fill them with chick-peas or kidney beans the moment my back is turned. And he doesn't know that some fine day I'll shoot him down for it."

"Jozú! Zeñó Rafaé! But what are you saying?"

And he wrung his hands desperately, looking at Sal- vatierra and protesting to him with childish vehemence:

"Don't believe him, Zeñó; he's a very bad man and says all this to get my blood boiling. By the health of my mother I swear it's all a lie. . . ."

And he explained the mystery of the two superposed hats that he wore almost upon his ears and which sur- rounded his roguish face with a nimbus of two colors. The lower one was his new hat, for holidays, and he wore it as his best when he went to Jerez. On workdays, he dare not leave it at the farm through fear of his mates, who permitted themselves all sorts of jokes at his expense, because he was "only a poor gipsy," so he covered it with the old hat lest it lose the gray, silky color that was his pride.

The steward continued to tease the gipsy with that peasant humor which takes pleasure in goading vagrants and the meek in spirit to fury.

"Listen, *Alcaparrón*, do you know who this man is? . . . Well, he's don Fernando Salvatierra. Didn't you ever hear speak of him? . . ."

The gipsy's countenance betrayed amazement, and he opened his eyes extraordinarily wide.

"I should say I have! Over at the workers' shelter they've been speaking for two hours of nothing else! Many years, Zeñó! I'm happy to know such a fine, noted person. It's easy to see that your grace is somebody; you've got the face of a ruler."

Salvatierra smiled at the fawning obsequiousness of the gipsy. That unfortunate fellow knew no categories; he judged by reputation, and believing the visitor a powerful personage, a man in authority, he trembled, concealing his perturbation behind the flattering smile of races eternally persecuted.

"Don Fernando," continued the steward, "you who have so many friends abroad could arrange for *Alcaparrón's* trip. Then we'd see if he would have as much luck in foreign lands as his cousins have had."

And he spoke of the *Alcaparronas*, dancing gipsies who had attained a great success in Paris and many cities of Russia whose names the steward could not remember. Their pictures figured even upon match boxes; the newspapers mentioned them; they had diamonds galore; they danced in theaters and at palaces, and one of them had made off with a grand duke, an *archipampano* or something of the sort that slipped Rafael's mind, and he had taken her to a castle where she lived like a queen.

"And all this, don Fernando, despite the fact that they are a couple of presumptuous monkeys, as homely and black as their cousin here; a pair of ungainly girls whom I remember as little ones at the farms hereabouts, robbing chick-peas and other seeds; a pair of frisky mice, with nothing more than a gipsy manner and a few shameful habits that make men blush. And is that what these foreign gentlemen so much admire? Really, man, it's too funny for anything! . . ."

And he laughed indeed, to think that these two copper-colored maidens whom he had seen stealing about the fields of Jerez, dirty and scabby, now lived like courtly dames.

Alcaparrón spoke with a certain pride of these first cousins, at the same time bemoaning the different lot of his family. They had become queens, and he, with his poor mother, his little sisters and Mari-Cruz, his poor little sickly cousin, earning two *reales* at the farm! And many thanks to them for giving them work every year, knowing that they were industrious toilers! . . . His cousins were a pair of unaffectionate ingrates who never wrote to the family, and never even sent them *this much.* (And he clicked one of his finger-nails against his horse-like teeth.)

"Zeñó; it seems impossible that my uncle should treat his own relatives so badly, seeing that he's a *cañí.* And to think how much my poor father loved him! . . .

But far from waxing indignant, he burst into eulogies of his uncle *Alcaparrón,* a man of initiative who, tired of starving at Jerez and ever facing the danger of going to prison every time an ass or a mule went astray, had slung his guitar across his shoulder, taking along all his cattle, as he called his daughters, and hadn't stopped until he arrived in Paris. And *Alcaparrón* laughed ironically at thought of the simplicity of the *gachés*—of all those persons who dominate the world and oppress the poor gipsies—recalling certain prospectuses and newspapers that he had seen with the portrait of his worthy uncle, showing his close-cropped cheek-whiskers, and his thievish face, under a conical hat that looked like a belfry, surrounded by columns of text printed in a strange language, in which the *mesdemoiselles Alcaparronas* were referred to, and their grace and beauty was lauded, with *olle! olle!* repeated about every six lines. . . . And his uncle, to add to his dignity, was called *captain Alcaparrón!* Captain of what? . . . And his cousins the *mesdemoiselles* had themselves abducted by gentlemen who feared their father, *the terrible hidalgo,* who had so often thrummed the guitar philosophically in the village inns, while the future *mesdemoiselles* had hidden themselves with some young men in the most distant rooms. *Josú,* what a joke! . . .

But the gipsy passed rapidly from smiles to tears, with the flighty incoherency of his bird-like soul. Ah, if only his father were alive—his father, who had been an eagle compared to that brother of his that had become so wealthy! . . .

"Is your father dead?" asked Salvatierra.

"Yes, seño: they needed one more in the holy field, and as he was good, he was called by the raven that sits there."

And *Alcaparrón* continued his lamentations. If only the poor old man hadn't died! Instead of his cousins, he and his brothers would be enjoying all that wealth. And he affirmed this in all good faith, discarding as an insignificant detail the difference in sex, and attributing no value to the piquant homeliness of the girls, believing that they owed their fortune to their skill in the *cante,* in which his poor old mother, his cousin Mari-Cruz, and he were much more expert than all the *Alcaparronas* that wandered over the earth.

The steward, seeing how sad the gipsy had become, offered him his protection. His fortune was made. Here was don Fernando, who, with his vast influence had a position already open for him.

Alcaparrón opened his eyes, afraid of a mocking jest. Yet fearing the consequences of a lack of respect toward that gentleman, he showered Salvatierra with fawning speech, while the latter looked at the steward, wondering how far Rafael would carry his joke.

"Yes, *gachó*," continued Rafael. "There's a position waiting for you. The gentleman will make you executioner for Seville or Jerez: whichever you choose."

The gipsy started, revealing his ludicrous indignation in a deluge of words.

"Wretch! Villain! May an evil bullet strike you in your black, black entrails, zeñó Rafaé!" . . .

He stopped for a moment in his malediction, seeing that his curses only added to the enjoyment of the steward, and he added, with malignant insinuation:

"I hope to God that when you go to don Pablo's vineyard the girl receives you with a long face."

Rafael ceased laughing. He feared that the gipsy would speak in don Fernando's presence of his love affair with his godfather's daughter, and he hastened to dismiss the fellow.

"Have a cigarette and be off . . . ill-omened rascal. Your mother's waiting for you."

Alcaparrón obeyed with the docility of a dog. Upon taking leave of Salvatierra he stretched out his tawny hand, repeating that they were waiting for him at the farmhands' dormitory and that the men and women were all excited to think that so lofty a personage was at Matanzuela.

When he had gone, the steward spoke to don Fernando of the *Alcaparronas* and other gipsies of the farm. They were familes who had worked years and years upon the same estate, as if they were part of it. They were much easier to manage, both the men and the women, than the other workers. There was no fear of rebellion, strikes or threats from them. They were beggars and a little thievish, but they grew humble before threatening glances with all the submissiveness of a persecuted race.

Rafael had seen gipsies engage in farm labor only in that part of Andalusia. The enthusiasm of people for horses seemed to have driven them out of this industry, which was theirs the world over, obliging them to seek their living on the farms.

The women were worth more than the men; they were withered, dark, angular, with men's trousers under their skirts, bending all day long at their work of weeding the wheat or sowing seed. At times, when they were not being closely watched, their racial indolence overcame them—the desire to remain motionless, gazing toward the horizon, seeing nothing and thinking of nothing. But the moment they divined the proximity of the steward, the alarm signal passed among them in that *caló* which was their only force of resistance—that which isolated them from the animadversion of their working companions:

"Cha: currela, que sinela er jambo!"

"Get to work, there, for the master is looking!" Whereupon every one fell to his task, with such ardor and such comic devotion, that many a time Rafael could not contain his laughter.

Night had fallen. The rain fell like watery dust upon the cobbles of the patio. Salvatierra spoke of going to the toilers' lodge, without heeding the protests of the steward. But really, was it right for a man of his kind to sleep there? . . .

"You know where I come from, Rafael," said the revolutionist. "For eight years I have been sleeping in worse places and among much more unfortunate creatures."

The steward made a gesture of resignation and called *Zarandilla*, who was in the stable. The old man would accompany don Fernando; Rafael would remain there.

"It doesn't befit me to enter the lodge, don Fernando. I must preserve a certain air of authority; otherwise they get too familiar and everything is lost."

And he spoke of the air of authority with firm conviction, respecting it as something necessary, after having violated it so many times in the rough adventures of his early youth.

Salvatierra and the old man went out through the patio amid the barking of the dogs, and following the outside wall, reached a lean-to that gave entrance to the workers' lodge.

Underneath the projection were ranged in a line various pitchers containing the farmhands' water supply. Those who felt thirst had to pass from the stifling heat of the lodge out into the cold of the night, and gulped down water that seemed like liquid ice, while the wind cut their perspiring backs.

As he crossed the threshold Salvatierra's lungs at once felt the lack of air, and at the same time his nostrils were assailed by a fetid odor of damp clothes, rancid oil, and a viscous agglomeration of mud and flesh.

The room was long and narrow, and appeared more spacious than it really was because of the density of the air and the poor light. At the rear was the fireplace, in which burned a fire of dry cow-dung, sending forth a pestiferous odor. A kitchen-lamp revealed a flame that looked like a red tear twinkling in the cloudy atmosphere. The rest of the room, in complete darkness, throbbed with palpitations of life in its obscurity. The presence of many persons could be divined under the shroud of the shadows.

Salvatierra, advancing to the middle of the wretched habitation, could see better. Over the fireplace boiled several pots tended by women upon their knees, and under the hanging lamp was seated the *arreador,* the second functionary of the house, who accompanied the laborers to their reaping and watched over their toil, urging them on with harsh words. IIe, together with the steward, formed what the workers called the *government* of the farm.

The *arreador* was the only person in the room who could boast a chair; the others, men and women, squatted upon the floor. Near him, seated in tailor fashion, were Manolo el de Trebujena and several friends, thrusting their spoons into a wooden bowl of hot *gazpacho.* The cloud was gradually dissipating before Salvatierra's eyes, which were by this time becoming accustomed to the asphyxiating atmosphere. Now he could make out in the corners groups of men and women seated upon the tamped earth or upon rush mats. The rain, interfering with their labors in mid-afternoon, had caused them to advance the time of their evening meal. Around the tubs of hot meat-scraps they laughed and chatted, dipping in their spoons with a certain tranquillity. They foresaw that the following day would be one of confinement, of enforced idleness, so they wished to remain awake until the night was well advanced.

The aspect of the laborers' quarters, the herding of the folk, evoked in Salvatierra's mind recollections of the prison. The same whitewashed walls, only less white here, rendered sooty by the nauseating vapor of the animal fuel, exuding grime because of continual contact with the unclean bodies. The same hooks upon the walls, and hanging from them the same outfit of poverty: saddle-bags, blankets, tattered clothes, torn mattresses, many-colored blouses, grimy hats, boots cumbered with countless patches fixed by sharp nails.

In prison each convict had his own pallet. In the workers' quarters only a few could permit themselves this luxury. The rest slept upon mats, without undressing, resting upon the hard earth the bones that had been wracked by exhausting toil. Bread, the cruel divinity that obliged them to accept this wretched existence, was scattered in crumbs upon the floor, or could be seen upon the pegs, among the ragged garments, in enormous six-pound loaves, like an idol who might be approached only after a day of wearisome genuflections.

Salvatierra peered closely into the faces of these persons, who eyed him with curiosity, for a moment suspending their meal, holding their spoons upraised in the air, motionless.

Under the misshapen hats were visible masks of poverty, of suffering and hunger. The younger toilers still retained the fresh vigor of their years. As they laughed, their eyes reflected the bantering spirit of the race, the joy of living without the burden of a family, the contentment of a single man who, however wretched he may consider himself, may nevertheless continue ever forward. But the adults revealed a premature age, broken down in their very prime, quivering like palsied old men; some, through eyes that flashed with the phosphorescent gleams of a wild beast, revealed a remnant of aggressiveness; others cringed with the resignation of him who awaits death as the only deliverance.

There were meager, sallow bodies, tanned by the sun,

with wrinkled skin. Between this and their skeletons, their poor, scant food had not succeeded in forming the slightest cushioning. Men who had not yet reached forty showed necks almost without flesh, with loose-hanging, swollen skin and the stiff tendons of old age. Their eyes, sunken deep in their sockets and surrounded by an aureole of wrinkles, shone like pale stars in the depths of a well. This bodily wretchedness was the consequence of years and years of physical fatigue, and of an insipid diet of bread, only bread. The rough, angular bodies seemed to have been chopped out by an ax; others were deformed and grotesque, as if fashioned by a potter; many, by their gnarled and twisted condition, recalled the trunks of the wild-olive trees in the pasture-grounds. The swarthy arms, with their sharp protuberances caused by enforced physical exertion, appeared like braided tendrils. And the herded mass of these unfortunates exhaled an acrid odor—that of hungry wretches' perspiration, of clothes that have not been removed from the body for months, of fetid breaths: all the pestiferous respiration of poverty.

The women looked worse than the men. Some were gipsies, as old and ugly as witches, with tanned, coppery skins that seemed to have passed through the flames of all the Witches' Sabbaths. The younger ones possessed the sad, faded beauty of anemia; flowers of life that withered before blooming; adolescents of pale skin, as white as paper which the sun had been unable to warm, staining it here and there with small, bran-colored patches. Virgins with their eyes extraordinarly wide open, as if amazed at having been born with blue lips and gums of a pale pink that betrayed the poverty of their blood. Their sad, lusterless hair peeked out in astonishment from under their kerchiefs, showing wisps of straw and particles of earth. The breasts of the majority displayed the unbroken flatness of the desert, and as they breathed, under their blouses appeared not the slightest trace of the seductive mounds that advance proudly like a heraldic glory of sex. They had large hands and arms as thin and bony as men's. When they walked, their skirts floated with a vacuous freedom, as if within them existed only air; and when they sat down, the cloth outlined sharp angles without a sign of curves. Hard labor and beastly toil had atrophied the development of feminine grace. Only a few revealed beneath their garments the attractions of sex; but they were very few.

Compelled to undergo the identical fatigue as the masculine drove, they remembered that they were women only in the advanced hours of the night, when, amid the darkness of the workers' quarters, as they lay huddled in their corners, they were disturbed in their heavy sleep—that of females of burden—by the impudence of the youths, who groped about for them, while the older laborers, cured of life's illusions, snored away outrageously, as if they wished to fall asleep as promptly as possible to recuperate their lost energy.

Salvatierra, noticing that the *arreador* had arisen and offered his seat, went over to the fire-place. Uncle *Zarandilla* squatted down upon the floor beside don Fernando, who, looking about, encountered the eyes of *Alcaparrón* and his equine teeth that glistened as their owner smiled to the revolutionist.

"Just look, your grace, *zeñó*, this is my mother."

And he pointed to an old gipsy, granny *Alcaparrona*, who had just fetched from the fire-place a stew of chick-peas that was being voraciously sniffed at by three youngsters, brothers of *Alcaparrón*, and a very slender, pale, large-eyed girl—his cousin Mari-Cruz.

"So your grace is that don Fernando who's so much

talked about?" commented the old woman. "May God grant you plenty of good fortune and a long life, that you may continue to be the father of the poor."

She deposited the pot upon the floor, and sat down together with all the family grouped around it. It was an extraordinary meal. The savory odor of the chick-peas roused a certain commotion in the lodge, attracting many envious glances toward the gipsy group. *Zarandilla* questioned the old woman jocularly. Had some fine-paying job turned up, eh? . . . The day before, when she went to Jerez, she certainly must have earned a few *pesetas* telling fortunes or selling magic powders to the lasses who complained of their lovers' indifference. Ah, old witch! It seemed impossible that she could be so clever, with that ugly face. . . .

The gipsy listened smilingly, without ceasing greedily to swallow the peas; but when *Zarandilla* touched upon her ugliness, she suddenly stopped eating.

"Quiet, blind fool, evil tongue. May God grant that you dwell under the earth all your life, like your brothers the moles. . . . If I'm ugly now, there were days when marquises used to kiss my shoes. And you know that well, you wretch. . . ."

And she added, sadly:

"I shouldn't be here now if the Marquis de San Dionisio were alive to-day—that charming *zeñó* who was the godfather of my poor little José María."

And she pointed to *Alcaparrón*, who dropped his spoon and straightened up with a certain pride upon hearing the name of his godfather, who, according to *Zarandilla*, was more closely related to him.

Salvatierra looked at the old woman's malignant, bleary eyes, at her nose, which resembled a he-goat's snout, contracting at every word with a repugnant ductility, and the two brushes of gray bristles that stuck out from her lips like cat's whiskers. And this monster had been a young and graceful woman, of the sort that caused the illustrious marquis to commit his wild escapades! And the witch had ridden countless times in the nobleman's coaches, to the strange tinkling of the mules' bells, with her flowery cloak falling across her shoulders, a bottle in her hands and a song upon her lips, through the very fields that now beheld her as wrinkled and repulsive as a caterpillar, sweating from sun to sun over the furrows and complaining of the pain in her "poor little loins!" She was not so old as she appeared, but to the wear and tear of fatigue was added the rapid decline suffered by the Oriental races in passing from youth to old age, like the splendid tropical days that leap from light to darkness with no intervening dusk.

The gipsies continued to devour their stew. After gently refusing the offers that came from all sides, Salvatierra drew from his pocket the package that contained his scant supper.

The group nearest to him, among which was Manolo, was comprised of former comrades, laborers with a bad reputation in the farms, some of whom addressed don Fernando with the familiar "tu," following the usage of the comrades of *the idea*.

As he munched his crust and his slice of cheese he wondered, with his customary uncertainty, whether he was appropriating food that others lacked, and thus his gaze fell upon the only one in all the lodge that was not busied with supper.

He was a youth of wasted body, with a red kerchief knotted about his neck and with only a shirt upon his chest. His companions were calling to him from the rear of the room, warning him that there was scarcely any *gazpacho* left, but he did not stir from his stump seat, under the oil-lamp, before a low table against which his knees were embedded as if in stocks. He wrote slowly and laboriously, with peasant-like obstinacy. Before his eyes was a part of a paper and he was copying off the lines with the aid of a pocket inkholder filled with slightly blackened water and a blunt pen that traced the lines with the same patience as a bullock opening furrows.

Zarandilla, who was beside don Fernando, spoke to him about the boy.

"That's our *Maestrico.* We call him the little teacher because he's so fond of books and papers. Hardly does he return from work when he's seized his pen and begun to scratch away."

Salvatierra approached the *Maestrico,* who, for a moment suspending his labors, turned and glanced at him. As he explained his desire to gain an education, and how he robbed hours from his sleep and from his rest, he expressed himself with a certain bitterness. He had been brought up as a beast; at seven he was already a herder in the farms or a shepherd in the mountains: hunger, blows and fatigue.

"And I want to know something, don Fernando; I want to be a man and not feel insulted, when I behold the mares trotting about the vegetable patch, at the thought that we're just as irrational as they. All the trouble of us poor folks is due to the fact that we don't know anything."

He eyed his companions bitterly—his companions of the laborers' quarters who were content in their ignorance and who poked fun at him, dubbing him the *Maestrico,* and even believed him crazy when they saw him, on returning from work, deciphering parts of newspapers or pulling forth from his sash his pen and his notebook, and writing obstinately before the wick of the oil-lamp.

He had never had a teacher; he was self-taught. He
suffered at the thought that others, with outside aid, had
easily conquered the obstacles which to him seemed in-
superable. But he had faith and struggled forward,
convinced that if everybody followed his example the
fate of the country would be changed.

"The world belongs to him who knows most. Isn't
that so, don Fernando? If the rich are strong and
trample upon us and do as they please, it's not only because they have the money, but because they know more
than we. . . . These unfortunates mock me when I advise them to study, and they mention the rich folks of
Jerez, who are more barbarous than their own toilers.
But that's no way of looking at it! The wealthy persons we see around us are nothing but puppets, and
above them are the others—the real rich—those who
know, those who make the laws of the world and maintain that crafty arrangement whereby a few have and
a vast majority have not. If the workingfolk knew as
much as these persons, they would not permit themselves
to be deceived; they would face them at every opportunity
and at last would compel them to divide power with
them."

Salvatierra admired the faith of this youth, who believed that he possessed the remedy for all the ills endured by poverty's vast horde. Education! Be men! . . .
The exploiters were but a few thousand and the slaves
numbered hundreds of millions. But scarcely were the
privileges of the few exposed to danger when ignorant
humanity, fettered to its servitude, was so idiotic, that
it allowed to be drawn from its own ranks the hangmen
and executioners—those who, wearing a bright-colored
uniform and pointing a gun, came with their bullets to
restore a rule of grief and hunger, whose consequences
they themselves suffered when they returned to the

lower stratum. Ah! If men did not dwell in blindness
and ignorance, how could this absurd state of affairs
continue? . . .

The ingenuous affirmations of the youth caused Salvatierra to 'reflect. Perhaps this simple fellow saw
more clearly than they—the men hardened in the struggle, who were interested in the propaganda of action and
immediate revolutions. He was a simple spirit, like the
adherents of primitive Christianity, who felt the doctrines of their religion with greater intensity than the
Fathers of the Church. His procedure was so slow that
it would require centuries for fulfillment; but its success
seemed certain. And the revolutionist, listening to the
farmhand, imagined himself in an epoch in which ignorance no longer existed, and the present beast of burden
—ill-nourished, his thought petrified, and with no other
hope than insufficient and degrading charity—had become
transformed into a man.

At the very first conflict between the fortunate and
the unfortunate the old world would crumble. The vast
armies organized by a society founded upon force would
serve to give it its death blow. The uniformed toilers
would seize possession of the guns that their exploiters
had given them for their defense, or would use these
arms for the purpose of imposing the law of happiness
for the majority upon the perverse shepherds who for
centuries had subjected the human flock to injustice.
The face of the globe would undergo a sudden change,
without shedding of blood or other catastrophe. Together with the armies and the laws manufactured by
the powerful, there would disappear all the impositions
and the cruelties that converted the earth into a prison.
There would remain only men. And all this could come
to pass as soon as the immense majority of human beings,
the innumerable army of poverty, should realize its

strength and refuse to maintain any longer the work of tradition! . . .

Salvatierra's humanitarian sentimentalism felt flattered by this generous dream of innocence. Change the world without bloodshed, with one dramatic stroke, using the magic wand of education, without the violent deeds that so repelled his sensitive soul and always led to the defeat of the lowly and the cruel reprisals of the powerful! . . .

The *Maestrico* continued to declare his convictions with a burning faith that illuminated his child-like eyes. Ah! If the poor only knew as much as the rich! . . . These are strong and govern, because knowledge is at their service. All discoveries and inventions of science fall into their hands, are for them alone, with hardly a few crumbs for those below. If any one rose from the wretched masses, elevating himself through sheer ability, then instead of remaining loyal to his origin and lending aid to his brothers, he deserted his post, turning his back upon a hundred generations of slaves crushed by injustice, and selling his body and his brains to the hangmen, begging a post among them. Ignorance was the vilest servitude, the most atrocious martyrdom of the poor. But isolated and individual instruction was in vain; this served only to form deserters, turncoats, who hastened to line up with the enemy. They must all learn at the same time; the great mass must acquire a realization of its own strength, and at a single stroke appropriate the great conquests of the human intellect.

"All! Do you understand, don Fernando? All at a time, crying, 'No more deceit; we refuse to serve you in order that *this* may continue.'"

And don Fernando noddingly approved. Yes, all at once; it must be so: all, sloughing their skins of resigned bestiality, the only garment that tradition cared to maintain across their shoulders.

But as his gaze turned back to the room, filled with gloom and smoke, he felt that it included all of exploited and unhappy humanity. Some had just finished eating their broth, with which they deceived hunger for a while; others, stretched out, belched contentedly, believing in a fictitious digestion that added nothing to their depleted vigor; all seemed stultified, antagonistic, without the will to emerge from their condition; they believed vaguely in some miracle as their only hope, or thought of a Christian alms that might permit them a moment's rest in their desperate wandering over the mountain of poverty. How much time would have to pass before these poor wretches should open their eyes and learn the road! Who could awaken them, infusing them with the faith of that poor youth who was groping along in the dark, his eyes fixed upon a distant star that he alone could see! . . .

The group of those who were devoted to *the idea*, abandoning the *gazpacho* bowl, which was now empty, ranged themselves upon the floor in a circle about Salvatierra. Solemnly they rolled their cigarettes, as if this operation absorbed their thoughts completely. Tobacco was their one luxury, and they had to calculate how to make their little package last all week. Manolo el de Trebujena had extracted from the bundle upon his donkey a small keg of brandy and was serving glasses of it in the center of a group. The older laborers, with their parchment-like faces and their matted beards, rushed over to him with the avidity of the ill, their eyes glowing with the solace of alcohol. From their sashes the younger element, after long hesitation, drew copper coins and bought drink, mentally justifying this extraordinary expenditure with the absurd thought that they were not going to work upon the following day. Some maidens of loose manners advanced cautiously, with cat-like tread, until they were lost amid the groups of young men; they screeched when, after countless pinches and shoves suggestive of brutal desire, they were offered a glass.

Salvatierra was listening to Juanón, a former comrade who was now working at the farm, and who had made a trip to Jerez for the express purpose of seeing him when he had returned from prison.

He was a massive fellow, muscular, with prominent cheek-bones, a square, proud jaw, rough skin and hair that invaded his forehead; his deep eyes, at certain moments, shone with a feline, greenish refulgency.

He had been a vine-dresser, but because of his reputation as a revolutionist and a quarrelsome fellow, he had been compelled to take up farm work, finding employment only at Matanzuela, thanks to Rafael, who protected him because he was a friend of his godfather. Juanón commanded the respect of every worker. He was of an impulsive nature, whose spirits suffered no depression: an energetic will that imposed itself upon all his companions.

Slowly and sententiously he addressed Salvatierra, at the same time eying the surrounding folk with an expression of superiority, reinforced by frequent expectorations upon the floor.

"All this has changed very much, Fernando. We're going backward and the rich are more our masters than ever."

He, too, in the manner of the *comrades* employed the familiar form of address. He spoke scornfully of the working class. Here were the youngsters of this place, believing themselves happy with a glass of brandy and without any other thought than to have their good times with their women companions in toil. It was necessary

only to notice the cool reception they had given to Salvatierra. Many were not even curious enough to draw
near to him; they had even smiled ironically, as if to say,
"Another impostor." To such 'as these, the periodicals
that the old men read in a loud voice were fraudulent;
those who spoke of the strength of union and of a possible revolt were impostors; the only real things to them
were their three *gazpachos* and their two *reales* per day.
Together with this, an occasional drunken spree, and
from time to time an assault upon one of the women
hands, whom they would afflict with the engendering of
a new unfortunate—and they considered themselves
happy as long as the optimism of youth and strength
endured in them. If they followed the impulse of the
strikes, it was only for the noise and the disorder that
these brought in their train. Of the older men, many
were still loyal to *the idea*, but their spirits had evaporated, and they had become timorous, bent beneath the
fear that the rich had known how to instill in them.

"We have suffered much, Fernando. While you were
languishing up yonder, our condition was transformed."

And he spoke of the reign of terror that reduced the
entire countryside to silence. The wealthy city, hated
by the serfs of the country, watched over them with
cruel and inexorable scowl to hide the fear it had of
them. At he slightest sign of trouble the masters were
on their guard. It was enough that a few workingmen
should get together with a certain air of mystery, at some
shepherd's lodge on a small farm of the district—whereupon at once the rich would sound the alarm in the
columns of the press throughout Spain, and reinforcements of soldiers would be dispatched to Jerez, and the
Civil Guard would scour the fields, threatening every
toiler who dared to rebel against the low wages or the
wretched food. *The Black Hand!* Always that same

specter, magnified by the exuberant Andalusian imagination, which the rich were careful to keep alive and kicking so that they could set it in motion the moment the toilers formulated the most insignificant demands.

In order to maintain their injustice and the traditional servitude of their employees, they required a state of war, feigning that they lived amid dangers and protesting to the government officials that they were being inadequately protected. If the laborers asked to be fed like human beings, to be permitted to smoke an additional cigarette during the hours of the burning summer sun, or to have their daily pay of two *reales* increased by a few *céntimos,* there rose a great shout from the employers, recalling *The Black Hand* and declaring that it was to be revived.

Juanón, impelled by his indignation, jumped to his feet. *The Black Hand!* What was it? He had been persecuted on suspicion of belonging to it, and even *he* was not sure what it consisted of. For month after month he had been in prison together with other unfortunates. At night they would take him out of his confinement and lead him to the dark solitude of the fields, where he would be flogged. The questions from the uniformed men were accompanied by blows from the butts of their guns that caused his very bones to creak— by savage assaults that increased in violence as a result of his negative replies. His body could still show the scars of these tokens of hospitality that he had received from the rich men of Jerez. They could have killed him before he would reply to the satisfaction of his torturers. He knew of societies for the defense of the workingmen and resistance to the masters' abuses; he belonged to them; but of *The Black Hand,* of the terror-inspiring association with its poniards and its vendettas, he knew not a word.

As a proof of its fictitious existence, there had been only a single death—a very common murder in a land of wine and blood: and for this homicide several toilers had been garrotted, and hundreds of unhappy wretches like himself had been confined to a cell, suffering tortures that cost a few of them their lives. But ever since that time the masters had a scarecrow to raise aloft as a banner—*The Black Hand*—and at the slightest movement of the poor to better their conditions, this lugubrious phantom, dripping blood, was summoned to arise.

The horrible recollection authorized everything. For the least fault a man was set upon in the fields; the toiler was a suspicious creature against whom it was permitted to indulge in anything. The authorities' excessive zeal was gratefully rewarded, and whoever dared to protest was silenced by the mention of *The Black Hand*. The younger folk were intimidated by this example; the older were afraid, and the rich, there in the city, with their imaginations fortified by the wine of their stores, added details to suit their fancy, embroidering new horrors and exaggerating the matter in such wise that the very persons who had been present at the birth of the fiction spoke of it as of something gruesomely legendary that had happened in remote ages.

Juanón ceased speaking, and his companions seemed rooted to the spot by that specter of the southern imagination which seemed to envelop the whole district of Jerez in its black folds.

After supper the toilers' quarters sank into the calm of night. Many of the men slept stretched out upon their mats, snoring wearily, breathing in from the floor the stifling emanations of the cow-dung embers. At the rear, the women, seated upon the ground with their skirts gathered like mushrooms, were telling stories or relating marvelous cures that had been effected in the mountains through the miraculous intervention of the Virgin.

A subdued humming arose above the buzz of the conversations. It came from the gipsies, who were still engaged with their extraordinary meal. Tía *Alcaparrona* had drawn from under her skirts a bottle of wine with which to celebrate her good fortune at the city. Her offspring had but a sip as their share on such occasions, but the mere sight of the wine was enough to cause an outburst of joy. *Alcaparrón,* his gaze fixed upon his mother, who was chief among those that claimed his admiration, was singing, accompanied by soft beating of palms on the part of the rest. The gipsy was bewailing "his burdens and his griefs," with that false sentimentality of the popular song, adding that "on hearing him, the feathers of a certain bird had fallen off in the thousands, from sheer emotion"; and the old woman and her family urged him on, praising his skill with as much enthusiasm as if they were praising themselves.

Suddenly, with the incoherence of a gipsy, who flits capriciously from one thought to another, *Alcaparrón* interrupted his song to have a word with his mother.

"Mother, how wretched we poor gipsies are! The *gachés* are everything: kings, magistrates, judges and generals. And we *cañís* are nothing."

"Hush, evil-tongue! Neither is any gipsy a jailer or a hangman. . . . Come, boy. Sing us another."

And the singing and hand-clapping were resumed with increased spirit.

A farmhand offered a glass of brandy to Juanón, who thrust it aside with his heavy hand.

"That's what is ruining us," he declared, sententiously. "Cursed drink."

And supported by the approving glances of the *Maestrico,* who had laid aside his writing implements and joined the group, Juanón inveighed against drunkenness. The wretched people forgot everything when they drank. If at times they succeeded in feeling that they were men, the rich had only to open the doors of their wine-stores, and the toilers were conquered.

Many in the gathering protested against Juanón's words. What could a poor fellow do to forget his misery, if not drink? The respectful silence imposed by the presence of Salvatierra was now broken, and many at a time burst forth into speech to express their griefs and their anger. Their food was getting poorer every day; the rich were abusing their power—that fear which they had instilled and spread.

Only during the thrashing season were they given chick-pea dishes; the rest of the year bread, only bread, and in many places even this was scantily provided. Even their most imperious necessities were exploited. Hitherto, when the ground was being plowed, for every ten plowmen there was a substitute whose duty it was to take the place of any worker who retired for a moment to attend to the calls of Nature. Now, in order to save the expense of this substitute, they gave the plowmen five *céntimos* extra, on condition that he would not leave his yoke even at the most cruel and insistent summons, and this, with sad irony, they called "selling the . . . most ignoble part of the body."

Each year brought an increasing number of women from the mountain down to the estate. They were submissive; feminine weakness made them fear the *arreador* and they worked as hard as they knew how. The *manijeros*—the recruiting agents—came down from the mountain at the head of their hunger-driven bands. In the villages they described the Jerez district as a place of abundance, and families confided to the *manijero* daughters scarcely entered upon the age of puberty, thinking with pitiless greed of the *reales* that the children would bring back after the working season was past.

The *arreador* of Matanzuela, and several of the group who were recruiting agents, protested. The men who had as yet not fallen asleep drew around Salvatierra.

"We are under orders," explained the *arreador*. "What can we poor fellows do? The fault lies with the masters; they're the ones that give the orders."

Old *Zarandilla,* too, put in a word, since he considered himself one of the farm *government.* The masters! . . . They could arrange everything, simply by giving a little thought to the poor; with charity, plenty of charity.

Salvatierra, who had been listening impassively to the discussion, started, breaking his silence upon hearing the old man's words. Charity! And what was the good of it? To keep the poor man enslaved, hoping for a few crumbs that stilled his hunger for a moment and prolonged his servitude.

Charity was egotism masquerading as a virtue; the sacrifice of a small share of the surplus divided at will. Charity? No. Justice! To each man what belonged to him!

And the revolutionist grew impassioned as he spoke; he abandoned his smiling apathy; behind the blue spectacles his eyes sparkled with the fire of revolt.

Charity had done nothing to raise man. It had reigned for nineteen centuries; the poets sang it as a divine inspiration; the fortunate lauded it as the greatest of virtues; yet the world was the same as on the day when it had appeared with Christ's doctrine. Experience with it had been long enough to demonstrate its futility.

It was the most anemic and weakest of the virtues. It had uttered kind words for slavery, but had not broken its chains; it offered a crumb to the modern serf, but did not dare to address the slightest reproach to the social organization that condemned him to poverty'for the rest of his days. Charity, sustaining the unfortunate wretch for an instant, that he might gather strength, was as virtuous as the peasant-woman who feeds the fowl of her corral and keeps them well fattened, until the moment when she is ready to eat them.

This so-called virtue had done nothing to liberate mankind. It was revolt—desperate protest—that had broken the fetters of the ancient serf, and the same power would emancipate the modern wage slave, flattered with every manner of ideal rights, except the right to bread.

Salvatierra, in the exaltation of his thought, desired to annihilate the phantoms with which the needy had for centuries been terrified or diverted so that they might not disturb the tranquillity of the privileged few.

Social Justice alone could save mankind, and Justice was not of heaven, but of earth.

More than a thousand years the outcasts had been resigned, with their thoughts centered upon heaven, confiding in an eternal compensation. But the sky was empty. What unfortunate could any longer believe in it? God had gone over to the side of the rich; He looked upon it as a virtue worthy of glory everlasting, whenever any of the wealthy, from time to time, shared a fragment of their fortune and preserved it intact, considering it a crime for those at the bottom to demand a decent livelihood.

Even if the sky did exist, the unfortunate worker would refuse to enter it, considering it an abode of injustice wherein he who dwells in luxury, enlivening his ennui with the voluptuousness of distributing alms, may enter the same as he who passes his life in suffering.

Christianity was simply one lie more, distorted and

exploited by those at the top in order to justify and sanctify their usurpations. Justice, not charity! Well-being upon earth for the unhappy, and let the rich reserve for themselves, if they so desired, the possession of heaven, first opening their hands and loosening their grip upon their earthly plunder!

The lowly could expect nothing from above. Over their heads existed only an infinity that was insensible to human despair; other worlds, which ignored the life of millions of wretched worms upon this sphere that was dishonored by selfishness and violence. The hungering many, those who thirsted for justice, must rely upon themselves alone. Forward, even unto death! Others would come after; they would sow the germinating seed in the furrows that had been fertilized with the blood of their predecessors. Up, then, poverty's horde, and forward march, with no other god than Revolution, with the road illuminated by the red star, the eternal devil of all religions, the leader in all the great movements of humanity! . . .

The audience of toilers heard the revolutionist in silence. Many followed his words with eyes wide agape, as if they wished to absorb them with their sight.

Juanón and Manolo nodded approval. They had read, in confused manner, all that Salvatierra was saying, but in his mouth the sentiments moved them like music vibrant with passion.

Old *Zarandilla* felt no compunction about throwing cold water upon the enthusiastic circle, interrupting with his practical sense.

"This is all very fine, don Fernando. But the poor man needs land to live, and the land belongs to the masters."

Salvatierra drew himself proudly erect. The land belonged to nobody. What men had created it, that they presumed to appropriate it as their own? The land belonged to those who tilled it.

The unequitable distribution of comfort; the increase of poverty with the advance of civilization; the seizure, by the powerful upper class, of all mechanical inventions, which had been planned to suppress physical labor and served only to render it more burdensome and stultifying than ever; all the evils of humanity proceeded from the appropriation of the land by a few thousand men who do not sow and nevertheless reap, while millions of human beings, toiling over the soil only to have its treasures of life miscarry, suffer a hunger that is centuries and centuries old.

Salvatierra's voice resounded through the silence of the room like a battle cry.

"The world is beginning to awaken from its thousand years' slumber; it protests against having been robbed in its infancy. The land is yours; nobody created it, and it belongs to you. If any improvement exists upon it, it is the work of your grimy hands, which are your titles of ownership. Man is born with a right to the air he breathes, to the sun that warms him, and he must demand the possession of the land that sustains him. The soil that you till, only to have another appropriate the harvest, belongs to you, even though you unfortunates, degraded by thousands of years of servitude, doubt your right and fear to stretch forth your hand lest you be called robbers. The man who seizes a piece of land, excluding all others from it—he who delivers it over to human beasts for them to cultivate while he remains idle—that man is he who really robs it from his fellow men."

CHAPTER IV

THE two mastiffs which, during the night, guarded the surroundings of the Marchamalo tower, awoke from their sleep under the portico of the wine-press house, with their bodies coiled into a circle and their ferocious jaws meeting their tails.

The two opened their eyes at the same time, sniffed the air, and after rising to their feet with a certain shakiness, barked loudly, and dashed precipitately down the slopes of the vineyard, scattering the earth with their paws.

They were almost savage animals, with fiery eyes and red mouths that bristled with teeth which made one shudder. The two darted toward a man who was crouching among the vines, off the road that led up a steep declivity from the highway to the tower.

The shock of the encounter was terrible; the man wavered, pulling at his cloak, which had been seized by one of the dogs. But suddenly the mastiffs stopped barking and whirling about him, ceased seeking a spot into which to sink their teeth, and placed themselves at his side, walking along with him and receiving the caress of his hands with barks of pleasure.

"Savages!" exclaimed Rafael in a low voice, continuing nevertheless to stroke them affectionately. "Evil wretches! . . . Don't you know me yet?"

They accompanied him to the foot of the terrace and returned to their place beneath the arcades, there to roll themselves again into a ball and renew their guarded sleep, which vanished at the slightest noise.

Rafael stopped for a moment in the little square to repair the evidences of his encounter. He placed his cloak properly across his shoulders and closed the knife that he had drawn in order to defend himself against the ferocious beasts.

Against the dark background, dimly illuminated by the light from the stars, stood out the silhouette of that new Marchamalo which don Pablo had had constructed.

In the center rose the stately tower, which could be seen from Jerez, dominating the hills that were covered with vineyards which made the Duponts the leading proprietaries of the district: a pretentious structure of red brick, with the base and the corners of white stone. The sharp merlons at the top were joined by an iron railing that converted the crown of this semi-feudal edifice into a vulgar platform. To one side was the best of Marchamalo—that to which don Pablo had devoted most of the attention he bestowed upon the new buildings—the spacious chapel, adorned like a great temple with columns and marbles. At the other side the former Marchamalo remained almost intact. Very slight repairs had strengthened this wing—low and arcaded—in which were the dwellings of the overseer and the dormitory of the vine-dressers, an ample, shelterless room, with a fireplace that blackened the walls with smoke.

Dupont, who had summoned artists from Seville to decorate his church, and had ordered from the Valencian dealers various dazzling images in gold and bright colors, felt a certain remorse before the old house of the toilers, not daring to lay hand upon it. It possessed so much *character;* this refuge of the laborers was a discreet restoration, with touches of reform. And the overseer continued to live in his dingy rooms, whose age María de la Luz concealed behind careful white-washing; and the workers slept in their clothes upon the rush mats that were granted to them by don Pablo's generosity, while the holy images dwelt amid marble and gildings, for entire weeks, without being seen by anybody, since the doors of the chapel were opened only when the master came to Marchamalo.

For a long while Rafael contemplated the structures, fearing lest some crevice suddenly light up in the obscure mass,—lest some window should be opened and the overseer appear, alarmed by the howling of the dogs. Several minutes elapsed without the least movement being noted about Marchamalo. The somnolent breathing of the fields submerged in the shadows rose to his ears; the stars twinkled intensely in the wintry heavens, as if the cold stimulated their refulgence.

The youth left the little square and, turning the corner of the old building, walked along through a lane that remained between the house and a compact row of prickly-pears. He stopped before a grating, and tapped lightly with his knuckles upon the wooden blinds; the blinds were opened, and the full bust of María de la Luz appeared against the dark background of the interior.

"How late you are, Rafael!" she said, in a soft voice. "What time is it? . . ."

The steward looked for a moment at the sky, reading the stars with the expertness of a country dweller.

"It must be something like half past two."

"And your horse? Where did you leave it?"

Rafael explained how he had come. The horse was at the "Crow" inn, a few paces away; a hut just off the highway. It needed a rest, for he had galloped all the way from the farmyard.

They had worked that Saturday. Many men and maidens of the toilers wished to spend Sunday in their mountain towns, and they had asked him for their pay, that they might take it to their families. Adjusting the accounts of these people, who always think they are being deceived, was enough to make a fellow crazy. Besides, he had been obliged to attend to a sick stallion— rub him down and give him other remedies, aided by *Zarandilla.* Then the fellows from the pasture-ground caused him suspicion, for they were certainly cheating the master out of charcoal. . . . In short, he had not stopped a moment at Matanzuela, and only after midnight, when those who remained at the lodge put out the lights, had he decided to gallop over. The moment it dawned, he would return to the inn, and mounting his horse, would present himself as if he had just arrived from Matanzuela, so that godfather wouldn't imagine they had been making love.

These explanations having been made, the two remained in silence, leaning against the grating, not daring to touch hands, gazing at each other closely by the pale light of the stars. It was the moment of mutual contemplation and silent timidity characteristic of all lovers who meet after a long absence. Rafael was the first to break the silence.

"And you've got nothing to say to me? After we haven't seen each other for a whole week, you can only stare at me like a ninny, as if I were a strange creature?"

"And what shall I say to you, naughty boy? . . . That I love you very, very much; that all these days I've passed with a deep, dark pain in my heart, thinking of my gipsy. . . ."

And the lovers, already launched into a passionate mood, lulled themselves with the music of their words, with all the verbose exuberance of the province.

Rafael, his hands grasping the bars, trembled with emotion as he spoke to María de la Luz, as if his words were not his own and disturbed him with a slight in-

toxication. The endearments of the popular songs, all
the bold expressions that he had heard, accompanied by
the strumming of the guitar, were mingled by him into
the amorous litany with which his murmuring voice enveloped his sweetheart.

"May all the burdens of your life descend upon me,
soul of my soul, and may you enjoy only happiness.
My gipsy darling, you've got God's own face; your lips
are the sweetest of arches, and when you look at me, it
seems that the good Jesus of the miracles is gazing at
me with his tender eyes. . . . I wish I were don Pablo
Dupont with all his wine-stores, so that I could spill
the wine out of the oldest butts he has—and they cost
thousand of *pesos;* and you'd put your pretty little feet
into the flood of wine and I would say to all Jerez:
'Drink, gentlemen, for this is glory.' And they'd all say:
'Rafael is right; it's as though they were the feet of
God's own mother!' Ah, little one, if you didn't love
me, what a fate would await you! You would have to
become a nun, for there'd be no fellow to ask your hand.
I'd plant myself before your door and I wouldn't let
God himself cross the threshold."

María de la Luz was flattered with the vehement expressions employed by her sweetheart at the mere thought
that another man could come courting her. The bru-
tality of his jealous threats pleased her even more than
his loving endearments.

"But you silly boy! I love only you! I'm just crazy
about my little steward and I yearn for the moment to
go to Matanzuela and see my handsome fellow as impatiently as one waits for the angels! . . . You know that
I could marry any one of those office-clerk friends of
my brother. The mistress sometimes speaks to me about
it. At other times she coaxes me to become a nun; one
of these grand nuns, with a large dowry, and she prom-

ises to pay all expenses. But I say, 'No, Señora, I've no ambition to be a saint; I'm awfully fond of men. . . .' But, heavens! What nonsense I'm talking! Not all men, no. Only one, only one: my Rafael, who, when he rides on his mare, looks as handsome as Saint Michael on horseback. But don't take flighty notions into your head because of this praise. It's all in jest! . . . I wish to be a farmwoman with my steward, and he must love me and say pretty things to me. I'd prefer wretched *gazpacho* with him to all the domains of Jerez. . . ."

"Blessings on your mouth! Go on, darling, for when you talk like that you just lift me to the sky! You'll lose nothing by loving me. I'm ready to do anything to keep you satisfied; and even if godfather gets angry, as soon as we marry I'll go back to smuggling and fill your apron with silver ounces."

María de la Luz protested, with a gesture of fear. That, never. She still shuddered with the recollection of that night in which she had beheld him arrive as pale as death and dripping blood. They would be happy in their poverty, without tempting God with new adventures that might cost him his life. What was the good of the money? . . .

"The important thing is to love each other, Rafael, and you'll see, you darling of my soul, how sweet I'll make life for you. . . ."

She, like her father, was of the country, and she wished to remain there. She was not at all frightened by the customs of the grange. At Matanzuela they surely must feel the lack of a mistress who would convert the steward's house into a "silver cup." He, who had become accustomed to the disordered smugglers' existence and to the care of *Zarandilla's* old wife, would learn what it meant to live really well. Poor fellow! She could easily see from his clothes how badly he needed a woman's care. . . . They would arise at break of day; he to go out and watch the toilers proceed to their daily tasks, she to prepare breakfast, tidy the house with the hands that God had given her, with no fear of hard work. Clothed in that country costume which became him so well, he would mount his horse, but not a button would be missing in his jacket, nor would there be the slightest rip in his trousers, and his shirt would always be as white as snow, as well ironed as any owned by a Jerez gentleman. And when he would return she would be at the gate waiting for him; poor, but as neat as a jet of water, well combed, with flowers in her hair and an apron so dazzling that it would blind him. The stew would perfume the whole house. And she had a gift for cooking! Her father sang her praises as a cook to everybody. . . . After having dined together, with the satisfaction of those who know that their bread is well earned, he would be off again to the fields, and she to her sewing, to attend the hen-roost, or to watch over the kneading of the brown-bread. And at night they would eat supper and go to rest with bones wearied by toil, but well satisfied with their labors; to sleep in the holy tranquillity of those who make good use of their day and do not feel the remorse of having wronged any one.

"Come closer!" murmured Rafael passionately. "You've left out the best part. Afterward we'll have little ones, mischievous tots that'll scurry about the farmyard. . . ."

"Stop, you bad boy!" exclaimed María de la Luz. "Don't run so fast, you'll fall. . . ."

And the two were silent, Rafael smiling at his sweetheart's blush, while she threatened him with one of her graceful hands for his boldness.

But the youth could not hold his tongue, and with the persistency of lovers he began to tell María de la Luz

about his early sufferings, when he became aware that
he was in love with her. The first time that he realized how much she meant to him was at Holy Week,
during the procession of the Interment. And Rafael
laughed, finding it very droll to have fallen in love amid
the terror-inspiring trappings of the fraternity monks,
the inquisitorial flickering of the tapers and the ear-
splitting noise of the trumpets and the drums.

The procession was parading late at night through the
streets of Jerez, amid a lugubrious silence, as if the end
of the world had come; and he, hat in hand, deeply affected, watched the passing of this ceremony that penetrated to his very soul. Soon, during a halt of the "Most
Sacred Christ of the Crown of Thorns" and "Our Lady
of the Greatest Affliction," a voice broke the silence of
the night—a voice that brought tears to the rough smuggler's eyes.

"And it was you, lass; your voice of spun gold that
simply turned the people crazy. 'That's the Marchamalo
overseer's daughter,' somebody said at my side. 'Blessings upon her beak: she's a nightingale.' And without
knowing why, I stifled with grief, and I saw you among
your friends, as pretty as a saint, singing the *saeta*, with
your hands clasped, gazing at the Christ with those mir-
ror-like eyes of yours, in which were reflected all the
candles of the procession. And I, who had played with
you when we were children, thought that you were somebody else—that you had suddenly been transformed; and
in my breast I felt something—as if I were being pierced
by a knife; and I took a good look at the Lord of Thorns
and envied him, for you were singing to him like a bird,
and your eyes were for him alone. And I came near
saying to him: 'Lord, have pity upon the poor and let
me take your place for a while upon the cross. It makes
no difference to me if they see me bare, in a kirtle and

limbs nailed to the cross, so long as María de la Luz does honor to me with her angel's voice. . . .' "

"Madman!" laughed the maiden. "Deceiver! That's how you madden me with all the lies you tell! . . ."

"Then I heard you again on the square before the Prison. The poor convicts, pressing against the bars, as if they were caged wild beasts, sang some pretty sad things to the Lord—about their chains and their griefs, and the mother that was weeping for them, and of their children whom they couldn't kiss. And you, my little soul, from below, answered with other verses, that was as sweet as an angel's sob, asking the Lord to have compassion upon the unfortunate prisoners. And then I swore that I loved you with all my soul—that you would have to be mine, and I was tempted to cry to the poor chaps behind the bars: 'Until later, friends. If this woman doesn't return my love, I'll commit some crime; I'll kill somebody and next year I'll be caged in with you and sing with you to the Lord of Thorns.' "

"Rafael, don't talk like a savage," moaned the maiden with a certain fear in her voice. "You mustn't say such things; that's tempting the Lord's patience."

"No, you little goose. That's only a manner of speaking. Why should I go to that horrible place? I'm going to glory, marrying my little brunette nightingale and taking her off to my little nest at Matanzuela. . . . But, ay, my darling! What I suffered ever since that day! The tortures I went through before 1 could pluck up the courage to say to you, 'I love you'? I came to Marchamalo afternoons, after I'd made a good smuggling haul, with a lot of hints in mind that I had prepared for the purpose of making you understand me. And you! Nothing! As if you were the Dolorosa, who looks the same during Holy Week as she does the rest of the year."

"But, my dear simpleton! I saw through you from the

very first! I guessed the love you bore me and I was as happy as could be! But it was my duty to hide my feelings. A girl mustn't wear her heart on her sleeve. That isn't proper."

"Hush, wicked soul! You made me suffer, those days! . . . I'd arrive on my horse, after having dangerously exposed myself in the mountains and exchanged shots with the guards, and to see you was to feel my very entrails open with a fear that made me shudder. 'I'll tell her this; I'll tell her that.' And seeing you and saying nothing were the same thing. My tongue would cleave to my palate, my mind would grow dark, as when I used to go to school; I was afraid you'd take offense and that godfather would give me a cudgeling, saying, 'Off with you, you shameless beast,' just like when a wandering dog shows up at the vineyard. . . . Finally it all came out. Do you remember? It cost something, but we reached an understanding. It was after I had been shot, when you cared for me like a little mother, and in the afternoons we'd sing a bit together, right near here, under the arcades. Godfather would pluck the guitar and I, without knowing how, would start *martinetes*, with my eyes fixed upon yours, as if I were going to eat them:

"Fragua, yunque y martillo rompen los metales,
Pero este cariño que yo te tengo no lo rompe nadie.
(Forge, anvil and hammer break metals,
But this love I bear thee none can break.)

"And while godfather answered '*tra, tra, tra, tra,*' as if he were striking iron with a hammer, you blushed and lowered your eyes, at last reading mine. And I said to myself: 'Good. This is going well.' And it *was* well; for somehow or other we told each other of our love.

Perhaps it was you, little rascal, who grew weary of making me suffer and shortened the road so that I might lose my fear. . . . And ever since that day there isn't in all Jerez or the countryside a happier, richer man than Rafael, the steward of Matanzuela. . . . Do you see don Pablo Dupont with all his millions? Well, aside of me, he's worth nothing! Absolutely nothing! . . . And all the other wine-merchants, nothing! . . . And my master, señorito Luis, with all his estate and his trail of women . . . nothing either! *I* am the richest man in Jerez, and I'm going to take to the farmhouse an ugly old brunette, who is blind—for you can hardly see the poor thing's eyes—and she has another defect, too: when she laughs such very pretty dimples form in her face, as if she were dotted with pock-marks."

And tightly clutching the bars of the grating he expressed himself so vehemently that it seemed he was trying to force his face between them, seeking that of María de la Luz.

"Quiet, now, eh?" said the girl with a smiling threat. "I'm going to stick you, with a hair-pin, if you don't act properly. You know, Rafael, that there are certain jokes I don't relish, and that I come to the grating because you promise to behave." The expression of María de la Luz and her threat to close the grille repressed Rafael's vehemence and he withdrew his body from the iron bars.

"Very good; just as you wish, evil heart. You don't know what it is to love, and that's why you're as cold and tranquil as if you were at mass."

"I don't love you? . . . Darling!" exclaimed the maiden.

And it was she who, forgetting her displeasure, began to express herself with an even greater passion than her sweetheart. She loved him as much as she loved her father. It was a different sort of love, but she was sure that if the two affections were placed in a balance, there wouldn't be the smallest difference between them. Her brother knew better than she how intensely she loved Rafael. How Fermín did tease her when he came to the vineyard and asked her questions about her affair! . . .

"I love you, and I believe I've always loved you, ever since we were tots and you arrived in Marchamalo, holding your father's hand, and got a place as a farmhand's assistant, with your simple mountain ways that used to make the señoritas and us laugh so much. I love you because you're alone in the world, Rafael, with neither father nor family; because you need a kind soul to keep you company, and I'm that soul. I love you because you've suffered a great deal to make a living—my poor boy! . . . because I saw you near death that night, and from that moment I knew that I carried you in my heart. Besides, you deserve to be loved for being so good and upright; because living like a wicked man among women and bullies, always out for good times, exposed to the peril of losing your hide with every silver ounce you earned, you thought of me, and in order to cause your little girl no more worry, you were willing to be poor and to work. And I'll reward you for all you've done, loving you much—oh, so much! I'll be both mother and wife to you, and everything else you need in order to live happy and content."

"Olé! Continue speaking through that pretty mouth of yours, my mountain maid!" cried Rafael, with a new impulse of enthusiasm.

"And I love you, too," added María de la Luz with a certain gravity, "because I am worthy of you; because I think I'm a good girl and I'm sure that as your wife I'll not cause you the slightest worry. You don't know me yet, Rafael. If I ever thought that I could hurt you in any way—that I didn't deserve a man like you—I'd turn my back upon you and drown with the sorrow of being left without you. And even if you came to me upon your knees, I would pretend to have forgotten your love. Now you can see whether I love you. . . ."

As she uttered these words her intonation was so sad that Rafael had to cheer her up. Who ever need think of such things? What could happen strong enough to part them? They knew each other well, and one was worthy of the other. Perhaps he, in view of his past life, did not deserve her love; but she was good and compassionate and granted him the royal alms of her affection. To live! To love each other boundlessly! . . .

And to flee from the gloom that her words had inspired, they directed the course of the conversation into other channels, speaking of the ceremony that don Pablo had financed for Marchamalo, which was to take place in a few hours.

The vineyard laborers, who every Saturday evening went off to Jerez to see their families, were now sleeping in the vicinity. They were more than three hundred; the master had ordered them to stay over, that they might attend mass and participate in the procession. With don Pablo would come all his relatives, the office force and many of the workingmen from the wine-stores. An important festival, at which her brother would necessarily be present. And she laughed to think what a face Fermín would have during the ceremony, and what he would say afterwards when he came to the vineyard and met Salvatierra, who, from time to time, with a certain caution, visited his friend the overseer.

Whereupon Rafael spoke of Salvatierra, of his unexpected visit to the farmhouse and of his extraordinary habits.

"That splendid gentleman is an excellent person, but he's more or less of a 'crank.' He has almost roused my whole gang of laborers to revolt. 'This is going bad; the poor must live,' and all that. No, matters aren't as well as they might be, but the chief thing in this world is to love one another and be willing to work. When we settle down at the farmhouse we'll not have more than our three *pesetas,* our bread and what goes with it. There isn't much in being a steward. But you'll see how well off we'll be, despite what señor Salvatierra says in his speeches and his inflammatory talk. . . . Don't let godfather know what I've said about his friend, however, for to him it's worse if I say a word against don Fernando than if I played you false, for example."

Rafael spoke of his godfather with mingled veneration and fear. The old man knew of his love, but he never mentioned this to either his daughter or the youth. He tolerated the affair in silence, with the grave countenance of the Latin type of father, certain of his authority, and convinced that with a single gesture he could frustrate all the hopes of the lovers. Rafael did not dare to broach the subject of marriage to him, and María de la Luz, whenever her sweetheart in a boast of bravery declared that he was ready to go to her father, dissuaded him, not without a certain fear.

They would lose nothing by waiting; their parents, too, had gone together for many years. Decent folks don't marry in a hurry. Señor Fermín's silence meant consent: they would wait, then. And Rafael, hiding from his godfather to court the daughter, waited patiently for the day when the old man would plant himself before him, saying in his coarse, peasant-like manner: "But what are you waiting for, you ninny? Why don't you carry her off? Take her, my boy, and may she make you happy."

It was beginning to dawn. Rafael could now make out more clearly the face of his sweetheart through the grating. The diffuse light of daybreak gave a bluish cast to her brown complexion, making the whites of her eyes shine with mother-of-pearl reflections and imparting a deep tone to the shadows underneath her eyes. Toward the direction of Jerez the heavens were parted by a large strip of violet light, which spread about everywhere, absorbing the stars within its bosom. Out of the mists of night rose the city in the distance, with the pine grove of Tempul and the groups of white cottages, in which the last gas lamps were flickering like agonizing stars. A chilling breeze was blowing; the earth and its plants seemed to perspire at contact with the light. A bird fluttered forth from the prickly-pears, with a sharp cry that caused the maiden to shudder.

"Go, Rafael," she said with the precipitation of fear. "Leave at once. Day is breaking, and my father gets up early. Besides, the laborers will soon be here. What would they say if they saw us at such an hour? . . ."

But Rafael was unwilling to leave. So soon! After such a sweet night!

The maiden became impatient. Why should he make her suffer, if they were going to see each other again so soon? He had only to run down to the inn and mount his horse as soon as the doors of the house were opened.

"I won't go. I won't go," he declared in a supplicating voice, with the light of passion in his eyes. "I won't go. . . . And if you wish me to go . . ."

He clutched the bars of the grating more tightly, murmuring timidly the conditions he exacted for leaving. María de la Luz started back in protest, as if she feared the advance of that mouth which was begging between the bars.

"You don't love me!" she exclaimed. "If you did, you wouldn't ask such things!"

And she buried her head in her hands, as if about to

burst into tears. Rafael thrust one of his hands through the bars and with a gentle pull separated the clasped fingers that concealed his sweetheart's eyes.

"It was only in jest, little girl! . . . Forgive me, for I'm awfully bad. Strike me. Slap me, for I deserve it very much indeed."

María de la Luz, her face slightly reddened from the pressure of her hands, smiled, conquered by the humility with which her suitor begged pardon.

"I forgive you, but be off at once. Hurry, for the men will be out directly! . . . Yes, I forgive you! I forgive you! Don't delay! Off, now!"

"Then just to prove that you really forgive me, give me a slap. Either you strike me, or I don't go!"

"A slap! . . . You're very clever, aren't you! I know what you want, naughty one. Here, and be off at once."

Through the bars, holding her body back, she extended an arm as soft as a cushion and pitted with charming dimples. Rafael seized it and caressed it passionately. Then he kissed the pink finger-tips, sucking at her fingers with an ardor that caused María de la Luz to tremble behind the grating.

"Let me go, wicked man! . . . Or I'll scream! . . ."

And with a strong tug freeing herself from the caresses that made her tremble with excitement, she suddenly closed the window. For a long time Rafael stood rooted to the spot, and did not depart until the impression left upon his lips by the hand of María de la Luz had faded away.

It was a long while after this that the inhabitants of Marchamalo gave any signs of life. The mastiffs jumped up, barking, when the overseer opened the door of the wine-press house. Then, with ill-humored faces, the vine-dressers obliged to stay over in Marchamalo to be present at the celebration, began to come out upon the terrace.

The sky was blue, without the trace of a cloud. Upon the edge of the horizon a band of red heralded the sunrise.

"May God grant us a good day, gentlemen," was the overseer's greeting to the men.

But the latter made wry faces or shrugged their shoulders, like prisoners who, in the sadness of their confinement, are little concerned with the state of the weather.

Rafael suddenly appeared on horseback, flying up the vineyard slope at a gallop, as if he had just arrived from the grange.

"You're a very early bird, my fellow," commented the godfather sarcastically. "It's well known that you lose sleep over the affairs of Marchamalo."

The steward hovered about the door without catching sight of María de la Luz.

When the morning was well advanced señor Fermín, who had been watching the highway from the crest of the hill, at last made out, at the end of the white ribbon that cut the plain, a large cloud of dust spotted by the black outlines of various carriages.

"They're here, boys!" he shouted to the men. "The master's coming. And now be sure to receive him in a manner worthy of you—like decent folks."

And the laborers, following the directions of the overseer, aligned themselves in two rows, one on either side of the road.

The great coach of the Duponts had been brought out in honor of the festivities. All the millionaire's teams of horses and mules, as well as his riding horses, had been taken from the stables that were situated at the rear of the wine-stores; and with them, the brilliant trappings and the vehicles of every class that he had bought in Spain or ordered from England, with all the prodigality of a wealthy man who is unable to display his opulence in any other manner.

Don Pablo stepped out of a large landau, giving his hand to a fat priest with a smiling face and silk vestments that glittered in the sun. After satisfying himself that this companion had descended without any mishap, he attended to his mother and to his wife, who were dressed in black, wearing their mantillas over their eyes.

The dressers, rigid in their double column, removed their hats and saluted their master. Dupont smiled with satisfaction, and the priest did likewise, sweeping the toilers with a glance of patronizing commiseration.

"Very good," he whispered into don Pablo's ear with fawning accent. "They seem to be good fellows. Everybody knows that they serve a Christian master who edifies them with his good example."

Other carriages were now arriving, with their noisy tinkling of bells and the dusty stamping of horses' hoofs over the Marchamalo slope. The terrace was filled with people. The Dupont retinue comprised all his relatives and the office force. Even his cousin Luis, who looked very sleepy, had at dawn forsaken the worthy company of his boon companions in order to be present at the festivities and thus please don Pablo, whose favor he needed in those days.

The master of Marchamalo, noticing María de la Luz underneath the arcades, went to meet her, joining the cook of the Duponts and a group of servants who had just arrived, laden with refreshments, and were asking the overseer's daughter to show them to the kitchen, where they were to prepare the banquet.

Fermín Montenegro stepped out of another coach, in the company of don Ramón, the office superintendent, and they walked to one end of the terrace, as if fleeing the authoritative Dupont, who was in the thickest of the crowd, distributing orders and flying into a rage upon noticing the omission of certain details.

The chapel bell commenced to swing in the belfry, striking the first call to mass. Nobody was expected from beyond the vineyard, but don Pablo desired three calls to be sounded, and that they be prolonged ones —as long as the bell-ringer could hold out. This metallic clangor filled him with joy; he believed that it was the voice of God spreading over his fields, protecting them as was His duty, in view of the fact that their owner was a loyal believer.

Meanwhile, the priest, who had come with don Pablo, seemed likewise to flee from the shouting and the angry gestures with which the latter accompanied his orders, and gently attached himself to señor Fermín, meditating upon the beautiful panorama afforded by the vineyards.

"How great is the providence of the Lord! And what beautiful things He creates! Isn't that so, my good friend? . . ."

The overseer knew the priest. He was don Pablo's latest fad—his most recent hobby: a Jesuit father of whom there was much talk, because of the striking manner in which he dealt in his sermons with the so-called social question, which to the impious was a tangle that could never be solved, but which the priest resolved in a jiffy, by the simple application of Christian charity.

Dupont was as capricious and willful as a lover in his passion for the people of the Church. For a season he would adore the Fathers of the Company, and be unable to consider a mass of any worth or a sermon of any distinction unless it were given in their church. Then he would soon weary of the soutane, attracted

by the monastic robe, according to the various colors, and
would open his safe and the doors of his hotel to the
Carmelites, to the Franciscans or to the Dominicans that
were established in Jerez. Every time he came to the
vineyard he would appear with a priest of another de-
nomination, from whom the overseer could guess his
present favorites. Sometimes they were friars with
white and black vestments; others, brown or chestnut
color; there had even been some with long, flowing
beards, who came from distant lands and could scarcely
jabber Spanish. And the master, with his lover-like enthusiasm, anxious to spread the merits of his latest passion, would tell the overseer in friendly confidence:

"He is a hero of the faith. He has converted many
infidels, and I believe that he has even worked miracles.
If it were not that I might hurt his modesty, I would
ask him to roll up the sleeves of his habit, so that you
could be overwhelmed at the sight of the scars left by
his tortures. . . ."

His differences with doña Elvira always consisted in
the fact that she, too, had *her* favorites, which rarely happened to coincide with those of her son. When he was
in the throes of his admiration for the Jesuits, the noble
sister of the Marquis de San Dionisio was eulogizing
the Franciscans, alleging their antiquity, and that all the
other foundations had come later.

"No, mamma!" he would exclaim, repressing his ire
through respect for his mother. "How can you compare
a set of beggars with the Fathers of the Company, who
are the sages of the Church? . . ."

And when the pious lady had gone over to the sages,
her son, almost weeping with emotion, spoke of the solitary saint of Assisi, and of his sons the Franciscans, who
could give the unfaithful true lessons in democracy and

who would, on the day least expected, settle the social question.

At the present moment the weather-vane of his fervor pointed in the direction of the Company, and he was unable to go anywhere without Father Urizábal—a Basque and a compatriot of the glorious St. Ignatius. This was merit enough for Dupont to sing his praises everywhere.

The Jesuit contemplated the vineyards with the ecstasy of a man accustomed to live within vulgar edifices, seeing only from time to time the splendor of Nature. He questioned the overseer upon the cultivation of the vineyards, praising the looks of those that belonged to Dupont; señor Fermín, flattered in his pride as a cultivator, told himself that those Jesuits were not at all so despicable as his friend don Fernando considered them.

"Listen, your grace, Father: there is only one Marchamalo. This is the best in all the Jerez countryside."

He enumerated the conditions necessary to a good Jerez vineyard—planted in calcareous soil, sloping, so that the rain should run down and not refresh the earth too much and deprive the must of strength. Thus was produced that cluster of grapes which was the glory of the district, with seeds as small as buckshot, transparent and as white as ivory.

Carried away by his enthusiasm, he related to the priest, as if the latter were a cultivator, all the operations that the soil had to undergo during the year, submitted to continuous care so that it should yield its sweet blood. During the three last months of the year they would dig the *piletas*—hollows around the vines so that they should receive the rain: this part of the work was called *Chata*. This was also the time for pruning, which provoked quarrels among the dressers and had occasionally been the cause of a murder—the fight starting over the question as to whether the pruning should be done

with shears, as the masters desired, or with the ancient
pruning-knives—short and heavy machetes—as the workers insisted. Then, during January and February came
what was called *Cava bien;* this leveled the earth, leaving
it as flat as if a strickle had been passed over it. Then,
the *Golpe lleno,* in March, to destroy the weeds that had
sprung up because of the rains, at the same time serving to sponge the soil; and in June and July, the *Vina,*
which pressed down the earth, forming a hard crust, so
that it would preserve all its sap, transmitting it to the
vine. Besides this, in May, when the grapes began to
appear, they sulphured the vines so as to avoid the
cenizo, a blight that hardened the seeds.

And señor Fermín, to demonstrate the unceasing care
required during the entire year by that soil, which was
like gold itself, bent down to scrape up a handful of
lime, and showed the fineness of its little white, powdery
particles, which did not reveal the slightest trace of any
parasitic growth. Between the rows of vines could be
seen the soil—pounded, smoothed and combed, with the
same polish as if it were the floor of a salon. And the
Marchamalo vineyard extended further than the eye
could reach, occupying several hills—which meant
enormous labor! . . .

Despite the harsh manner in which the overseer treated
the vine-dressers during their hours of labor, now that
they were not present he expressed compassion for their
lot. They earned ten *reales*—an exorbitant wage compared to that of the farmhands; but their families lived
in the city, and besides, they paid for their meals, getting
together for the purchase of *costo,* the bread and pottage
that was brought from Jerez every day upon two horses.
Their implements were their own: a nine-pound hoe
which they had to handle as easily as if it were a cane,
from sun to sun with no rest outside of an hour for

breakfast, another for dinner, and a few minutes here and there granted by the overseer who, with his stentorian voice, would shout the order for a smoke.

"Nine pounds, father," added señor Fermín. "That's easy to say, and for a short while it's merely a toy. But you ought to see how a good Christian looks after raising and lowering the implement all day long. At the close of the day it weighs *arrobas*. . . . *Arrobas?* What am I talking about? Tons, I should say. When you move it, it seems as if you're lifting all Jerez in the air."

And since he was speaking to a friend of the master's, he did not conceal the tricks that were employed in the vineyards to hasten the work and get the most out of the day's labors. The fastest and strongest worker was selected, and was promised an increase of one *real*, being placed at the head of a line. This man was known as *hombre de mano*. The robust fellow thus chosen, in gratitude for the increase in his pay, attacked the soil with his hoe with hardly time for a breath between one blow and another, and the other unfortunates had to follow his pace, managing, with superhuman efforts, to keep up with the companion who served as their spur.

At night, thoroughly exhausted, they whiled away the time before their final meal by playing cards or singing. Don Pablo had severely prohibited the reading of newspapers. Their sole joy was Saturday, when at nightfall they left the vineyard, bound for Jerez, to *hear mass*, as they said. Until Sunday night they remained with their families; their savings—that part of their pay which remained after they paid their share of the *costo*—they gave to their wives.

The priest expressed surprise at noticing that the men had remained at Marchamalo, since it was Sunday.

"Because they are very good, father," explained the overseer in hypocritical tones. "Because they are very fond of their master, and it was enough for me to tell them, on don Pablo's behalf, about the ceremony, for the poor fellows to remain behind of their own account, giving up their weekly visit to their homes."

The sound of Dupont's voice calling his illustrious friend, Father Urizábal, caused the latter to leave the overseer and make his way to the church, escorted by don Pablo and his entire family.

Señor Fermín at this moment caught sight of his son walking along a path with don Ramón. They discussed the beauty of the vineyards. Thanks to the initiative of don Pablo, Marchamalo was regaining the position it held in its most famous days. Phylloxera had killed many of the vines that were the glory of the house of Dupont, but the present head had planted upon the slopes that had been devastated by the plague, the American vine—an absolute innovation in Jerez—and the renowned farm would return to its glorious times without fear of new invasions. This was the reason for the ceremony: so that the blessing of the Lord might cover with His eternal protection the hills of Marchamalo.

The office superintendent grew enthusiastic as he contemplated the undulating vineyards, and burst forth into lyric eulogies. He was in charge of the firm's publicity, and from his pen—that of an old, luckless journalist and submerged intellectual—sprung the prospectuses, the leaflets, the advertisements on the fourth page of the newspapers—all of which trumpeted the glory of the house of Dupont, in such a pompous, solemn, puffed-up style that it was hard to tell whether it was sincere, or a jest that don Ramón permitted himself at the expense of his employer and the public. As one read it, one must perforce come to the conclusion that the wine of Jerez was quite as indispensable as bread, and that those who did not drink it were condemned to an early death.

"Just look, Fermín, my boy," he declaimed with oratorical intonation. "What a beautiful expanse of vineyards! I am proud to lend my services to a house that
is the proprietor of Marchamalo. Such a glory is not
found in any nation, and when I hear persons talk of the
political progress of France, of the military power of
the Germans or the naval superiority of the English, I
reply: 'This is all very well. But where have they wines
as good as those from Jerez?' It is impossible to speak
too well of this wine so pleasant to the eye, so odorous to
the nostrils, the delight of the palate and the support of
the stomach. Don't you agree with me? . . ."

Fermín nodded affirmation and smiled, as if he had
known in advance just what don Ramón would say. He
knew by heart the pompous phrases of the firm's
prospectuses, considered by don Pablo as the most
glorious models of secular literature.

Whenever he found the opportunity, the old employee
repeated them in declamatory fashion, intoxicated with
the taste of his own work.

"Wine, dear Fermín, is the universal beverage par
excellence—the most healthful of all that man employs
for either nutrition or recreation. It is the beverage that
attained to the honor of creating a pagan deity of intoxication. It is the drink sung by the Greek and Roman
poets, celebrated by artists, lauded by physicians. In
wine the poet finds inspiration, the soldier courage, the
toiler strength, the invalid health. In wine man finds
pleasure and joy, and from it the old imbibe vigor.
Wine stimulates the intelligence, quickens the imagination, fortifies the will, maintains energy. We can understand the Greek heroes and their poets only by the
stimulus of the wines of Cyprus and Samos; and the
license of Roman society is utterly incomprehensible to
us without the wines of Falernus and Syracuse. It is

possible to explain the heroic resistance of the Aragon-
ese peasant during the siege of Zaragoza—without rest
or food—only by remembering that in addition to the
admirable moral power of their patriotism they counted
for physical stimulation upon their jug of red wine. . . .
But within the field of wine production, which comprises
many countries, what an astounding variety of classes
and types, of colors and bouquets—and how Jerez stands
at the very head of the wine aristocracy! Don't you
agree, Fermín? Isn't all this praise that occurs to me
just and well expressed? . . ."

The young man assented. He had read all this many
times in the Introduction to the firm's large catalogue:
a brochure containing views of the Dupont wine-stores
and the numerous other buildings, accompanied by a
history of the firm and eulogies upon its growth; this was
don Ramón's masterpiece, which the master presented
to his customers and his visitors bound in white and blue,
the colors of the Purísimas painted by Murillo.

"The wine of Jerez," he continued, with solemn accent, "is not an upstart—an article elevated by the
caprices of fashion; its reputation is of well proved
antiquity—not only as a grateful beverage, but as a
therapeutic agent that knows no substitute. The guest
in England is received with a bottle of Jerez wine; likewise, with a bottle of Jerez wine the convalescent in the
Scandinavian countries is put on the road to recovery,
and in India the English soldiers recuperate the strength
that has been robbed by fever. With Jerez wine the
sailors fight the scurvy, and through its aid the pious
missionaries have in Australia reduced the cases of
anemia brought on by the climate and the privations. . . .
And why indeed, gentlemen, should not such prodigious
results be realized by a Jerez wine of sound, authentic
source? In it are found the legitimate, natural alcohol

of the wine with the minerals proper to it; astringent tannin and stimulating ethers, inducing appetite for the nourishment of the body and sleep for its restoraticn. It is at the same time a stimulant and a sedative—excellent advantages not to be found combined in any other product which is, at the same time, like our own Jerez wine, grateful to both the palate and the sight."

For a moment don Ramón ceased, to take breath and rest in the echo of his eloquence, but a few instants later he resumed, eying Fermín intently, as if the latter were an enemy, most difficult to convince.

"Unfortunately, many persons imagine that they are tasting Jerez wine when they are drinking only impure adulterations. In London, under the name of Sherry, they sell heterogeneous liquids. We cannot compromise with this fraud, gentlemen. Jerez wine is like gold. We can admit that gold is pure, medium or of lowest quality. What we cannot admit, however, is that mere plating should be called gold. That is properly called Sherry which is produced by the vineyards of Jerez—which is grown and aged by its wine-dealers and which is exported under their honorable name by houses of unassailable credit, as for example the firm of Dupont Brothers. No establishment may be compared to theirs; it includes every branch; it cultivates the vine and develops the must; it stores and ages the wines; it even assumes charge of selling and exporting, and in addition distills musts, producing its famous cognac. Its history goes back more than a century and a half. The Duponts constitute a dynasty; its power admits neither auxiliaries nor associates; it plants its vines upon its own soil, and they are previously born in the Duponts' own hothouses. The grapes are pressed in Dupont wine-presses and the casks in which the wine matures are made by Dupont. In Dupont warehouses the wine is stored and aged under the vigilance of a Dupont, and by Dupont it is bottled and exported without the intervention of any other interests. Ask, therefore, for the legitimate Dupont wines with the security that it is the firm which preserves them pure and genuine."

Fermín laughed to hear his superintendent launch into a speech composed of fragmentary sentences from the prospectuses and the advertisements, which he knew by heart.

"But, don Ramón! I'm not on the market for a single bottle! . . . I belong to the establishment!"

The publicity director seemed to awake from his oratorical nightmare, and laughed as heartily as his subordinate.

"Perhaps you have read a good deal of this in the firm's publications, but you must agree with me that it's not at all bad. Besides," he added, ironically, "we great men dwell under the weight of our greatness, and as we cannot escape from it, we repeat ourselves."

He gazed across the vine-clad tracts and continued in tones of sincere delight:

"I'm happy to see that they've replanted the vineyards that were devastated by the Phylloxera with American vines. I advised don Pablo very often to do so. In that way our production will very shortly increase, and business, which is going well, will go still better. Then let the plague return whenever it pleases; it will pass over these parts."

Fermín turned to him with an expression that invited confidence.

"Frankly speaking, don Ramón, in which do you believe most—in the American vine or the benediction that this father is going to pronounce over the vine-stocks? . . ."

Don Ramón eyed the young man very closely, as if

he desired to see his own reflection in the speaker's pupils.

"My dear boy! My dear boy!" he exclaimed severely.

Then, looking about him with a certain alarm, he continued in a low voice, as if the very vines might hear him:

"You know me: I deal in confidence with you because I know that you are above going around gossiping and because you've seen a bit of the world and have shed your simple notions abroad. Why ask me questions? You know that I keep quiet and let matters take their course. I have no right to more. The firm of Dupont is my refuge; if I were to leave it, I'd have to return, with all my family, to the wretched poverty of Madrid. Here I am like a wanderer who finds rest and takes gratefully what is given to him, without indulging in the criticism of his benefactors."

The recollection of the past, with its illusions and his boasts of independence, awoke a certain humiliation in him. In order to justify himself he desired to explain the radical transformation that had come over his life.

"I retired, Fermín, and I'm not sorry. There are still many of my former comrades in poverty and enthusiasm who continue faithful to the past, with the most obstinate indifference to consequences. But they were born to be heroes and I'm only a man that considers eating the primary function of life. . . . Besides, I got tired of writing for fame and for ideals, of sweating for others and living in perpetual poverty. One day I told myself that it's possible to labor for one of two things only: to become a great man or to eat. And since I was convinced that my withdrawal would cause the world not the slightest emotion—in fact, that it had never even learned of my existence—I laid aside my tools of the Ideal, decided to eat, and taking advantage of certain 'boosts' that I had given to the firm of Dupont in the newspapers,

I accepted a lifelong position in it, and I can't complain."

Don Ramón imagined that he discerned a certain repugnance in Fermín's eyes for the cynicism with which
he expressed himself, and he hastened to add:

"I am what I am, my dear fellow. Just scratch me, and
my former self will appear. Believe me: he who bites
into the fatal apple of which those friends of our master
speak, never can remove the taste from his lips. He
may change his garb so as to continue living; but his
soul, never! He who once doubts, and reasons and
criticizes, can never again believe with the faith of the
sincerely devout; he believes either because his reason
counsels him to, or because his personal advantage forces
him to. Therefore, when you hear a fellow like me discussing faith and creed, tell him that he lies because
it's to his advantage, or that he's deceiving himself for
the peace of his mind. . . . Fermín, my boy; I don't
earn my bread in untroubled ease, but at the cost of
vile degradations of my soul, which shame me in my own
eyes. I, who in *my day* bristled like a hedgehog with
pride and virtue! . . . But remember that I've got my
daughters on my hands—that they must eat and dress
and all the rest that's necessary to bag a husband with,
and that until such a fellow comes along I've got to support them, even if I must steal to do so."

Don Ramón believed that he again caught a glimpse
of commiseration in his hearer's eyes.

"Despise me as much as you please: young folks can't
understand certain things. You may remain pure without anybody but yourself suffering for it. . . . Besides,
my boy, I do not repent of what they call my apostasy. I
am a disillusioned man. . . . Sacrifice myself for these
people? Much good that does! . . . I've spent half my
life raving with hunger and hoping for the great revolution. Now, let's see; suppose you tell me when this

country ever really revolted? When did we ever have a revolution? . . . The only genuine one was in the year 1808, and if the country rose at that time it was only because a few princes and *infantes* that were born simpletons, and evil from inherited instincts, were kidnapped from them. And the popular beast shed its blood to have these fellows returned to the throne; and the rulers showed their gratitude for so many sacrifices by sending some to prison and others to the gallows. A wonderful people! Go and sacrifice yourself and expect something from them! . . . Ever since then there haven't been any revolutions. There have been army uprisings or mutinies, which were of indirect value, if any, by influencing public opinion. And since in these days generals no longer revolt, because they have everything they desire, and because the rulers, having learned their lesson from history, take care to flatter them, it's all up with the Revolution! Those who work for it sweat and labor with as much success as carrying water in a sieve. . . . I salute these heroes from the door of my seclusion! . . but I take not a step to accompany them. I am not of their glorious race. I am a quiet, well-fed domestic bird, and I'm not sorry for it, either, when I look at my former comrade Fernando Salvatierra, your father's idol, dressed winters in summer fashion, and summers in winter fashion, living upon bread and cheese, with a cell reserved for him in every prison of the Peninsula, and bothered by the police at every step. . . . It's all very fine; the papers print the hero's name, and perhaps some day history will speak of him, but I prefer my office desk, my chair which makes me think of the canons gathered in the choir, and the generosity of don Pablo, who is as lavish as a prince with those who know how to get around him."

Fermín, offended by the sarcastic tone in which this

victim, content with his servitude, referred to Salvatierra,
was about to answer him when from the end of the walk
sounded the imperious voice of Dupont and the loud
hand-clapping of the overseer summoning his men.

The church bell was filling the air with its third call.
Don Pablo, from the steps of the chapel, swept his gaze
across his flock of employees and then entered hurriedly,
since he desired to edify the people by aiding in the mass.

The crowd of workers filled the chapel.   They all remained standing, with a sullen expression upon their
faces that at certain moments made Dupont lose all hope
that these fellows would ever appreciate the concern he
gave himself about their souls.

Near to the altar, seated upon red chairs, were the
women of the family; behind were the relatives and the
office force. The altar was bedecked with mountain
grasses and flowers from the Dupont conservatory at
the hotel. The pungent perfume of the wild branches
mingled with the odor of tired, perspiring flesh that was
exhaled by the multitude of laborers.

From time to time María de la Luz left the kitchen
to run to the door of the church and hear a "snatch of
mass." She stood upon tip-toe, and her gaze would
rise above all the heads to fix itself upon Rafael, who
was at the overseer's side, upon the steps leading to the
altar, standing like a barrier between the upper class
persons and the poor folk.

Luis Dupont was slouching behind his aunt's seat, but
the moment he caught sight of María de la Luz he made
various gestures to her, even threatening her with his
hand. The wretched fellow! Always the same. Up to
the very moment when mass was to begin he had been
in the kitchen importuning her with his jests, as if they
were still at their childhood games. Several times she

had been forced to warn him, half smilingly and half in offense, that he must keep his hands away.

But María de la Luz could not remain long in the same place. She was called by the kitchen folk, who could not find certain of the ingredients most indispensable to their dishes.

The mass advanced. The widow Dupont felt her heart soften as she beheld the humility, the Christian grace with which her Pablo changed the position of the missal or managed the wine-vessels. A man who was the foremost millionaire of his country, affording the poor such an example of humility before the priests of God; serving as an acolyte to Father Urizábal! If all the rich were to do likewise, there would be a different frame of mind among the toiling masses, who felt only hatred and desire for vengeance. And overcome by her son's grandeur, she lowered her eyes, sighing and upon the verge of tears.

The mass terminated, there came the moment for the great ceremony. The vineyards were to be blessed so as to be rendered immune from the peril of Phylloxera . . . after having been planted with American vines.

Señor Fermín hurriedly left the chapel and had several bundles, which had been brought from Jerez the previous day, dragged up to the door. They were filled with candles, and the overseer began to distribute them among the laborers.

Under the glowing light of the sun there commenced to shine, like red, opaque brush strokes, the flames from the wax tapers. The workers formed in two lines and, guided by señor Fermín, began a slow procession down the slope.

The women, grouped in the little square, together with all their maids and María de la Luz, watched the departure of the procession, the slow progress of the two rows of men, their heads lowered and the tapers in their hands, some in brown jackets and others in their shirts with a red kerchief around their necks, all of them bearing their hats placed against their breasts.

Señor Fermín, who walked at the head of the procession, was already at the middle of the hill, when there appeared a more interesting group in the door of the chapel: Father Urizábal, with a pluvial of gold, embroidered with red carnations, and at his side, Dupont, grasping his taper as if it were a sword, looking about him in all directions, imperiously, so that the ceremony proceed without a hitch and the slightest detail be not overlooked.

Behind, like an honorary escort, marched all his relatives and office employees, with unctuous countenance. Luis appeared the most solemn of all.

He scoffed at everything, except matters pertaining to religion, and this ceremony, by its extraordinary character, was affecting him deeply. He had received excellent training at the hands of the Fathers of the Company. "And he had such a good start," as don Pablo was wont to say when report came to him of his cousin's wild escapades.

Father Urizábal opened the book which he bore close to his chest—the *Roman Ritual,* and commenced to recite the *Litany of the Saints*—the Great Litany as the church folk call it.

Dupont with his glances ordered all those about him to follow him faithfully in his responses to the priest.

"*Sancte Michael!* . . ."

"*Ora pro nobis,*" replied the master with a firm voice, looking around at his group.

Those near Dupont repeated the same words, and the *Oro pro nobis* advanced like a roar as far as the head

of the procession, where señor Fermín seemed to beat
the time for the voices of the laborers.

"*Sancte Raphael!* . . ."

"*Ora pro nobis.*"

"*Omnes sancti Angeli et Archangeli!*"

Now, instead of a single saint being invoked, there
were many, so Dupont raised his head and shouted more
loudly than ever, for every one to hear, that no mistakes
should be made in the response:

"*Orate pro nobis.*"

But only those in the immediate vicinity of don Pablo
could follow his indications. The rest of the procession
advanced slowly, and each successive response that came
like a roar from the files of men was increasingly disordered, with burlesque sonority and ironic tremblings.

After a few sentences of the litany had been recited
the workers, bored by the ceremony, holding their candles
with the wick downward, replied automatically, sometimes imitating the noise of thunder and other times
an old woman's high-pitched scream, so that many of
them had to bring their hats to their mouths to stifle
their laughter.

"*Sancte Jacobe!*" sang the priest.

"*No-o-o-bis!*" bellowed the men, with burlesque in-
flexions of the voice, without relaxing the gravity of their
grimy faces.

"*Sancte Barnaba!* . . ."

"*Obis! Obis!*" replied the toilers from afar.

Señor Fermín, himself beginning to feel bored by the
ceremony, pretended anger.

"See here, now! Let there be order!" he shouted, facing the most serious offenders. "You confounded fellows, can't you see that the master will understand you're
making fun of him? . . ."

But the master was aware of nothing; he was overcome

by his emotions. The sight of the two rows of men marching between the vines, and the solacing chant of the priest, moved his soul. The candle flames burned without color or light, like glowworms delayed upon their journey and overtaken by day: the Jesuit's cape glittered under the sun like the shell of an enormous insect— white, red and gold. The sacred ceremony moved Dupont to the point of wiping the tears from his eyes.

"Very beautiful, isn't it?" he sighed during a pause of the litany, unable to see any one of the group about him, and uttering the expression of his enthusiasm to no one in particular.

"Sublime!" the superintendent of the office hastened to murmur.

"Cousin . . . first-rate!" added Luis. "This is like a theatrical spectacle."

Dupont, despite his emotion, did not forget to make the responses to the litany or to assist the priest. He took him by the arm to guide him over the uneven surface of the earth; he kept the raised embroidery of his cape from catching upon the runners.

"*Ab ira, ab odio, et omni mala voluntate!* . . ." chanted the priest.

It was now the time for varying the response, and Dupont, with all his associates, replied:

"*Libera nos, Domine.*"

Meanwhile, the rest of the procession continued, with ironic tenacity, to answer with its *Ora pro nobis*.

"*A spiritu fornicationis!*" said Father Urizábal.

"*Libera nos, Domine,*" replied, with deep contrition, Dupont and all those who understood this supplication to the Almighty, while half of the procession roared from the distance:

"*No-o-obis . . . obis!*"

The overseer was now marching up the slope, leading his men toward the terrace.

The vine-dressers formed in groups about the cistern, which reared its great iron circle above the square and was topped by a cross. As the priest and his cortège reached the terrace, Dupont laid aside his taper to take from the chapel warden the hyssop and the vessel of holy water. He would serve as sacristan to his learned friend. His hands trembled with emotion as he grasped the sacred objects.

The overseer and many of the toilers, aware that the supreme moment of the ceremony had arrived, opened their eyes very wide, hoping to see something extraordinary.

In the meantime the priest turned the leaves of his book, without being able to find the prayer befitting the occasion. The Ritual was exceedingly precise, down to the last detail. The Church worms its way into every avenue of life: prayers for women about to give birth, for water, for light, for new homes, for recently constructed vessels, for the bed of the newly-wed, for those about to undertake a voyage, for bread, for eggs, for every sort of eatable. At last he discovered in the Ritual what he was looking for: *Benedictio super fruges et vineas.*

And Dupont experienced a certain pride to think that the Church had its Latin prayer for the vineyards, as if it had foreseen many centuries ago that there would be born in Jerez a servant of the Lord, a great wine producer, who was going to need its prayers.

"Adjutorium nostrum in nomine Domine," recited the priest, looking at his wealthy acolyte through the corner of his eye, ready to aid him with the response.

"Qui fecit caelum et terram," answered Dupont with-

out hesitating, remembering the words that he had carefully memorized.

He even responded to two other invocations by the priest, who was now slowly reading the *Oremus*, begging the Lord's protection of the vineyards and beseeching Him to guide the grapes to maturity.

"*Per Christum Dominum nostrum . . .*" concluded the Jesuit.

"*Amen,*" replied Dupont with contracted features, struggling to restrain his tears.

Father Urizábal grasped the hyssop, moistening it in the copper vessel, and drew himself erect as if the better to dominate the extension of vineyards that spread before him from the terrace.

"*Asperges . . .*" and mumbling the rest of the invocation between his teeth, he cast a spray of water into the space before him. "*Asperges . . . Asperges . . .*" and he sprayed the water to right and to left.

Then, gathering his cape and smiling to the women, with the satisfaction of one who has completed his labors, he turned to the chapel, followed by the sacristan, who was again carrying the hyssop and the copper vessel.

"Is it all over?" asked an old, solemn-faced husbandman phlegmatically of the overseer.

"Yes. It's over."

"And the father priest has nothing more to say? . . ."

"I believe not."

"Good. . . . And can we be off now?"

Señor Fermín, after exchanging a few words with don Pablo, returned to the groups of laborers, clapping his hands to get their attention. Fly away! The festivities had come to an end as far as they were concerned. Now they could go to the other *mass,* to see their wives; but they must all return to the vineyard that night, ready to get to work early next morning.

"Take the candles with you," he added. "Your master presents them to you so that your families may keep them as souvenirs."

The laborers commenced to file by Dupont, with their extinguished candles.

"Many thanks," said some, raising their hands to their hats.

And the tone of their voices was such that those about Dupont wondered whether or not he would take offense.

Don Pablo, however, was still under the pressure of his emotions. Within the tower the preparations for the banquet were coming to a close, but he would not be able to eat! "What a day, my friends! What a sublime spectacle!" And gazing upon the hundreds of toilers who were filing down the slope among the vines, he gave free vent to his feelings of enthusiasm.

They had just witnessed an image of what society ought to be. The masters and the servants, the rich and the poor—all united in God, loving one another with Christian brotherhood, each one preserving his place in the hierarchy and the share of well-being that the Lord was pleased to grant him.

The workingmen hastened on their way. Some were running to outdistance their companions, and to reach the city as soon as possible. They had been waited for in Jerez since the previous night. They had passed the week looking forward to Saturday and to their return to their homes and the warmth of the family circle, after six days of herding together.

This was the sole consolation of the poor worker— the sad rest after a week of fatigue—and he had been robbed of a day and a morning. Only a few hours remained to the men; as soon as night came on they would have to return to Marchamalo.

As they cleared the territory of the Duponts, and found

themselves upon the highway, the men burst into conversation. For a moment they stopped to take a look at the top of the hill, where the forms of Dupont and his office force stood out against the sky, diminished by the distance.

The youngest of the laborers looked scornfully at the candles that had been presented to them, and placing them under their abdomens, moved them cynically, pointing to the top of the hill.

"Here's to you! . . . To you! . . ."

The older men broke into muffled threats.

"May a sharp knife get you some day, you old bigot! May they riddle you, you old thief! . . ."

And Dupont, from above, swept the fields with a tearful glance as he gazed down at his hundreds of toilers who had stopped on the road, doubtless to salute him. Then he communicated his enthusiasm to the friends about him.

"A wonderful day, my friends! A touching spectacle!" All that the world needed in order to get along well was to organize itself on the basis of sane traditions. . . . Just like his firm.

CHAPTER V

ONE Saturday morning, Fermín Montenegro, upon leaving the office, met don Fernando Salvatierra.

The leader was taking a long walk, bound for the environs of the city. For the greater part of the day he worked at translations from the English, or at writing articles for newspapers devoted to *the idea;* labors that brought him just enough for his bread and cheese, permitting him in addition to help out the *comrade* that he sheltered in his rickety house, as well as other no less needy *comrades* who besieged him frequently, asking succor in the name of solidarity.

His sole pleasure, after work, was walking; his walks, however, lasted hours, and amounted almost to a journey, extending well into the night, when he would appear most unexpectedly at farms situated several leagues from the city.

His friends fled from accompanying this walking enthusiast upon his excursions—this fellow with tireless legs, who recommended walking as the most efficacious of remedies, and spoke of Kant, adducing as examples the four-hour promenades which the philosopher used to take daily. Thanks to this tranquil exercise the sage attained to a ripe old age.

Salvatierra, upon learning that Fermín had no immediate work on hand, invited him to come along. He was going toward the plains of Caulina. He preferred the Marchamalo road, and was sure that his former comrade, the overseer, would receive him with open arms;

but he knew the feelings of the Duponts toward him and desired to avoid unpleasantness.

"Even you, my boy," continued don Fernando, "expose yourself to a sermon, if Dupont should learn that you walk with me."

Fermín shrugged his shoulders. He was accustomed to his employer's reprimands, and a few hours after having heard him, he no longer remembered the words. Besides, it was some time since he had conversed with don Fernando, and it would be a pleasure to accompany him on this balmy spring afternoon.

The two left the city, and after following the hedges of some small vineyards with their little recreation houses amid groups of trees, they beheld the plains of Caulina, extending before their vision like a green steppe. Not a tree, not a structure. The land disappeared toward the mountains, which, hazy in the distance, blotted out the horizon; an uncultivated, wild prairie, with the monotonous solemnity of abandoned soil.

Thick clumps of undergrowth covered the ground; spring tinted their dark green with the red and white of wild flowers. The agaves and the prickly-pears—the coarse, repulsive plants of abandoned land—heaped up upon the borders of the road a sharp, aggressive vegetation. Their straight or arched stalks, with their white tufts, were the substitutes for trees in this flat, unvaried immensity that was disturbed by not the slightest undulation. Scattered at long intervals, the shacks and huts of the herders, made of branches and very low-roofed, so that they seemed to harbor reptiles rather than men, were scarcely visible, and appeared like black warts. Ring-doves were winging in the smiling afternoon sky. The clouds displayed a golden lining, reflecting the setting sun.

Endless wires stretched from post to post, almost on a

level with the ground, marking the boundaries of the
plain, which was parceled off in gigantic proportions.
And within these enclosures of indefinite limits, which
it was impossible to follow with the eye, were the bulls,
moving about with slow steps, or motionless upon the
ground, rendered diminutive by the distance, as if they
had just fallen out of a box of toys. The bells upon the
bell-oxen filled the silence of the afternoon with faint
vibrations, adding a new melancholy note to the dead
landscape.

"Look, Fermín," said Salvatierra ironically. "Happy
Andalusia! Fertile Andalusia! . . ."

Thousands upon thousands of men, victims of day-
labor, suffered the tortures of hunger because they had
no fields to cultivate, and the land was reserved for
beasts, in the very suburbs of a civilized city. Nor was
the dominating animal of that plain the peaceful steer
that provides meat for man's sustenance; it was the wild
bull, destined to fight in the arenas, whose savagery was
cultivated by the breeder, who bent every effort toward
increasing it.

The immense tract of land was easily enough to provide room comfortably for four towns and food for
hundreds of families; but the land belonged to the
animals, whose ferocity was nurtured by man to amuse
idlers, and their trade was invested with a patriotic
character.

"There are visionary folk," continued Salvatierra,
"who dream of bringing to these plains the water that
is lost in the mountains and of establishing upon their
own land the entire horde of the disinherited who deceive hunger with the *gazpacho* they get at the workers'
dormitories. And they hope to accomplish this within
the present order of things! And yet many of them call
me deluded! . . . The rich man has his granges and his

vineyards and has need of Hunger, which is his ally, so that it may give him his wage-slaves. The cattle-raiser, on his side, needs plenty of uncultivated land for the production of his beasts, who pay not with their meat, but by virtue of their ferocity. And the powers that possess the money are interested in the continuation of such a state of affairs, and it will continue."

Salvatierra laughed as he recalled what he had read upon the progress of his country. On the farms could be seen agricultural machines of the most recent models, and the newspapers, paid by the rich, dissolved into eulogies of the great initiative of their supporters regarding agricultural advance. Lies—all lies. The earth was cultivated worse than in the time of the Moors. Fertilizers were unknown; they were mentioned with disdain, as modern inventions contrary to all tradition. Intensive cultivation as practiced by other peoples was considered a dream. They plowed here in Biblical fashion; the land was left to produce as it pleased, and the scant harvest was compensated for by the vast extension of the properties and the ridiculously low wages.

The triumphs of mechanical progress had been accepted only as a weapon against the enemy—against the laborer. The one modern tool that was to be found on every farm was the thrasher. It was the heavy artillery of large property. Thrashing after the old system, with its droves of mares turning about the thrashing floor, consumed entire months, and the laborers selected this season in which to ask for some improvement in their conditions, threatening a strike, which would subject the harvest to the dangers of bad weather. The thrashing-machine, which accomplished in two weeks the labor of as many months, assured the owner of his gathering. Besides, he saved the expense of so many hands, and this in itself was a vengeance upon the discontented, mutinous tribe that molests decent persons with its impositions. And in the *Círculo Caballista* the chief landed proprietors spoke of the progress of the country and of their machines, which served only to gather and assure the harvests, and never to sow and raise them; and this artifice of war was hypocritically presented as an example of disinterested progress.

Great property was impoverishing the country, subjecting it like a helpless victim beneath its brutal weight. The city was the *urbs* of the Roman times, surrounded by leagues and leagues of territory, without a town or a hamlet, and no other groups of living beings beside the farmhouses, with their wage-slaves, mercenaries of poverty, who beheld themselves replaced as soon as age or exhaustion appeared in them; they were situated worse than the ancient slave, who at least was sure of bread and shelter until he died.

Life was concentrated in the city, as if war had devastated the fields and security might be had only within city walls. The ancient latifundium, dominating the land, populated the country with hordes when they were needed for the work. And when the task was done, a deathly silence fell over these immense solitudes, and the bands of toilers retreated to their mountain towns, to curse from afar the tyrannical city. Others begged in the city, seeing close at hand the wealth of their masters and their barbaric display, which gave rise in the hearts of the poor to a desire to exterminate all.

Salvatierra paused for a moment to turn back and contemplate the city, whose white groups of houses and garden trees stood out against the rose and gold of the sunset.

"Ah, Jerez! Jerez!" apostrophized the rebel. "City of millionaires, surrounded by a vast army of beggars! . . .

The strange part of it is that you are still here, so white and pretty, smiling at all their wretchedness, without their having long ago set fire to you. . . ."

The country, dependent upon the city and embracing almost a province, was in the hands of only eighty proprietors. Throughout the rest of Andalusia it was the same. Many families of deep-rooted nobility had retained their feudal property—the vast extensions acquired by their ancestors only at the cost of galloping along, lance in socket, slaying Moors. Other great properties had been formed by the purchasers of national estates, or by the political agitators who were rewarded for their services in the elections by a State gift of mountains and public lands, upon which entire towns were situated. Upon certain sites of the mountains could be met abandoned villages with crumbling houses, as if an epidemic had passed through the place. The population had fled far away, in search of day-labor, before the sight of these public lands, which provided bread for their families, being converted into pasture-ground for a wealthy man of influence.

And this incubus of property, vast and barbarous in character, was rendered somewhat tolerable in certain sections of Andalusia because the masters were absent, living in Madrid upon the rentals sent to them by associates or administrators, content with the income from estates which they had never seen and which, because of their immensity, brought many returns from various sources.

But in Jerez the rich man was at all hours upon the poor man's back, to make the wretch feel his influence. He was an uncouth Centaur, proud of his strength, seeking combat, intoxicated with his power; he enjoyed defying the hungry fellow's anger, so that he might

master him as if he were one of the wild colts being subjected to branding.

"The rich man hereabouts is more of a commoner than
the toiler," averred Salvatierra. "His lusty, impulsive
bestiality renders the wretchedness of the poor more
grievous than ever."

Wealth was more evident in these parts than anywhere
else. The wine growers, the owners of the warehouses,
the exporters, with their extraordinary fortunes and their
ostentatious living embittered the poverty of the unfortunate.

"Those who give a man two *reales* for a whole day's
work," continued the revolutionist, "pay almost fifty
thousand *reales* for a noted horse. I have been through
the workers' quarters and through many of the stables
of Jerez, where these useless animals are kept, serving
only for the flattery of their owners. Take my word
for it, Fermín: there are thousands of rational beings
in this land, who, upon arising with aching bones from
their mat at the farm, would gladly be transformed into
horses."

He by no means abhorred these vast properties. They
represented an easy transition into communism of the
land, a generous dream whose realization he often believed near. The fewer the number of landowners, the
easier it would be to solve the problem and the less the
interest aroused by the clamors of the dispossessed.

But the solution was far, far away, and in the meantime he was rendered indignant by the increasing poverty
—the moral debasement of the slaves of the soil. He
was amazed at the blindness of the fortunate classes,
who were fettered to the past. Giving over the land
in small parcels to the workers, as in other parts of
Spain, would have the result of retarding the revolution
in the fields by centuries. The small cultivator who

loves his piece of land, like a prolongation of the family, is bitter and hostile to every revolutionary innovation—more so even than the genuine rich man. Every new idea is considered by him a danger to his meager comfort and he repels it forcibly. Giving over the possession of the land to such persons as these would delay the moment of supreme Justice that filled all Salvatierra's dreams; but even if this should happen, his kind soul found consolation in the fact that poverty would obtain momentary alleviation thereby. Towns would spring up amid solitudes, the isolated granges would disappear, with their gloomy aspect of a garrison or a penitentiary, and the beasts would return to the mountains, leaving the plains for the sustenance of man.

But Fermín, as he listened to his former teacher, shook his head in token of denial.

"Everything will continue as before," said the youth. "The rich care nothing about the future, nor do they believe any precaution necessary to retard it. Their eyes are at the back of their head, and if they do see anything, it's behind. As long as the governing element comes from their class and hold at their service the rifles that we all pay for, they will laugh at the rebels from below. Besides, they know the people."

"That's just as you say," agreed Salvatierra. "They know the people, and do not fear them."

The revolutionist thought of the *Maestrico*—the boy whom he had seen writing so laboriously under the light of the oil-lamp, in the workers' quarters at Matanzuela. Perhaps this ingenuous soul saw the future more clearly through his simple faith than he, with his indignation, longing to destroy all evil at a single blow. It was first necessary to create new men before setting about to overcome the decrepit world. And as he thought of the poverty-stricken, spiritless masses, his voice echoed with a certain sadness.

"It is in vain that revolutions have been attempted in this country. The soul of our people is the same as it was in feudal days. Within its depths it retains the resignation of the serf."

That land was the land of wine, and Salvatierra, with the impassivity of the abstainer, cursed the power that alcoholic poison wielded over the people, transmitting its evil from generation to generation. The wine-warehouse was the modern counterpart of the feudal fortress that held the masses in slavery and abjection. Their enthusiasm, their crimes, their joys, their love—all were the product of wine, as if those persons, who learned to drink almost at the moment when their lips left the mother's breasts, and counted the hours of the day by the number of glasses, lacked their own passions and affections, and were unable to move or feel from their own impulse, having to resort to drink for all their actions.

Salvatierra spoke of wine as of an invisible, all-powerful personage, who intervened in all the deeds of these automatons, suggesting their very thoughts, as limited and capricious as those of a bird, and plunging them into despair as well as into disordered happiness.

Intelligent men who could serve as leaders for those below revealed generous aspirations in their youth, but scarcely did they become of age when they fell victims to the epidemic of the land: they were converted into renowned "wine-growers," and their brains were unable to function unless stimulated by alcohol. In the very prime of life they became decrepit, with trembling hands—almost paralytic—red eyes, obscured sight and confused thoughts; as if the fumes of the alcohol had shrouded their minds in clouds. And having become joyous victims of this slavery, they lauded wine as the most certain aid to a long robust life.

The horde of the poor could not enjoy this pleasure of the rich; but they envied the wealthy, dreaming of intoxication as the greatest of joys. During their moments of protest or anger it was enough for wine to be placed within their reach, whereupon they would all smile at beholding the cause of their undoing gold and luminous through the full glass of sparkling liquid.

"Wine!" exclaimed Salvatierra. "That is the chief enemy of this country: it destroys our energy, it creates false hopes, it brings premature old age; it ruins everything—even love."

Fermín smiled as he listened to his master.

"Not so bad as all that, don Fernando! . . . I admit, nevertheless, that it is one of our vices. It may be said that we carry our love of it in our very blood. I confess my own weakness: I'm fond of a glass offered me by my friends. . . . It's the national disease."

The revolutionist, impelled by the tumultuous course of his thoughts, forgot wine and launched an attack against another enemy: resignation in the face of injustice—the Christian humility of the oppressed.

"These people suffer in silence, Fermín, because the teachings they inherited from their ancestors are stronger than their own anger. They go barefoot and hungry before the image of Christ; they are told that He died for them, and it doesn't occur to the wretched flock that centuries have gone by without the fulfillment of anything that He promised. The women, with that feminine sentimentalism that has supreme faith in the supernatural, still admire his eyes that they don't see, and await a word from his mouth—forever mute through the most colossal of calamities. Beseech not the dead; dry your tears and seek in the living the remedy for your ills."

Salvatierra grew exalted, raising his voice in the silence of the dusk. The sun had concealed itself, leaving over the city an aureole of flame. From the direction of the mountain the first star, like a harbinger of the night, stood out against a violet sky. The revolutionist gazed at it, as if it were the star that was to guide toward broader horizons the masses, with their tears and their griefs—the star of Justice, pale and vacillating, illuminating the slow departure of the rebels, and gradually growing as they approached it, scaling heights, overthrowing privileges, dethroning gods—until it was converted into a sun.

The great dreams of poesy came to Salvatierra's mind, and he spoke of them to his companion in the muffled, quivering voice of a prophet in the throes of his vision.

A trembling of the bowels of the earth had one day shaken the ancient world. The trees groaned in the forests, waving their leafy manes like desolate mourners; a funereal wind ruffled the lakes and the blue, luminous surface of the classic sea that had for centuries upon the Greek shores crooned its accompaniment to the dialogues of the poets and the philosophers. A death-lamentation rent the air, reaching the ears of all men: *The great Pan has died!* . . . The sirens sank forever into the glaucous depths; the nymphs fled in terror into the bowels of the earth, never to return; and the white temples, which like hymns of marble sang the joy of life beneath the sun's torrent of gold, grew overcast and fell into the august silence of ruins. *Christ is born,* sang the same voice. And the world became blind to all that was without, concentrating its sight upon the soul; and it abhorred matter as a vile sin, and repressed the purest sentiments of life, making a virtue of its amputation.

The sun continued to shine, but it seemed less luminous to humanity, as if between mankind and that body had been placed a funereal veil. Nature continued its creative labors, insensible to the madness of men; but the latter loved no flowers other than those through which the light filtered across the stained-glass of the arched windows, and admired no trees other than the palms of stone that supported the vaults of the cathedrals. Venus hid her marble nudity in the ruins of the conflagrations, hoping to be reborn after a sleep of centuries, under the plow of a rustic. The model of beauty was now the fruitless, ailing virgin, weakened by fasts: the pious nun, as pale and drooping as the lily that she held in her waxen hands, with tearful eyes enlarged by the ecstasy and the pain of the hidden hair-shirt.

The dark slumber had lasted for ages. Men, denying Nature, had sought in privation, in a tortured, deformed life, in the deification of grief, the remedy to their ills— the longed-for human brotherhood, believing that the hope of an after-life and charity upon earth were enough for the happiness of Christians.

And now the same lamentation that had announced the death of the great god of Nature was sounding once more, as if it were regulating, at intervals of centuries, the vast mutations of human existence. "Christ has died! . . . Christ has died!"

"Yes," continued the rebel, "He has been dead for some time. In their moments of despair all souls hear this mysterious cry. In vain do the church-bells ring every Easter announcing that Christ is risen. . . . He is reborn only for those who live upon His heritage. Those who feel the hunger of justice, and have been awaiting their redemption for thousands of years, know that He is really dead and that He will never return,

even as the cold and willful Greek divinities never return."

Men, following Christ, had not gazed upon a new
horizon: they had journeyed over beaten paths. Only
the exterior had been changed—the name of things.
Humanity, by the fading light of a religion that curses
life, looked upon the same sight that it had beheld
previously, in the innocence of its infancy. The slave
redeemed by Christ was now the modern wage-slave,
with his right to die of hunger, without the bread and the
pitcher of water that his predecessor had found in his
cell. The merchants that had been thrust out of the
Temple were now assured of entering into glory eternal
and were the very pillars of all virtue. The privileged
classes spoke of the kingdom of heaven as if it were one
more pleasure to add to those they enjoyed upon earth.
The Christian peoples exterminated one another, not
because of the whims and the hostility of their leaders,
but for something less concrete—for the prestige of a
floating rag, whose colors turned them mad. Men who
had never met slew each other in cold blood, leaving
behind uncultivated fields and abandoned families; yet
they were brothers of misfortune in the chain of labor,
with no other differences than those of tongue and race.

On winter nights the great poverty-stricken mob
swarmed in the streets of the city, foodless and without
shelter, as if it were in the midst of a desert. The children cried with cold, snuggling their hands under their
armpits; the women, with brandy-soaked breath, stole
into a doorway to spend the night there; the breadless
vagrants gazed at the illuminated windows of the man-
sions or followed the procession of fortunate persons,
who, wrapped in their furs, comfortably seated within
their carriages, were departing from the festivities of

the rich. And a voice, perhaps the very same, repeated in their ears, which were buzzing from weakness:

"Abandon your hope. Christ has died!"

The toiler out of work, upon returning to his cold hovel where the questioning eyes of his emaciated wife awaited him, sank upon the floor like an exhausted beast, after an all-day search to still the hunger of his family. "Bread! Bread!" groaned the little ones, hoping to find it under his threadbare smock. And the father heard that same voice, sounding like a lament that effaced all hope: "Christ has died!"

And the toiler in the country who, ill-fed upon meat scraps and bread crumbs, sweated beneath the sun and felt upon the verge of suffocation, when he stopped a moment for breath in this furnace-like atmosphere, told himself that all this talk of the brotherhood of man preached by Jesus was a lie, and that this god who had performed no miracle, leaving the ills of the world the same as he had found them, was likewise false. . . . And the toiler, garbed in a uniform, obliged, in the name of things which he did not understand, to kill men who had done him no harm, as he lay for hour after hour in a trench, surrounded by the horrors of modern warfare, fighting an enemy too far away to be seen, watching thousands of his fellow-beings fall shattered by the hail of steel and the explosion of black spheres—this man, too, thought with shudders of terror: "Christ has died! Christ has died!"

Yes; he was indeed dead. His life had not served to alleviate a single evil that afflicts humanity. On the other hand, he had wrought incalculable damage to the poor by preaching humility to them, by inculcating into their spirits submission and the belief in the reward of a future world. The debasement of alms and the hope of justice beyond this earth had kept the poor in their poverty for thousands of years. They who live in the shadow of privilege, however much they adore the Crucified One, were insufficiently appreciative of his function as a guardian angel during nineteen centuries.

But the unfortunate were shaking off their lethargy: the god was a corpse. Away with resignation. Before the dead Christ must be proclaimed the triumph of Life. The huge cadaver still weighed upon the earth, but the deceived masses were already stirring, ready to bury it. On all sides were heard the cries of a world that had just been born. Poetry, which had vaguely prophesied the coming of Christ, was now announcing the appearance of the great Redeemer, who was not to be confined within the weakness of one man, but who would be embodied in the immense horde of the disinherited, the sad, under the name of Revolution.

Mankind was about to begin anew its march toward fraternity, the ideal of Christ. But now it would abhor meekness, despise charity as debasing and fruitless. To each man what belonged to him, with neither concessions that degrade him nor privileges that awaken hatred. The true brotherhood was Social Justice.

Salvatierra ceased to speak, and noticing that night was falling, turned about and began to retrace his journey.

Jerez, like a vast black mass, revealed the outlines of its towers and its roofs against the dying splendor of the twilight, while below, the red stars of its street-lanterns perforated the darkness.

The shadows of the two men were delineated upon the white surface of the road. The moon came out over their shoulders, climbing the heavens.

When they were still far from the city they heard a noisy tinkling of bells, which caused the carts that were slowly returning from the farms with the muffled crunching of their wheels, to turn to one side of the road.

Salvatierra and his disciple, taking refuge in the road drain, saw four spirited horses with flying tassels and strings of strident bells, pulling at a coach crowded with people, prance by. The occupants were singing, shouting, clapping hands, filling the road with their mad merriment, scattering the scandal of the *juerga* across the dead plains, which appeared sadder than ever under the light of the moon.

The carriage sped past like a flash amid clouds of dust, but Fermín was able to recognize the driver. It was Luis Dupont who, standing upon the coach-box, was with word and whip lashing the four beasts, who were dashing at almost runaway speed. A woman beside him was likewise shouting, inciting the animals with a mad fever of velocity. This was the *Marquesita*. Montenegro thought that she had recognized him, for as the coach disappeared, she waved her hand through the cloud of dust and shouted something that he could not hear.

"They're out for a good time, don Fernando;" said the young man, after silence had resumed its sway over the road. "The city seems too small for them, and since to-morrow is Sunday, they wish to spend the day in Matanzuela at their ease."

Salvatierra, on hearing the name of the farm, recalled his companion of the "Jackdaw"—that invalid who desired his presence as the best remedy. He had not seen him since the day on which the storm had obliged him to take refuge in Matanzuela, but he thought of him often, proposing to repeat his visit the next week. He would prolong one of his extended walks and stretch it out as far as the sick man's cabin, where he was awaited as a solace.

Fermín spoke of Luis's recent love affairs with the *Marquesita*. Friendship had at last brought them to a pass which both seemingly desired to avoid. She was no longer with the uncouth hog-dealer. She was once more "attracted to the nobility," as she put it, and she shamelessly boasted of her new relations, living at Dupont's house and together with him giving herself up to the most scandalous festivities. Her love seemed to them insipid and monotonous if they did not season it with intoxication and escapades that stirred the hypocritical calm of the city.

"Two insane persons have joined lots," continued Fermín. "Some day they will quarrel, coming out of one of their festivities covered with blood; but in the meantime, they think they are happy and display their good fortune with admirable shamelessness. I believe that what gives them most amusement is the indignation of don Pablo and his family."

Montenegro related the most recent adventures of this enamored couple, which had alarmed the city. Jerez was too narrow to contain their joy, so they ran about to the nearby estates and towns, reaching as far as Cádiz, followed by a suite of singers and bullies that always accompanied Luis Dupont. Several days before they had given a most noisy celebration at Sanlúcar de Barrameda, at the conclusion of which the *Marquesita* and her lover, getting one of the waiters drunk, cut off all his hair with a pair of shears. At the *Círculo Caballista* the young members laughed as they gossiped about the doings of this pair. But what a splendid chap was this Luis! And what a woman was the *Marquesita!* . . .

And the two lovers, submerged in a continuous intoxication that was renewed upon the first sign that it was wearing off—as if they feared to lose their illusion by contemplating themselves coldly without the deceitful joy of wine—whirled hither and thither like a whirlwind of scandal, amid the plaudits of the young set and the indignation of their families.

Salvatierra listened to his disciple with an ironic expression. Luis Dupont interested him. He was a good example of the idle rich youth that owned all the country.

By the time the two travelers had reached the outlying houses of Jerez, the carriage of Luis Dupont, whirling along vertiginously in the wake of the fiery steeds who were running as if mad, was already in Matanzuela.

The farm dogs barked furiously as they caught sound of the horses' hoofs, gradually coming nearer, accompanied by shouting, the strumming of guitars and songs of prolonged lamentations.

"Here comes the master," said *Zarandilla*. "It can't be anybody else."

He called the steward and both stepped into the road to watch the arrival of the noisy carriage under the light of the moon.

The graceful *Marquesita* jumped down from the coach-box, and gradually all of the suite extricated themselves from the mass of flesh that filled the interior. The young master handed over the reins to *Zarandilla* after having reminded him several times to take good care of the animals.

Rafael removed his hat and stepped forward.

"Is that you, my handsome fellow?" asked the *Marquesita* brazenly. "Every time I see you, you're better looking than before. If it weren't that I did not care to hurt María de la Luz, some day we would deceive this fellow."

But "this fellow," by whom she meant Luis, laughed at his cousin's indecency, without at all concerning himself with the silent comparison, to which Lola's eyes seemed to be given over, between his emaciated, "high liver's" body and the powerful physique of the steward.

The young owner reviewed his group. None had been lost on the journey; they were all present; *la Moñotieso,* renowned singer of Andalusian popular songs, and her brother; her father, a veteran of the classic dance who had made the platforms of all the cafés chantants in Spain thunder beneath his heels; three protégés of Luis, with solemn countenances and eyebrows that formed a single line, their hands upon their hips and their eyes rolled upward, as if they dared not look at one another lest they be horrified, and a plump-faced fellow with a priestly double-chin and tufts of hair stuck to his ears, holding a guitar under his arm.

"Here you have him!" exclaimed the master to his steward, indicating the guitar player. "Señor Pacorro, alias the Eagle, the foremost player in the world. Give me *Guerra* when it comes to killing bulls, and this friend when it comes to playing guitar. . . . He is unsurpassed !"

And as the farm head stood staring at this extraordinary creature, whose name he had never heard, the player bowed ceremoniously like a man of the world expert in social formalities.

"Happy to make your acquaintance. . . ."

And without saying another word he entered the farmhouse, following the other members of the party, who were being piloted by the *Marquesita.*

Zarandilla's wife and Rafael, assisted by this troupe, put the master's rooms in order. Two sooty table lamps lighted the large salon with its whitewashed walls decorated by chromographs of saints. Don Luis's "confidential men," bending their backs with a certain lazy reluctance, brought forth from hampers and boxes all the supplies that had been taken along in the carriage.

The table was filled with bottles, through which the

light shone; some were of hazel color, others of pale
gold. *Zarandilla's* old wife went into the kitchen, accompanied by some of the other women, while the young
proprietor asked the steward about the farm laborers.

Almost all the men were absent from the farm. As
it was Saturday, the toilers who lived in the mountain
had gone off to their towns. There remained only the
gipsies and the groups of girls that came down from the
mountains for the weeding season, under the care of their
manijeros.

The master received this news with satisfaction. He
never cared to amuse himself in the presence of the laborers; they were envious persons with a hard heart,
and flew into a fury at the sight of somebody else's joy,
afterwards spreading the silliest sort of gossip. He liked
to have the farmhouse all to himself. Wasn't he the
master? . . . And flitting from one thought to another
with his incoherent frivolity, he turned to his associates.
What were they doing there, anyway, sitting down,
neither drinking nor talking, as if they were watching
the dead? . . .

"Let's have something from those golden fingers of
yours, master," he said to the player, who, with the
guitar upon his knees and his eyes staring at the ceiling,
was amusing himself by strumming arpeggios.

The master Eagle, after coughing a few times, commenced a florid piece, interrupted now and then by the
squeaking scales of the first string. One of Luis's
myrmidons opened some bottles and arranged the rows
of cañas, offering to the audience these crystal tubes,
filled with bubble-crowned, golden liquid. The women,
attracted by the guitar, came running from the kitchen.

"Step forward, *Moñotieso!*" shouted the proprietor.

And the singer broke into a *soleá,* with a penetrating,
powerful voice, which, after swelling her neck as if it

were about to burst, reverberated throughout the hall and echoed all over the house.

The honorable parent of la *Moñotieso*, like a man who knew his duties, waited for no further invitations and pulled his other daughter into the center of the room, beginning to dance with her.

Rafael, after having drunk a few glasses, prudently slunk away. He did not care to disturb the celebration with his presence. Besides, he desired to make the rounds of the farmhouse before night should come on, fearing that the master might, in a drunken caprice, be seized with a desire to inspect it.

In the yard he stumbled against *Alcaparrón*, who, attracted by the noise of the festivities, was waiting, with his parasitic adhesiveness, for an opportunity to introduce himself into the hall. The steward threatened to club him if he dared to remain there.

"Off with you, you rascal. These gentlemen don't want any gipsies around."

Alcaparrón withdrew with a humble air, ready, however, to return the moment Rafael disappeared; the latter went into the stable to see whether the master's horses were being well cared for.

When, an hour later, the steward returned to the scene of the festivities, he saw the table strewn with empty bottles.

The guests were the same as before, as if the liquid had been poured upon the floor; only the guitarist was strumming more violently, and the others were beating their palms with wild fervor, at the same time shouting encouragement to the old dancer. The worthy father of the *Moñotiesos,* opening his black, toothless mouth and uttering feminine shrieks, moved his scrawny hips, at the same time collapsing his stomach so as to make the opposite part stand out in greater relief. His own

daughters, laughing at the top of their lungs, applauded
these exploits of a degenerate old age.

"Olé, how graceful! . . ."

The old man continued to dance like a feminine caricature, urged on by the salacious incitation of the *Marquesita.*

San Patrisio!

Que la puerta se sale del quisio!

And as he sang these words he writhed in such a manner that it seemed he was about to unhinge the lower
part of his back, while the men threw their hats at his
feet, roused to enthusiasm by this infamous dance, the
disgrace of sex.

After the dancer had returned to his seat, perspiring
and begging a glass, a long silence followed.

"There are more women needed here. . . ."

It was *el Chivo* who spoke, after having spat through
the corners of his lips, with the solemn gravity of a bully
who is not prodigal with words.

The *Marquesita* protested.

"And what do you call *us,* you scarecrow?"

"Yes, that's the point. What do you call us?" echoed
the two *Moñotiesos.*

El Chivo condescended to explain. He had not meant
to be lacking in respect to those ladies who were present;
he merely meant to say that in order for the entertain-
ment to proceed to best advantage more women folk
were necessary.

The young master resolutely arose to his feet. More
women? . . . He had 'em. There were all kinds of 'em
at Matanzuela. And seizing a bottle, he ordered Rafael
to accompany him to the workers' quarters.

"But, señorito, what is your grace going to do?"

Despite the steward's protests, Luis compelled Rafael

to show the way, and they were followed by the entire party.

The happy band, upon entering the quarters, found them almost deserted. It was a spring evening; the *manijeros* and the *arreador* were squatting upon the floor, near the entrance, gazing out across the fields that slumbered silently beneath the bluish light of the moon. The women were dozing in the corner, or had formed in small groups and were listening in religious silence to tales about witches and miracles performed by saints.

"The master!" announced the steward as he entered.

"Get up! Wake up! Who'd like some wine?" shouted the young proprietor gayly.

All jumped to their feet, smiling at the unexpected apparition.

The women gazed in wide-eyed astonishment at the *Marquesita* and her two companions, admiring their Chinese flower-embroidered silk shawls and their shining coiffures.

The men meekly bowed before the master, who was offering them glasses of wine, while their eyes sought the bottle that he held in his hands. After feigned refusals, they all drank. It was rich man's wine, of the sort they did not know. Oh! This don Luis was indeed a man! Somewhat light-headed; but youth was his excuse, and besides, he was generous-hearted. If only all masters were like him! . . .

"That's what you call wine, friend!" said some to others, wiping their lips with the backs of their hands.

Tía *Alcaparrona* drank, too, and her son, who had at last succeeded in joining his master's suite, walked back and forth before him, displaying his horses' teeth through his very best smiles.

Dupont, brandishing his bottle aloft, was making a speech. He had come to invite all the maidens of the

lodge to his banquet—but only the good-looking ones.
That was his way: open and frank. Long live democracy! . . .

The maidens, blushing in the presence of their master, whom many were beholding for the first time, drew
back, their gaze directed to the ground and their hands
clasped before their skirts. Dupont indicated his selec-
tions. This one! That one! . . . And he chose, among
the others, Mari-Cruz, *Alcaparrón's* cousin.

"You, my gipsy girl; you, too! You're a bit ugly but
there's something nice about you and you'll sing for us."

"Like the very seraphim, zeño," corroborated her
cousin, attempting to make use of the relationship so as
to obtain admission to the feast.

The maidens, rendered suddenly timid, as if they were
threatened by some danger, recoiled and refused to accept the invitation. They had already had supper, many
thanks! A few moments later, however, they were smiling and whispering contentedly, upon beholding the wry
faces made by certain of their companions who had not
been chosen by the master or his friends. *Alcaparrona*
scolded them for their timidity:

"Why are you afraid to go? Along with you, lassies,
and if you have no desire to fill yourself with good
things, save a little of what the master gives you. More
than a few times I was wined and dined by the señor
Marquis, the papa of this shining sun here!"

And as she spoke she pointed to the *Marquesita,* who
was examining some of the young girls as if she desired
to divine the beauty beneath their tattered clothes.

The recruiting agents, aroused by the master's wine,
which had merely awakened their thirst, intervened pa-
ternally, prompted by the thought of other bottles. The
girls could with perfect security go with don Luis; they,

who were charged with watching over the girls, assured them of it, and would be responsible to their families.

"He's a gentleman, girls, and besides, you're going to dine with these ladies. All of them decent persons."

The maidens' resistance was of short duration and at last a group of them left the lodge, escorted by the master and his guests. Those who remained in the shelter began to hunt in the corners for a guitar. There would be a good time to-night! As the master was leaving, he had told the steward to send the laborers all the wine they desired. Oh, what a princely don Luis! . . .

The table was set by *Zarandilla's* wife, assisted by the young mountain girls, who had acquired a certain self-possession upon entering the master's rooms. Moreover, the young man, with a frankness that flattered them, causing waves of blood to mount to their cheeks, went from one to the other with his bottle and the tray of glasses, urging them to drink. The father of the *Moñotiesos,* with his indecent tales, made them blush and burst into laughter that sounded like the clucking of hens.

There were more than twenty for supper, and tightly pressed around the table they commenced to eat the dishes that *Zarandilla* and his wife served with great difficulty, passing them over the guests' heads.

Rafael remained standing near the door, undecided whether to leave or to keep in sight out of respect to his master.

"Take a seat, man," ordered don Luis magnanimously. "I permit you to."

And as the persons at the table crowded more tightly than ever together to make room for him, the *Marquesita* arose, calling him. Right there, at her side! The steward, as he took his place, felt that he was sinking into the skirts and the rustling underclothes of the beauty, as if stuck to her, in burning contact with one side of her body.

The girls affectedly refused the first offerings of the young master and his companions. Thanks; they had already supped. Besides, they were not accustomed to the rich food of the gentlemen and ladies, and it might do them harm.

But the aroma of the meat, of the sacred meat, always seen by them from a distance, and spoken of in the workers' lodge as if it were a food of the gods, seemed to overcome them with an intoxication more intense than that induced by the wine. One after the other they threw themselves upon the plates, and having lost their first scruples, began to devour it as if they had just come from protracted fasts.

The young master rejoiced at the voracity with which those jaws were grinding; he felt a moral satisfaction almost equal to that which virtue affords. Such was his way! He was fond of mingling with the poor from time to time!

"Ho for the women with good appetite. . . . And now for a drink to wash the meat down."

The bottles were emptied and the lips of the maids, shortly before blue with anemia, became red with the juice of the meat and glittered with the drops of wine that trickled down to the points of their chins.

Mari-Cruz, the gipsy-maid, was the only one that did not eat. *Alcaparrón* beckoned to her, hovering around the table like a dog. The poor girl had always had such a poor appetite! . . . And with his gipsy skill, he seized everything that Mari-Cruz furtively offered to him. Then he went out into the yard to gobble it down at a single gulp, while his sick cousin drank and drank, admiring the rare wine as the chief surprise of the banquet.

Rafael, bewildered by the proximity of the *Marquesita*, could barely take a bite. He was tormented by contact with this body that had been made for love—by the ravishing perfume of fresh skin purified by a cleanliness that was unknown in the country. She, on her side, seemed to inhale with delight, through her pink, vibrating nostrils, the masculine atmosphere, the odor of leather, of sweat and of the stables, that was given off at every movement from the spirited youth.

"Drink, Rafael. Be lively. Look at *my man* over there, making love to his mountain girls!"

And she pointed to Luis, who, attracted by novelty, had forgotten her and commenced to court her neighbors; two country maidens that offered the charm of an ill-washed, rustic beauty; two belles of the farm in which he thought he perceived the acrid perfume of the pasture-grounds, the animal odor of the flocks.

The supper came to an end at about midnight. The atmosphere of the room had become heated and was almost suffocating.

The strong smell of spilled wine and of the superfluous food that had been heaped in a corner was mingled with the stench from the table-lamps.

The girls, their faces red from the food they had eaten, could hardly breathe and relieved themselves by loosening their clothing, opening their waists at the neck. Far from the vigilance of the agents, and upset by the wine, they forgot their woodland-virgin modesty. They gave themselves over with veritable fury to this extraordinary feast, which was like a flash of light in their dark, gloomy lives.

One of them, finding that a glass had been spilled upon her dress, arose and threatened the other with her nails. They felt upon their bodies the pressure of manly arms and smiled with a certain joy, as if absolving themselves in advance of any contact that they might suffer in this sweet abandonment to pleasure. The two *Moñotiesos,* drunk and furious to see the men paying attentions only to the *payas,* spoke of undressing *Alcaparrón* and tossing him up in a blanket, and the boy, who had slept all his life in his clothes, ran off, trembling for his gipsy modesty.

The *Marquesita* kept edging closer and closer to Rafael. It seemed that all the warmth of her organism had concentrated upon the side that grazed against the steward, and that the opposite side remained cold and insensible. The youth, obliged to drink the glasses that were offered to him by the lady, felt that he was becoming intoxicated—but with a nervous sort of intoxication that caused him to drop his head and knit his eyebrows fiercely, as if desiring to engage in a fight with one of the bullies that accompanied don Luis.

The feminine heat of this gentle skin, which caressed him with its touch under the table, irritated him like a danger that is hard to conquer. He tried several times to arise, pretending that he had things outside demanding attention, but he felt himself clutched by a small hand filled with nervous strength.

"Keep your seat, you rascal; if you stir the slightest bit I'll tear out your soul."

As drunk as the others, resting her auburn head on one hand, the *Marquesita* gazed at him with rolling eyes; blue, frank eyes, which appeared never to have been darkened by the cloud of an impure thought.

Luis, enthused by the admiration of the two girls seated beside him, wished to reveal himself in all his heroic grandeur, and suddenly dashed a glass of wine into the face of *el Chivo,* who happened to be sitting before him. The wild beast of the penitentiary contracted his horrible, mask-like features and made a gesture as

if to jump to his feet, darting a hand into the interior
of his jacket.

There was a moment of oppressive silence, but the
bully, after his first impulse of anger had subsided, remained in his seat.

"Don Luis," he said, with a grimace of adulation,
"you're the only man that can do such a thing. You're
as good as my father."

"And because I'm braver than you, too!" shouted the
young master, arrogantly.

"That, too," granted the bully, with another fawning
smile.

The young man cast his triumphant glance over the
faces of the terrified girls. Eh? . . . There was a man
for them!

The *Moñotiesos* and their father, who, from having accompanied don Luis everywhere as pupils of his generosity, "knew their parts by heart," hastened to conclude
the scene, raising a great racket. Hurrah for real, brave
men! More wine! More wine!

And all, even the formidable thug, drank to the health
of the master, while he, as if suffocated by his own greatness, removed his jacket and his waistcoat, rose to his
feet and grasped hold of his two companions. What
were they doing there, jammed close to the table, looking at one another? Out into the yard! Let them run
about, play, and continue their festivities in the moon-
light, since the night was so beautiful! . . .

Whereupon all filed out in the greatest disorder, jostling one another and anxious, because of the suffocation
of drunkenness, to breathe the free air of the patio.
Many of the girls, upon leaving their seats, staggered
about, being forced to lean their heads upon some man's
breast. Señor Pacorro's guitar emitted a sad complaint
as it struck against the hinges of the door, as if the open-

ing were too narrow for the instrument and the Eagle who carried it.

Rafael, too, was about to arise, but he was again restrained by the nervous little hand.

"You stay here," commanded the marquis's daughter, "and keep me company. Let those people amuse themselves. . . . But don't run away from me, evil fellow! I seem to scare you."

The steward, freed from the pressure of those who had been sitting next to him, had pushed back his chair. But the woman's body pursued him, leaned against him, and however much he withdrew his own person he could not deliver himself from its soft burden.

Outside in the patio resounded señor Pacorro's guitar, and the singers, hoarse with wine, accompanied him with shouts and hand-clapping. The girls, pursued by the men, ran by the open door, laughing with nervous outbursts, as if they were tickled by those who were giving them chase. They were discovered in all the hiding-places to which they ran—the stable, the granaries, the oven, and the other departments of the farmhouse that communicated with the patio. In these obscure rooms there were encounters, suffocated laughter, shouts of surprise.

Rafael, in his drunken condition, thought of only one thing: he must free himself from the audacious hands of the *Marquesita*, from the weight of her body—that tempting perfume, against which he waged dispirited combat, certain of being conquered.

He was silent, overwhelmed by the extraordinary aspect of the adventure, repressed by his respect for social hierarchies. The daughter of the Marquis de San Dionisio! This alone kept him rooted to his seat, defending himself weakly against a woman whom he could repel with a simple wave of one of his strong hands. At last he was forced to speak.

"Let me go, your grace! . . . Doña Lola . . . it can't be!"

Beholding him shrink from her with all the modesty of a virgin, she erupted into insults. He wasn't the brave fellow of other times, when he used to smuggle and had dealings with all sorts of women in the inns about Jerez! That brat of a María de la Luz had bewitched him! A wonderfully virtuous girl, who lived in a vineyard surrounded by men! . . .

She continued to shower insults upon Rafael's sweetheart, but the young man uttered not a word. The steward preferred to see her in this mood; now he felt stronger to resist temptation.

The *Marquesita,* dead drunk, persisted in her insults with all the ferocity of a scorned woman, but she clung to him nevertheless.

"Coward! Am I not to your taste? . . ."

Zarandilla entered the room hurriedly, as if he desired to have word with the steward, but he stopped. Outside, near the door, the voice of the master sounded with irritated tone. With Rafael in there, there was no steward or anybody to give orders except himself! . . . "Do as I say, you blind old fool! . . ."

And the old man left as hurriedly as he had entered, without speaking a word to the steward.

Rafael grew vexed at the stubbornness of this woman. If it were not for his fear that she would embroil him with his master, causing him to lose his post at the grange, which was the chief hope of his sweetheart and himself! . . .

She continued to upbraid him, but her ire was subsiding, as if her intoxication deprived her of the power of movement, and her desire could now vent itself only

in words. Her head slipped down upon Rafael's bosom;
she bent over, with her eyes rolled upward, inhaling that
masculine perfume, which seemed to lull her to sleep.
Her bust had fallen against the peasant's knees, and
she still kept heaping insults upon him, as if this afforded
her an exquisite delight.

"I'm going to take off my skirts and have you put
them on. . . . Simpleton! . . . They ought to call you
María, just like that blockhead sweetheart of yours. . . ."

The patio suddenly resounded with a shriek of terror,
followed by explosions of brutal laughter. Then there
was a noisy running about, the shock of bodies against
the walls, and a din of danger and fear.

Rafael bounded to his feet, paying no heed to the
Marquesita, who rolled over on the floor. At the same
moment three maidens dashed in with such speed that
they overturned several chairs. Their faces were white
with a deathly pallor; their eyes were distended with
fear; they stooped, as if with the intention of hiding
underneath the table.

The steward went out into the yard. In the middle
of it a beast was bellowing, looking at the moon as if he
were surprised to find himself at liberty.

Before his legs lay stretched something white, which
scarcely stood out against the ground.

From the shadows of the roofs, along the walls, came
the harsh laughter of men and the shrill shrieks of
women. Señor Pacorro, the Eagle, sat impassively upon
his stone seat, strumming his guitar with the serenity
of a solemn drunkard, proof against all manner of surprises.

"Poor little Mari-Cruz!" whimpered *Alcaparrón.*
"The beast is going to kill her! He's going to kill
her! . . ."

The steward took the situation in at a glance. . . .

What a witty master! To afford a surprise to his
friends and laugh at the fright of the women, he had
compelled *Zarandilla* to free a young bull from the
stable. The gipsy-girl, reached by the beast, had fainted
from the shock. . . . The feast was a tremendous success!

CHAPTER VI

MARI-CRUZ was dying. *Alcaparrón*, regardless of his mother's protests, whimperingly announced the news to all the farm folk.

"What do you know, blockhead! . . . My godmother pulled others through who were much farther gone. . . ."

But the gipsy, scorning the blind faith of señora *Alcaparrona* in her godmother's wisdom, foresaw the death of his cousin with all the clairvoyance of affection. At the farmhouse and in the fields he related the origin of her illness to everybody.

"The cursed joke of the señorito! . . . The poor thing has never been very strong—always ailing—and the fright she got from that bullock has done for her. May God . . . !"

Respect for the wealthy, however, and the traditional submission to his master, kept the gipsy malediction from rising to his lips.

That fatal raven which, according to him, summoned good persons whenever the graveyards needed another soul, must now be awake, preening its black wings with its beak and preparing to utter the caw that would call his cousin. Ay, poor little Mari-Cruz! The best one of the family! . . . And lest the girl divine his thoughts, he kept away, watching from a distance, without daring to approach her corner in the workers' lodge, where she lay stretched upon a mat that had been generously ceded to her by the day-laborers.

When *señá Alcaparrona,* two days after the nocturnal festivities, had seen her niece feverish and too weak to go to the fields, she had diagnosed the illness, with all her experience as an arbiter of good fortune and as a witch who cured diseases. It was the fright caused by the young bull "that had remained *inside* of her."

"It's the bad blood that's risen to her breast and is choking her. That's why she's always asking for a drink, as if a river weren't enough," said the old woman.

And, when at daybreak she departed for the fields, in which she worked together with her family, the only medicine she left for the girl was a jar of water beside the tattered bedclothes. This was to be kept full all the time.

The girl passed the greater part of the day in the darkest corner of the laborers' dormitory. One or other of the farm dogs, coming in now and then, would circle about her with a muffled growl of surprise, and after attempting to lick her pale face would dart off, repelled by the bloodless, translucent, infantile hands.

At noon, when a sunbeam would introduce its golden shaft into the penumbra of this human beings' stable, the first spring flies would make their way to the obscure corner, enlivening the solitude with their buzzing.

From time to time *Zarandilla* and his mother would visit Mari-Cruz.

"Courage, little girl; you look better to-day. The important thing is to get rid of all this evil stuff that's risen to your breast."

The sick maiden, smiling weakly, would stretch out her thin arms to grasp the jar, and she would drink and drink, in the hope that the water would melt the burning, stifling lump that made it so hard for her to breathe, transmitting the fire of fever to the rest of her body.

When the sunbeam would withdraw, and the buzzing of the flies ceased, and the stretch of sky framed by the door took on a soft, violet shade, the invalid grew happy.

This was the best of hours; her people would soon return. And she smiled at *Alcaparrón* and her brothers, who squatted upon the floor in a semi-circle, saying not a word to her, gazing at her with questioning eyes, as if they wished to trap her fugitive health. The first thing her aunt asked her every afternoon when she came back from work was, whether she had cast out *that*, for the old gipsy expected the sick girl to expel through her mouth all the blood that her fright had caused to accumulate in her bosom.

The spirit of the invalid was furthermore raised by the presence of her working companions—the laborers who, before eating their evening *gazpacho*, stopped for a moment with her and tried with their rough words to give her courage. The redoubtable Juanón spoke with her every night, proposing energetic measures, as befitted his character.

"What you need, my child, is to eat: to fill up. The only trouble with you is that you're hungry."

And following up his words, he offered her as many rare foods as his companions had: even a slice of cod and a black pudding that had by some miracle been preserved in the lodge. . . . But the gipsy refused everything with a grateful expression.

"You're missing a good thing. It's given to you with all our heart. That's why you're so skinny and sickly, and you'll die, because you don't eat."

Juanón grew confirmed in his belief when he noted the emaciated condition of the girl. There no longer remained upon her the slightest vestige of flesh; her flabby, bloodless muscles had wasted away. There was left only the skeleton, revealing its sharp angles underneath the whitish skin, which seemed to have grown as delicate as a gossamer covering.

Her entire life seemed to be concentrated in her sunken

eyes, which seemed to grow blacker, with a brighter glow in their centers, like two drops of tremulous clay in the depths of the livid orbits.

At night *Alcaparrón,* crouching before her, avoiding her glance that he might weep freely, could see the light of the lamp through her ears and her nostrils, which were as transparent as the Host.

The steward, alarmed by the appearance of the invalid, spoke of fetching a doctor from the city.

"This isn't Christian treatment, aunt *Alcaparrona.* The poor creature's dying like a beast."

The old gipsy, however, objected indignantly. A doctor? That was all right for gentlemen—for the rich. And who was going to pay him? . . . Besides, she had never needed a doctor all her life, and she was an old woman. The persons of her race, although poor, had their little bit of learning, which the *gachés* often sought.

And she had her godmother summoned, whereupon there came to the farm an extremely aged gipsy, who enjoyed great repute in Jerez and the countryside as a witch-doctor.

After hearing *Alcaparrona's* account, sne felt the sick girl's wretched frame, approving all of her friend's words. She had not been mistaken: it was the shock— the bad blood that had risen to her breast and was throttling her.

For an entire afternoon both the gipsies wandered over the neighboring hills seeking herbs, and they solicited from *Zarandilla's* wife the craziest ingredients for a wonderful cataplasm that they wished to prepare. That night the men in the dormitory, with all the credulous awe of country folk before the miraculous, silently watched the manipulations of the two witches about a pot placed over the fire.

The invalid submissively swallowed the concoction

and received upon her bosom a plaster, handled mys-
teriously by the two old women, as if it contained a
supernatural power. The godmother, who had performed miracles, was ready to deny her learning if within two days she did not succeed in melting the ball of
flame that was stifling the girl.

The two days went by, and two more, without any
relief for Mari-Cruz.

Alcaparrón continued his sobbing outside of the shelter,
so that the sick girl should not hear him. She was
getting worse and worse! She couldn't lie down! She
was choking! Her aunt no longer went to the fields;
she remained in the lodge, nursing her. Even while she
slept they had to hold her in a sitting posture, while her
bosom heaved with the rattle of a broken bellows.

"Ay, Lord!" groaned the gipsy, losing her last hope.
—"The same as the birds when they're wounded! . . ."

Rafael dare not advise the family, nor did he go in to
see the sick girl, except during working hours, when the
toilers were in the fields.

Mari-Cruz's illness and the young master's wild es-
capade at the grange had brought about strained relations
between him and all the laborers.

Some of the girls, upon recovering their senses after
the intoxication of that night, had refused to remain at
the farm any longer and had gone back to the mountains.
They condemned the recruiting agents, in whom their
families had reposed all confidence, and who had been
the first to advise them to follow the master. And after
having spread among the workers who returned to
Matanzuela Sunday night, news of what had happened
the previous evening, they alone undertook the return
to their homes, telling everybody the scandals that had
taken place at the farm.

The laborers, upon their return to Matanzuela, did not

see their master. He and his retinue, after having slept off their intoxication, had returned to Jerez as happy as ever, with scandalizing merriment. The toilers, in their indignation, held the steward and the rest of the farm administration responsible. The master was far away, and besides, it was he who gave them their bread.

Some of the men who were at the farm on the night of the festivities had to settle accounts and go hunting for work at other farms. Their companions were incensed. Daggers would yet be drawn. Drunkards! For four bottles of wine they had sold girls who might have been their own daughters. . . .

Juanón came face to face with the steward.

"So you," he began, spitting upon the floor with an air of scorn, "you were the fellow that divided the girls among the men for them to have a good time with? . . . You'll get on in the world, Rafael. Now we know what you're good for."

The steward recoiled as if he had been struck by a knife.

"I'm good for whatever I'm good for. And I'm ready for a fight to the death if any man dares insult me."

Wounded in his pride, he glared defiantly at Juanón and the other men, his knife ready in his jacket pocket, poised to fall upon them at the slightest provocation. In order to show that he had no fear of these persons who were anxious to give vent to their old grudges against the superintendent of their labors, Rafael tried to justify his master.

"It was a joke. Don Luis let the bull loose just to have a little fun, without intending harm to any one. What happened then was an accident."

And through pride he did not add that it was he who had replaced the beast in the stable, liberating the gipsy from the horns that were madly tearing her clothes.

He likewise maintained silence as to his quarrel with the master, after saving Mari-Cruz—the frankness with which he had censored his conduct and the rage of don Luis, who tried to strike him, just as if he were one of the bullies of his suite.

Rafael had squeezed Luis's hand in his powerful clutch, shaking him as if he were a child; at the same time, with his free hand the steward had sought his knife with so resolute a mien that *el Chivo* held back, despite the urgent cries of the master that they should kill this fellow.

The selfsame bully, fearing the steward, had set the matter right by declaring that the three were equally brave fellows and that among brave men there should exist no quarrels. And together they had drunk the last glass, while the *Marquesita* was snoring under the table, and the girls, terrified by the encounter, fled to the lodge.

When, one morning, Rafael was summoned to the master, he took the road to Jerez in the firm belief that he would never return to Matanzuela. The summons was undoubtedly to inform him that another steward had been found for his place. . . . But the madcap Dupont received him with a merry countenance.

The day before he had definitely broken off with his cousin. He was tired of her whims and her scandals. He now desired to turn over a new leaf, so as to spare any further displeasure to don Pablo, who was like a father to him. He was thinking of entering politics, of running for Deputy. Other men of the district had succeeded, with no other merit than a fortune, and birth no greater than his own. Moreover, he counted upon the support of the Fathers of the Company, his former preceptors, who would shower him with congratulations when they beheld him at his cousin's hotel, transformed into a serious man, occupied in defending the sacred interests of society.

But he soon wearied of holding forth in this strain and eyed his steward with a certain curiosity.

"Rafael, do you know that you're a brave chap? . . ."

This was his sole allusion to the scene of that night. Then, as if he regretted having given so absolute a testimonial of bravery, he added modestly:

"I, you and *el Chivo* are the three manliest men in Jerez. Let any fellow dare to face us! . . ."

Rafael listened to him impassively, with the respectful mien of a loyal servant. The only matter that interested him in all this was the certainty that he would retain his position in Matanzuela.

Now the master asked news of the farm. His powerful cousin, who had learned of everything, had also, when he scolded him for that good time which was the talk of Jerez (he mentioned this with no little pride), referred to a gipsy ill with fright. How about this? And with a bored air he listened to Rafael's account.

"In short, nothing; we know how those gipsies exaggerate. That'll go by. Fright at a bullock let free. . . . Why, that joke is the regular thing!"

And he enumerated all the banquets in the country, at the homes of wealthy persons, that had been concluded with this ingenious jest. Then, in magnanimous manner, he issued orders to his steward.

"Give those poor people all they need. Pay the girl her wages while she's ill. I want to convince my cousin that I'm not so bad as he believes, and that I, too, can give charity, when it's my turn."

Rafael left his master's house and spurred his horse, ready to make a visit to Marchamalo before returning to the farm. He was halted, however, in front of the *Círculo Caballista*.

The wealthiest young men of Jerez abandoned their glasses of wine and dashed into the street, surrounding the steward's horse. They desired to learn the details of what had occurred at Matanzuela. That chap Luis at times exaggerated so much when he recounted his exploits! . . . And at Rafael's curt, grave responses, they all laughed loudly, finding their information confirmed. The bullock set free, pursuing the drunken maidens, brought wild outbursts of laughter to these youths, who, drinking wine, breaking in horses and discussing women, awaited the moment when they would inherit the wealth and the land of all Jerez. . . . But what a splendid chap was this Luis! And to think they had missed that gorgeous sight! Some recalled remorsefully that he had invited them to the feast, and regretted that they had not accepted.

One of them asked whether it was certain that a girl was ill from fright. Upon hearing from Rafael that she was a gipsy, many shrugged their shoulders. A gipsy! She'd soon get well. Others, who knew *Alcaparrón* through his many pilferings, laughed upon hearing that the invalid was of his family. And all, forgetting the gipsy, resumed their comment upon the gay old time that "crazy Dupont" had given, besieging Rafael with new questions, asking what the *Marquesita* was doing while her lover was freeing the bullock, and if she had run much.

When Rafael had nothing further to tell, all the young men went back to the club without saluting him. Now that their curiosity was satisfied, they looked with scorn upon the mere laborer who had caused them to abandon their tables so hurriedly.

The steward spurred his mount to a gallop, wishing to arrive in Marchamalo as soon as possible. María de la Luz had not seen him for two weeks and received him with a wry face. Even here there had arrived, exaggerated by popular commentary, news of what had happened at Matanzuela.

The overseer shook his head in disapprobation of the event, and his daughter, taking advantage of some moments during which señor Fermín was absent, rebuked her sweetheart, as if he were the sole person responsible for the farmhouse scandal. Ah, the wicked fellow! That's why he hadn't put in an appearance at the vineyard for so many days! The señor was returning to his former gay habits; he was converting into an abode of shame that farmhouse of which she dreamed as a nest of lawful love.

"Enough, shameless fellow. You can't come back here. I know you. . . ."

And the poor steward almost burst into tears, wounded by his sweetheart's injustice. To treat him so . . . after the temptation to which the *Marquesita's* drunken indecency had subjected him, in regard to which he maintained silence out of respect for María de la Luz! . . . He offered his position as an excuse. He was only a servant, who must close his eyes to many things, in order to keep his place. What would her own father do if the owner of the vineyard was a young man of his master's sort? . . .

Rafael left Marchamalo; his sweetheart's ire had cooled down, but he carried in his thoughts, like a heavy burden, the asperity with which she had repelled him. Heavens—that master of his! And what trouble Luis's diversions gave him! . . . He turned slowly toward Matanzuela, thinking of the laborers' hostile glances, of that girl who was dying rapidly, while there in the city the idlers spoke of her and her shock with loud laughter.

Hardly had he set foot upon the ground when he saw

Alcaparrón, who was wandering about the farmyard
with the expression of a madman, as if the exuberance
of his grief was too great to be confined under the roofs.

"She's dying, *zeñó Rafaé.* This makes a week that
she's been suffering. The poor girl can't lie down, and
day and night she sits with her arms stretched out,
moving her hands like this . . . like this; as if she's
looking for her health that's gone forever. Ay, my poor
Mari-Cruz! Cousin of my soul! . . ."

And he uttered these cries as if they were roars, with
the tragic expansion of the gipsy race, which needs much
room for its griefs.

The steward entered the shelter, and before he came
close to the sick girl's heap of rags, he heard the sound
of her labored breathing—a dolorous puffing of disordered bellows, which dilated and contracted the
wretched sides of her body.

Her fight for air forced her to open, with shudders of
agony, the wretched clothes that covered her frail body,
revealing a consumptive, undeveloped chest, as white as
paper, with no signs of sex other than two sunken brown
circles between her ribs. As she breathed she moved
her head from side to side, as if trying to absorb all the
air. At certain moments her eyes expanded with an
expression of horror, as if she felt the touch of something cold and invisible upon the shriveled hands that
she extended before her.

Old *Alcaparrona* now appeared less confident than
during the early days of the illness.

"If she could only throw up the evil thing she's got
inside!" she exclaimed, looking at Rafael.

And after wiping the cold, viscous sweat from the sick
girl's face she offered her the jar of water.

"Drink, daughter of my bosom! My white dove! . . ."

And the wretched dove, wounded unto death, after

having drunk thrust her tongue between her violet lips, as if she desired to prolong the sensation of coolness: a dry tongue, of baked red, like a slice of roasted meat.

At times her noisy respiration was interrupted by a dry cough, and she spat mucus streaked with blood. The old woman shook her head. She was looking for something black and monstrous—a putrid ejection which, upon being expelled, would take with it all the maiden's illness.

The steward spoke to old *Alcaparróna* about five *duros* that he was to give her on behalf of the master, and the old woman's eyes grew tender.

"No. Don Luis is a thorough gentleman! It was the poor girl's bad luck—cursed accident. May God reward the master for his kindness! . . ."

And the old woman abandoned the sick girl to accompany the steward to the door, murmuring praises of her master and asking when she could come to the farmhouse for the money.

Two days passed. Ten days had already gone by since Mari-Cruz had fallen ill. The laborers lodged in the dormitory seemed to have accustomed themselves to the sight of the gipsy seated upon her heap of tatters and to the sound of her labored puffing. From time to time some of them spoke of going to Jerez for help, of bringing a physician; but the others replied with a shrug of their shoulders, as if they believed that this could go on indefinitely.

At night the toilers were rocked to sleep by the panting of the broken bellows that issued from one of the corners. They had grown so hardened to the sight of the invalid that they could pass her by, smiling and conversing in loud tones, without seeing her. They only turned their heads in her direction with a certain disquietude when the painful panting would cease for a few moments.

The *Alcaparrón* family, stupefied by nights of sleep-lessness, remained motionless, all seated upon the floor about the sick girl, without daring to go to the fields and earn their day's pay.

One afternoon the old woman burst into shrieks. The girl was dying; she was choking. She, so weak that she could scarcely move her hands, was twisting her bony skeleton with the extraordinary strength of pain, and such were her contortions, that the woman could scarcely restrain her in her grasp. Supporting herself upon her heels, the sick girl managed to rise, doubling over like an arch, her chest panting and heaped in a ball, her face blue and shriveled.

"Jozé María!" groaned the old woman. "She's dying! . . . She's dying in my arms! Here, son!"

But *Alcaparrón*, instead of answering his mother's call, dashed like a madman out of the lodge. He had seen a man pass by, an hour before, on the Jerez highway, bound for the "Jackdaw."

It was he—the extraordinary being of whom all the poor folks spoke with such deep respect. Suddenly the gipsy had felt himself inflamed with that faith which the leaders of the masses cast about them, like an aureole of supernatural confidence.

Salvatierra, who was in the tavern speaking with *Maracardillos,* his suffering comrade, recoiled with sur-prise at the precipitous entrance of *Alcaparrón.* The gipsy looked in all directions, the light of madness in his eyes, and finally threw himself at don Fernando's feet, clutching his hands with supplicating vehemence.

"Don Fernando! Your grace can do everything! . . . Your grace performs miracles if he wishes! My cousin . . . my Mari-Cruz . . . she's dying, don Fer-nando, she's dying! . . ."

Salvatierra did not know just how he left the tavern,

pulled along by the feverish hand of *Alcaparrón,* or how he arrived in Matanzuela with dream-like rapidity, running after the gipsy, who tugged at him, at the same time calling him his God, certain that he would work the miracle.

The rebel soon found himself in the semi-darkness of the dormitory, and by the light of the oil-lamp, held by several of the gipsies, he could distinguish the bluish, agonizing mouth of Mari-Crúz, contracted in the supreme spasm, her eyes increased in size by the darkness of grief, with an expression of infinite anguish. He lowered his ear to the damp, slimy skin of that breast which seemed upon the point of bursting. The examination was brief. As he lifted his head he instinctively removed his hat, remaining standing and bareheaded before the poor girl.

There was nothing that could be done. It was the last agony, the tenacious, horrifying, supreme struggle that awaits the end of all existence.

The old woman explained to Salvatierra her opinions upon the cause of the illness, hoping that he would approve of them. It was the blood that had been poisoned by the shock, and now it couldn't get out and was killing her.

But don Fernando shook his head. His devotion to the study of medicine, his desultory but extensive reading during the long years of seclusion, his continuous contact with misfortune, were enough to enable him to recognize the ailment at first sight. It was consumption —rapid, brutal, fulminating, spreading the tuberculosis with all the fertile growth of the plague: phthisis in its stifling form—the terrible *glanulia,* which had arisen as the result of a strong shock in this poor organism, open to all diseases, offering a ready haven to their germs. He examined from head to foot this fleshless body of sickly white, of which the bones seemed to be as fragile as paper.

Salvatierra asked in a low voice about her parents. In this agony he seemed to discern the remote influence of alcohol. Old *Alcaparrona* protested.

"Her poor father drank like everybody else, but he was a man of powerful endurance. His friends called him *Damajuanja*. But drunk? . . . Never."

Salvatierra sat down upon a stump, following the course of the agony with a sad glance. He wept the death of this creature, whom he had seen only once; the wretched offspring of alcoholism, who was leaving the world, impelled by the bestiality of a night of intoxication.

The poor thing was struggling in the arms of her people, in all the horrors of asphyxia, stretching her hands forward.

A veil seemed to float before her eyes, making her pupils grow smaller. Her breathing bubbled like boiling water, as if the air in her throat encountered the opposition of foreign matter.

The old woman, finding no other remedy at hand, gave her water to drink, and it fell into her stomach noisily, as if into the bottom of a hollow vessel; it struck against the walls of the paralyzed œsophagus, making them sound as if they were of parchment. Her face lost its general features; her cheeks grew dark; her temples flattened; her nose grew thin with a cold slenderness; her mouth twisted to one side into a horrible grimace.

Night was beginning to fall and the laborers began to return to the dormitory; the men and women grouped themselves silently at a short distance from the dying girl, their heads lowered and restraining their sighs.

Some of the toilers went back to the fields to hide their emotion, which was not unmingled with fear.

Christ! And that's how persons died! That was the cost of losing one's life! . . . And the certainty that all of them would have to pass through that terrible ordeal, with its contortions and its tremblings, made them look upon the life of toil through which they dragged on their existence as tolerable and even happy in comparison.

"Mari-Crú! My little dove!" sighed the old woman. "Do you see me? Here we are—all of us!"

"Answer, Mari-Crú!" entreated *Alcaparrón,* whimpering. "I'm your cousin, your José María. . . ."

But the gipsy answered only with raucous rattling, scarcely opening her eyes, showing between her motionless eyelids her corneas, which were the color of clouded glass. In one of her convulsive fits she thrust forth from her tattered covering a bony, tiny foot, completely black. The lack of circulation was gathering the blood at her extremities. Her ears and her hands likewise were becoming purple.

The old woman broke into lamentations. It was just what she had said! The *corrupted blood;* the accursed shock that had not come out, and now, with the approach of death, was spreading all through the body! And she hovered over the agonizing child, kissing her with mad avidity, as if biting her to bring her back to life.

"She has died, don Fernando! Can't your grace see? She is dead! . . ."

Salvatierra bade the old woman keep silent. The dying girl no longer saw; her cavernous respiration was gradually slackening, but her sense of hearing was still preserved. It was the final resistance of the senses against death; it was retained while the body kept sinking into the dark abyss of unconsciousness. There remained to her only the last labored tremblings of vegetative existence. Her convulsions slowly ceased, together with the agitation of her wretched body. Her eyelids opened with a last shudder, showing the pupils dilated with a dull, glassy luster.

The revolutionist took between his arms this body that was as light as a child's, and asking the relatives to stand aside, slowly laid it out in the heap of tatters.

Don Fernando trembled; his blue spectacles grew moist, disturbing his sight. The cold impassivity that had characterized him during so many hazards of his career, melted before this little corpse, as light as a feather, which he was laying out upon the bed of its misery. There was in his expression and about his hands something priestly, as if death were the only injustice before which his eternal rebel's anger prostrated itself.

When the gipsies beheld Mari-Cruz stretched out motionless, they remained for a long while in silent stupor. In the rear of the lodge sounded the women's sobs, and the fervent murmur of a prayer.

The *Alcaparrones* contemplated the corpse from a distance, without kissing it or venturing the slightest contact, with that superstitious awe which death inspires in all of their race. But the old woman soon raised her shriveled hands to her face, scratching it, sinking her fingers into her oily hair, which was of a jet black that defied the years. The thin strands of hair flew about her face and her strident shriek sent a shudder through all.

"Aaaay! My daughter is dead! My little white dove! My April rose! . . ."

And these wails, in which vibrated the ostentatious exuberance of Oriental grief, she accompanied with scratches that filled the wrinkles of her face with blood. A muffled shock at the same time shook the earth of the tamped floor. It was *Alcaparrón,* who, fallen prostrate, was striking the ground with his head.

"Aaay! Mari-Crú is gone!" he bellowed like a wounded beast. "The best one of the house! The most decent of the family! . . ."

And the little *Alcaparrones,* as if in sudden obedience to a racial rite, arose and commenced to run about the farm and its vicinity, shrieking and clawing their faces.

"Ay! Ay! Our poor little cousin is dead! . . . Ay! Mari-Crú has left us! . . ."

It was a mad dash of elfs through all the dependencies of the farm, as if they desired even the humblest of the animals to learn of their misfortune. They penetrated into the stables, they scurried between the legs of the animals, repeating their lamentations over the death of Mari-Cruz; they ran along, blinded by their tears, stumbling against corners of the walls and door-casings, overturning in their path a plow here, a chair there, and followed by the unleashed dogs, who tagged at their heels throughout the farmyard, adding their barks to the desperate wailing.

Some of the laborers stopped the little demons in their wild race, raising them in the air; but even thus imprisoned, they kept waving their arms and legs and crying incessantly:

"Ay! Our cousin is dead! The poor little Mari-Crú!"

Exhausted from weeping, from scratching themselves, from striking their heads against the ground—crushed by their noisy grief—the entire family returned to the corpse, forming a circle about it.

Juanón spoke of watching over the dead with some companions until the following morning. Meanwhile the family could sleep outside of the dormitory, for they all needed rest badly. But the old gipsy protested. She did not care to have the corpse remain in Matanzuela any longer. To Jerez at once! They would bear her in a cart, upon a mule, on their shoulders if it proved necessary—she and her sons.

They had their house in the city. Did they think the *Alcaparrones* were vagabonds? Her family was numerous, infinite; from Córdoba to Cádiz there was never a live-stock fair without one of them present. They were poor, but they had relatives that could cover them from head to foot with silver ounces; rich gipsies who trotted over the roads followed by regiments of mules and horses. All the *Alcaparrones* loved Mari-Cruz, the sickly virgin with the gentle eyes. And if she had lived like a beast of burden, she should be buried like a queen.

"Let us go," said the old woman, with great exaltation in her voice and her manner. "Let us be off to Jerez at once. I wish all of our people to see her before dawn, as pretty and neat as the very Mother of God. I wish her grandfather to see her—my father, gentlemen: the oldest gipsy in all Andalusia; and I wish him to bless the poor little creature with his hands of a Holy Father, which tremble and seem to shine with light."

The laborers approved the desires of the old woman, with the egotism of weariness. They could not resuscitate the dead, and it was better, for their tranquillity, that this noisy family which disturbed their slumber should leave as soon as possible.

Rafael intervened, offering one of the farm's carts. Old *Zarandilla* was going to get it ready, and before half an hour they could take the corpse to Jerez.

The aged *Alcaparrona*, at sight of the steward, gathered courage and her eyes glowed with hatred. At last she had found some one upon whom to fasten responsibility for her misfortune.

"It's you, is it, you wretch? Now are you satisfied, treacherous steward? Take a look here at the poor girl you killed!"

Rafael answered ill-humoredly:

"Less of your words and insults, old witch. As far as that night is concerned, you were more to blame than I."

The old woman, with the infernal joy of having some one upon whom to vent her grief, was about to attack him.

"Pimp! . . . It's you that did it all! Cursed be your soul and that of your wretched master!"

At this point she hesitated for a moment, as if in regret at having named the master, always respected by those of her race.

"No; not the master. For after all, he's young, he's rich, and those young men have nothing to do but amuse themselves. Cursed be *you,* who oppress the poor and drive them on as if they were black slaves, and divide the girls among the visitors so as to hide your own robbery the better! I want none of your money; take the five *duros* you gave me; here they are, you thief! Take them, you pimp!"

And struggling in the grasp of the men who were holding her back from attacking Rafael, she sank her hands into her tatters, seeking the money with feigned haste, with the firm purpose of never finding it. Her attitude, however, was none the less dramatic on this account.

"Take it, you mangy cur! . . . Here it is, and may every *peseta* turn into a devil that'll gnaw at your heart!"

And she opened her shriveled hands as if she were casting something upon the floor, yet threw nothing, accompanying these beatings of the air with proud grimaces, as if the money had really rolled upon the ground.

Don Fernando intervened, placing himself between

the steward and the witch. She had said enough already; she must be silent.

Despite this the old woman became more insolent than ever, finding herself protected by Salvatierra's body, and thrusting her harpy-like mouth over one of his shoulders, she continued insulting Rafael.

"May God send death to the one you're most fond of! . . . May you see the girl you love some day stretched out stiff and cold, like my poor little Mari-Cruz!"

Up to this moment the steward had listened to her with cold disdain, but when these words were uttered it was he who had to be held back by the men.

"Old witch!" he roared. "Say what you please to me, but don't put that other person on your lips or I'll kill you!"

And so intense was his desire to carry his threat into execution that the laborers had to use all their strength to drag him out of the place. Who paid any attention to women? . . . Let him leave the old woman alone; she was crazed with grief. When, conquered by Salvatierra's advice and the shoves of so many arms, he crossed the threshold of the dormitory, he could still hear the piercing voice of the gipsy, which seemed to follow him.

"Flee, you false person, and may God punish you by taking away your vineyard sweetheart! May a señorito rob her from you! . . . May don Luis enjoy her, and you learn of it!"

Ah! What will-power Rafael needed to summon, in order not to turn upon his steps and strangle the old witch! . . .

Half an hour later *Zarandilla* backed his cart against the door. Juanón and some companions wound the corpse in a sheet and carried it from its bed of rags.

She weighed even less than at the time of her death. She was, according to these men, a feather, a wisp of straw. It seemed that together with her life all her substance had evaporated, leaving only her frame, which scarcely revealed the slightest bulk under its shroud.

The vehicle started on its journey, jouncing over the ruts of the road with sharp creaks of the axle.

Close behind the cart walked the old woman and her little ones. In the rear marched *Alcaparrón*, at the side of Salvatierra, who desired to accompany these humble folk to the city.

At the door of the workers' shelter the laborers crowded together; the weak light of a lamp shone amid their black mass. With silent attention they all followed the squeaking of the cart, which was invisible in the darkness, and the lamentations of the gipsy band, which rent the calm of the fields that lay blue and lifeless under the cold light of the stars.

Alcaparrón felt a certain pride at walking with that personage of whom folks spoke so much. They had reached the main road. Upon its white sash stood out the silhouette of the cart, which scattered upon the silence of the night the languid jangling of the horses' bells and the wails of those who walked behind.

The gipsy was sighing, like an echo of that grief that bellowed before him, and at the same time he spoke to Salvatierra of his dead beloved.

"She was the best one in the family, zeñó . . . and that's why she's gone. The good ones go first. Here you have my cousins the *Alcaparronas,* a couple of public women that are the disgrace of the family, and the strumpets have money by the fistful, and coaches, and the papers speak of them. And poor little Mari-Crú, who was better than the wheat, dies after a life of hard labor."

The gipsy moaned, looking at the sky, as if in protest against this injustice.

"I loved her so much, zeñó; if I ever wished for anything good, it was to share it with her. Better still: to give it all to her. And she, the little dove that didn't have an unkind word in her, the tender April rose—how good she always was to me!—taking my part as if she were my little virgin! . . . Whenever my mother was angry because of something I had done, it was Mari-Crú who defended her poor little José María. . . . Ay, my darling cousin! My sweet little saint! My brown little sun with those eyes that were just like a blaze! What wouldn't this wretched little gipsy have done for her? . . . Listen, your grace, zeñó. I've had a sweetheart; I mean, lots of them; but this particular one was a *gachi* that didn't belong to our caste; a *calé* without a family, and with a house of her own in Jerez. A wonderful beauty, zeñó, and what's more, just crazy for me, from what she said, because I sang her sweet things so nicely. And when we were ready to get married, I said to her: '*Gachi,* the house will be for my poor little mother and my cousin Mari-Crú. Since they've worked so hard and lived a dog's life in the workers' shelters, let them live well and at their ease for a while. You and I are young and strong, and we'll be able to sleep in the corral.' And the *gachi* refused and threw me into the street; and I wasn't sorry, because I had my mother and my cousin, and they're worth more—ay!—than all the women in the world. . . . I've had sweethearts by the dozens, and I've been on the point of marrying, for I like the girls . . . but I love Mari-Crú as I'll never love any other woman. . . . How can your grace explain this—you who know so much? I love the poor little darling that's riding there ahead of us, in a way I simply can't explain . . . yes!—like the priest loves the Mother of God when he says mass to her. I was so fond of looking into her eyes and listening to her golden little voice; but as to touching a stitch of her clothes? It never occurred to me. She was my little virgin, and just like those in church, she had only a head for me; the pretty little head that was made by the very angels. . . ."

The thought of the departed one caused him to sob anew, and he was answered by the chorus of lamentations that escorted the cart.

"Aaay! My child is dead! My shining sun! My gentle treasure! . . ."

And the little ones responded to their mother's wail with an outburst of dolorous cries, so that the obscure earth, the blue space and the stars with their sharp refulgence should surely learn that their cousin, the sweet Mari-Cruz, had died.

Salvatierra felt overcome by this tragic, noisy grief that poured forth into the night, breaking the silence of the fields.

Alcaparrón ceased his moaning.

"Tell me, your grace, zeñó—you who know so much. Do you believe that I'll ever see my cousin again? . . ."

He needed to know this; he was assailed by the anguish of doubt, and suddenly stopping, he looked entreatingly at Salvatierra with his Oriental eyes, which shone with pearly glints into the gloom.

The rebel was touched by the anguish of this simple soul, who in his grief was imploring a crumb of consolation.

Yes, he would see her again; Salvatierra affirmed this with solemn gravity. And more; he would be at all hours in contact with something that had formed part of her being. All that exists remains in the world; it simply changes form; not an atom is lost. We live surrounded by that which has been the past and that which will be the future. The remains of those we loved and the components of all those who in turn will love us, float in the air about us, maintaining our existence.

Salvatierra, under the pressure of his thoughts, felt the necessity of confessing himself to some one—of speaking to this simple creature of his own weakness and his vacillations before the mystery of death. It was a desire to vent his thoughts (with a certainty of not being understood)—of bringing his soul to light, similar to what he had seen in the great Shakespearian characters —kings in misfortune, leaders persecuted by fate, who confide their ideas fraternally to fools and madmen.

This gipsy, whom everybody made fun of, seemed all at once to have been rendered great by grief, and Salvatierra felt impelled to communicate his thoughts to him, as if he beheld in him a brother.

The rebel, too, had suffered. Grief had cowed him; but he felt no remorse, since in his weakness he had found the balm of consolation. Men admired his strength of character—the stoicism with which he faced persecution and physical ordeals. But this was only in his struggle against men. Before the mystery of Death— cruel, invincible, inevitable—all his strength was shattered.

And Salvatierra, as if he had forgotten the presence of the gipsy and were talking to himself, recalled his proud departure from the penitentiary, defying persecutions anew, and his visit to Cádiz, to see a certain corner of earth near a mud wall, among crosses and marble slabs. And was this all that remained of the being that had filled his thoughts? Did there remain of mamma, of that woman as kindly and sweet as the sacred women of all religions, only that plot of earth and the wild daisies that blossomed on its borders? Was the gentle glow of her eyes lost forever? The echo of her caressing voice, cracked by old age, which with its child-like lisping called to Fernando, her "darling Fernando?"

"*Alcaparrón*, you can't understand me," continued Salvatierra in a quivering voice. "Perhaps your greatest fortune is this simple soul of yours, which permits you to be as light and capricious as a bird in all your griefs and your joys. But hear me, even if you don't understand. I don't deny all that I've learned; I don't doubt that which I know. Future life is a lie—a proud illusion of human egotism; the heaven of the religions is likewise a deception. They preach these things to people in the name of a poetic spiritualism, and their life eternal, their resurrection of the dead, their pleasures and punishments of beyond the grave, are of a materialism that gives one nausea. There exists for us no other life than the present; but, ah! before the sheet of earth that covers mamma, for the first time I felt my convictions waver. When we die, that is the end of us; but something of us remains about those who succeed us upon the earth; something that is not merely the atom that nourishes new lives; something impalpable and undefinable, that was the personal seal of our existence. We are like the fishes of the sea. Do you understand me, *Alcaparrón?* The fishes live in the same water in which their ancestors were dissolved and in which throb the spawn of their successors. Our water is the ambient in which we exist: space and earth: we are surrounded by those that were and those that will be. And I, *Alcaparrón* my friend, whenever I am seized with a desire to weep at the recollection of the nothingness beyond that heap of earth, and the sad insignificance of the little flowers that surround it—I tell myself that not all of mamma is there—that something of her has escaped and is circulating through life, that it brushes against me, attracted by a mysterious sympathy and accompanies me everywhere, enveloping me in a caress as soft as a kiss. . . . 'It's a lie!' cries a voice within my thoughts. But I do not listen; I wish to dream, to invent new lies for my consolation. Perhaps in this very breeze that strokes our faces there is something of the gentle hands that caressed me for the last time just before I went to prison."

The gipsy, gazing at Salvatierra through his African eyes distended with amazement, had ceased to moan. He did not understand most of the speaker's words, but he glimpsed a hope in them.

"According to what you say, do you believe that Mari-Crú is not entirely dead? That I'll be able to see her some time, when I'm overcome by memory of her? . . ."

Don Fernando felt himself influenced by the lamentations of the family, by the anguish he had witnessed, by the wretched poverty of that corpse which was jouncing along in the cart before them. The sad poetry of the night, with its silence now and then broken by cries of grief, overflowed his soul.

His affirmation was clear. Yes; *Alcaparrón* would feel his dead beloved near him. Something of her would rise to his face like a perfume, when he would be hoeing the soil, and the new furrow would send to his nostrils the fresh odor of newly removed earth. There would be something of her soul, too, in the ears of grain, in the poppies that stained the golden corn with bright red drops, in the birds that sang at dawn when the human flock went forth to the cutting, in the mountain thickets, over which the insects circled, frightened by the galloping mares and the roaring bulls.

"Who knows," continued the rebel, "whether in those stars that seem to blink from above, there is not at this very moment something of the light from those other eyes that you loved so much, *Alcaparrón?* . . ."

But the gipsy's glance revealed an astonishment that was not unmingled with compassion, as if he believed Salvatierra mad.

"You are stupefied by the vastness of the universe compared with the smallness of your poor little dead beloved, and you recoil. The vase is far too large for a tear; that's certain. But the drop of water, too, is lost in the ocean, and yet, none the less it is there."

Salvatierra continued to speak, as if desiring to convince himself. What did vastness or smallness signify? In a drop of liquid there exist millions and millions of beings, all possessing their own life; as many as there were men upon the planet. And a single one of these infinitesimal organisms was sufficient to kill a human being, and to decimate a nation by an epidemic. Then why should not men, the microbes of the infinite, influence this universe in whose bosom remained the strength of their personality? . . .

Then the revolutionist seemed to doubt his own words, to regret them.

"Perhaps this belief is tantamount to cowardice. You can't understand me, *Alcaparrón.* But, ah! Death! The unknown, who spies upon us and follows us, scoffing at our pride and our contentment! . . . I despise it, I mock it, I await it fearlessly so that I may have rest at last; and many await it even as I. But we men love, and love makes us tremble for those that surround us; it saps our energy, it makes us fall prostrate, like trembling poltroons, before this black witch, and we invent a thousand illusions to console us for her crimes. Ah! If only we did not love! . . . What a brave, rash animal would man be then!"

The cart, in its jolting progress, had left Salvatierra

and the gipsy behind. They had stopped to converse and could no longer make out the vehicle. They were guided along, however, by its distant squeaking and the lamentations of the family that walked behind, beginning the chant of its grief anew.

"Good-by, Mari-Crú!" the little ones were shrieking, like acolytes of a funereal religion. "Our cousin is dead! . . ."

And when for a moment they were silent, the voice of the old woman could be heard, despairing, strident, like a priest of grief.

"The white dove is leaving us; the gentle gipsy; the rose-bud that hadn't yet opened! . . . Lord in heaven! What can you be thinking of when you take only the good away? . . ."

CHAPTER VII

By the time September had brought the gathering season, the rich men of Jerez were more concerned with the attitude of the toilers than with the results of the harvest.

Even the gayest young men of the *Círculo Caballista* forgot the merits of their horses, the excellencies of their dogs and the style of the women whose ownership they disputed, and spoke only of the folk that had been bronzed by the sun, exhausted by their labors, filthy, evil-smelling and with sullen eyes, who lent their arms to land that belonged to others.

In the numerous societies that occupied the lower sections of almost all the buildings on la Calle Larga, they spoke of nothing else. What more did the vineyard workers desire? . . . They earned ten *reales* per day, they ate their tubs of pottage which they took care of all themselves without the intervention of the owner; they had an hour's rest in winter and two in summer, lest they fall overcome by the heat upon the limy earth, which shot sparks; they were granted eight cigarettes per day and at night they slept upon rush mats, most of the men having a sheet. These toilers were regular sybarites; and yet they had the presumption to complain and demand reforms, threatening a strike! . . .

At the *Caballista,* the vineyard owners seemed suddenly stricken with compassion, and spoke of the farmhands. Now *these* poor fellows really deserved better treatment! Two *reales* per day, insipid food and forced to sleep on the ground, dressed, with less shelter than the beasts. It was only logical that these should complain; but not the workers in the vineyards, who, when compared to the farmhands, lived like lords.

But the proprietors of the farms, in their turn, protested indignantly, upon beholding that the burden of the danger was cast upon them. If they did not pay the laborer better it was because the product of the farm did not warrant any more. Could the wheat, the barley and the live-stock be compared to those world-famous vineyards that simply spurted gold from their vines, and during certain years brought easier profits to their owners than if they were to take to the highway as bandits? . . . When folks enjoyed such good fortune they ought to be generous, and give a small share of their income to those who sustained them with their efforts. The toilers were right to complain.

And the gatherings of the rich were taken up by continuous argument between the proprietors of the two industries.

Their life of ease had become paralyzed. The roulette wheel was motionless; the decks of cards remained unopened upon the green tables; pretty girls passed by on the sidewalk without attracting to the windows a group of heads that shouted flirtatious comment and cast meaningful glances.

The janitor of the *Caballista* went about like mad looking for the key to what was pompously called "the library" in the statutes of the society; a closet hidden in the most obscure corner of the house, as bare as a poor man's cupboard, revealing through its dusty panes, overgrown with spiders' webs, a few dozen books that nobody had ever opened. The worthy members all at once felt impelled to instruct themselves, to master what folks called the social question, and every afternoon they looked at the closet as if it were a tabernacle of science, hoping that the key would appear so that they might seek within it the light they desired. They were really in no great hurry, however, to become informed upon these matters of socialism that had caused the revolt of the workers.

Some of them grew indignant at the books before even opening them. Lies! All lies! They did not read, and they were happy. Why didn't those country bumpkins have the same sense, instead of robbing themselves of hours of sleep at night, forming a circle about the comrade who read to them from newspapers and pamphlets? The less a man knew, the happier he was. . . . And they cast glances of abomination at the bookcase, as if it were a depository of ills, while the unhappy piece of furniture continued to guard within its entrails a treasure of inoffensive volumes, for the most part presented by the Ministry at the instance of the Deputy from that district; verses to the Virgin Mary and collections of patriotic songs; guides for the breeding of canaries and rules for the production of the domestic rabbit.

While the wealthy disputed among themselves or waxed indignant at the claims of the toilers, the latter continued in their attitude of protest. The strike had partially begun, with a lack of cohesion that proved the spontaneity of the resistance. In several vineyards the proprietors, prompted by the fear of losing the vintage, "gave in to everything," cherishing in their rancorous minds, however, hopes of reprisal the moment the clusters were in the wine-press.

Others, richer than these, "were ashamed," as they declared with noble arrogance, denying any arbitration with the rebels. Don Pablo Dupont was the most spirited among them. He would sooner lose his whole winery than lower himself to that mob. The idea of coming with demands to him—the father of his toilers, who took care not only of their bodily sustenance, but also of the health of their souls, delivering them from "crass materialism"!

"This is a 'matter of principle,'" he asserted in his office to his force, who all nodded their heads affirmatively even before he spoke. "I am in a position to give them what they ask and even more. But let them not ask me for it! Let them not make demands! For that is to deny my sacred rights as master. . . . Money matters very little to me, and the proof of that statement lies in the fact that sooner than yield, I'd lose the Marchamalo crop."

And Dupont, aggressive in defense of what he called his rights, not only refused to give ear to his laborers, but even discharged from the vineyard all those who had made themselves conspicuous as leaders long before the revolt was attempted.

Few vine-laborers remained in Marchamalo, but Dupont had substituted the strikers with gipsies from Jerez and girls that came from the mountain, caught by the bait of good pay.

As the vintage required little strength, Marchamalo seethed with women bending over its slopes, cutting down the grape-clusters, while from the roadway the strikers, deprived of work by their "ideas," taunted them with insults.

The rebellion of the workers had coincided with what Luis Dupont was pleased to call his era of seriousness.

The madcap had finally astonished his powerful cousin with his new conduct. No more women or scandals! The *Marquesita* no longer remembered him. Offended by his evasions, she had returned to her hog-dealer—"the only man who could manage her."

The young man seemed to grow moody when people spoke to him of his notorious banquets. All that had now passed forever; one could not be young all one's life. Now he was a man; and a serious, dignified man. He had *something* inside his head; his former teachers, the Fathers of the Company, had recognized that. He did not intend to stop on his upward march until he conquered a position in politics as high as that of his cousin in industry. Others, worse than he, managed the affairs of that district, and were listened to by the government yonder in Madrid, as if they were viceroys of the country.

Of his past life he retained friendship only with his cronies, reinforcing his retinue with several new braggarts. He flattered and maintained them with the purpose of making use of them in his political career. Who would dare oppose him in his first campaign, seeing him in such honorable company! . . . And in order to entertain his worthy suite, he continued to dine at the taverns and to get drunk with them. This did not serve to injure his respectability. A good time now and then could scandalize nobody. It was the custom of the place! Besides, this won him a certain popularity.

And Luis Dupont, convinced of his personal importance, went from one club to the other speaking upon the "social question," with vehement gestures that endangered all the bottles and glasses arrayed upon the tables.

At the *Círculo Caballista* he avoided the groups of young men, who recalled his past escapades only to applaud them, proposing even more extravagant ones. He sought the conversation of the "solemn fathers"—the great wine-dealers and the wealthy farmers, who began to listen to him with a certain attention, admitting that this scatter-brained chap had a good head on his shoulders.

Dupont swelled with vehement oratory as he spoke of the country's laborers. He repeated what he had heard

from his cousin and from the priests that frequented the
Duponts; but he exaggerated the solutions, however, with
an authoritative, brutal ardor, much to the pleasure of
his hearers, who were as rough as they were rich, and
found pleasure in conquering bulls and taming wild
colts.

To Luis the question was very simple. A little charity, and then religion—plenty of religion; and a big stick
for the recalcitrant. This was enough to finish the so-
called social question, and everything would be as smooth
as silk. What cause had the toilers for complaint when
there existed men like his cousin and many of those present (at this point there were grateful smiles and a stir
of approbation), who were benevolent to the point of
excess and could not look upon misfortune without
plunging their hands into their pockets and giving a *duro*
or even two? . . .

To this the rebels replied that charity was not enough,
and that, in spite of it, many people lived in poverty and
wretchedness. And what could the masters do to remedy the irremediable? There would always exist rich
and poor, sated and hungry; only madmen or criminals
could dream of equality.

Equality! . . . Dupont employed an irony that roused
his hearers to enthusiasm. All the jests that had been
inspired in his cousin Pablo and his retinue of priests
by the noblest of human aspirations, were by Luis repeated with the firmest conviction, as if they were the
summary of human thought. What was all this talk
of equality about? . . . Somebody could then take possession of his house, if he pleased; and he, in turn, could
appropriate his neighbor's jacket, because he needed it;
and another would fasten his claws upon the other fellow's wife, because she appealed to him. A fine mix-

up, gentlemen! . . . Didn't folks that spoke of such
equality deserve to be shot or put in strait-jackets?

And the laughter of the orator was swelled by the
guffaws of the entire membership. Down with Socialism! How witty and clever was this young fellow! . . .

Many of the older men nodded their heads with a
patronizing air, recognizing that Luis was needed else-
where—that it was a pity his words should be wasted in
this atmosphere of tobacco, and that his desire must be
satisfied at the first opportunity, so that all Spain should
hear from the parliamentary tribune this just and sparkling critic.

Dupont, inspired by the general sentiment, continued
to speak, but now his tone became grave. What the
lower classes needed even more than wages was the
solace of religion. Without religion one lived like a
madman, the prey to every misfortune; this was the case
with the laborers of Jerez. They believed in nothing,
they did not attend mass, they scoffed at the priests, and
thought only of the social revolution, of butchering and
shooting down the citizens and the Jesuits; they had no
hope of a future life—that consolation and compensation of all miseries here below, which are insignificant,
since they endure but a few score years—and as the logical result of so much impiety, they found their poverty
harder to endure, and gloomier than ever.

This sad, godless flock deserved its punishment. Let
them not complain of the masters, for these did their
best to put them upon the right path! Let them seek
out those who were truly to blame—Salvatierra and others of his stripe, who had robbed them of their faith!

"Moreover, gentlemen," perorated the young man,
with forensic intonation, "what are they going to gain
by an increase in wages? It will foment vice, that is all.
These persons do not save; these folk have never saved.

Let us see. Let them bring forward a single day-laborer who has laid aside anything from his earnings."

All were silent, nodding their heads in assent. Nobody brought forward the laborer demanded by Dupont, and he smiled triumphantly, awaiting in vain the miraculous being who could accumulate a fortune upon his daily pay of several *reales*.

"In these parts," he continued solemnly, "there is neither devotion to task nor the spirit of saving. Look at the toiler in other lands; he works harder than our own, and lays aside a tidy sum for old age. But here! . . . Here the only thing the young farmhand thinks of is to catch a girl off her guard in some straw-loft or in the dormitory while she's asleep; and when he gets old, the moment he gets a few *céntimos* together he spends it on wine and gets drunk."

And with a single impulse, as if they had suddenly lost their memories, they began with great severity to anathematize the vices of the working folk. What could be expected of a mob that had no other aim in life than to drink? . . . Dupont was right. The drunkards! The base tribe that perpetuated the poverty of their condition, violating women as if they were animals! . . .

The young speaker knew how to end all this anarchy. The government was in large measure to blame. At this very moment, since the strike had already begun, there should be a battalion in Jerez—an army, if necessary—and cannon, plenty of cannon. And he complained bitterly of the men at the top, as if the only mission of the Spanish army was to guard the wealthy men of Jerez and see that they lived undisturbed, and it was a felony not to fill the streets and fields with red pantaloons and glittering bayonets the moment the toilers showed any signs of discontent.

Luis was liberal, very liberal. He disagreed on this

point with his masters of the Company, who spoke enthusiastically of Don Carlos, affirming that he was the
"sole banner." He was with those that ruled, and not
once did he mention the royal personages without pre-
fixing *Their Majesty* to the names, as if they could hear
from afar these marks of exaggerated respect and reward him for them with the position he desired. He
was liberal; but his liberty was that of decent persons.
Liberty for those who had something to lose; and for
the lower classes, all the bread possible, and the stick—
plenty of it—the only means of defeating the evil that
is born in man and develops without the check of religion.

He knew history; he had read much more than those
who were listening to him and with patronizing bounty
he deigned to impart some of his knowledge to them.

"Do you know," he asked, "why France is more
wealthy and further advanced than we? . . . Because it
laid heavy hands upon the bandits of the *Commune,* and
in a few days disposed of more than forty thousand of
them. It used the cannon and the mitrailleuse to finish
them off all the more quickly, and everything was clean
and quiet. . . . As for myself," the young man continued with a professorial air, "I am not pleased with
France because it is a Republic and because there the
respectable folk forget the Lord and mock his ministers. But I would wish for this country a man like
Thiers. That's what we need here—a man who could
smile and mow down the rabble with guns."

And he smiled, to show that he was as capable as any
other of being a Thiers.

He could settle the Jerez conflict in twenty-four hours.
Let them give him full authority and they would see.
The immediate, thorough executions of *The Black Hand*
had given some results. The rebels were cowed by the

sight of the corpses strung up before the Prison. But
this was not enough. They needed a copious bleeding
to sap the strength of the rebellious beast. If he were
at the helm, the leaders of all the country workingmen's
societies that had overturned the city would be behind
the bars.

But this, too, seemed merely anodyne and insufficient,
and straightway he corrected himself by adding more
ferocious proposals. It would be better to forestall the
rebels, to cause a miscarriage of their plans, to "punc-
ture them so that they'd come out prematurely," and once
they rose in revolt, let not a single one be left! Plenty
of the Civil Guard, plenty of cavalry, plenty of artillery.
This was why the wealthy bore the burden of the taxes,
the greater part of which went to the army. If this were
not the case, then what good were the soldiers, who
cost so dear, in a country that had no wars to fight? . . .

As a preventive means, they must suppress the perverse shepherds who incited the poverty-stricken flock.

"For every one of the men that goes through the fields,
from shelter to shelter, giving out vile sheets and poi-
sonous books, four shots. For those who deliver
harangues and shout monstrosities at the secret meetings that are held at night in a barn or around some village tavern, four shots. And the same for those who,
in the vineyards, disobeying their masters and with the
pride of knowing how to read, inform their comrades of
the nonsense printed in the papers. . . . For Fernando
Salvatierra, four shots. . . ."

But scarcely had the young man uttered these final
words, when he seemed to regret them. An instinctive
hesitation stemmed his eloquence. The generosity and
the virtues of this rebel inspired him with a certain respect. The very listeners who approved his plans remained silent, as if they were repelled by the inclusion

of the revolutionist in the prodigal distribution of shots.
He was a madman who imposed admiration, a saint who
did not believe in God; and these men of the land felt
for him a respect similar to that of the Moor before the
demented dervish who curses him and threatens him
with his staff.

"No," resumed the young man, "for Salvatierra a
strait-jacket, and let him spread his doctrines in a madhouse as long as he lives."

Dupont's audience approved these solutions. The
owners of the horse-stables, old men with grayish side-
whiskers who passed hour after hour staring at their
bottle in sacerdotal silence, broke their solemnity to smile
at the young man.

"The boy has talent," said one. "He speaks like a
Deputy."

And the others agreed with him.

"His cousin Pablito will see to it that we nominate him
when the elections come around."

At times Luis felt wearied by the triumphs that he
reaped in the clubs—of the astonishment caused in his
former companions by his sudden seriousness. His predilection for amusing himself with common folk was reborn in him.

"I'm tired of upper class young men," he said with the
displeasure of a superior man to his acolyte *el Chivo*.
"Let's go to the country; a bit of a spree makes a fellow
feel good."

And with the aim of keeping in the good graces of his
powerful cousin, he went to spend the day at Marchamalo, feigning interest in the result of the grape-gath-
ering.

The vineyard was filled with women, and Luis enjoyed
mingling with these mountain girls, who smiled at the
young man and felt grateful for his generosity.

María de la Luz and her father received Luis's assiduous visits to the vineyard as an honor. Of the scandalous adventure at Marchamalo hardly a faint recollection remained. That was the señorito's affair! These folk, accustomed by tradition to respect the rough pleasures of the rich, excused them as if this sowing of wild oats was a duty of their youth.

Señor Fermín had learned of the great transformation that was coming over don Luis—of his pretensions to dignity—and it was with pleasure that he beheld the young man flee the temptations of the city and come to the vineyard.

His daughter, too, received the young man cordially, addressing him with the familiar pronoun as in their childhood, and laughing at all his jokes. He was Rafael's master, and some day she would be his servant at that farmhouse which she always beheld in her mind's eye as the very nest of her happiness. She hardly recalled the stormy banquet that had so greatly incensed her against the steward. The young man was plainly repentant of his past, and everybody, at the end of a few weeks, had completely forgotten the accident at the farmyard.

Luis exhibited intense fondness for life at Marchamalo. More than once night overtook him there and he remained to spend the night in the Dupont tower.

"I'm just like a patriarch there," he would tell his friends in Jerez. "Surrounded by maidens who love me as if I were their papa."

The friends laughed at the bounteous tones in which the addlepated fellow spoke of his innocent diversions with the flock of vintagers. Besides, he was fond of staying over at the vineyard for the night air.

"This is what you call living, señor Fermín," he said once upon the terrace, under the light of the stars, as he breathed in the evening breeze. "At this time the young members of the *Caballista* must be roasting out on the sidewalk."

The evenings passed in patriarchal tranquillity. The young owner offered the guitar to the overseer.

"Come here! Let's have something from those golden hands!" he would shout.

And *el Chivo*, obeying his orders, would go off in search of a few bottles of the best Dupont wine in the carriage boxes. A real good time! But quiet, respectable, orderly, without loose words or suggestive gestures that would affright the spectators, who were girls that had heard talk of the terrible don Luis in their home towns. Beholding him from near, they lost their fears, agreeing that he was not so black as he was painted.

María de la Luz sang, the young proprietor sang, and even the heavy-browed *Chivo*, obeying his master, released the voluminous stream of his harsh voice, singing coarse recollections of prison life and gallant duels in defense of one's mother or one's beloved.

"Olé, my fine fellow!" shouted the overseer, ironically, to that horrifying figure.

Then the young proprietor would take María de la Luz by the hand, and draw her into the center of the group; they would break into a Sevillian dance, with a grace that elicited shouts of enthusiasm.

"God's own grace!" exclaimed the father, strumming the guitar with renewed energy. "There's a pair of doves for you! . . . That's what you call dancing!"

And Rafael the steward, who came to Marchamalo only from week to week, upon seeing the dance done twice, felt proud of the honor being shown by his master to his sweetheart. His master was not at all a bad sort; all that had gone before was merely the madcap pranks of youth; but now that he was settling down he was a really fine fellow. And with such taking ways! And how fond he was of mingling with the lower classes, as if they were his equals. He encouraged the pair of dancers, without the slightest twinge of jealousy; he, who was capable of drawing his knife if any one dared cast a glance at María de la Luz. He felt only a sort of envy of his master for not being able to dance with his grace. His life had been devoted to the conquest of bread, and he had had no time for acquiring such accomplishments. He only knew how to sing, but in a rough, wild voice, such as he had been taught by his smuggling companions when they trotted along on their mares, arched over their bundles, filling the silence of the sierra's gorges with couplets.

Don Luis reigned over the vineyard as if he were the owner. The powerful don Pablo was away. He was spending the summer with his family on the Northern coast, taking advantage of his trip to visit Loyola and Deusto, his good counselors' centers of sanctity and wisdom. The madcap, in order to prove once more that he was a dignified, serious man, wrote long letters to him, referring to his visits to Marchamalo, the vigilance that he exercised over the vintage and the happy outcome of the latter.

And he was genuinely interested in the gathering. The animosity he felt against the workers—his desire to conquer the strikers—awoke him to persistency and industry. At last he established himself definitely in Marchamalo tower, vowing that he would not leave the place until the vintage was over.

"Things are moving," he said to the overseer, winking slyly. "Those bandits will gnash their teeth when they see that with the women and a few of our loyal workingmen we've finished the work without need of them. At night, a ball and a respectable good time, señor

Fermín. So that those outlaws may learn of it and burst with rage."

And thus the vintage was carried on, amid music and merriment, with the best wine generously distributed.

At night the house containing the wine-presses, which during don Pablo Dupont's presence was so ordered and silent that it possessed a conventual atmosphere, resounded with festal din up to a late hour.

The day-laborers forgot sleep to drink the lordly wine that was so prodigally poured. The girls, habituated to the poverty of the workers' lodges, opened their eyes wide with amazement, as if the largess of the marvelous tales they heard in their evening groups had come true. The supper was worthy of upper class gentlemen. Don Luis paid royally.

"See here, señor Fermín. Have some meat brought from Jerez; let all these girls eat till they burst; let them guzzle; let them get drunk; I'll stand all expenses. I wish that rabble to see how we treat loyal workers who know their place."

And facing the grateful multitude, he said, modestly:

"When you come across any of the strikers, tell them how the Duponts treat their laborers. The truth; only the truth."

During the day, when the sun beat down upon the earth, baking the white slopes of Marchamalo, Luis dozed under the arcades of the house, with a bottle at his side, distilling coolness, and from time to time holding out his cigar for *el Chivo* to light.

He had found a new pleasure in playing master of the immense estate; he believed in all faith that he was discharging an important social function in contemplating from his shaded retreat the labor of so many persons, bent and panting beneath the sun's rain of fire.

The maidens extended along the slopes with their colored skirts, like a flock of blue and pink sheep. The men, in their shirts and drawers, advanced crouchingly like white lambs. They went from one vine to another, dragging their bodies over the baked earth. The runners spread their red and green over the surface of the ground, and the grapes rested upon the lime, which up to the last moment communicated to them its generous heat.

Other maidens were carrying the large baskets of gathered clusters up the hill to the wine-presses, and passed in a continuous rosary before the señorito who, reclining upon his rush sofa, smiled at them patronizingly, thinking of the beauty of labor and the perversity of the rabble who were intent upon overturning so wisely organized a world.

At times, bored by the silence, he would call the overseer, who was going from hill to hill watching the work.

Señor Fermín squatted down before him and they discussed the strike and the news that came from Jerez. The overseer did not conceal his pessimistic views. The resistance of the working men was growing gradually stronger.

"There is a great deal of hunger, señorito," he said with the conviction of rustic folk, who appreciate the stomach as the source of all activity. "And hunger means disorder, clubs and riots. Blood is going to flow, and in the prison they're making room for more than one. . . . It will be a miracle if this doesn't end with the carpenter raising scaffolds in the prison square."

The old man seemed to scent catastrophe; but he beheld it approach with egotistical serenity, since the two men who possessed his affection were far away.

His son had gone to Málaga, on behalf of his employer, to represent the firm as its confidential spokesman in a bankruptcy case. He would remain there for

some time, going over accounts and discussing matters
with other creditors. Would that he'd not come back for
a year! Señor Fermín was afraid that should his son
return to Jerez he would compromise himself by siding
with the strikers, impelled by the teachings of his master Salvatierra, which would draw him into the camp
of the lowly and the rebellious. As for don Fernando,
many days before, he had left Jerez under escort of the
Civil Guard.

At the very beginning of the strike the wealthy proprietors had given him indirectly to understand that it
would be for his good to get out of the province of Cádiz
as soon as possible. He, he alone, was responsible for
what had occurred. His presence incited the working
folk, rendering them as audacious and rebellious as in the
times of *The Black Hand*. The chief agitators of the
workingmen's societies, who revered the revolutionist,
had entreated him to flee, as they feared for his life. The
hints from the powerful interests were equivalent to a
death threat. The laborers, accustomed to repression
and violence, trembled for Salvatierra. Perhaps the
enemy would kill him some night on some street or other,
without Justice ever being able to lay hands upon the assassin. It was even possible that the authorities, taking
advantage of Salvatierra's extended excursions about the
countryside, would subject him to mortal torture or *suppress* him with a bastinado in some deserted field, as they
had done with more humble toilers.

But don Fernando replied to these admonitions with
unshaken refusals. There he was, of his own accord,
and there he should stay. . . . At last the authorities ex-
humed one of the many charges that they had held pend-
ing against him owing to his propaganda of social revolt, and a judge summoned him to Madrid; don Fernando undertook the journey with great resolution, ac-

companied by the Civil Guard, as if it were his fate always to travel between a pair of guns.

Señor Fermín was happy at this solution. And now if they would only take up a good deal of his time, so that he couldn't return inside of a year! He knew Salvatierra, and he knew that if the rebel remained in Madrid it would not be long before the insurrection of the hungering ranks would break out, followed by cruel reprisals and a prison sentence for don Fernando, perhaps for life.

"This will all lead to bloodshed, señorito," continued the overseer. "Up to the present moment they are content with hissing the strikebreakers in the vineyards, but let your grace remember that this is the worst month of the year at the farms. The thrashing is over everywhere, and until sowing begins there will be thousands and thousands of men going around idle, ready to dance to the tune that's played to them. You'll see how quickly one group joins another, and then the trouble will commence. Already many strawlofts have been set on fire in the country, and the hand that lighted them hasn't been caught."

Dupont grew excited. All the better. Let them all unite, let them rise in rebellion as soon as they pleased; then they would be slashed and sent back to obedience and tranquillity. He desired the rebellion and the clash even more than did the toilers.

The overseer, astonished to hear the young man speak so, shook his head.

"Bad, very bad, señorito. Peace by blood is an evil peace. It's better to reach a friendly agreement. Let your grace take the word of an old man who has gone through the sufferings of Cain, mixed up in all these uprisings and revolutions."

On other mornings, when Luis Dupont did not feel

like holding converse with the overseer, he would enter
the house and seek out María de la Luz, who worked
in the kitchen.

The maiden's joyous spirits, the freshness of her dark
brown skin, produced a certain emotion in the young man.
The voluntary chastity that he was observing in his retirement caused the peasant girl's charms to appear considerably exaggerated. He had always felt a certain predilection for the girl, finding in her a modest attraction,
yet powerful and piquant, like the perfume of the herbs
in the fields. But now, in the solitude, María de la Luz
appeared to him superior to the *Marquesita* and all the
other singers and impulsive maids of Jerez.

But don Luis restrained his impulses, and concealed
them beneath a merry air of intimacy—the recollection
of their childhood companionship. When, instinctively,
he permitted himself some liberty that offended the girl,
he recalled these childhood days. Were they not like
brother and sister? Hadn't they been brought up together? . . . She should not look upon him as a distant
gentleman, the master of her sweetheart. He was,
rather, the same as her brother Fermín; she should consider him as one of the family.

He feared to compromise himself by some rash deed
in that house, which belonged to his severe cousin. What
would Pablo say, who through respect of her father
considered the overseer and his children a humble branch
of his own family? Besides, that famous night at
Marchamalo had done him great harm, and he did not
care to compromise his growing reputation as a dignified personage by another scandal. This thought
caused him to be timid with the grape-gatherers that attracted him, and he limited his pleasures to an intellectual perversion, making them drink at night to see them
in merry mood, without the inhibitions of modesty, chat-

tering among themselves, pinching and pursuing one another, as if they were alone.

Toward María de la Luz he was equally circumspect. He could not look at her without uttering a shower of praises for her beauty and her grace. But this did not alarm the maiden, who was accustomed to the vociferous expressions of gallantry characteristic of the province.

"Thanks, Luis," she would say, smiling. "And how very, very kind the señorito is! . . . If you keep this up I'm going to fall in love with you and we'll wind up by eloping together."

At times Dupont, influenced by solitude, which incites one to the greatest audacities, and by the perfume of a virgin skin that seemed to exhale life during the hours of intense heat, permitted himself to be drawn along by his instincts and cleverly placed his hands upon that body.

The girl bounded away, knitting her brows and tightening the corners of her mouth with an aggressive expression.

"Luis! Keep your hands off. What do you call this, señorito? Do that again and I'll give you a slap that'll be heard as far as Jerez."

And by her hostile glance and her menacing hand she displayed her firm intention of delivering that fabulous slap. It was then that he would recall, as an excuse, their childhood intimacy.

"But, you silly, wicked girl! I meant nothing by it; only a joke, just to see what a pretty face you make when you get angry! . . . I've already told you I'm your brother. Fermín and I—the same thing."

The girl seemed to regain her composure, but without abandoning her hostile attitude.

"Very good; then let this brother of mine put his

hands where they belong. You can loosen your tongue all you please; but if you show your claws, boy, then you'd better order another face, for I'll disfigure this one for you in a single blow."

"Olé, what a formidable maid!" exclaimed the señorito. "That's how I like to see my little girl! Shooting sparks, and everything! . . ."

When Rafael would come to Marchamalo, his young master did not on this account deprive himself of the pleasure of this continuous courtship.

The steward received all his master's praises of his sweetheart with innocent satisfaction. At last the señorito was like a brother to him, and this relationship made Rafael feel proud.

"Bandit, you!" the señorito would say to him with feigned indignation, in the presence of the girl. "You're going to carry off the best thing we've got here, the pearl of Jerez and its countryside. Do you see all the vineyard of Marchamalo, which is worth a cool million? . . . Well, it amounts to nothing aside of this little girl here, who's the very image of grace. And you're carrying her off, you robber . . . shameless wretch!"

And Rafael, as well as señor Fermín, laughed like one possessed. How witty and good this don Luis was! The señorito, continuing in this tone of mock gravity, turned to his steward.

"Laugh, you lubber. . . . Just look how content the fellow is with the envy that other persons feel of him! Some fine day I'll do away with you and take Mariquita de la Luz for my own, and I'll place her upon a throne in Jerez, right in the center of la plaza Nueva, and at her feet will be all the gipsies of Andalusia, playing and dancing before her, outvying one another in their songs to the queen of beauty and of grace, just as she de-

serves. . . . That's what I, Luis Dupont, will do, even
if my cousin excommunicates me."

And in the same style he kept embroidering a row of
hyperbolic, incoherent compliments, amid the laughter of
María de la Luz and the others, who were flattered by
the intimacy of the young man.

At the end of the vintage Luis swelled with pride, as
if he had completed a great task.

The gathering had been accomplished by the employment of women, and the strikers, despite their profuse
threats, did not dare to appear. This was no doubt due
to the fact that he was there watching over the vineyard;
because it was enough that they should know don Luis
and his friends were defending Marchamalo for nobody
to dare approach with the intention of disturbing the
work.

"Eh, what do you say, señor Fermín?" he said, petu-
lantly. "They did well not to come, for I would have
received them with bullets. Will my cousin ever repay
me for what I'm doing for him? Repay me! Why, it
would be just like him to say that I'm good for nothing.
. . . But this time he'll be forced to admit my worth.
This very day I'm going to Jerez, and I'll take along the
best there is in the wine-vaults. And if Pablo fumes
when he gets back, let him fume. He must pay me
something for my services. And to-night, a good time
. . . the best of the season; to last until sunrise. I wish
these girls, when they go back to the mountains, to return happy and with pleasant memories of the señorito.
. . . And I'll bring players, so that you can take a rest,
and singers, so that Mariquita won't have to do it all.
. . . You don't care to have that kind of women at
Marchamalo? Afraid my cousin will find out? . . .
Very good, then; they won't come. You, señor Fermín, are a stale old chap; but just to please you the sing-

ers will be left out of it. And when you come to think
of it, we won't be lacking women, here where you've got
so many that it looks like a seminary. But music and
wine over your head! And genuine country dancing;
and society dances, too, with the couples tightly clasped
together, just like fashionable folk. Oh, you'll see what
a time we have here to-night, señor Fermín!"

And Dupont rode to the city in his carriage, which
enlivened the entire length of the highway with the jangling of its bells. He returned well after nightfall. It
was a summer night; hot, without the slightest whiff of
a breeze stirring the air.

The earth exhaled a warm vapor; the blue of the sky
dissolved into a faint, whitish tint; the stars seemed to
be veiled by the dark clouds. Through the silence of
the night sounded the crackling of the shoots as their
bark expanded, split by the heat. The grasshoppers
shrilled furiously in the furrows, burned by the heat;
the frogs croaked from afar, as if kept awake by the
lack of coolness in the pond.

Dupont's companions, in their shirt sleeves, were lining up under the arcades the numerous bottles brought
from Jerez.

The women, in light dress, wearing only a percale
skirt, revealing their bare arms beneath the kerchief
crossed over their chests, took charge of the baskets of
food, admiring them and heaping praises upon the magnanimous señorito. The overseer lauded the quality of
the cold meats and the olives, which served to rouse
thirst.

"What a lordly banquet the señorito is preparing for
us!" exclaimed the old man, laughing like a patriarch.

The chief attraction of the sumptuous supper, which
was held in the middle of the terrace, was the wine.
Men and women ate standing, and when they held the

full glass in their hands, they advanced to a table occupied by don Luis, the overseer and his daughter, and lighted by two oil-lamps. The ruddy flames, whose sooty tongues rose in the air of the night without the slightest tremor, illuminated the golden transparency of the wine. But what was this? . . . And all, after admiring the beautiful color, resumed their drinking and opened their eyes wide in grotesque astonishment, seeking words, as if they could not express the veneration with which the portentous liquid inspired them.

"This is made from the very tears of Jesus," exclaimed one, smacking his lips piously.

"No," replied the others. "It's the very milk of the Mother of God. . . ."

And the young man laughed, enjoying the wonderment of the peasants. It was wine from the "Dupont Brothers'" stores: a very high-priced, venerable wine which only the milords yonder in London could afford to drink. Every drop was worth a *peseta*. Don Pablo guarded it like a treasure; very likely he would be wroth to know the havoc that his scatter-brained relative was wreaking with it now.

But Luis was by no means repentant of his generosity. He rejoiced to craze the wretched flock with the rich men's wine. It was the pleasure of the Roman patrician, intoxicating his clients and his slaves with beverages fit for emperors.

"Drink, my children," he urged with paternal accent. "Seize the opportunity, for you'll never get another. Many of the young men of the *Caballista* would envy you this chance. Do you know what all these bottles are worth? A fortune. This stuff is dearer than champagne; every bottle costs I don't remember how many *duros.*"

And the humble threw themselves upon the wine,

drinking and guzzling gluttonously, as if fortune itself were gliding down their throats.

At don Luis's table the bottles were served after having for a long while remained in ice-filled tanks. The wine flowed through the drinker's mouth, leaving it insensible with the pleasant paralysis of coolness.

"We're going to get drunk," pronounced the overseer sententiously. "This goes down without your feeling it. It's nice and cool in your mouth and turns to fire in your stomach."

He continued to fill his glass, however, between one bite and another, tasting the cold nectar and envying the rich, who could daily permit themselves this pleasure of the gods.

María de la Luz drank as much as her father. Scarcely did she empty her glass, when the señorito hastened to fill it.

"Don't pour me any more, Luis," she begged. "See, I'm getting drunk. This drink is treacherous."

"You silly goose. It's just like water! And even if you do begin to feel tipsy, it passes in a moment! . . ."

When the supper had come to an end, the guitars began to sound, and the guests formed a group, squatting down upon the ground before the chairs occupied by the musicians, the señorito and his companions. They were all drunk, but they continued to drink. How hot it was! Their skin dripped with perspiration; their chests heaved, as if they could find no air. Wine! More wine! There wasn't a better antidote for the heat; it was the genuine Andalusian beverage.

Beating their palms, while others clinked the empty bottles as if they were castanets, they applauded the famous Sevillian dances of María de la Luz and the señorito. She danced in the center of the group, before Luis, with her cheeks flaming and a strange glint in her eyes.

Never had they seen her dance with such grace and abandon. Her bare arms, as white as pearls, rose above her head like voluptuously curved pearl handles. Her percale skirt, between the rustle that revealed the adorable contour of her legs, showed beneath its hem a pair of diminutive feet, as scrupulously shod as those of a señorita.

"Ay! I'm exhausted!" she soon gasped, stifling from the exertions of the dance.

And she sank into a chair, feeling that from the whirling of the dance everything was beginning to revolve about her: the terrace, the people and even the great tower of Marchamalo.

"It's the heat," said her father gravely.

"A little drink and it'll pass," assured Luis.

He offered her a glass filled with that bubble-crowned liquid gold, which dimmed the sides because of its coolness. And Mariquita drank eagerly, with a raging thirst, desirous of renewing the sensation of coolness in her mouth, which seemed to burn as if her stomach were afire. From time to time she protested.

"I'm going to get drunk, Luis. I believe I'm drunk already."

"What of it!" exclaimed the young man. "I'm soused, too, and your father, and the whole gang of us. That's what the feast is for. Another glass! There's a brave girlie! On with the festivities!"

Some girls were dancing in the middle of the group, with all the awkwardness of peasants, facing the vintagers who were no less rustic.

"This isn't worth a straw!" shouted the señorito. "Away! Off with you! See here, master *Eagle*," he added, turning to the guitarist. "A real society dance. A polka, a waltz; anything. We're going to dance tightly clasped to each other, like the upper class folk."

The girls, upset by the wine, seized one another or stumbled into the arms of the young vineyard-toilers. All began to revolve to the sound of the guitar. The overseer and don Luis's acolytes accompanied the tune, marking time with the empty bottles or tapping the ground with their canes, laughing like children at this evidence of their musical skill.

María de la Luz felt herself dragged forth by the señorito, who seized her by one hand, at the same time clasping her around the waist. The girl refused to dance. Whirl about, while everything was going around and around before her eyes! . . . But at last she consented, giving herself up to her partner.

Luis perspired, wearied by the maiden's inertia. What a heavy girl! As he pressed against this helpless body his chest felt the contact of elastic protuberances. Mariquita let her head fall upon his shoulder, as if, overcome by the dizzying spectacle, she no longer cared to see. Only once did she draw herself up straight, to look at Luis, and a faint glimmer of revolt and protest shone in her eyes.

"Let me go, Rafael; this isn't proper."

Dupont burst into laughter.

"Rafael, she says! . . . Well, that *is* funny! The girl is pretty far gone! My name is Luis! . . ."

The girl's head drooped again upon his shoulder, as if she had not understood the young man's words.

Every moment she felt more and more overcome by the wine and the motion. With her eyes shut and her thoughts whirling around like a crazy wheel, she thought that she was suspended in emptiness, in a gloomy cavern, with no other support than the man's arms. If he let go, she would fall and fall without ever reaching the bottom. Instinctively she grasped her support.

Luis was no less overcome than his partner. He

breathed in gasps, suffocated by the weight of the girl.
He trembled at contact with her soft, pink arms, with the
perfume of her robust beauty, that seemed to gush forth
in a voluptuous stream from the low neck of her dress.
The breath from her lips caused the skin of his neck to
bristle, sending a shudder throughout his body. . . .
When, exhausted with fatigue, he brought Mariquita
back to her seat, the girl staggered, pale and with eyes
closed. She sighed and raised her hand to her forehead,
as if it pained her.

In the meantime the couples danced away with mad
shouting, jostling against one another, shoving against
others intentionally, with lurches that almost threw over
the spectators, forcing them to withdraw their chairs.

Two young vine-dressers began a quarrel, each tugging
at the arm of the same girl. Wine lighted their eyes
with a homicidal flame, and at length they went off to the
wine-press house in search of the pruning-knives—the
short, heavy machetes—that killed with a single blow.

The señorito barred their passage. What was this?
Killing themselves for the sake of dancing with a girl,
when so many of them were waiting for a partner? Silence, and let them continue with their good time. He
compelled them to shake hands and drink out of the same
glass.

The music had ceased. All eyes were turned anxiously toward that part of the terrace where the brawlers
were.

"On with the good time, I say," ordered Dupont, like
a bounteous tyrant. "Nothing's happened here."

Again the music resounded; the couples resumed their
dancing and the young man returned to his group.
Mariquita's chair was vacant. He looked around, but
could not see the girl anywhere.

Señor Fermín was absorbed in watching the agile fin-

gers of Pacorro, the Eagle, with all the admiration of
an old guitar-player. Nobody had noticed the withdrawal of María de la Luz.

Dupont entered the wine-press house, tip-toeing along,
opening the doors with feline caution, without knowing
why.

He went through the overseer's rooms. Nobody. He
thought that the door to Mariquita's room was closed,
but it yielded at the first thrust. The bed was unoccupied and the room in order, as if nobody had entered.
The same solitude in the kitchen. He gropingly crossed
the spacious room that served as the toilers' dormitory.
Not a soul! Then he thrust his head into the wine-press
department. The diffuse light from the heavens, penetrating through the windows, cast a few pale rays upon
the floor. Dupont, amid this silence, imagined that he
heard the sound of breathing—the slight stirring of some
one stretched upon the floor.

He went forward. His feet stumbled across some
sacks, and a body was lying upon them. As he kneeled
down to see better, he divined, by touch rather than sight,
María de la Luz, who had taken refuge hither. Doubtless she revolted against hiding in her own house in such
a shameful condition.

At the touch of Luis's hands, this flesh, sunk in the
stupor of intoxication, seemed to awake. The enchant-
ing body turned around; her eyes glistened for a moment,
struggling to remain open, and the burning mouth murmured something in the señorito's ears. He thought he
heard her say:

"Rafaé. . . . Rafaé! . . ."

But she said no more.

Her bare arms wound about Luis's neck.

María de la Luz fell deeper and deeper into the black

pit of unconsciousness, and as she descended she clutched
this support desperately, concentrating upon it every
atom of her will, leaving the rest of her body in insensible
abandon.

CHAPTER VIII

By the beginning of January the strike of the laborers had spread throughout the Jerez countryside. The farm-hands made common cause with the vineyard men. As agricultural labors were of little importance during the winter months, the landowners bore the conflict without impatience.

"They will surrender," they said. "It's a hard winter and hunger is widespread."

In the vineyards, the care of the vines was given over to the overseers and the toilers who had remained loyal to their employers, thus arousing the indignation of the strikers, who taunted them with accusations of treachery, threatening collective vengeance.

The wealthy class, despite their arrogant manners, betrayed a certain fear. As was their custom, they had made the Madrid newspapers comment upon the strike and paint it in somber colors, exaggerating it to the proportions of a national calamity.

The government officials were censured because of their neglect, but in such urgent terms that it appeared every rich man was besieged in his own home, defending himself with gun in hand against a wild, starving mob. The government, as usual, had sent an armed force to choke off the lamentations of these beggars of authority, and there arrived at Jerez reinforcements of the Civil Guard, two companies of line infantry and a troop of cavalry that joined the horsemen from the stallions' stable.

Decent folk, as Luis Dupont called them, smiled beatifically upon beholding so many red pantaloons upon the streets. The clanking of sabers over the sidewalk sounded like the best of music to their ears. As they entered their various clubs their souls expanded upon sight of the officers' uniforms around the tables.

Those who some weeks before were importuning the government with their wailing, as if they were at the point of death, strangled by those crowds that remained in the country with their arms crossed, not daring to enter Jerez, now appeared arrogant and boastful to the point of cruelty. They scoffed at the frowning faces of the strikers and at their eyes, which had the sickly squint of hunger and despair.

Moreover, the authorities believed that the moment had arrived in which they must impose their rule by fear, and the Civil Guard was arresting all who figured at the head of the workingmen's societies. Men were packed into jail every day.

"There are more than forty of them behind the bars already," announced the best informed at the evening meetings. "When the number has reached to a hundred or two, the whole matter will settle like a pool of oil."

At midnight, when the men left their club-rooms, they would find women in tattered coats or with their skirts raised to shelter their heads, huddling together and stretching out their hands.

"Señor, we haven't anything to eat. . . . Señor, we're dying of hunger. . . . I've three little ones and my husband, who is on strike, doesn't bring home any bread."

The gentlemen would laugh and hasten their steps. Let Salvatierra and the other preachers give them bread. And they gazed with almost amorous affection upon the soldiers that promenaded through the street.

"A curse on you!" roared the women in their despair.

"God grant that some day we poor are in the saddle! . . ."

Fermín Montenegro watched sadly the course of this silent conflict, which must surely come to a head with a terrible outbreak; but he watched from a distance, avoiding all intercourse with the rebels, since his master Salvatierra was no longer in Jerez. At the office, too, he maintained silence whenever in his presence the friends of don Pablo manifested the cruel desire for measures of reprisal that would terrify the toilers.

Since he had returned from Málaga his father, every time they met, counseled him to be very prudent. He must keep silent; after all, they both ate the bread of the Duponts and it wasn't right to side with the poor folk, even if they complained with good reason. Besides, for señor Fermín all human aspirations were summed up in don Fernando Salvatierra, and that man was away. They were detaining him at Madrid, under constant surveillance lest he return to Andalusia. And the Marchamalo overseer, with his don Fernando absent, considered the strike devoid of interest, and the strikers an army with neither chief nor banner: a mob that would perforce be decimated and sacrificed by the rich.

Fermín obeyed his father, holding prudently aloof. He made no reply to the gibes of his office mates who, knowing of his intimacy with Salvatierra, poked fun at the rebels so as to gain the favor of their employer. He avoided la plaza Nueva, where the strikers of the city would gather, motionless and silent, following with hostile glances the gentlemen who purposely passed by with their heads in the air and a defiant expression in their eyes.

Montenegro soon stopped thinking of the strike, attracted by other matters of greater interest.

One day, as he was leaving the office for his lunch at

the house where he was stopping, he met the steward of Marchamalo.

Rafael seemed to be waiting for him, leaning against one of the corners of the square, opposite the Dupont buildings. Fermín had not seen him for a long time. He seemed to have changed considerably; his features had become wan and his eyes were sunk in a dark circle. His country costume was black with dust; he wore it carelessly as if he had forgotten that proud carriage that caused him to be considered the most gallant of the country horsemen.

"Are you ill, Rafael? What's the matter?" exclaimed Montenegro.

"Troubles," replied the steward, laconically.

"I didn't see you at Marchamalo last Sunday, nor the previous one, either. Have you had a falling out with my sister? . . ."

"I've got something to talk over with you; and it'll take a long time—a long time!" said Rafael.

He couldn't discuss the matter there on the square; not at the boarding-house, either. What the steward had to say to him must be kept secret.

"Very good," said Fermín jestingly, guessing that it was a question of a lovers' quarrel. "But, my sad fellow, since I've got to eat, let's go to the *Montañés*, and there you can let out all the little griefs that are crushing you, while I feed the inner man."

At the *Montañés* restaurant, as they passed the main hall of the establishment, they heard the strumming of a guitar, the clapping of palms and the joyous shouts of women.

"That's young Luis Dupont," the waiter told them. "He's there with some friends and a 'swell' woman they brought from Seville. The fun's beginning now. . . .

There'll be a gay old time until to-morrow morning, at least."

The two friends sought out the most distant room, so that the noise of the festivities should not interrupt their conversation.

Montenegro ordered his lunch and the waiter brought the table into that room, which smelled of wine and seemed like a berth, so scantily was it furnished. Shortly afterwards he returned, carrying a large tray filled with glasses. It was a present from don Luis.

"The señorito," explained the waiter, "learned that you were here and he sends you this. He also says that the gentlemen may order whatever they please, and that it's all paid for."

Fermín requested him to tell don Luis that he would see him as soon as he had finished eating. The waiter closed the door, and Fermín was left alone with Rafael.

"Come, now," he invited, pointing to the plates. "Try some of this."

"I won't eat," answered Rafael.

"Won't eat? So . . . you'll live on air, I suppose, like all lovers. . . . Well, you'll drink, at least!"

Rafael made a strange grimace, as if surprised at the superfluousness of the question. And without raising his glance from the table he began to drain the glasses before him ravenously, one after the other.

"Fermín," he soon said, gazing at his friend with reddened eyes. "I'm crazy . . . stark mad."

"I can see that," answered Montenegro phlegmatically, without interrupting his meal.

"Fermín, it seems as if a demon were whispering the most atrocious barbarities into my ear. If your father weren't my godfather, and if you weren't who you are, I would have killed your sister, María de la Luz, days ago. I swear it to you by this, by my best friend, the only inheritance from my father."

And with a great creaking of springs he opened a knife with well-worn handles, imprinting a fierce kiss upon the smooth blade whose designs were colored by the reddish rust.

"Man, you don't mean all of that," said Montenegro, looking fixedly at his friend.

He had dropped his fork and a red cloud passed over his forehead. But this hostile attitude lasted only a second.

"Bah!" he added. "You certainly *are* crazy. And whoever takes any stock in what you say is even crazier."

Rafael suddenly burst into weeping. At last his eyes could give passage to the tears that rushed to them; they rolled down his cheeks and fell into the wine.

"It's true, Fermín. I'm crazy. I brag and brag, and when it comes down to the fine point, I'm a coward. Just look at my condition. A child could knock me over. Why kill Mariquita? I wish I had the courage for it. Then I'd kill you, too, and all of us would be at rest."

The distant strumming of the guitar and the voices that interrupted its rhythm, applauding the skill of a dancer, seemed to accompany the tears that fell from the youth's eyes.

"But let's hear your story!" exclaimed Fermín impatiently. "What's this all about? Speak, and stop your crying, for you look like a pious woman in the procession of the Holy Interment. What's the trouble between you and Mariquita? . . ."

"She doesn't love me any more!" cried the steward in accents of despair. "She's through with me! We've split, and she don't care to see me any more! . . ."

Montenegro smiled. And was that all? Mere lovers' quarrel; maidens' whims, feigning anger so as to enliven the monotony of a long courtship! The ill wind would blow over. He knew all about it from hearsay. He expressed himself with the skepticism of an experienced young man, in *English* fashion, as he said. He was opposed to the ideal love affairs that lasted for years and were part of the country's traditions. He had never had any love affair in Jerez. He was content to satisfy his desires with whatever he found good from time to time.

"This always satisfies the body," he continued. "But relations for good, with sighs, griefs and jealous fits! Never! My time is needed for other matters."

And Fermín, in a jesting tone, tried to console his friend. This bad squall would pass. Mere women's caprices—getting angry and pretending displeasure so that they'll be all the more loved! On the day he least expected it he would find María de la Luz coming to him, telling him it had all been a joke, meant to test his affection, and that she loved him more than ever.

But the youth shook his head in token of denial.

"No. She doesn't love me. It's all over, and I'm going to die."

He told Montenegro how his love affair had come to an end. She called him one night for a conversation at the grill, and in a voice and with an expression the recollection of which still brought shudders to the poor fellow, she announced that all was over between them. Christ! What news to receive so suddenly! . . .

Rafael clutched at the bars to keep from falling. Then there followed everything: entreaties, threats, tears; but she was inflexible, smiling in a fearful fashion, refusing to continue their relations. Ah! Women! . . .

"Yes, my boy," corroborated Fermín. "A shameless

tribe. Although it's here a matter of my sister, I make no exception of her. That's why I take from them what I need and flee from the rest. . . . But what excuse did Mariquita offer you? . . ."

"That she's stopped loving me; that her affection for me has suddenly gone out. That she hasn't the slightest trace of feeling for me and doesn't care to lie by feigning to care for me. . . . As if love could go out in a jiffy, like a light! . . ."

Rafael then recalled the conclusion of his last visit. Wearied with supplicating, with weeping, clutching against the bars of the grating, kneeling like a child, his despair caused him to burst into threats. Fermín must pardon him, but in that moment he had felt capable of the crime. The girl, tired with his prayers, frightened by his curses, had suddenly closed the window. And that was the condition of things at the moment!

Twice he had gone, during the day, to Marchamalo, under the pretext of seeing señor Fermín; but no sooner did she hear his horse coming along the road than María de la Luz ran into hiding.

Montenegro listened to him meditatively.

"Can she have another sweetheart?" he asked. "Can she have fallen in love with somebody else?"

"No. Not that," Rafael hastened to reply, as if this conviction served him as a consolation. "I thought the same thing myself at first, and I could already see myself in jail at Jerez and afterwards in the penitentiary. I'll kill the man who takes my Mariquita away from me. But, ay! Nobody has taken her away from me; it's she herself that's going. . . . I spent days watching Marchamalo tower from a distance. The glasses I've gulped down in the road tavern! And how they turned to poison whenever I saw anybody descend or climb the vineyard hill! . . . I've spent whole nights stretched between

the vines, with my gun at my side, ready to shoot full of
mold-shot the first fellow who'd approach the grating.
. . . But I saw only the dogs. The window was closed.
And in the meantime the Matanzuela grange was without a head, although with this strike going on I'm not
very much missed. I'm never there now; poor *Zarandilla* takes charge of everything; if the master ever found
it out, he'd discharge me. I've got eyes and ears only to
watch your sister, and I'm positive there's no other fellow—that she loves nobody else. I'm almost ready to
wager that she still has a little affection left for me.
Now judge whether I haven't gone mad! . . . But the
cursed girl flees at sight of me, and says she no longer
loves me."

"But have you done anything to rouse her resentment,
Rafael? May she not be offended at something you've
committed?"

"No, not that, either. I'm more innocent than the
child Jesus and the lamb he has at his side. Ever since
I've been going with your sister I haven't looked at any
other girl. They all appear ugly to me, and Mariquita
knows it. The last night that I spoke with her, when I
begged her to forgive me, without knowing what for,
and asked her whether I had offended her in any way,
the poor girl started to cry like the very Magdalen. Your
sister knows full well that I haven't been unfaithful to
her by a hair's breadth. She herself admitted it: 'Poor
Rafael! You're so good! Go and forget me. You'll be
unhappy with me.' And then she closed the window in
my face. . . ."

As he related this the poor fellow began to groan,
while his friend, who had by now finished his meal,
leaned his forehead pensively upon his hand.

"Then, to tell the truth, boy," murmured Fermín, "I
can't see through this puzzle. Mariquilla is leaving you,

yet she has no other sweetheart; she pities you, tells you that you're good, showing that she still has some affection for you, and then closes the window upon you. It takes the very devil to understand the women! And what evil souls the wretches possess at times! . . ."

The din in the room where the feast was being given grew louder, and the voice of a woman, sharp and with a metallic quiver, reached the ears of the two friends.

> She left me . . . the evil gipsy!
> At the moment I loved her most. . . .

Rafael could listen to no more. The popular song tore at his very soul with its ingenuous sadness. He burst into tears and cried like a child, as if the couplet summed up his entire history—as if it had been composed after he had been dismissed from that grating behind which was his life's happiness.

"Do you hear, Fermín?" he asked, between sobs. "I'm the fellow in that song. The same thing is happening to me as happened to the poor chap of the couplet. People have pity on a puppy, and love him, and don't desert him, and his cries inspire pity; and here I am, a man, a creature of God—out into the street with you! If I once loved you, I don't love you any longer! Burst with grief! . . . Christ! It's a miracle I haven't died already! . . ."

For a long while they were silent. Engrossed in their thoughts, they no longer heard the tumult of the festivities and the woman's voice continuing the popular couplets.

"Fermín," said the steward at length, "you are the only one who can settle this matter."

This was why he had waited for him at the door of the office. He knew Fermín's powerful influence upon the rest of the family. María de la Luz respected him even more than her father, and his wisdom was much spoken of everywhere.

His education in England, and the praises of the overseer, who looked upon his son as an intellect almost as great as his master's, influenced the girl, who mingled with her sisterly affection a large share of admiration. Rafael did not dare to speak with his godfather; he was afraid of him. But he placed his entire faith in Fermín and hoped that he would arrange everything.

"Whatever you tell her to do, she'll do. . . . Fermin-illo, don't forsake me; help me out. You're my patron saint; I'd gladly place you upon an altar and light candles before you and pray a litany to you. Fermín, my little saint, don't abandon me; defend me. Soften that heart of stone; hold me firmly, or else I'll fall and go to prison or to the madhouse."

Montenegro ridiculed the whimpering exaggerations of his friend.

"Very good, man; I'll do what I can, but stop your crying and all this praying, for you remind me of my employer don Pablo, when they speak to him of God. I'll see Mariquita; I'll speak to her about you; I'll tell the bad girl what she deserves. There! Are you satisfied? . . ."

Rafael dried his tears and smiled with childish naïveté, showing his finely chiseled teeth of dazzling white. But his happiness was most impatient. When was Fermín thinking of going to Marchamalo?

"Man, I'll go to-morrow. We're very busy at the office with the closing of our books for the year. The English accounts are giving me a great deal of bother."

The youth made a grimace of dissatisfaction. To-morrow! . . . One night more of sleeplessness, of bemoaning his misfortune, of cruel uncertainty, not knowing whether to expect any results.

Montenegro laughed at the steward's unhappy frame of mind. What love made of men! He felt like giving this chap a spanking, as if he were an overgrown, petulant child.

"No, Fermín; I ask it for your own good. Do something for me; go at once, and you'll release a soul from agony. They won't say anything to you at the office. Those men are fond of you; you're their favorite."

And he besieged the girl's brother with ardent prayers, with affectionate words, to visit his sister at once. Montenegro yielded, conquered by the youth's anxiety. He would go to Marchamalo that very afternoon; he would lie to the superintendent, saying that his father was ill. Don Ramón was a good fellow and would wink the other eye.

Impatient Rafael then reminded him of how short January afternoons were, and the necessity of acting at once.

Fermín summoned the waiter, who was astonished at the parsimony of the two friends, and urged them to order more. It was all paid for! Don Luis had an open account! . . .

Rafael went directly to the street, afraid lest his master see him with reddened eyes. Fermín thrust his head through the doorway of the room where the feast was being given, and after having accepted a glass from Dupont hurriedly escaped from the latter, who tried to seize him by the lapel and keep him there.

Before the afternoon was half over Fermín arrived in Marchamalo. Rafael had taken him on the haunches of his horse. His impatience caused him to move his heels nervously, and he spurred the animal.

"You're going to kill the poor beast, you savage!"

shouted Fermín, pressing his chest to the horseman's back. "The two of us make a heavy weight!"

Rafael, however, was thinking only of the approaching interview.

"I wish I could take you on the very chariot of Elijah, Ferminillo, so that you could see the girl as soon as possible."

They stopped at a roadside inn, near the vineyard.

"Do you wish me to wait for you?" asked the steward. "I'll wait here for you gladly, until the Day of Judgment."

He was anxious to know the girl's attitude. But Fermín did not desire him to wait. He wished to spend the night at the vineyard. And he continued the way on foot, while Rafael shouted after him that he would come to see him the following day.

When señor Fermín noticed his son approaching, he asked him with a certain anxiety whether any trouble had occurred at Jerez. "Nothing, father." He had come to spend the night with the family, since they had been given leave at the office, through lack of work. The old man was gratified with the visit, yet he could not shake off the uneasiness that his son's arrival had caused in him.

"When I saw you coming I imagined that there was trouble in Jerez; but if nothing's happening there as yet, be sure it will break out very soon. Even from here, I know all about it; there's always a friend from one of the other vineyards that brings me a breath of what the strikers are planning. And then, at the tavern, the muleteers repeat what they hear at the meetings."

And the overseer spoke to his son of the great mass-meeting that the workingmen were going to hold on the following day upon the plains of Caulina. Nobody knew who had given the orders, but the call was being circulated from mouth to mouth through the countryside

and the mountain district, and thousand upon thousands
of men would get together, arriving from as far off as
the province of Málaga—all who earned their living in
the Jerez district.

"A genuine revolution, my son. And at the back of
it all is a stranger, a young fellow they call the
Madrileño, who speaks of slaying the rich and dividing
up all the city's treasures. The people seem to have gone
crazy; they all believe that to-morrow victory will be
theirs and that poverty will be a thing of the past. The
Madrileño uses Salvatierra's name, as if working under
his orders, and many persons say, just as if they had
seen him, that don Fernando is concealed in Jerez and
that he'll show up the moment the revolution breaks
out. What do you know about this? . . ."

Fermín shook his head incredulously. Salvatierra had
written to him a few days before, and had mentioned
nothing about returning to Jerez. He doubted very
much whether he had come. In addition, this attempt
at an insurrection seemed unlikely. It would turn out
to be one more of the many alarms invented by the despair of the starving workers. To attempt an invasion
of the city while the troops were quartered in it would
be sheer madness.

"You'll see, father; when they get together at Caulina
the whole thing will resolve itself into shouts and threats,
similar to their secret meetings. And as to don Fernando, don't you worry. I am certain that he is in
Madrid. He isn't so foolish as to compromise himself
in a wild plan of this sort."

"That's just what I think, my son; but whatever happens, you try not to get mixed up to-morrow with these
madmen, if they should actually get as far as the city."

Fermín looked in all directions, seeking his sister. At
last María de la Luz came out of the house, smiling at

her brother and receiving his visit with exclamations of happy surprise. The young man gazed at her intently. Nothing! If Rafael had not spoken to him, he could not have divined any evidence of their love affair's sad breaking off.

More than an hour elapsed without his being able to talk alone with his sister. In Fermín's fixed glances the maiden seemed to guess something of his thoughts. She tried to appear impassive, but her countenance would suddenly turn as pale and transparent as wax, and as suddenly flush with a wave of blood.

Señor Fermín walked down the hillside, to meet some muleteers that were passing by on the road. His sharp sight, characteristic of country folk, had recognized them from above. They were friends of his, and he wished to learn from them what was being said at the secret gatherings regarding the mass-meeting of the following day.

When brother and sister were left alone their glances met, amid embarrassing silence.

"I've got something to talk over with you, Mariquita," said the young man at last, resolutely.

"Then begin whenever you please, Fermín," she replied, in calm tones. "I could see, the moment you came, that something was on your mind."

"No; not here. Father might return, and what we have to discuss requires time and calm. Let's take a walk."

Brother and sister began to stroll downhill, on the slope opposite the highway. They descended between the vines, behind the tower, toward a row of prickly-pears that bounded the vast vineyard on this side.

María de la Luz tried several times to halt, not caring to walk so far. She wished to speak as soon as possible so as to come out of her oppressing uncertainty. But her brother refused to begin the conversation as long as they trod upon soil that was under their father's supervision.

They stopped at the row of prickly-pears, near a wide opening through which could be seen a dense olive-grove, whose branches were gilded by the setting sun.

Fermín had his sister sit down upon the hillock, and planting himself in front of her, he began, with a gentle smile intended to win her confidence:

"Now let's see, my light-headed girl: you're going to tell me why you broke with Rafael; why you dismissed him like a dog, inflicting such grief that the poor fellow's ready to die."

María de la Luz tried to treat the entire matter as a jest, but she was pale and her smile was as rigid as a sad grimace.

"Because I don't love him; because I've tired of him. There! He's a simpleton, and he bores me. Haven't I the right to love whatever man I please? . . ."

Fermín chided her like a rebellious child. She was lying: her face showed it. She couldn't hide the fact she still loved Rafael. There was something behind all this that he must know, for the good of both lovers, to bring them together again. All this talk of being bored was a pretense! And this swaggering air with which Mariquita expressed herself in attempting to justify her break with Rafael was likewise assumed! She wasn't so bad as all that; she couldn't treat her former sweetheart so cruelly. What! Was this the way to break off a love affair that had begun in childhood? Was this a way to send off a fellow after having had him for years and years, so to speak, tied to her apron strings? There was something inexplicable to him about her conduct, and she must tell. Wasn't he her only brother, and the best of her friends? Didn't she confide to him all the

things she feared to tell her father, because of the awe
with which the latter inspired her? . . .

But the girl was unresponsive to her brother's affectionate, persuasive tone.

"Nothing of the sort," she replied vehemently,
straightening out as if she were about to arise. "You've
invented the whole business. The simple truth of the
matter is that I'm wearied with the courtship, that I
don't care to marry—that I intend to spend my life beside father and you. Who is there better than you?
No more lovers!"

The brother received these words with an expression
of incredulity. Another lie! How had she so soon tired
of the man she loved so much? What powerful cause
could so quickly have undone their affection? . . . Ah,
Mariquita! He wasn't such a simpleton as to swallow
nonsensical explanations.

And as the girl raised her voice to hide her perturbation, repeating vehemently that she was mistress of her
will and could do as she pleased, Fermín began to lose
patience.

"Ah, false maiden! Heart of stone! Harsh soul!
Do you imagine that you can drop a man whenever you
please, after having entertained him for years at the
grating, maddening him with words of honey, vowing
that you loved him more than life itself? For much
less some women have been stabbed in the heart. . . .
Shout all you wish; repeat that you will do as you please.
But I am thinking of that poor fellow who, while you're
speaking like a shameless hussy, is going about in dis-
traction, crying like a child, despite the fact that he's the
manliest man in all Jerez district. And all because of
you . . . because of you, who act worse than a gipsy!
Because of you, fickle girl! . . ."

Roused to a high pitch by his anger, he spoke of Ra-

fael's sadness, of the weeping countenance with which
the steward had implored his aid, of the anguish in which
he was awaiting the result of his mediation. But he
could speak no more. María de la Luz, passing suddenly from resistance to collapse, had burst into tears,
and her groans and tears increased with every word that
Fermín uttered in his tale of her lover's despair.

"Oh, the poor fellow!" moaned the girl, forgetting all
dissimulation. "Oh, Rafael of my soul! . . ."

The brother's voice became tender.

"You love him. Don't you see? You love him. You
yourself reveal it. Why make him suffer, then? Why
this obstinacy, that plunges him into despair and causes
you tears?"

And the youth, bending over his sister, alternately besieged her with entreaties or shook her shoulders violently, filled with a presentiment of how serious the secret
was that Mariquita was hiding, and that he must learn
at all costs.

The maiden was silent. At the sound of her brother's
voice she sobbed, as if each word penetrated into her soul,
causing it to contract with the pain of the open wound;
but she did not part her lips; she feared to speak too
much, and she continued to weep, filling the afternoon
silence with lamentations.

"Speak!" commanded Fermín imperiously. "Say
something. You love Rafael; you love him perhaps more
than ever. Why, then, do you leave him? Why do you
send him away? That's what interests me; your silence
frightens me. Why? Why? Speak, woman; speak, or
I'm liable to kill you."

And he gave María de la Luz a rude shove. The
maiden, as if she could no longer sustain herself under
the burden of her emotion, had fallen prostrate upon the
ground, her face hidden in her hands.

The sun was beginning to set. The cerise-colored disk could be seen between the foliage of the olive grove, as through a green jalousie. Its last beams, almost on a level with the soil, colored with an orange splendor the colonnade of olive-tree trunks, the clumps of bushes and the outline of the maiden stretched upon the ground. The sharp pellicule of the prickly-pears bristled like a luminous skin.

"Speak, Mariquita," roared Fermín's voice. "Tell me why you act so. Tell me, as you value your life! Can't you see you're driving me mad! Tell your brother, your Fermín!"

The voice of the maiden issued from that extended form, thin, shameful, distant.

"I don't love him . . . because I love him very much. I can't love him, because I love him too much to make him unhappy."

And as if after these confused words she gathered courage, Mariquita arose, gazing fixedly at Fermín through her tear-filled eyes.

Let him strike her, let him kill her; but she did not wish to speak to Rafael again. She had sworn many a time that if she should ever consider herself unworthy of him, she would forsake him, even if she would destroy her soul by so doing. It was a crime to reward that man's love by introducing into his future existence something that might insult Rafael, who was so good, so noble, so loving.

There was a protracted silence.

The sun had disappeared. Now the black foliage of the olive grove stood silhouetted against a violet sky, over a delicate rim of gold on the horizon.

Fermín was silent, as if he were terrified by contact with the mysterious truth, whose approach he could feel.

"According to what you say," he began with solemn

calm, "you consider yourself unworthy of Rafael. You flee because there is something in your life that might bring shame upon him, and make him unhappy."

"Yes," she replied, without lowering her glance.

"And what is that? Speak. I believe a brother is entitled to know."

María de la Luz again hid her head between her hands. Never; she would not say a word; she had said enough. It was an ordeal beyond her strength. If Fermín loved her even a little bit, he must respect her silence, leave her in peace, for she had much need of it. And the clamor of her weeping rent the silence of the twilight anew.

Montenegro was as upset as his sister. After his access of indignation he felt weak, softened, overwhelmed by that mystery which he had been able only to discern dimly. He spoke very gently, even humbly, recalling to the young girl the intimate affection that joined their lives.

They had not known their mother, and Fermín had filled for the little girl the void which that woman had left when she died. They could scarcely recall her sad, generous features. How many times, at an age when other children are lulled to rest in a warm lap, had he been a mother to her, rocking her while he was exhausted for lack of sleep, putting up with her crying and her cuffing. How many times, during the days of their poverty, when their father could not find work, he had stifled his hunger in order to give his sister the bread that had been given to him by other children, his play-mates! . . . When she was suffering the ills of infancy, her brother, who barely reached to the edge of the bed, had watched over her, and had even slept with her without fear of contagion. They were more than brother and sister; they had spent half of their lives together, in

contact from head to foot, mingling their breath and
their perspiration. Neither of them knew what in their
bodies was their own or had been assimilated from the
other.

Later, when they had grown up, this fraternal love
had increased, welded by the griefs of a sad childhood.
He gave no thought to marrying, as if his mission upon
earth were to live at the side of his sister, seeing her
happy with a good, noble fellow like Rafael, devoting
his life to her children. . . . Mariquita had no secrets
from Fermín. She would run to him, in moments of
doubt, sooner than to her father. . . . And now, the
ingrate, as if her soul had suddenly hardened, allowed
him to suffer while she looked impassively on, without
revealing to him this mystery of her life!"

"Ah, evil heart! Wicked sister! . . . How little I
knew you!"

These reproaches from her brother, spoken in a
choked voice, as if he were on the verge of tears, produced a greater effect upon María than all the threats
and violent actions of before.

"Fermín. . . . I desired to remain mute and save you
suffering, for I know that the truth will hurt you. Ay,
Jesus! To wreck the souls of the two men I love
best! . . ."

But since her brother insisted, she would confide in
him, and let happen what God pleased. . . . She had
arisen again, and spoke without a gesture, almost without
moving her lips, with her gaze lost in the horizon, as if
she were dreaming, and relating the history of another
person.

Night was beginning to fall and to Fermín it seemed
that all the darkness of twilight had crept into his brain,
clouding his thought and plunging it into the somnolence
of a painful stupor. An intense, paralyzing cold, as if

from a tomb, pierced his back. It was the soft evening
breeze, but to Fermín it seemed an icy blast, a glacial
jet that came from the North Pole for him, only for him.

María de la Luz continued her calm account, as if she
were relating the misfortune of another woman. Her
words summoned rapid images to her brother's thoughts.
Fermín could behold everything: the general intoxication
of that last night of the vintage—the girl's drunkenness
—her collapse like an inert body into the corner of the
wine-press house, and then the arrival of the señorito to
take advantage of her condition.

"Wine! The cursed wine!" cried María de la Luz
angrily, placing the blame for her misfortune upon the
golden liquid.

"Yes, wine," repeated Fermín.

And there came to his mind the figure of Salvatierra,
and his anathema against the maleficent divinity that
regulated all the actions and affections of a people that
was enslaved to it.

His sister's words brought vividly before his eyes the
horror of her awakening, after the sad illusion of intoxication had disappeared; the indignation with which
she repelled the man she did not love, and who seemed
more repugnant than ever to her after his facile conquest.

All was over for María de la Luz. The firmness of
her speech showed this fully. She could not now belong
to the man she loved. She must appear cruel, must
feign repulsion, and like a light-headed coquette make
him suffer, rather than tell him the truth.

She was dominated by the prejudices of the common
woman who confuses love with physical virginity. A
woman could be the wife of a man only if she brought
to him as a token of submission the integrity of her
body. She must be like her mother, like all the good

women she knew. The virginity of the flesh was as
important as love; and when that was lost, even through
no fault of the woman, against her will, she must resign
herself, bow her head, bid farewell to happiness and
continue on life's journey alone and sad, while her unhappy lover wandered off in a different direction, seeking another urn of love, which should be sealed and
inviolate.

In the eyes of María de la Luz the evil was irremediable. She loved Rafael; the steward's despair height-
ened her passion; but never should she speak to him
again. She was content to be thought a cruel woman,
rather than deceive the man she loved. What did Fermín say to this? Should she not repel her sweetheart,
even if it broke her heart?

Fermín remained silent, his chin against his chest and
his eyes closed, as motionless as death. He looked like
a standing corpse. Suddenly there awoke in him the
human beast that stamps and roars before misfortune.

"Ah, you unchaste bitch!" he stormed. "Evil woman!
You . . . !"

And the most grievous insult to woman's virtue was
discharged from his lips against María de la Luz. He
advanced a step, with his gaze wandering and his fist
raised. The girl, as if the painful revelation had plunged
her into a torpor, did not shut her eyes or move her head
to avoid the blow.

Fermín's hand, however, fell to his side without striking her. It had been a flash of ferocity; nothing more.
Montenegro recognized that he had no right to punish
his sister. Through the blood-colored mist that passed
before his eyes he thought he could see the gleam of
Salvatierra's blue spectacles and his cold smile of infinite
tenderness. What would the master do in his place? . . .
Pardon, undoubtedly; enfold the victim in the boundless

commiseration that the sins of the weak inspired in him. Besides, the wine was the chief culprit here: that golden poison, that amber-colored demon, scattering madness and crime with its perfume.

Fermín was for a long while silent.

"Not a word of this to father," he said at last. "It would kill the poor old man."

Mariquita nodded assent.

"If you should see Rafael," he continued, "not a word to him, either. I know him. The poor fellow would be sent to prison on your account."

The admonition was unneeded. To avoid Rafael's vengeance, she had lied, pretending her cruel fickleness.

Fermín continued to speak in somber tone, yet imperiously, without admitting of reply. She would have to marry Luis Dupont. . . . She abhorred him, did she? She had shunned him ever since that terrible night, had she? . . . Well, this was the only way out. No señorito could with impunity tamper with his family's honor. If she did not marry him for love she would at least tolerate him through a sense of duty. Luis himself would seek her out and beg her hand.

"I hate him! I detest him!" cried Mariquita. "Let him not come. I don't care to see him! . . ."

But her protests were shattered against her brother's unbending will. She was mistress over her affections, but above these was the honor of the family. To remain a spinster, concealing her dishonor, with the cold consolation of having deceived Rafael, might satisfy her. But what of him, her brother? How could he endure meeting Luis Dupont continually, without demanding reparation for the outrage he had committed, and with the feeling that the young blade was inwardly laughing at the deed, every time they encountered each other.

"Silence, Mariquita," he counseled harshly. "Silence and obedience. Since you have been unable to take care of yourself as a woman, at least let your brother defend the honor of the family."

Night had fallen and the brother and sister walked up the hill back to their house. It was a slow, painful ascent; their legs trembled, their ears buzzed, and their chests heaved as if a huge burden oppressed them. It seemed that they were bearing upon their shoulders a giant corpse—something that would weigh upon the rest of their existence.

They passed a bad night. During the evening they suffered the torture of having to smile at their poor father and follow his conversation about the events that were being hatched for the next day; and Fermín was forced to express his opinion as to the mass-meeting of the strikers upon the plains of Caulina.

The young man could not sleep. He could divine Mariquita's sleeplessness upon the other side of the thin wall; he could hear the continuous tossing about of her body in the bed, and her outbursts of violent sobbing.

Shortly after daybreak Fermín left Marchamalo, bound for Jerez, without taking leave of his father and sister. As he came down to the main road the first person he met, in the vicinity of the roadside inn, was Rafael, upon his horse, planted like a Centaur in the middle of the highway.

"Seeing that you come so early, you must have good news for me!" exclaimed the steward with an ingenuous confidence that almost drew tears from Fermín. "Open that mouth of yours, Ferminillo. What's the result of your mission? . . ."

Montenegro had to employ a violent effort to lie, concealing his perturbation beneath vague words.

The affair was progressing so-so; not at all badly.

Rafael could rest easy; mere woman's whims, without any foundation whatsoever. He would insist that everything be straightened out. The important thing was that Mariquita loved him the same as ever. He could be certain of this.

What a radiant, joyous expression appeared on the countenance of the steward, who beamed like an angel in heaven!

"Here, Ferminillo; jump up on the horse's haunches, my clever fellow! My brainy Ferminillo! I'm going to take you to Jerez quicker than you can say Jesus. You've got more talent, more eloquence, and more sense in that head of yours than all the lawyers of Cádiz, Seville and even Madrid put together! . . . I knew what door I was knocking at when I sought out your help! . . ."

The horse galloped along, spurred on by the steward. The happy peasant felt that he must dash along, take deep breaths of air, and sing to give vent to his joy, while Fermín, behind him, was almost weeping to see how joyous the innocent fellow was, singing couplets to his sweetheart, as if thanks to her brother she was once again his. In order to keep his position upon the horse's haunches Fermín had to grasp the steward's belt tightly; he did this, however, with a certain remorse, as if ashamed of the contact with this kind, simple-hearted being whose confidence he was forced to deceive.

They parted just outside of Jerez. Rafael went off to the farmhouse. He desired to be there, since he had been notified of what was afoot on the Plains of Caulina.

"There's to be a great time, with plenty for all. They say that to-day everything's going to be divided up, and that they're to set fire to the whole city, and that more heads will be cut than in a battle with the Moors. . . . I'm off to Matanzuela, and the first fellow that shows

up with evil intentions will be received with a bullet.
After all, the master is the master, and that's what
don Luis has me there for: to guard his interests."

It was an added torment for Fermín to behold the
pride with which the youth left—the firm tranquillity
with which he spoke of risking his life in combat with
any who dared make the slightest attempt against his
master's property. Ah! If this innocent, spirited fellow knew what *he* knew! . . .

Fermín spent the entire day at the office working,
with his thoughts far, far away; he translated his letters
mechanically, without paying any heed to the sense of
the words, and wrote down numbers like an automaton.

At times he would raise his head, remaining motionless and staring at don Pablo Dupont through the open
door of his private office. The head of the firm was engaged in discussion with don Ramón and other gentlemen—wealthy dealers who arrived with a certain air of
fear, yet soon becoming reassured and not long after
that laughing loudly, after listening to the millionaire's
vehement words.

Montenegro gave no attention to the discussion, despite
the fact that don Pablo's voice, high-pitched with anger,
from time to time rang through the office. They must
be speaking of the mass-meeting at Caulina; word had
come from the country to the city.

Several times, when Dupont had been left alone in his
study, the employee was tempted to enter . . . but he
restrained himself. No; not there. He must speak with
him alone. He knew the man's violent character. The
surprising news would cause him to explode into shouting, and the entire office force would hear everything.

Late that afternoon Fermín, after having wandered
a long while about the streets, so as to allow some time
between his departure from the office and his visit to his

employer, directed himself to the widow Dupont's ostentatious hotel.

He walked through the door and the archway with the ease of an old employee of the firm. For a moment he paused in the patio, amid its white arcades and its clumps of plantain trees and palms. In the center of one of the galleries played a water-fountain, falling into a deep basin. The fountain aspired to monumental proportions; it was a heap of stalactites forming a vaulted grotto, within which was lodged the Virgin of Lourdes, executed in white marble. It was a mediocre statue, with the prim exterior of French sculpture, which the proprietor of the hotel looked upon as a masterpiece of art.

Fermín had only to announce himself, whereupon he was led to the master's study. A servant parted the curtains of the windows so as to admit the afternoon light. Don Pablo, leaning against the wall, was stooping before a telephone, with the receiver to his ear. He motioned his employee to take a seat, and Fermín, sinking into a chair, allowed his glances to wander about the room. This was the first time he had been there.

A spacious apartment finished in gilded wood-carving, ornamented with the head of St. Peter and the pontifical coats-of-arms, contained the most glorious diploma of the firm—the Brief presenting the papal benediction to all the Duponts in the hour of their death, down to the fourth generation. Then, in other rooms no less dazzling, appeared all the distinctions conferred upon don Pablo, as honorable as they were sacred: parchments with huge seals or inscriptions in red, blue or black; titles as Knight Commander of the Order of St. Gregory, of the *Pro Ecclesia et Pontifice,* and of the Piana; diplomas as Knight Hospitaller of St. John and of the Holy Sepulcher. The letters that bore the cross of Carlos III and

of Isabel the Catholic, granted after their visit to the
warehouses of the Duponts, hung upon the obscurest
walls, placed in less attractive frames, with the modesty
that civil power must display before the representatives
of God—yielding place, as if abashed, to all the honorary
titles invented by the Church and which, without a single
omission, had been showered upon don Pablo.

Dupont had refused of Rome only the title of nobility.
His friends there placed at his disposal all the pomp of
heraldry: he could have been a Count, Marquis, Duke—
whatever he pleased. The Holy Father would have
made him even a Prince, by the grace of God; and as for
the title, if it didn't satisfy him, all he had to do was
to lay hands upon any of the innumerable saints in the
calendar.

But doña Elvira's son obstinately refused this distinction. The Church above all! . . . But historic nobility
was also the work of God. And proud of his mother's
lineage, he would smile ironically upon speaking of the
papal nobility, scorning the industrial heads and the
newly rich who flaunted Roman titles. Later, there
would be solicited for him the glorious, established mar-
quisate of San Dionisio that had been without succession
since the death of his famous uncle Terreroel.

Don Pablo, leaving the telephone, greeted Fermín, and
with a gesture prevented his rising from the seat.

"What is it, my boy? Do you bring news? Do you
know anything about the mass-meeting at Caulina? . . .
They've just been telling me that groups are pouring in
from every direction. There are about three thousand
of them already."

Montenegro appeared indifferent. He was not interested in the mass-meeting. He had come on another
matter entirely.

"I'm glad that you're indifferent," said don Pablo,

sitting down before his desk, at the foot of the papal Brief. "You've always been somewhat *green;* you know that I understand you, and I'm pleased to note that you're not mixed up in any of these scrapes. I tell you this because I'm fond of you, and because these other fellows are going to get a drubbing—an awful drubbing."

And he rubbed his hands, as if rejoicing in anticipation of the punishment that the rebels were going to suffer.

"You, who so much admire Salvatierra, your father's good friend, may congratulate yourself upon the fact that he's not at present in Jerez. Because if he were, this would be his last exploit. . . . But let's get down to business, Ferminillo. What brings you here? . . ."

Dupont looked intently at his employee, who commenced to explain himself with a certain timidity. He knew the long-standing affection which don Pablo and all his family felt for that of the poor overseer of Marchamalo. It was a lordly, magnanimous fondness that they, poor and humble, could not appreciae too highly. Besides, Fermín admired his employer's character: his piety, incapable of compromising with vice or injustice. That was why, in a moment of extreme difficulty for his family, Fermín came to him, in search of advice and moral support.

Dupont stared at Montenegro with widened eyes, telling himself that only something of extreme importance could have brought his visitor.

"Very well," he said, impatiently. "Let's get to the point and not lose any time. Remember, this is a very important day. I'm liable to be called on the telephone any moment."

Fermín remained with lowered head, hesitating, with a dolorous expression, as if his words burned his tongue. At last he began the account of what had happened at Marchamalo on the last night of the vintage.

The irascible, impetuous, fulminating character of Dupont seemed to swell with anger during the narrative, until at the close of the tale it exploded thunderously.

His egotism centered his first thoughts upon himself and what this attack meant to the honor of his house. Moreover, he felt wounded by his cousin's lack of respect, affirming that in this indecent crime there was an element of profanation of his own person.

"Such abominations, and at Marchamalo!" he exclaimed, bounding from his chair. "The tower of the Duponts; my house, whither I often take my family, converted into a den of vice! The demon of impurity indulging in his sins within two paces of the chapel, of God's house, wherein wise priests have pronounced the most beautiful sentiments in the world! . . ."

He was stifled by indignation. He coughed, grasping the sides of the desk, as if his fury threatened him with an attack of apoplexy and he feared to fall in a heap upon the floor.

Then came the lamentations of the business man. This was what had been accomplished by the raid upon his best wines committed in his absence by his iniquitous relative! Such a mad pillage could not have had any other results. To intoxicate a whole mob of coarse, ordinary persons with the wine of the rich! He had given his cousin a good scolding when he returned to Jerez; and now, after he had forgotten the felonious deed, he was apprised of its final consequence—a disgrace that would keep him from ever setting foot in Marchamalo. Jesus! Jesus! What a shame for the family! . . .

"Pity me, Fermín," groaned don Pablo. "Have compassion upon me; consider the cross I bear on my shoulders. The Lord has showered all his gifts upon me, his unworthy servant. I possess wealth, a mother who is a saint, a Christian wife and obedient children; but in this vale of tears happiness cannot be complete. The All-Highest must put us to proof, and my chastisement comes from the daughters of the Marquis and this don Luis, who is the prey of the devil. We are the best of families, but these madcaps take it upon themselves to bring us tears, to afflict us with the torments of disgrace. Pity me, Fermín; have compassion upon the most unhappy Christian on earth, who none the less does not complain of his lot, but praises the Lord."

The exalted fanatic reappeared in don Pablo, who was on the verge of delirium as he spoke of God and the fate of His creatures. And he begged for Fermín's compassion in such an entreating manner that the young man feared he would kneel down before him, his hands clasped, supplicating his forgiveness.

At certain moments Montenegro, despite his sadness, was seized with the desire to laugh at the extraordinary aspect of the situation. This powerful man was begging for pity. Then what should *he* beg, who had come likewise impelled by a family disgrace? . . .

Dupont sank breathlessly into his chair, his head buried in his hands, with that ease with which his character passed from disordered, impulsive action to cowardly abjection.

He sighed gloomily:

"My family! . . . My family! . . ."

But as he raised his glance he met Fermín's eyes, which were contemplating him in surprise, as if asking when the moment would come that he would cease asking pity for himself and be disposed to pity his clerk.

"And you," he asked. "What do you think I can do in the matter? . . ."

Montenegro cast aside all diffidence and answered his employer firmly. If he had known what to do he should

not have come to bother don Pablo. He was there to be
advised by him; even more—to have him remedy the
evil, like a Christian and like a gentleman, since these
two titles were always upon his tongue.

"You are the head of your family and that is why I
have sought you. You possess the means of bringing
about the proper state of affairs and returning to a
family its honor."

"The head! . . . the head!" murmured don Pablo
ironically.

And he remained silent, as if seeking a solution of the
affair.

Then he spoke of María de la Luz. She had sinned
deeply and had much to repent. Her unusual condition at
the time and her lack of will-power might serve her as
excuse before God; but drunkenness was no virtue, and
carnal sin was none the less a sin. . . . The poor girl's
soul must be saved, and she must be provided with means
for concealing her disgrace.

"I believe," he added, after long meditation, "that the
best thing would be for your sister to enter a convent. . . . Don't make such a wry face; you mustn't
imagine I mean any convent at all. I will speak to my
mother; we know how to arrange matters. She will go
to a high-class convent where there are none but distinguished ladies and we'll attend to the financial end
of it. You know that I never stop at expense. Four
thousand, five thousand *duros* . . . whatever it will be.
Eh! It seems to me that's not at all a bad solution!
There, in retirement, she will cleanse her soul of sin.
Then, I shall be able to take my family to the vineyard,
without fear of them having to rub elbows with an unfortunate maiden that has committed the vilest of sins,
and she will live like a grand lady, like a distinguished
bride of God, surrounded by every comfort—even serv-

ants, Fermín! And you must admit that this is far better than remaining at Marchamalo and eating the laborers' mess."

Fermín had jumped to his feet, pale and frowning.

"Is that all you have to say?" he demanded, in a choked voice.

The millionaire was taken aback by the youth's attitude. What! Didn't he think this sufficient? Did he have any better solution? And with intense amazement, as if he were mentioning some unheard-of, insane project, he added:

"You surely cannot have thought of having my cousin marry your sister! . . ."

"He can do nothing else. This is the logical, the natural way out—this is what honor advises, and the only thing a Christian like you could countenance."

Dupont grew excited anew.

"Ta, ta! So this is *your* interpretation of Christianity! You *green* fellows who know religion only from the outside, select certain of its exterior aspects to cast into our faces whenever it suits your purpose. It is clear, of course, that we are all the children of God, and that the good children will have an equal share in His glory; but while we dwell upon earth, the social order, which comes from on high, requires the existence of hierarchies, which must be respected and not be permitted to intermingle. Just take up the matter with a learned man— a truly learned one; with my friend, Father Urizábal, or some eminent priest, and you will see how he answers you: the same as I. We must be good Christians, forgive our neighbors, aid them with charity and help them save their souls; but each one must remain in the social circle that God designated for him, in the family into which he was brought at birth, without overleaping the dividing barriers through false notions of liberty, whose real name is libertinism."

Montenegro contained his anger only at the cost of violent efforts.

"My sister is good and honorable, despite everything," he declared, glaring boldly at don Pablo. "My father is the most generous and peaceful toiler in all the Jerez countryside; I am young, but I have never harmed a soul, and my conscience is clear. We Montenegros may be poor, but that gives no one the right to scorn us or dishonor us with the egotism of pleasure. Nobody! Do you understand me, don Pablo? Nobody! And whoever tries it shall not escape unpunished. We are as good as the best of them, and my sister, although poor, is well worthy of entering by the front door into a family which, though it possess millions, holds in its bosom men like Luis and women like the *Marquesitas*."

At any other moment Dupont would have fumed with rage before the insolent threats of his clerk. Now, however, he seemed to be intimidated by the youth's glance, by the accent of his voice, which quivered with menacing portent.

"Man! Man!" he exclaimed, trying without success to whip himself into indignation, and consequently adopting a good-humored gentleness.

"Consider what you are saying. I know that my cousin and the two women you name are a bad sort. Many's the pang they've given me! But they bear my name, and because they belong to my family you must speak of them with greater courtesy. Besides, what do you know of the punishment that is held in store for them by the grace of the All-Highest? . . . The Magdalen was worse than these unfortunate women—much worse—and she died like a saint. Luis may be bad, but some of our saints raised even greater scandals in their youth. Take Saint Augustine, for example—a father of the Church, a pillar of Christianity. When Saint Augustine was a young man . . ."

The ring of the telephone bell interrupted Dupont, who was about to launch upon the story of the great African's life, without having noticed Fermín's indifference.

Dupont remained for several minutes at the telephone, from time to time uttering a joyous exclamation, as if highly satisfied with what he was hearing.

When he returned to Montenegro he no longer seemed to remember what had brought the young man.

"They are approaching us, Fermín," he exclaimed, rubbing his hands. "I've been told, on the part of the magistrate, that the Caulina mob is beginning to march on the city. A little uneasiness at first, and then *pum, pum, pum!* the punishment that they need so badly— imprisonment, and even a couple of executions, so that they'll get back their senses and leave us in peace for a while."

Don Pablo was going to give orders to have the doors and the low windows of his hotel closed. If Fermín did not wish to remain, he had better leave as soon as possible.

The master spoke hurriedly, with his thoughts centered upon the imminent invasion of the desperate working-men, and thrust Fermín forward, accompanying him to the door, as if he had forgotten entirely their previous conversation.

"Well, how does the matter stand, then, don Pablo?"

"Oh, yes! Your affair . . . concerning the girl. We'll see. Come again. I'll talk it over with my mother. Sending her to a convent is best of all; take my word for it."

And as he noticed Fermín's features cloud over with

an expression of protest, he resumed his humble manner.

"Man, give up all thought of their marrying. Have pity upon me and my family. Haven't we suffered enough? Here are the Marquis's daughters, who shame us by wallowing about with the rabble; Luis, who seemed to have turned over a new leaf, and now confronts us with this adventure. . . . And do you wish to add to the affliction of my mother and myself, by asking a Dupont to marry a vineyard girl? I imagined you thought better of us. Have pity upon me, man; have compassion."

"Yes, don Pablo, I pity you," replied Fermín, ironically, pausing upon the threshold. "You well deserve compassion for the state of your soul. Your religion is different from mine."

Dupont recoiled, at once forgetting his preoccupations. He had been touched in the vulnerable spot of his garrulousness. And an employee of his dared to address such words to him! . . .

"My religion . . . my religion?" he exclaimed furiously, not knowing where to begin. "What have you to say against it? We'll settle that to-morrow at my office . . . and if not, why, this very moment . . ."

But Fermín did not permit him to continue.

"It will not be very easy to-morrow," he said, calmly. "We'll not see each other to-morrow. And perhaps never again. It can't be now, either. I'm in a hurry. . . . Good-by, don Pablo! I will not bother you any more; you won't have to ask me any more to pity you. What I've got to do I'll attend to myself."

And he dashed precipitously out of the hotel. When he reached the street it was beginning to grow dark.

CHAPTER IX

BEFORE the afternoon was half over the first groups of workingmen had arrived at the immense plain of Caulina. They appeared like black flocks, rising from every direction of the horizon.

Some came down from the mountains, others from the granges of the plain or from the districts situated beyond Jerez, arriving at Caulina after having circled about the city. There were men from the confines of Málaga and from the vicinity of Sanlúcar de Barrameda. The mysterious call had flown from the taverns to the hovels, across the entire countryside, and all the toilers hastened to the meeting-place, believing that the moment of vengeance had arrived.

They looked with savage glances toward Jerez. The triumph of the poor was near, and the white, smiling city—the city of the rich, with their wine-stores and their millions—was going to burn, illuminating the night with the splendor of its ruins.

Those who had lately arrived grouped themselves at one side of the road, on a part of the plain covered with bushes. The bulls that were grazing here retreated to the rear, as if they were intimidated by this dark mass, which grew and grew, augmented incessantly by new bands.

Poverty's entire horde was coming to the meeting. There were tanned men, meager, without the slightest cushion of fat beneath their lustrous skins; strong skeletons revealing under the tightly-drawn skin their sharp outlines and obscure hollows; bodies in which there was more waste than nutrition, and whose absence of muscle was supplied by the bundles of tendons that had been swollen by hard labor.

They were clothed in tattered garments covered with patches and spreading an odor of poverty, or else stood shaking in the cold, with no other protection than a ragged jacket. Those who had come from Jerez to join them could be distinguished by their capes, and by their appearance as city workers; their manners, too, were urban rather than rustic.

The hats—some of them brand new, others faded and misshapen, with fallen brims and hanging fringes, covered features in which appeared all the gradations of human expression, from stupid, beast-like indifference to the aggressiveness of one who is born well prepared for the struggle for existence.

These men recalled their ancient animal lineage. Some had a long, bony countenance with bovine eyes and a gentle, resigned expression; they were the cattle men, desirous of stretching out upon the furrow and chewing their cud without the slightest idea of protest, in solemn motionlessness. Others revealed the mobile, hairy lip and the phosphorescent eyes of the cat; these were the wild-beast men who quivered, dilating their nostrils as if they scented the odor of blood. The majority, with dark bodies and limbs as twisted and as angular as twigs, were plant-men, forever rooted to the earth whence they had sprouted, incapable of either movement or thought, resigned to die upon the same spot, contentedly feeding their lives upon what the strong cast off.

The stirrings of revolution, the passionate lust for vengeance, and the intense desire of improving their condition seemed to make them all equal, producing a family resemblance. Many, upon abandoning their dwelling, had been obliged to tear themselves out of the arms of their wives, who wept with the presentiment of danger; but on beholding themselves among their comrades they drew themselves proudly erect, looking toward Jerez with braggart glances, as if they were about to eat it.

"Just see!" they exclaimed to one another. "How inspiring it is to behold so many poor persons gathered together, ready to act like men for their rights! . . ."

There were more than four thousand. Every time a new group arrived, the various men composing it, curling up in their torn cloaks so as to lend greater mystery to their question, would turn to those already there and ask:

"What's up? . . ."

And those who heard the question seemed to answer with their glances: "Yes, what's up?" They were all there without knowing the why or wherefore; without knowing for certain who had called them together.

Through the country there had been circulated the rumor that on that afternoon, toward nightfall, the great revolution would take place, and they had hastened to the mass-meeting, exasperated by the ordeals and the persecution of the strike, carrying in their sashes an old pistol, sickles, knives or the terrible pruning-shears, which with a single thrust could lop off a head.

They brought something more: the faith that accompanies all crowds in the early moments of rebellion —that credulity which enthuses them with the most absurd news, each one exaggerating on his own account so as to deceive himself, believing that in this manner he forces reality with the impulse of his nonsensical fancies.

The credit for having set the meeting afoot and spread the first news of it, they imputed to the *Madrileño*— a young outsider who had appeared in the Jerez countryside at the very height of the strike, emboldening the simple toilers with his bloodthirsty harangues. Nobody knew him, but he was a youth with a fine gift of speech and of some account, judging from the friendships of which he boasted. Salvatierra had sent him, he averred, to substitute him in his absence.

The great social movement that was to change the face of the earth was destined to start in Jerez. Salvatierra and other men no less famous were already concealed inside the city, ready to appear at the psychological moment. The troops would join the revolutionists as soon as the latter entered the town.

And the credulous toilers, with the imaginative exuberance of their race, embellished the news, adorning it with all manner of detail. A blind confidence spread through the various groups. Only the blood of the rich would flow. The soldiers were with the poor; the officers, too, were on the side of the rebels. Even the Civil Guard, so deeply hated by the laborers, for the moment received their sympathy. For the fellows with the three-cornered hats were also on the people's side. Salvatierra was behind all this, and his name was enough to induce all to accept the truth of this unheard-of miracle.

The older men, who had been present at the September uprising against the Bourbons, were the most credulous and confident of all. They *had seen,* and did not need any one to prove the miracles. The rebellious generals and the admirals of the fleet had been mere puppets in the hands of the greatest man in the country. Don Fernando had done it all: he had caused the vessels to mutiny, he had thrown the battalions at Alcolea against the troops from Madrid. And what he had done to dethrone a queen and prepare the abortion of a seven-months republic, could he not repeat when it was a matter of nothing less than conquering bread for the poor? . . .

The history of that district, the tradition of the province of Cádiz—the home of revolutions—influenced the credulity of the men. They had seen, from one night to the following morning, thrones and ministries destroyed with such ease that none doubted the possibility of a revolution that should exceed all the previous ones in importance and assure forever the welfare of the unfortunate.

Three hours passed and the sun was beginning to set. Still the crowd did not know with any certainty what it was waiting for and how long it would have to remain there.

Old *Zarandilla* went from one group to another to satisfy his curiosity. He had run off from Matanzuela, after a quarrel with his wife, who tried to bar his way, and despite the advice of the steward, who warned him that his years were not for adventures. *Zarandilla* desired to have a close view of what a *rigolution* of the poor really looked like; he was anxious to be present at the blessed moment (if it really were coming) in which the toilers of the soil would wrest it from the rich, dividing it into small parcels and peopling the immense, uninhabited properties, thus realizing their dream.

He tried to recognize some of the men with his weak eyesight, and was surprised at the motionlessness of the groups, their uncertainty and lack of plan.

"I've been a soldier in my day, boys," he said. "I've been to war, and what you're preparing now is the same as a battle. Where is your flag? Where is the general? . . ."

Wherever he turned his dim glance he could see only throngs that seemed fascinated by an endless hope. No general, no banner!

"Bad, bad," mused *Zarandilla*. "I think I'll go back to the farmhouse. The old woman was right; this will end in a drubbing."

Another inquisitive spirit was gliding from group to group, listening to the conversations. It was *Alcaparrón*, with his double hat pushed down over his ears; he moved his body, enveloped in ragged clothes, with a feminine carriage. The laborers received him with laughter. He here, too? . . . They would give him a gun when they entered the city; they'd see if he would battle with the citizens like a brave fellow.

But the gipsy replied to these suggestions with exaggerated gestures of fear. His race had no liking for warfare. He, take a gun! Had they ever seen many soldier-gipsies? . . .

"But you'll certainly not object to robbing," said others to him. "When the moment for dividing up comes around, you just bet you'll be there, my boy!"

And *Alcaparrón* smiled like an ape, rubbing his hands at the mention of plunder, flattered in his atavistic race instincts.

A laborer who had formerly worked on the Matanzuela estate reminded him of his cousin Mari-Cruz.

"If you're a man, *Alcaparrón*, to-night you can get your revenge. Take this sickle and plunge it into the stomach of that villain, don Luis."

The gipsy refused the deadly weapon, fleeing from the group to hide his tears.

Night was rapidly falling. The laborers, wearied with waiting, began to stir. breaking forth into protests. See here! Who was in charge of all this? Were they going to stay all night at Caulina? Where was Salvatierra? Let him show up! . . . Without him they would go nowhere.

Impatience and dissatisfaction gave birth to a leader.

Juanón's thunderous voice was heard above the shouts of the men. His powerful arms rose over their heads.

"Who gave the order for this meeting? . . . The *Madrileño?* Very well; let him appear; have him sought out."

The city toilers, who formed the nucleus of the comrades of the *idea* that had come from Jerez, and were supposed to return thither at the head of the country folk, gathered about Juanón, instinctively foreseeing in him the leader that would harmonize all their wills.

At last the *Madrileño* was located, and Juanón accosted him to learn what they were all doing there. The stranger expressed himself very volubly, but without saying anything.

"We have come together for the revolution; that's it, for the social revolution."

Juanón stamped with impatience. But what about Salvatierra? Where was don Fernando? . . . The *Madrileño* had not seen him, but he knew—that is, he had been told—that he was in Jerez awaiting the arrival of the people. He also knew—or rather, he had been told—that the troops would come over to their side. The prison-warden, moreover, was also in the plot. They needed only to appear, and the soldiers themselves would open the gates, freeing all their imprisoned comrades.

The giant remained for a moment in meditation, scratching his forehead, as if he thus wished to hasten the progress of his confused thoughts.

"Very well," he exclaimed after a long pause. "This is a matter of being men or not; of entering the city no matter what the outcome, or else of sneaking off to bed."

His eyes shone with steely resolution—the fatalism of those who resign themselves to being leaders of men. Upon him reposed the responsibility of a rebellion that he had not prepared. He knew no more about the seditious movement than did these poor people, who seemed to have sunk into the shades of the twilight without being able to discover what they were doing there.

"Comrades," he shouted imperiously. "On to Jerez, those of you who have any 'guts'! We're going to empty the jail of all our brothers . . . come what may. Salvatierra is there."

The first to approach the impromptu chief was Manolo el de Trebujena, the rebel toiler, boycotted at every farm, who traveled over the countryside selling brandy and revolutionary periodicals.

"I'm with you, Juanón, seeing that comrade Fernando is waiting for us."

"Every man among you that can feel the lash of shame, follow me!" continued Juanón at the top of his lungs, without any clear idea as to whither he was leading his comrades.

But in spite of his call to manhood and shame, the majority of the men recoiled instinctively. A hum of mistrust, of intense disillusionment, arose from the swarm. Most of them passed suddenly from noisy enthusiasm to suspicion and fear. Their southern imaginations, ever predisposed to belief in the unexpected and the marvelous, had led them to have confidence in the appearance of Salvatierra and other renowned revolutionists, all mounted upon fiery chargers, like proud, invincible chieftains, followed by an army that had sprung miraculously from the earth. The rest was merely a matter of accompanying these powerful aids on their entrance into the city, reserving for themselves the simple task of slaying the conquered and apportioning their wealth. And instead of this, here they were talking of having them enter alone into that city which stood silhouetted against the horizon, athwart the dying splendor of the sunset, and seemed to blink at them satanically through the reddish eyes of its lights, as if luring them on to an ambush. They were no fools. Life was hard with its excess of toil and its constant hunger; but it was worse to die. Home, then! Home! . . .

And the groups commenced to break up, filing off in the direction opposite to the city; they were lost in the gloom, not caring to linger and hear the insults of Juanón and the more enthusiastic of the men.

The latter, fearing lest immobility lead to more desertions, gave the command to march.

"To Jerez! On to Jerez. . . ."

They began their journey. There were about a thousand in all; the city toilers and the beast-men, who had come to the meeting with the scent of blood in their nostrils, and could not withdraw, as if impelled by an instinct superior to their will.

At the side of Juanón, among the most spirited of the regiment, marched the *Maestrico*—the youth who spent his nights in the workers' shelter teaching himself how to read and write.

"I'm afraid we're going about this wrong," he said to his vigorous companion. "We're proceeding blindly. I've caught sight of men hastening to Jerez to give warning of our arrival. They're expecting us; and for nothing good, either."

"Shut up, you, *Maestrico*," replied the chief imperiously; for, proud of his position, he received the slightest objection as a piece of irreverence. "Just shut up, d'you hear? And if you're afraid, sneak off like the others. We wish no cowards here."

"I, a coward!" exclaimed the youth ingenuously "Forward, Juanón. To the very death! . . ."

They tramped along in silence, their heads lowered, as though about to attack the city. They marched as if they desired as soon as possible to emerge from the uncertainty that accompanied their project.

The *Madrileño* explained his scheme. First of all, to the prison, to release their incarcerated comrades. There the troops would join them. And Juanón, as if no orders could be given except by his voice, repeated at the top of his lungs:

"To the prison. To free our brothers!"

They took a roundabout course so as to enter the city by a lane, as if ashamed to tread the wide and well-lighted thoroughfares. Many of these men had been in Jerez but a few times and followed their leaders with flock-like docility, considering uneasily how best to get out of the place if they should be compelled to take to flight.

The black, mute avalanche advanced with a muffled tramping of feet that shook the pavement. As they approached, house doors were closed and lights were extinguished. From a balcony came a woman's taunts:

"Rabble! Common herd! I hope they hang you, for that's what you deserve! . . ."

And upon the stones of the pavement resounded the crash of an earthen vase as it shattered into fragments without striking anybody. It was the *Marquesita*, who, from the balcony of the hog-dealer's home, was venting her indignation against this drove of men, so repelling to her because of their commonness, which dared to threaten decent folk.

Only a few raised their heads. The majority marched on, insensible to the ridiculous attack, desirous of coming as soon as possible to the rescue of their friends. The city toilers recognized the *Marquesita*, and as they marched on their way they replied to her insults with words as classic as they were indecent. But what a sour thing she was! If they weren't in such a hurry, they'd have given her a good currying under the skirts. . . .

The column suffered a certain set-back upon ascending the slope that led to the prison square: the most somber spot in the city. Many of the rebels recalled their comrades of *The Black Hand;* it was here that they had been garrotted.

The square was deserted; the ancient convent that had been converted into a prison had all its windows closed, and not a light shone through the bars. Even the sentinel had hidden behind the large door of the inner court.

The leader of the regiment stopped as they entered the square, resisting the thrusts of those who came behind. Nobody! Who was going to help them? Where were the soldiers that were supposed to join them? . . .

They did not have to wait long for an answer. From one of the lower windows shot a darting flame—a red line that dissolved in smoke. A loud, dry discharge shook the square. Then followed another and another, until there had been nine in all, although they seemed infinite to the toilers, who stood there motionless with surprise. It was the guard, firing upon them before the workers even raised their guns.

Surprise and terror infused some with an all-forgetting heroism. They advanced shouting, with their arms outspread.

"Don't shoot, brothers, for we've been betrayed! . . . Brothers! We don't mean any harm! . . ."

But the brothers were hard of hearing and continued to shoot. The terror of flight soon arose in the mob. All began to rush down the hill, coward and hero alike, jostling against one another, stumbling along, as if the shots that continued to reverberate in the deserted square were whipping them on.

Juanón and the more energetic of the strikers succeeded in stemming the torrent of men as soon as they had turned a corner. The groups formed anew; this time, however, they were smaller, and less compact. Only six hundred were left. The credulous leader blasphemed under his breath.

"Well, now; let the *Madrileño* come and explain this to us."

But they searched for him in vain. The *Madrileño* had disappeared in the rout, and, like all who knew the city, had scurried off through the lanes the moment the shots had resounded. There remained with Juanón only those who came from the mountains; they groped along the streets, amazed to discover nobody, as if the city had been abandoned.

"Salvatierra is not in Jerez, nor does he know a thing about this," said the *Maestrico* to Juanón. "It seems to me we've been tricked."

"I think the very same," replied the giant. "And what are we going to do about it? As long as we're here, let's go to the heart of the city—la Calle Larga."

They began a disordered march through the inner section of the city. What calmed them somewhat, infusing them with a certain courage, was the fact that they encountered neither obstacles nor enemies. Where was the Civil Guard? Why were the troops in hiding? The mere circumstance that they remained shut up in their barracks, leaving the city in the strikers' power, instilled in the rebels the absurd hope that it was still possible for Salvatierra to appear, at the head of the mutinous soldiers.

They arrived without any opposition at la Calle Larga. No precautions against their coming. The street was clear of pedestrians; but the balcony-windows of the casinos were lighted; the lower floors had no other fastening than the glass doors.

The rebels passed by the wealthy men's clubs with glances of hatred, yet scarcely stopping. Juanón was momentarily expecting the miserable flock to give vent to an outburst of rage; he was even ready to intervene, by virtue of his authority, and quell the outbreak.

"Those are the rich fellows!" was heard from some of the groups.

"The chaps that fatten us on *gazpachos* fit for dogs."

"The men that rob us. Just look at them drinking our blood! . . ."

And after a brief halt they would continue their hurried march, as if they were bound for a certain place and feared to arrive late.

They grasped their terrible pruning-shears, their sickles, their knives. . . . Let the rich bandits come out and they'd see how their heads should roll on the pavement. But it would have to be in the street, for all of them felt a certain aversion to forcing the glass doors, as if they formed an impregnable wall.

As these rough toilers confronted their oppressors, they were bowed down by the weight of long years of submission and cowardice. Besides, they were intimidated by the light of the large street—its broad sidewalks with their rows of lamps, and the red splendor of the balconies. All mentally formed the selfsame excuse for their weakness. If only they had these people in the open country! . . .

As they passed by the *Círculo Caballista* there appeared behind the glass doors several heads of young men. They were señoritos who followed the procession of the strikers with ill-disguised anxiety. But as they saw the toilers go by without stopping they glanced at them with a certain irony, recovering confidence in the superiority of their caste.

"Long live the Social Revolution!" shouted the *Maes-*

trico, as if it grieved him to march by the nest of the rich in silence.

The inquisitive onlookers disappeared, laughing as they did so, greatly rejoicing at the acclamation. As long as they were content with just shouting! . . .

The toilers arrived in their purposeless procession at la plaza Nueva, and upon noticing that the leader had stopped, they gathered about him with interrogating glances.

"And what shall we do now?" they asked, innocently. "Where shall we go?"

Juanón glowered with a ferocious expression.

"You can go wherever you please. Much we're accomplishing! . . . As for me, I'll take the fresh air."

The men dispersed into small groups. Leaders arose, each guiding his comrades in a different direction. The city was theirs; the best part of it was to begin! There now reappeared the atomic instinct of the race, incapable of group action, destitute of collective effort, strong and enterprising only when each individual can work after his own inspiration.

La Calle Larga had grown dark; the casinos were closed. After the terrible shock the rich had suffered at sight of the threatening procession, they feared a change of heart upon the part of the wild beast, who might repent of his magnanimity. Whereupon all the doors were barred.

A numerous group set out for the theater. That's where the wealthy and the bourgeois were. They must all be slain: a *real* drama. But as the laborers approached the illuminated entrance they stopped, halted by a fear that did not lack a certain religious element. They had never been inside of this place. The air, warm and charged with gaseous emanations, and the buzz of countless conversations that escaped through the crevices of the doors, intimidated them as if it were the breathing of a monster concealed behind the red curtains of the vestibule.

Let them come out! Let them come out and they'd get all they were looking for! . . . But to go in? . . .

Various spectators came to the door, attracted by the news of the invasion that had spread through the nearby streets. One of them, dressed in a cape and wearing a gentleman's hat, dared to advance toward several of the cloaked men who formed a group before the theater.

They fell upon him, surrounding him and raising their pruning-shears and sickles aloft, while the other spectators fled, taking refuge within the theater. At last the toilers had what they were looking for! It was the bourgeois, the sated bourgeois, who must be bled that he might return to the people all the substance he had sucked in. . . .

But the "bourgeois," a robust young man of calm, frank gaze, restrained them with a gesture.

"Eh, comrades! I'm a workingman like yourselves!"

"Your hands, then! Let's see your hands!" roared some of the laborers, without lowering their threatening weapons.

And from the folds of the cape appeared a pair of strong, calloused hands, with the nails flattened by toil. One after the other these men filed by, feeling his palms and assaying his hard skin. He had callouses; then he was one of theirs. And the menacing implements went back to their hiding place under the cloaks.

"Yes, I'm one of you," continued the young man. "I'm a carpenter, but I like to dress like the gentlemen, and instead of spending the night at a tavern, I go to the theater. Everybody has his own tastes. . . ."

This disillusionment so discouraged the strikers that

many of them withdrew. Christ! Where were the
wealthy fellows hiding? . . .

They filed through the broad streets and through the
side lanes, in small groups, waiting for some one to come
by that they might make him show his hands. This was
the best way of recognizing the poor man's enemies.
But whether with callouses or without, nobody passed
their way.

The city seemed to have been deserted. The inhabitants, seeing that the armed forces still remained hidden
in the barracks, fled to their homes, exaggerating the
importance of the invasion and believing that millions of
men had occupied the streets and the environs of the
city.

A group of five laborers stumbled against a young man
in a side street. They were among the most ferocious
of the band: men who experienced a homicidal impatience upon noticing that the hours were flying by
without bloodshed.

"Your hands; show us your hands," they bellowed,
surrounding him and raising their shining weapons.

"My hands!" answered the young man ill-humoredly,
opening his cape. "And why should I show them? I
don't feel like it."

But one of the men had seized the youth's arms in his
powerful clutches, and with a violent pull forced him to
show his hands.

"He hasn't any callouses!" they exclaimed with grim
joy.

And they stepped backward, as if to fall upon him
with greater force. They were restrained, however, by
the calmness of the youth.

"I haven't any callouses? Well, what of it? I'm a
workingman like you, just the same. Salvatierra hasn't

any, either. And you're not any more revolutionary
than he! . . ."

The name of Salvatierra seemed to detain the heavy
knives in the air.

"Let the fellow go," came Juanón's voice from
behind. "I know him, and will answer for him. He is
a friend of comrade Fernando; he's a follower of the
idea."

It was not without a certain pang of regret that the
barbarous group forsook Fermín Montenegro, angered
at the miscarriage of their anticipated pleasure. Juanón's
presence inspired respect. Besides, there was another
young fellow coming up the street. He surely did not
belong to the *idea;* he must be some scion of the bour-
geoisie returning home.

While Montenegro was thanking Juanón for his op-
portune arrival, which had saved his life, the encounter
of the toilers and the passer-by took place somewhat
further down the street.

"Your hands, bourgeois; show us your hands."

The bourgeois was a thin, pale young man—a boy of
sixteen with a threadbare suit, but wearing a large collar
and a bright tie: the poor man's luxuries. He trembled
with fright as he showed his delicate, bloodless hands—
the hands of a clerk who is shut up in an office cage
during the hours of sunlight. He wept, excusing himself with interrupted words, and glaring at the pruning-
shears with his terror-stricken eyes, as if he were
hypnotized by the cold steel. He was just coming from
the office . . . he had worked overtime . . . they were
drawing up their balances. . . .

"I make only two *pesetas* a day, gentlemen . . . two
pesetas. Don't hurt me . . . let me go home. My
mother is waiting for me. Aaay! . . ."

It was a cry of pain, of terror, of despair, that aroused

the whole street. A hair-raising shriek, followed by a crack as of a broken pot, and the young man fell backward to the ground.

Juanón and Fermín, frozen with horror, ran toward the group. In the center lay the boy with his head in a black pool that kept growing larger and larger, and his legs contracting stiffly in the agony of death. A pruning-shears had opened his cranium, cracking his skull.

The brutes seemed satisfied with their work.

"Look at him," said one of them. "The apprentice of the bourgeois is dying like a chicken! . . . After him come the masters."

Juanón burst into curses. Was this all they could do? Cowards! They had passed by the casinos, where the rich folk were—the real enemy—and it hadn't occurred to them to do anything but shout, and they were afraid to break the glass doors—the only barrier between them and the wealthy. All they were good for was to assassinate a mere child, a workingman like themselves, a poor office clerk who earned two *pesetas* per day and perhaps supported his mother.

Fermín was afraid that the giant would draw his knife and fall upon his comrades.

"What are you going to do with savages like these!" roared Juanón. "Would to God or the devil that we were all caught and hanged. . . . And me first of all, because I'm such a stupid beast; because I ever thought that you fellows were good for anything."

The unhappy fellow went off, desiring to avoid a clash with his brutal comrades. The latter, too, made their escape, as if the words of the giant had brought back their reason.

Montenegro, finding himself alone before the corpse, was seized with fear. Following upon the precipitous flight of the murderers there came the noise of windows being opened, and he was afraid that the neighbors would surprise him near the victim.

He did not stop in his flight until he reached the main streets. There he thought he would be better protected from the wild beasts who were at large, everywhere demanding that folks show their hands.

After a short while it seemed to him that the city was awakening. From the distance came a discharge that shook the earth, and following close upon it was heard the trot of lancers upon la Calle Larga. Then, at the further end of this street there began to glisten rows of bayonets as the infantry advanced in rhythmic step. The façades of the large houses seemed to be infused with new spirit and of a sudden all doors and windows were opened.

The armed forces spread all over the city. The light from the lanterns was reflected in the helmets of the horsemen, the bayonets of the infantry and the polished three-cornered hats of the Civil Guard. Against the semi-darkness stood out the red of the soldiers' trousers and the yellow leather-straps of the guards.

Those who had deemed it advisable to hold these forces in check now judged that the moment had come to release them. For several hours the city had yielded without resistance, wearied with monotonous waiting because of the rebels' mild actions. But blood had begun to flow. A single corpse was sufficient—the corpse that would justify cruel reprisals which should arouse authority from its voluntary slumber.

Fermín thought with deep sadness of the unfortunate bookkeeper, stretched out there upon the street—a victim exploited even in death, since he provided the pretext that was being sought by the powerful.

Throughout Jerez the man-hunt began. Platoons of the Civil Guard and of line infantry stood rigidly on guard at the openings of all streets, while the cavalry and strong foot-patrols scoured the city, detaining all suspicious characters.

Fermín went hither and thither without encountering opposition. His outer appearance was that of a young gentleman, and the armed forces were giving chase only to cloaks, to country hats, to coarse jackets; to all who looked like laborers. Montenegro saw them pass by in a row, on the way to the prison, between the bayonets and the horses—some dejected, as if surprised by the hostile appearance of the armed force that "was supposed to join them"; others stupefied, unable to understand how the gangs of prisoners could arouse such joy in la Calle Larga, when a few hours before they had marched through like conquerors, without permitting themselves the slightest abuse.

There was an unending procession of prisoners, taken at the moment in which they were attempting to escape from the city. Others had been seized at the taverns where they were in hiding, or were accidentally encountered in the search that included every street.

Some came from the city. They had left their houses shortly before, upon seeing that the invasion had come to an end, but their poor appearance was enough to lead them to be detained as rebels. And the groups of prisoners kept passing by incessantly. The prison was too small for so many, and considerable numbers had to be taken to the troops' barracks.

Fermín felt tired. Ever since nightfall he had been hunting throughout Jerez for a certain man. The entrance of the strikers, the uncertainty of the outcome, had for several hours taken his mind away from his own affairs. But now that the matter was over, his nervous excitement vanished and weariness overpowered him.

For a moment he thought of retiring to his room. But his affairs were not of the sort that could be postponed to the following day. He must finish that very night, at once, the matter that had sent him forth like a madman from the hotel of don Pablo, whom he had seen for the last time.

He began to wander anew through the streets in search of his man, without paying any attention to the ranks of prisoners that passed by him.

In the vicinity of la plaza Nueva the desired meeting occurred.

"Long live the Civil Guard! Hurrah for respectable folk! . . ."

It was Luis Dupont shouting in the midst of the silence that so many guns in the streets imposed upon the city. He was drunk; this was easily to be inferred from his shining eyes and his fetid breath. Behind him marched *el Chivo* and a tavern waiter, with glasses in their hands and bottles in their pockets.

Upon recognizing Fermín, Luis threw himself into the young man's arms and tried to kiss him. What a day, eh? . . . What a victory! And he spoke as if he alone had routed the strikers.

Upon learning that the herd was entering the city, he had gone with his valiant acolyte to the *Montañés* tavern, shutting the doors securely against all disturbance. They must gather courage—drink a bit before getting down to business. There was plenty of time for them to get out and send the rabble flying before their pistols. He and *el Chivo* were enough for the task. Let the enemy be misled into confidence, until the moment when they would emerge, like two ministers of death. And at last, they had come out with a revolver in one hand and a knife in the other; the end of the world! But such ill luck! For they found the troops already in the street. Even then, they had done something.

"I," declared the drunkard proudly, "helped to capture more than a dozen of 'em. Besides, I delivered I don't know how many punches among these low-down chaps, who, even after they had been corraled, continued to speak ill of respectable folk. . . . A fine drubbing they're going to get! . . . Long live the Civil Guard! Hurrah for the rich!"

And as if these acclamations had dried his windpipe, he beckoned to *el Chivo,* who came to his rescue with a couple of glasses of wine.

"Drink," Luis ordered his friend.

Fermín hesitated.

"I don't feel like drinking," he replied, in a choked voice. "What I *do* wish, however, is to have a talk with you, and at once, on a very interesting subject. . . ."

"That's all right; we'll see to that," answered the young man without attributing any importance to the request. "We'll talk for three days in succession. But first we've got to fulfill our duty. I'm going to treat all the brave chaps who together with me saved Jerez to a glass of wine. For, believe me, Ferminillo, it was I, and I alone, who resisted those brutes. While the troops were in the barracks I was at my post. I believe the city ought to show its appreciation by giving me some office! . . ."

A platoon of cavalry trotted by. Luis advanced toward the officer, raising a glass of wine aloft; but the soldier rode on without noticing the offer, followed by his men, whose horses almost trampled upon Luis.

This slight, however, did not dampen his enthusiasm.

"Hurrah for the graceful horsemen!" he cried, throwing his hat at the hind legs of the horses.

And as he picked it up he straightened out, saluted,

and, assuming a serious expression, brought one hand to his chest and shouted:

"Hurrah for the army!"

Fermín did not care to leave him, and forcing himself to be patient, accompanied him on his journey through the streets. The señorito halted before the various squads of soldiers, ordering his two men to advance with their glasses and bottles.

"Hats off to the brave fellows! Hurrah for the cavalry . . . and the infantry . . . and the artillery, too, even if it's not here! . . . Have a glass, my dear lieutenant."

The officers, in a bad humor because of the stupid day's work, which had lacked both danger and glory, refused the drunkard with a rude glance. Off with him! Nobody drank there.

"Well, since you can't drink," insisted the youth with the obstinacy of a drunkard, "I'll drink for you. Here's to the health of the handsome fellows! . . . Death to the rabble!"

A group of the Civil Guard attracted his attention at the end of the street. The sergeant who was at the head of it—an old man with wiry, grayish mustache—likewise refused Luis's treat.

"Here's to the men with 'guts'! A blessing on the mother of every one of you! Hurrah for the Civil Guard! Come, have a drink on me. *Chivo*, serve these gentlemen."

The veteran again excused himself. Orders . . . the care of the body. . . . But his firm refusal was accompanied by a generous smile. He was speaking to a Dupont, to one of the wealthiest men in the city. The sergeant recognized him, and despite the fact that a few moments before he had been striking with the butt end of the gun all passers-by that wore laborers' clothes, he tolerated the young man's toast resignedly.

"Go on, don Luis," he advised in tones of entreaty. "Better go home; this is no night for celebrations."

"Good, then. . . . I'll go, honorable veteran. But first I'll have another drink . . . and another; one for each of you. I'll do the drinking, seeing that you can't, all on account of the silly regulations; and may it help you all. . . . To your health, then! Clink, Fermín; you, too, *Chivo*. Now, then, all repeat after me: Hurrah for the guards! . . ."

At last he tired of going from group to group and having his offers refused, and decided that the celebration was over. His conscience was clear; he had honored all the heroes who, supporting his own valor, had saved the city. Now to the *Montañés* to finish the night.

When Fermín found himself in a room of the tavern before more bottles, he decided that the moment for broaching his matter had arrived.

"I had something exceedingly important to talk over with you, Luis. I believe I mentioned it to you."

"I remember . . . you had something to say to me. . . . Speak as long as you please."

He was so drunk that his eyes could not remain open, and his voice whined like that of an old man.

Fermín looked at *el Chivo*, who had as usual sat down beside his patron.

"I've got something to say to you, Luis, but it's a very delicate matter. . . . No third party."

"Are you referring to *el Chivo?*" exclaimed Dupont, opening his eyes. *"El Chivo* and I are one and the same; he knows all of my affairs. Even if my cousin Pablo came here to talk about his business, *el Chivo* would remain to hear everything. So speak without fear, man! I haven't any secrets from this friend."

Montenegro resigned himself to suffering the presence of this sycophant, not wishing to delay the desired discussion by any scruples as to the man.

He spoke to Luis with a certain timidity, veiling his thoughts, weighing his words well, that they might be understood by only the two of them, leaving the bully in ignorance.

If he had sought him out, then Luis might well understand why. . . . *He knew everything.* Surely the recollection of what had happened at Marchamalo on the last night of the vintage had not passed from his memory. Very well, then; he had come to see that the evil done that night should be remedied. He had always looked upon Luis as a friend, and hoped that he would show himself such now . . . for if he didn't . . .

Exhaustion and the nervous excitement of a turbulent night precluded any extended dissimulation on Fermín's part, and the threat leaped to his lips at the same time as it flashed from his eyes.

The wine he had drunk was burning his entrails, as if it had turned to poison because of the repugnance with which it had been accepted from those hands.

Dupont, as he listened to Montenegro, pretended to be drunker than he really was, so as to hide his perturbation.

Fermín's threat caused *el Chivo* to abandon his silence. The hector believed that the moment had arrived for his fawning intervention.

"No threatening here, do you understand, my fine fellow? . . . Nobody can say anything to this gentleman while *el Chivo's* around."

Fermín leaped defiantly to his feet, casting a challenging glance at the sinister beast.

"You shut your mouth!" he ordered. "You stick your tongue in . . . your pocket or wherever else you please.

You're nobody here; and before you address me, ask my permission."

The bully hesitated, as if overcome by the young man's defiance, and before he could recover from the attack, Fermín continued, addressing Luis:

"And you're the man who thinks himself so brave? . . . A hero, and yet everywhere you go you take a companion with you, like the school-children. Brave man, and yet you're afraid to separate from him even for a private chat with a gentleman! You ought to be wearing short pants."

Dupont forgot his drunkenness, casting it aside to rise before his friend in all his valor. Man! He had been wounded in his most sensitive spot! . . .

"You know, Ferminillo, that I'm braver than you, and that all Jerez is afraid of me. You'll see whether I need companions or not. You, *Chivo,* clear out."

The bully grumblingly objected.

"Clear out!" repeated the señorito with the arrogance of impunity, as if he were about to kick the fellow.

El Chivo left, and the two friends resumed their seats. Luis no longer seemed intoxicated; on the contrary, he summoned every effort to appear sober, opened his eyes extraordinarily wide, as if trying to fell Montenegro with a glance.

"Whenever you please," he declared in a low voice, intended to inspire greater fear, "we can go out and settle this with a duel. Not here, because *el Montañés* is a friend of mine and I don't care to compromise him."

Fermín shrugged his shoulders, as if he scorned this ludicrous attempt to terrify him. They would see about the duel, afterwards, according to how the conversation turned out.

"Now, to the point, Luis. You know the evil you

committed. What are you thinking of doing to remedy it?"

The señorito felt his courage ebb again upon seeing that Fermín attacked the much-feared question directly. Man alive, the fault wasn't entirely his. It was the wine, the cursed carousal, accident . . . being too good altogether; for if he hadn't been at Marchamalo, superintending the interests of his cousin (and damned if he appreciated it!), nothing would have happened. But anyway, the harm was done. He was a gentleman, and this concerned a friendly family and he would face the music. What did Fermín desire? . . . His fortune, his person—all was at his disposition. He thought that the best thing would be for them to agree upon a certain sum of money; he promised to collect it, no matter how large it was, and give it to the girl as a dowry; she'd easily catch a good husband with that bait.

Why did Fermín make such a wry face? Had he uttered some piece of nonsense? . . . Well, if this solution wasn't to his taste, he could suggest another. María de la Luz could come and stay with him. He would set her up in a fine city house, and she'd live like a queen. He was fond of the girl; he was very sorry for the trouble he had brought upon her since that night. He would do all in his power to make her happy. Many rich men of Jerez lived in this way with their women, who were respected by all as if they were legitimate wives; and if they didn't marry the women, it was only because the latter were of the lower class. . . . He didn't care for this arrangement, either? Well, let Fermín propose something and they would settle it at once.

"Yes, we must settle it at once," repeated Montenegro. "And in as few words as possible, for it hurts me to speak of this. What you're going to do is, go to-morrow to your cousin and tell him that, stricken with shame at your sin, you are to marry my sister, as a gentleman should. If he gives his consent, all the better; if not, it doesn't matter. You marry her, settle down, and do your best not to make her unhappy."

The señorito had thrust his chair back, replying with a round negative. He could not marry. What about his career? And his future? Why, that very moment his family, in agreement with the Fathers of the Company, was arranging for his marriage to a wealthy young lady from Seville, a former spiritual daughter of Father Urizábal. And he needed the union badly, for his fortune was very much depleted after such heavy inroads, and his political ambitions required wealth.

"Marry your sister? No," concluded Dupont. "That's nonsense, Fermín; think it over; sheer folly!"

Fermín's anger rose as he replied. Folly! Yes, a folly on the part of poor Mariquita. A happy lot, indeed, to put up with a man of his kind, a pool of vices not fit to live with the coarsest women of the town! To María de la Luz this marriage was another sacrifice; but there was nothing to do but to undergo it.

"Do you imagine that I have any genuine desire to be related to you, and that the thought gives me pleasure? . . . Then you're mistaken. Would to God you never had the evil thought that has made my sister unhappy! If this hadn't arisen, I wouldn't accept you as a brother-in-law even if you came to me on your knees with millions. . . . But the harm is done, and it must be remedied in the only way possible, though we all burst with anguish. . . . You know my views, and that I laugh at matrimony: it's one of the many illusions that exist in the world. What is necessary for happiness is Love . . . and nothing more. I can say so because I'm a man, because I scoff at society and what 'they' say. But my sister is a woman and in order to live a peaceful life must command respect and do as other women do. She must marry the man that has abused her, even if she doesn't feel a jot of affection for him. Never shall she speak again to her former sweetheart; it would be a crime to deceive him. You may say, let her continue as an old maid, since nobody knows what happened. But everything that happens gets to be known. You yourself, if I were to leave matters alone, would finally, on some night of intoxication, reveal your good luck and the fine drink you had at your cousin's vineyard. Christ! Anything but that! There's no way out of this except your marrying her."

And with even stronger words he grasped Luis tightly, as if forcing him to accept this solution.

Dupont defended himself with the anguish of one who sees that he has been cornered.

"You're all mixed up, Fermín," he said. "I see more clearly than you. . . ."

And to escape the predicament he tried to defer the conversation until the following day. They would then look more closely into the matter. . . . Fear of finding himself forced to agree to Montenegro's proposals made him insist upon his refusal. Anything but marriage. . . . It was impossible; his family would renounce him; people would laugh at him; his political future would be ruined.

The brother, however, insisted with an inflexibility that terrified Luis.

"You shall marry her; there is no other way. You shall do your duty, or else one of us is superfluous in this world."

Luis's mania of bravado reappeared. He felt strong at the thought that el Chivo was near,—that perhaps the bully heard his words from the nearby corridor.

Threats, to him? There wasn't anybody in all Jerez

that could threaten him with impunity. And he brought his hand to his pocket, fondling the invincible revolver that had almost saved the city, with Luis alone repelling the invasion. Contact with the barrel of the weapon seemed to communicate new courage to him.

"Bah! We're through. I'll do all I can to see that she's well provided for, like the gentleman I am. But I'll not marry her, do you understand? I will not marry her. . . . Besides, how is it certain that I am the guilty party?"

Cynicism twinkled in his eyes. Fermín gnashed his teeth and thrust his hands into his pockets, recoiling as if he feared the words that the señorito was about to utter.

"And how about your sister?" he continued. "Isn't she to blame at all? You're a simpleton, a mere child. Believe me; a girl that isn't willing, isn't forced. I'm a rake; agreed. But your sister . . . your sister herself is something of a . . ."

He uttered the insulting word, but it was scarcely audible.

Fermín rushed upon him so violently that the chairs rolled over and the table shook, sliding toward the wall from the force of his thrust. In his hand flashed Rafael's knife,—the selfsame weapon the steward had forgotten two days before in that same tavern.

The señorito's revolver remained at the opening of his pocket, for his hand lacked the strength to draw it.

Dupont staggered, then uttered the shriek of a slaughtered beast; a growl that hastened the bubbles of dark blood which spurted from his neck like from a broken glass.

At last he fell prostrate upon the floor, amid a loud crash of glasses and bottles that followed him in his descent, as if the wine wished to mingle with his blood.

CHAPTER X

THREE months had gone by since señor Fermín left the Marchamalo vineyard, and his friends could scarcely recognize him as they saw him sitting in the sun, before the wretched shanty where he lived, together with his daughter, in one of the suburbs of Jerez.

"Poor old Fermín," the people would say at sight of him. "He isn't even the shadow of his former self."

He had fallen into a silence that approached imbecility. For hours at a time he would remain motionless, with his head lowered as if overcome by memories. When his daughter approached on her way into the house, or to tell him that the meal was ready, he seemed to awake and become aware of his surroundings, and his eyes followed the girl with a severe glance.

"Wicked woman!" he would murmur. "Cursed female!"

She, she alone was guilty of the disgrace that weighed upon the family.

His anger,—that of the ancient type of father, incapable of tenderness or pardon,—his virile pride that had always caused him to consider woman as an inferior creature, capable of nothing but bringing misfortune to man, pursued poor María de la Luz. She, too, had suffered in health, and had become pale and thin, her eyes made larger by the traces of tears.

In the new existence that she led with her father, she was forced to resort to prodigies of economy. And in addition to the straits and preoccupations of poverty, she had to endure the mute reproach of her father's

347

eyes, the shower of muffled curses which he seemed to pour upon her every time she drew near, rousing him from his meditation.

Señor Fermín lived with his thoughts centered upon the terrible night of the strikers' invasion.

For him, nothing of importance had occurred since then. It seemed that he could still hear the doors of Marchamalo shaking, an hour before dawn, under the furious blows of a stranger. He arose, with his gun held ready, and opened a grated window. But it was his son, his Fermín, hatless, his hands stained with blood and a gash across his face, as if he had engaged in struggle with many persons.

His words were few. He had killed señorito Luis, and had afterwards escaped by wounding the bully that always accompanied Dupont. This slight scratch bore witness to the scuffle. He must flee,—seek safety at once. His enemies would surely suspect that he had hastened to Marchamalo, and by daybreak the horses of the Civil Guard would come dashing up the hillside.

There was a moment of mad confusion, which the poor old man thought would never end. Whither could he go? . . . His hands opened the drawers of the bureau, fumbling through the clothes. He was seeking his savings.

"Take it, my son; take it all."

And he filled Fermín's pockets with *duros* and *pesetas,* —all his silver, which had become moldy from being stored away, having been gathered slowly during the course of the years.

When he thought that he had provided his son with sufficient funds, he hurried him out of the vineyard. Rush! It was still night and he could get out of Jerez without being seen. The old man had his plan. They must hunt up Rafael at Matanzuela. The young steward still maintained friendly relations with his former smuggling companions, and he would guide him over the secret mountain passes to Gibraltar. There he could sail for any country he had a mind to; the world is large.

And for two hours father and son had hurried along, almost running, without feeling any fatigue, spurred on by fear, and darting out of the road every time they heard the sound of distant voices or the noise of a horse.

Ah, what a cruel journey, with its grievous surprises! This was what had undone him! As it grew light, about half way on their flight, he could catch a look of his son, whose face was that of a dying man, stained with blood and with all the aspect of a fugitive assassin. It grieved him to see Fermín in such a condition, but the case was by no means desperate. After all, he was a man, and men kill more than once without losing their honor. But when his son explained, in a few words, *why* he had killed, the old man thought he would drop dead upon the spot; his legs shook beneath him and it was all he could do to keep from falling prostrate in the middle of the highway. It was Mariquita, his daughter, who had provoked all this! Ah, the cursed bitch! And as he thought of what his son had done, he admired him all the more for it, and his rough, peasant soul was filled with gratitude for the sacrifice.

"Fermín, my son . . . you've done well. There was nothing else left but revenge. You're the best one in the family. Better than I, who wasn't equal to keeping an eye on the girl."

Their entry into Matanzuela was tragic; Rafael was overwhelmed with surprise. They had killed his master, and it was he,—Fermín,—who had committed the crime!

Montenegro grew impatient. He wished to be taken

to Gibraltar without being seen. Less talk. Did Rafael
care to save him, or did he refuse? The steward's only
reply was to saddle his brave steed and another one of
the horses. He would rush Fermín to the mountains
immediately, and once there, other men would take him
in charge.

The old overseer watched them gallop away, and began his return, bent by sudden old age, as if his whole
life were speeding off with his son.

His later existence had gone by as in the clouds of
a dream. He could recall that he had at once left
Marchamalo, to take refuge in the suburbs, in the hovel
of one of his wife's relatives. He could not remain at
the vineyard after what had happened. Between his
family and the master's there was blood, and before they
would cast it in his face he would leave.

Don Pablo Dupont managed to convey to him offers
of alms to sustain his old age, although he considered
the overseer chiefly to blame for what had occurred,
since he had not brought his children up in religious
ways. But the old man refused all aid. Many thanks,
sir; he was grateful for the offer, but he would sooner
die than accept money from the Duponts.

Several days after Fermín's flight he was visited by
his godson Rafael. The steward was out of a position;
he had abandoned the farmhouse. He had come to inform him that Fermín was in Gibraltar, and that one of
those days he would sail for South America.

"You, too," said the old man sadly, "have been stung
by the cursed snake that has poisoned us all."

The youth was in a gloomy, dispirited mood. As he
spoke to the old overseer at the door of the shanty, he
cast anxious glances within, as if he feared that María
de la Luz would appear. During their escape through

the mountains Fermín had told him everything . . . everything.

"Ah, godfather, what a blow it was! I believe I'm going to die. . . . And not to be able to avenge myself! To think that the shameless wretch is dead without my knife having plunged into him! And to be unable to bring him back to life so as to kill him all over again! . . . How often the thief must have scoffed at me, seeing how innocent I was of the whole affair, and what a fool he had made of me! . . ."

In his strong, masculine heart the one thing that caused him deep despair was the ridiculous situation he had been in, all the while serving his betrayer. He bemoaned the fact that *his* hand had not executed vengeance.

He had lost all desire to work. What use was it to be good? He would go back to his smuggler's life. Women? . . . good for a short while, and then to whip like indecent, heartless beasts. . . . He wished to declare war against the whole world,—against the rich, against the rulers, those who inspire fear with their guns, and are responsible for the poor being trampled upon by the powerful. Now that the poor folk of Jerez were going about crazed with terror, and labored in the fields without raising their eyes from the ground, and the prison was crowded, and many who before were violently radical went to mass so as to avoid suspicion and persecution,—now *he* was only beginning. The rich class would see what a beast they had let loose upon the world when one of them had destroyed his illusions.

His taking up smuggling was only temporary,—a mere byplay. Later, when they would be gathering the harvests, he would set all the straw-lofts afire, and the farmhouses, too, and would poison the animals on the pasture-grounds. Juanón, the *Maestrico,* and all the other unfortunates who were in prison awaiting execution, and would die at the garrotte, would have in him their avenger.

If he could find men with enough courage to follow him, he would organize a troop of horsemen, leaving José María *el Tempranillo* like a child at the breast. Not for nothing did he know the mountain country. Let the wealthy be on their guard. He would slash the evil fellows from top to bottom, and the good men among them would be able to save their hides only by giving him money for the poor.

As he vented his anger through these threats he grew exalted. He spoke of becoming a highwayman, with that enthusiasm which rustic horsemen feel for adventures on the road. To him it seemed that the only vengeance open to an aggrieved man was to turn bandit.

"They'll kill me," he continued. "But before they do, godfather, you may be sure that I'll have done with half Jerez."

And the old man, who shared the youth's views, nodded approval. He was doing well. And if he himself were young and strong, Rafael would have one companion more in his troop.

Rafael had not returned. He fled from the temptation of meeting María de la Luz face to face, by some trick of the devil. For upon confronting her he was liable to slay her, or burst into tears like a child.

From time to time some old gipsy woman would come in search of señor Fermín; at other times it would be one of the *mochileros* who sold his scant supply of tobacco in the cafés and the clubs.

"Here, gaffer; this is for you. . . . From Rafael."

It was money from the smuggler, which the old man received and silently handed over to his daughter. The youth never appeared. At rare intervals he would come to Jerez, and this was enough to cause *el Chivo* and the other sycophants that formerly buzzed about Luis Dupont to hide in their homes, avoiding the taverns and the cafés frequented by the smuggler. That *gachó* had murder in his eye and bore them a grudge because of their former friendship with his master. Not that they were afraid of him. Oh, no! They were brave fellows . . . but city folk, and they weren't going to measure their strength against a brute that spent the week sleeping in the mountains with the wolves.

Señor Fermín let the time fly by without displaying any interest in what was going on or being said around him.

One day the gloomy silence of the city roused him from his lethargy for a few hours. They were about to garrote five men for the invasion of Jerez. The trial had proceeded very quickly; the punishment was urgent, so that the propertied classes be put at ease.

The entry of the rebellious laborers had with the passing of time grown to the proportions of a revolutionary reign of terror. Fear silenced all tongues. The very persons who had seen the strikers file by the wealthy men's houses without any hostile intent, silently accepted this outrageous imposition of an excessive penalty.

People spoke of two murders having been committed on that night, coupling the drunken señorito with the unfortunate bookkeeper. Fermín Montenegro was sought on a charge of homicide; his trial was to be held separately, but this did not prevent people from exaggerating the events of that night, placing another murder against the account of the revolutionists.

Many had been sentenced to prison. The penalties scattered chains right and left, with terrifying prodigality, upon the wretched flock, all of whom seemed to ask themselves in amazement what they could have done that evening. Of the five condemned to death, two were the murderers of the young office clerk; the other three were going to their end because they were considered dangerous characters,—because they had spoken and threatened, and believed vehemently that they had a right to a share of the world's happiness.

Many persons blinked maliciously upon learning that the *Madrileño,* who had instigated the invasion of the city, was going to prison for only a few years. Juanón and his comrade el de Trebujena awaited their last moment resignedly. They had lost all desire to live. Life nauseated them after the bitter disillusionment of that famous invasion. The *Maestrico* opened his girlish eyes in astonishment, as if refusing to believe in the wickedness of men. They lusted for his life because he was a dangerous creature, because he dreamed of a Utopia in which the learning of the few would become, in the hands of the vast horde of the unfortunate, an instrument of redemption! And, a poet without knowing it, his spirit, garbed in a coarse exterior, rose upon the flames of faith, consoling the anguish of his last moments with the hope that others would come after him, pushing the cause along, as he said, and that these others would at length succeed in winning out by force of numbers, even as the drops of water that form the flood. They were slain because they were few. Some day they would be so many that the powerful, wearied of assassinating them, terrified before the immensity of their bloody task, would at last lose heart and surrender.

Of this excitement señor Fermín could perceive only the hush of the city, which seemed ashamed of itself,— the terrified looks upon the poor folk; the cowardly submission with which all spoke of the upper class.

A few days later he had forgotten all about the event. A letter had come to him: it was from his son, from his Fermín. He was in Buenos Aires, and he wrote with confidence in his future. At first he had had to struggle hard, but over there, with faithful work, he was almost sure of success, and he harbored the certainty that he would make his way.

Ever since that day señor Fermín had something to occupy his mind, and he shook off the stupor in which grief had plunged him. He wrote to his son and waited anxiously for his letters. How far away he was! If only he could go there! . . .

On another day he was shaken by a new surprise. Seated in the sun, before his door, he noticed the shadow of a motionless man beside him. He raised his head and uttered a cry. Don Fernando! . . . It was his idol, the good Salvatierra, but grown old, sadder than ever, with a dull glance behind his blue spectacles, as if all the misfortunes and the iniquities of the city weighed heavily upon him.

They had released him,—they now allowed him to live at ease, knowing that wherever he went he would be unable to find a corner where he could build his nest, and that his words would be lost in the silence of terrror.

When he had returned to Jerez his former friends had fled from him, not wishing to compromise themselves. Others eyed him with hatred, as if he, in his enforced exile, were responsible for all that had occurred.

But señor Fermín, his old-time comrade, was not of these. As he beheld Salvatierra, he straightened up and fell into his arms, with that sob of the strong who choke without being able to cry.

Ay, don Fernando! . . . Don Fernando! . . .

Salvatierra comforted him. He knew everything.

Courage! He was a victim of the social maladjustment, against which the rebel thundered with all his ascetic ardor. He could still begin life anew, followed by his children,—the world is large. Where his son could make a living, there he, too, should seek it.

And some mornings Salvatierra would return to visit his old comrade. Soon, however, he disappeared. Some said he was in Cádiz; others, that he was in Seville, wandering through the province of Andalusia, which, together with the recollection of his exploits and his generosity, harbored the remains of the only being whose love had sweetened his existence.

He could not live in Jerez. The powerful employers cast defiant glances at him as if they were ready to jump upon him; the poor folk shunned him, avoiding all encounter.

Another month elapsed. One afternoon, as María de la Luz happened to come to the door, she met a sight that caused her almost to fall to the ground in a swoon. Her legs began to tremble; her ears buzzed; all her blood rushed to her face in a burning wave and then receded, leaving her with a greenish pallor. . . . It was Rafael there before her, enveloped in a cloak, as if waiting for her. She tried to flee,—to take refuge in the furthest room of the house.

"Maria de la Lú! . . . Mariquilla! . . ."

It was the same tender, entreating voice that she had heard when they used to meet at the grating, and without knowing how, she wheeled about, approaching him timidly, fixing her tearful glance upon the eyes of her former sweetheart.

He, too, was sad. A melancholy gravity seemed to impart a certain elegance to him, refining his rough, mountaineer's exterior.

"Maria de la Lú," he murmured. "Two words, that's

all. You love me and I love you. Why spend the rest of our lives in pain, like a pair of unhappy souls? . . . Until a short while ago I was so savage that the mere sight of you would have filled me with thoughts of murder. But I've been talking to don Fernando, and his wisdom convinced me. It's all over."

And he affirmed this with energetic mien. Their separation was at an end; no more stupid jealousy of a wretch that was dead for good and whom she had never loved; his rancor over a misfortune in which she was not at all to blame had vanished entirely.

They would flee the place. He hated the country so deeply that he did not even care to do it any harm. To abandon it altogether was the best thing; to place between it and them many, many leagues of land and water. Distance would efface their unpleasant memories. Out of sight of the city, of the fields, they would forget completely the ills they had suffered there.

They would go in quest of Fermín. He had enough money to pay the traveling expenses for all of them. His latest smuggling ventures had netted him fat sums; rash exploits the audacity of which astounded the officials: interminable processions of horses over the mountain roads, under shelter of his gun. They hadn't been able to kill him, and his good luck inspired him with fresh courage to undertake the long voyage that would alter his entire existence.

He knew the young world of America, and thither would go his mate, his godfather and he. Don Fernando had described this paradise to him. Infinite droves of wild horses who were awaiting the educative legs of the horseman; vast extents of lands without an owner, without any tyrant over them, longing for the hand of man to deliver them of the life that burgeoned in their entrails. What better Eden for a spirited, powerful countryman, until then a slave in body and soul to those who do not toil! . . .

They would be free and happy in the bosom of Nature, there where the primitive solitude had preserved a piece of the world clean of the crimes of civilization and of man's selfishness; where everything belonged to everybody, with no other privilege than that of labor; where the land was as pure as the air and the sun, and had not been dishonored by monopoly, nor parceled up and debased by the cry of "This belongs to me . . . and let the rest die of hunger."

And this life,—primitive, yet free and happy,—would in time refashion the virginity of their souls. They would become new beings, innocent and industrious, as if they had just sprung from the soil. The old man would close his eyes forever gazing sunward, with the tranquillity of one who fulfills his duty, returning to the earth whence he came; they, too, when their hour arrived, would likewise close their eyes, loving each other to the very last moment, and above their graves the task of labor and liberty would be carried on by their children and grandchildren, who would be happier than they, strangers to the cruelties of the old world, regarding the idle rich and the malignantly powerful as children regard the ogres of the fairy tales.

María de la Luz listened to him, deeply moved. Flee from this place! Leave so many memories behind! . . . Had the wretch who caused her family's ruin still lived, she would have persisted in her simple woman's obstinacy. She could belong to none other than the man who had robbed her of her virginity. But since the thief was dead, and Rafael, from whom she had withheld nothing, accepted the situation generously, pardoning her, she was ready to assent to everything. . . . Yes; they should flee the place. The sooner, the better! . . .

The youth went into details. Don Fernando had taken it upon himself to win over the old man; besides, the revolutionist would give him letters to friends of his in America. Inside of two weeks they would sail from Cádiz. Flee, flee as soon as possible from a land of gibbets, where guns answered the cry of hunger, and the rich deprived the poor of life, honor and happiness! . . .

"As soon as we land," added Rafael, "you will become my wife. We will repeat our conversations at the grating. Better still: I'll be more affectionate than ever, so that you'll see not a bitter recollection remains. It's all over. Don Fernando is right. The sins of the body represent very little. . . . It's love that counts; all the rest is a matter of animal preoccupations. Your dear little heart is mine? Then I own it all. . . . María de la Lú! My soul's mate! We'll march face to the sun; now we are truly reborn; to-day our love just begins. Let me kiss you for the first time in my life. Embrace me, sweet companion, let me see that you are really mine, that you will be the prop of my strength,—my support when the struggle commences over yonder. . . ."

And the man and woman embraced before the entrance to the house, joining their lips without the tremor of carnal passion, for a long time remaining thus, as if they scorned the persons who looked at them in amazement,—as if with their love they defied the horrified protest of an old world that they were leaving forever.

Don Fernando accompanied his loyal friend señor Fermín to Cádiz, to the gangplank of the trans-Atlantic liner; the old man was leaving with Rafael and María de la Luz for the New World.

Farewell! They would never see each other again.

The world is too large for the poor, who ever remain in one spot, rooted by necessity.

Salvatierra felt that tears were coming. All his friendships, the memories of the past, were vanishing, scattered by death or misfortune. He was left all alone amid a people that he had tried to free, and who no longer recognized him. The rising generation looked upon him as a madman who inspired a certain interest because of his ascetic habits, but they did not understand his words.

Several days after the departure of these friends he left his retreat at Cádiz and hastened to Jerez. He had been summoned by a dying friend,—a comrade of the good old days.

Señor *Matacardillos,* owner of the "Jackdaw," was this time surely at the point of death. His family begged the revolutionist to come, looking upon his presence as a final ray of joy for the invalid. "This time he's really going, don Fernando," his sons had written, and don Fernando hurried to Jerez, setting out upon the Matanzuela road,—the same he had followed one night, in a different direction, behind the corpse of a little gipsy maiden.

Arriving at the tavern, he learned that his friend had died several hours before.

It was a Sunday afternoon. Within, in the only room of the cabin, the swollen body was laid out upon a poor bed, with no other company than the flies, which darted hither and thither above its purple countenance.

Outside, the widow and her children, with the resignation of a misfortune that has long been expected, were filling glasses and attending to the customers seated near the little tavern.

The Matanzuela day-laborers were gathered in a wide circle, drinking. Don Fernando, standing in the door of the hut, contemplated the vast plain, without a man, without a beast, sunk in the monotonous solitude of Sunday.

He felt alone, completely alone. He had just lost the last of the friends of his revolutionary youth. Of all those who had fired their guns on the mountain range and faced death or the penitentiary in their romantic ardor for the revolution, not one remained at his side. Some had taken desperate flight to the other side of the ocean, spurred on by poverty; others were rotting in the bosom of the earth, without the consolation of having seen Justice and Equality reign over men.

How much useless effort! How many sterile sacrifices! . . . And the heritage of all this labor was to be lost forever! The new generations did not recognize the old,—they scorned to receive from their wearied, feeble hands the burden of hatreds and hopes.

Salvatierra looked sadly at the group of laborers. They did not know him, or pretended not to. Not a glance had rested upon him.

They were discussing the great tragedy, which still seemed to hold the people of Jerez under its heavy pall: the execution of the five workingmen for the nocturnal entrance into the city. But they spoke calmly, without passion or hatred, as if the men executed had been bandits surrounded by a halo of popularity.

They revealed some vehemence only when they appraised the manner in which the men had faced death,— the way in which they had walked to the gallows. Juanón and el de Trebujena had gone to their doom like the fellows they were: brave men incapable alike of fear or braggadocio. The other two assassins had died like brutes. And the recollection of the poor *Maestrico* almost roused them to laughter, with his quivering anguish and his hurrahs for the Revolution, so as to give himself courage and restrain the nervousness of his sensitive soul.

Of the powerful interests, of those who had ordered the exaggerated and unjust punishment, of those who perhaps had prepared the instigating deed so as to justify their later repression,—not a word. Servile fear and the intention of doing no thinking were reflected in the eyes of all. They grew silent and resumed their drinking.

A man approached Salvatierra. It was *Zarandilla;* his sight had become weaker than ever. He had not recognized the revolutionist until the tavern folk had told him that don Fernando was there.

He asked with great interest after Rafael. Ay, don Fernando! How things had changed at Matanzuela, after the departure of that boy! Now the farm belonged to don Pablo Dupont, and the new steward was a harsh, unyielding fellow, a slave-driver who tormented him and everybody else.

But as for the laborers. Well, he could see them over there! More satisfied than ever, content with the new master, and blushing with the bashfulness of a child whenever they approached any man that had been stigmatized with the hatred of the rich. They had recognized Salvatierra, and were doubtless pretending never to have seen him. They feared to compromise themselves.

There was a new caste of laborers upon which *Zarandilla* looked with amazement. They were enthusiastic about their raise in pay. They earned now not two *reales,* but two and a half, and attributed this increase to their submission and their good behavior. "If you'll just be good fellows, you'll get more than if you start trouble," they had been told. And this they repeated, thinking with scorn of the malicious agitators who tried to incite them to revolt. If they continued to be obedient and submissive, perhaps in time they would even get three *reales*. A veritable state of felicity! . . .

They looked upon the farm of Matanzuela as a paradise. Benevolent Dupont displayed unheard-of generosity. He saw to it that the toilers heard mass every Sunday; and from month to month he organized communions for the laborers. Those who, upon days of rest, did not go home, but remained at the farm to hear the religious sermons of a priest from Jerez, were in the afternoon treated to several glasses at the inn by the master.

Dupont, as he himself averred, was a *modern* believer. Any road at all was good if it led to the winning of souls.

And the laborers, as *Zarandilla* confessed, "allowed themselves to be wooed," prayed and drank, chaffing the proprietor with mock solemnity and calling him "cousin."

Zarandilla's long stay at Salvatierra's side, and the curiosity inspired by the rebel, at last overcame the aloofness of the laborers. Some approached, and gradually a circle was formed about the revolutionist.

One of the oldest of the toilers addressed him in a sarcastic tone. If don Fernando was scouring the countryside with the purpose of inciting the men as in the olden days, he was wasting his time. The people were cautious: it was like the scalded cat of the popular song. And it wasn't because the laborers were so well off, either. They simply made a living,—that was all. But the poor lads that had been sentenced at Jerez were worse off than they.

"We old fellows," continued this rustic philosopher, "still feel a certain respect for your grace and those of your day. We know that you haven't grown rich from your speeches, as a good many others have. We know that you've suffered and that you've been severely punished. . . . But just take a look at these fellows."

And he pointed at those who had remained seated without caring to draw near to Salvatierra; they were all young men. From time to time they cast insolent glances at the revolutionist. "A rank impostor, like all the other fellows who came looking for the toilers. Those who had followed his doctrines were now rotting in the earth of the cemetery, and he was still here. . . . Less sermons and more wheat. . . ." They were clever chaps; they had seen enough to know the true from the false, and they sided only with the man who brought them some profit. The true friend of the laborers was the master with his pay; and if on top of this he gave wine, better still. Besides, of what concern could the lot of the toilers be to this fellow who dressed like a gentleman,—even if his clothes were as ragged as a beggar's,—and had no callouses on his hands? What he was after was to live at their expense; he was a pretender like the rest.

Salvatierra could divine these thoughts in the hostile eyes.

The old rustic's voice continued to vex him with its crafty philosophy.

"Why should your grace be so deeply concerned with what happens to the poor, don Fernando? Let them alone. If they are content, you be content, likewise. Besides, we've learned from experience. Let your grace, who knows so much, first win over the Civil Guard, and when you come to us at the head of the three-cornered hats,—have no fear,—we'll all fall in behind."

The old man filled a glass of wine and offered it to Salvatierra.

"Drink, your grace. And don't lose your health in trying to adjust matters that can't be adjusted. In this

world there's no truth but this. Friends,—false; family
. . . good to eat with potatoes. All this business of
revolutions and dividing-up—lies, mere words with which
to deceive the simple. This is the only truth: Wine!
From one gulp to another it gladdens us until death.
Drink, don Fernando; I offer it to you; it's ours,—because we've earned it. It's cheap; it costs only one
mass."

Salvatierra the impassive trembled with anger. He
felt like thrusting the glass aside, smashing it upon the
ground. He cursed the golden beverage, the alcoholic
demon that spread its amber wings over that debased
flock, fettering its will and instilling it with slavery to
crime, madness and cowardice.

Digging the soil, sweating over its furrows, leaving in
its bowels the best of their existence, they produced this
golden liquid; and the powerful rich used it to intoxicate them, to hold them in the enchantment of an illusory joy.

And yet they laughed! And counseled him to submit,
scoffing at his altruistic efforts and lauding their oppressors! . . . Must, then, their slavery be unending? Were
human aspirations to cease forever in this ephemeral joy
of the sodden, satisfied brute? . . .

Salvatierra felt his anger disappear; faith and hope
were returning.

Dusk was beginning to fall; night was approaching,
like the harbinger of a new day. The twilight of human
aspirations, too, was but ephemeral. Justice and Liberty
slept in the conscience of every man. They would yet
awake.

Beyond the fields there were cities,—vast agglomera-
tions of modern civilization,—and within them were
other flocks of sad unfortunates; but these repelled the
false solace of wine, and laved their new-born souls in

the dawn of a new day, feeling upon their brows the first beams of the sunrise, while the rest of the world lay still in darkness. They would be the elect; and while the rustics remained in the country, with the resigned gravity of the cattle, the disinherited of the city were awakening and rising to their feet, ready to follow the sole friend of the wretched and the famished,—the friend who crosses the history of all religions, insulted by the name of Devil, and who now, casting off the grotesque garb that had been foisted upon him by tradition, dazzles the sight of some and terrifies others with the proudest of beauties,—the beauty of the angel of light who was once called Lucifer, and is now called Revolution. . . . Social Revolution!

THE END

GLOSSARY

NOTE—Only those words are here elucidated that are not explained by the context or made evident from the manner in which they are used. It is interesting to note that the nicknames (which are so frequent in most of Blasco Ibáñez's fiction) possess their own connotation. Thus *Alcaparrón* signifies a caper; *el Chivo* is equivalent to our "the Kid"; *Damajuanja* is our friend Demijohn; *Zarandilla* properly refers to a frisky fellow.

Afición: literally, affection, attachment, fondness; the regular term by which the national sport of bullfighting is referred to.

Archipampano: the title of any imaginary dignity.

Arreador: literally, a muleteer; here equivalent to a taskmaster.

Arroba: as a liquid measure, about 4 gallons; as a dry measure, 25 pounds.

Arrumbador: as here employed the term means either a cask piler or one who transfers the various wines in blending a new mixture.

"Boca Abajo!": literally, face downward.

Bodega: any place where wine is stored, either above or below ground.

Bota: as a liquid measure, about 125 gallons.

Caló: gipsy cant.

Céntimo: 100th of a *peseta*.

Círculo Caballista: Horsefanciers' Club; Jockey Club.

Duro: a silver coin worth five *pesetas;* nominally equivalent to about a dollar.

Flamenca: refers to a type of dubious Andalusian female.

367

Garrocha: a sort of goad-stick. For the type of *garrocha* used in the bull-fight see the author's "Blood and Sand" (Sangre y Arena).

Gazpacho: an Andalusian dish made of biscuit, oil, vinegar, onions and garlic; also plain crumbs of bread fried in a pan.

Infante: any son of the King of Spain, except the heir apparent; any daughter of the King; wife of the prince-royal.

Juerga: a "good time," with all its graded implications, from that of a simple feast to a wild carousal.

Montañés: highlander; native of the province of Santander.

Madrileño: here, "the fellow from Madrid."

las Navas de Tolosa: a famous battle in the Sierra Morena; it took place on July 16, 1212, and the victory of the Christians over the Almohades decided the fate of Spain.

Plaza Nueva: "New Square."

Peseta: 100 centimos; worth about .193 cents. (cf. the franc.)

Peso: five *pesetas.*

Real: A coin varying in value from 12½ to 10 cents.

Soleá, Andalusian for *soledad* (solitude) and referring to a type of song as well as dance.

Solera: "The wines, which are stored in bodegas or sheds above ground, are reared for a number of years as *soleras.* These *soleras* consist of various characters of sherry, the style of which is unvaryingly kept up, and whenever a quantity is drawn off they are filled up with wines of the same description." (Enc. Brit., article "Wine.")

Saeta: an arrow; also refers, as here, to pious songs, often of an improvised character.